Little MONSTERS

LITTLE MONSTERS VOL. 2. First printing. August 2023. Published by Image Comics, Inc.
Office of publication: PO BOX 14457, Portland, OR 97293. Copyright © 2023 171 Studios &
Dustin Nguyen. All rights reserved. Contains material originally published in single magazine
form as LITTLE MONSTERS #7-13. "LITTLE MONSTERS," its logos, and the likenesses of all
characters herein are trademarks of 171 Studios & Dustin Nguyen, unless otherwise noted.
"Image" and the Image Comics logos are registered trademarks of Image Comics, Inc. No part
of this publication may be reproduced or transmitted, in any form or by any means (except for
short excerpts for journalistic or review purposes), without the express written permission of
171 Studios & Dustin Nguyen, or Image Comics, Inc. All names, characters, events, and locales
in this publication are entirely fictional. Any resemblance to actual persons (living or dead),
events, or places, without satirical intent, is coincidental. Printed in the USA. For international
rights, contact: foreignlicensing@imagecomics.com. ISBN: 978-1-5343-9968-6

Publication design by Steve Wands

JEFF LEMIRE writer

DUSTIN NGUYEN artist & cover

STEVE WANDS letterer & designer

GREG LOCKARD editor

special thanks to KAELI NGUYEN

SHIRLEY WU background assistant

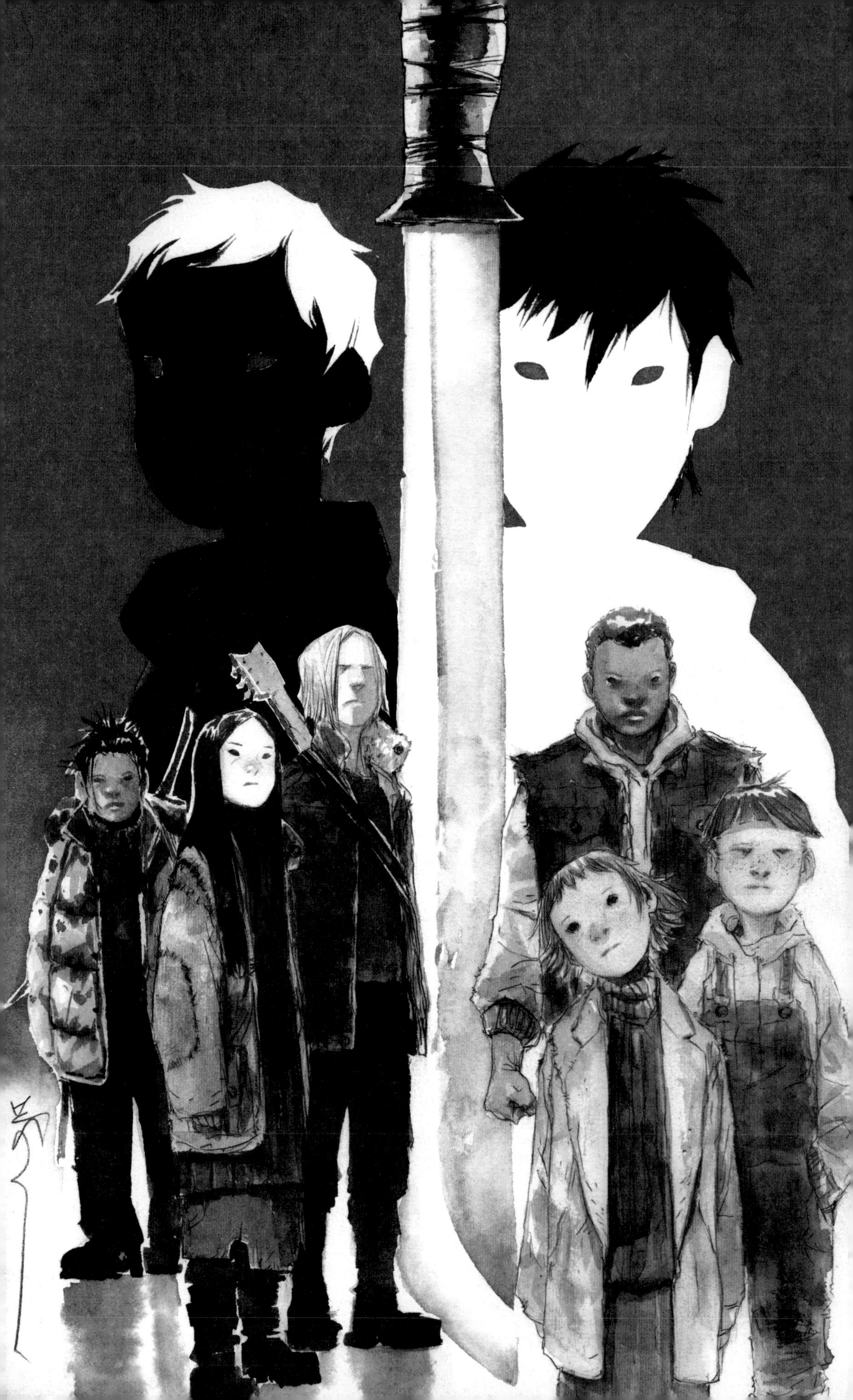

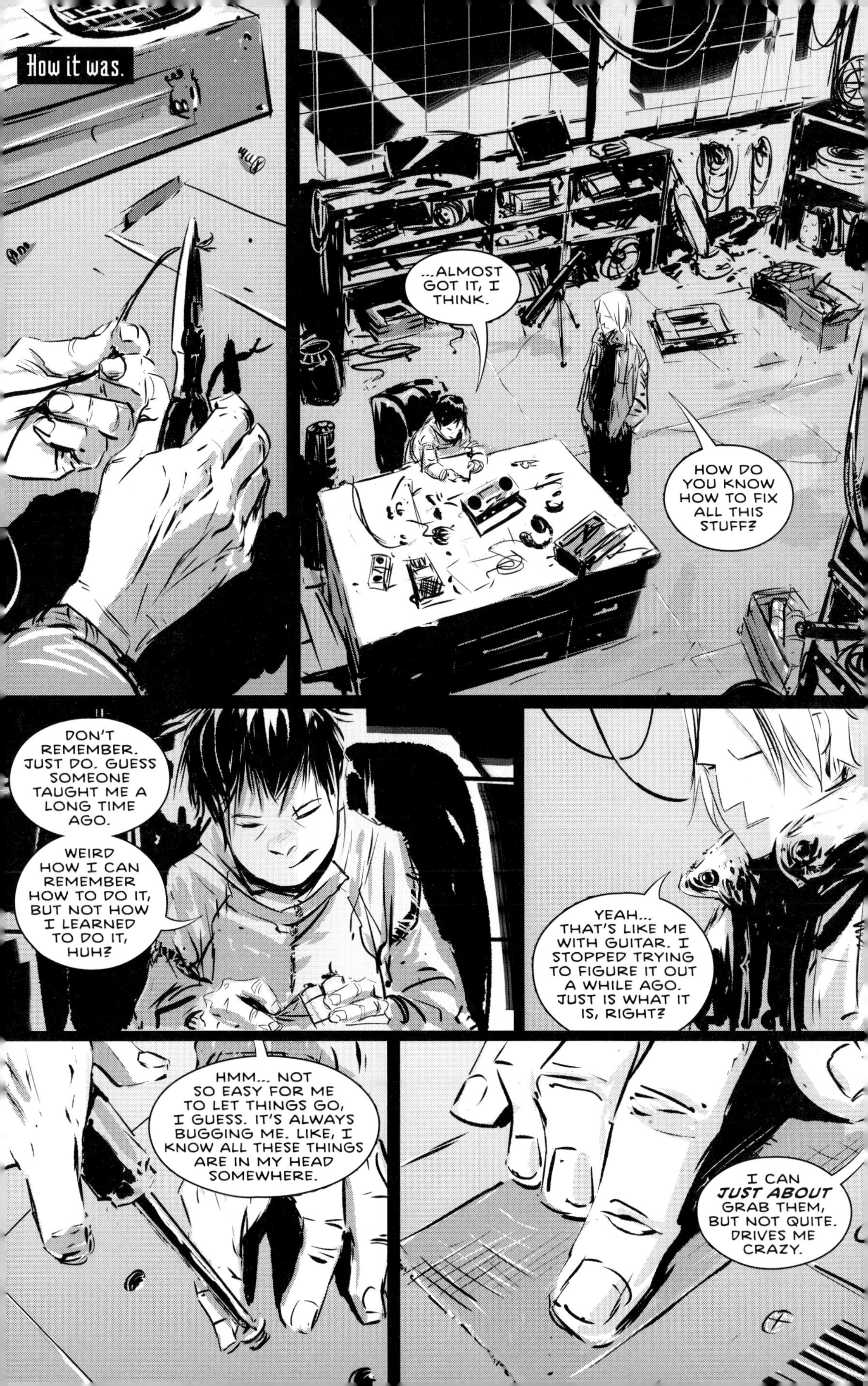
How it was.
...ALMOST GOT IT, I THINK.
HOW DO YOU KNOW HOW TO FIX ALL THIS STUFF?
DON'T REMEMBER. JUST DO. GUESS SOMEONE TAUGHT ME A LONG TIME AGO.
WEIRD HOW I CAN REMEMBER HOW TO DO IT, BUT NOT HOW I LEARNED TO DO IT, HUH?
YEAH... THAT'S LIKE ME WITH GUITAR. I STOPPED TRYING TO FIGURE IT OUT A WHILE AGO. JUST IS WHAT IT IS, RIGHT?
HMM... NOT SO EASY FOR ME TO LET THINGS GO, I GUESS. IT'S ALWAYS BUGGING ME. LIKE, I KNOW ALL THESE THINGS ARE IN MY HEAD SOMEWHERE.
I CAN *JUST ABOUT* GRAB THEM, BUT NOT QUITE. DRIVES ME CRAZY.

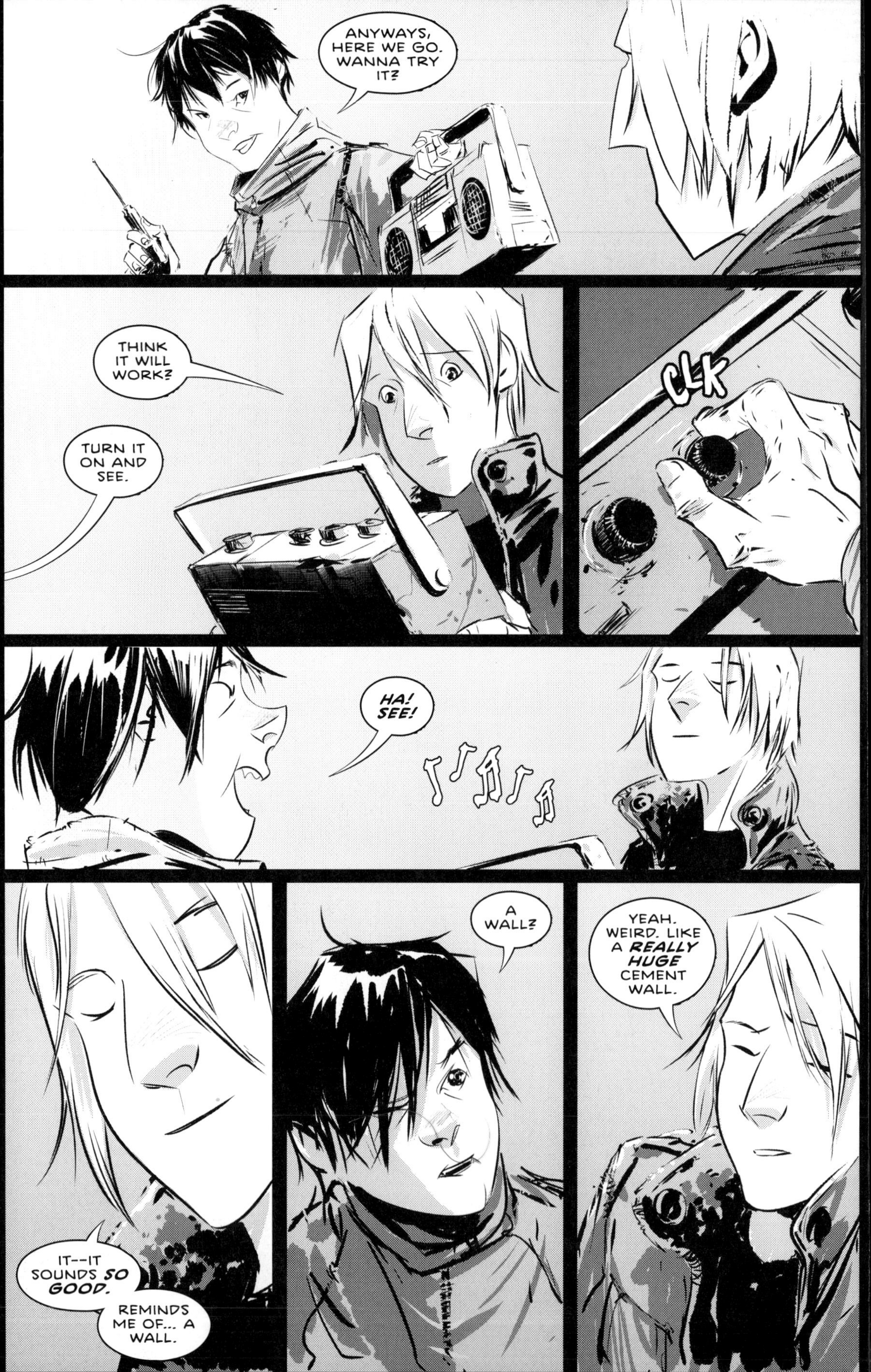
ANYWAYS, HERE WE GO. WANNA TRY IT?
THINK IT WILL WORK?
TURN IT ON AND SEE.
CLK
HA! SEE!
IT--IT SOUNDS ***SO GOOD.***
REMINDS ME OF... A WALL.
A WALL?
YEAH. WEIRD. LIKE A ***REALLY HUGE*** CEMENT WALL.

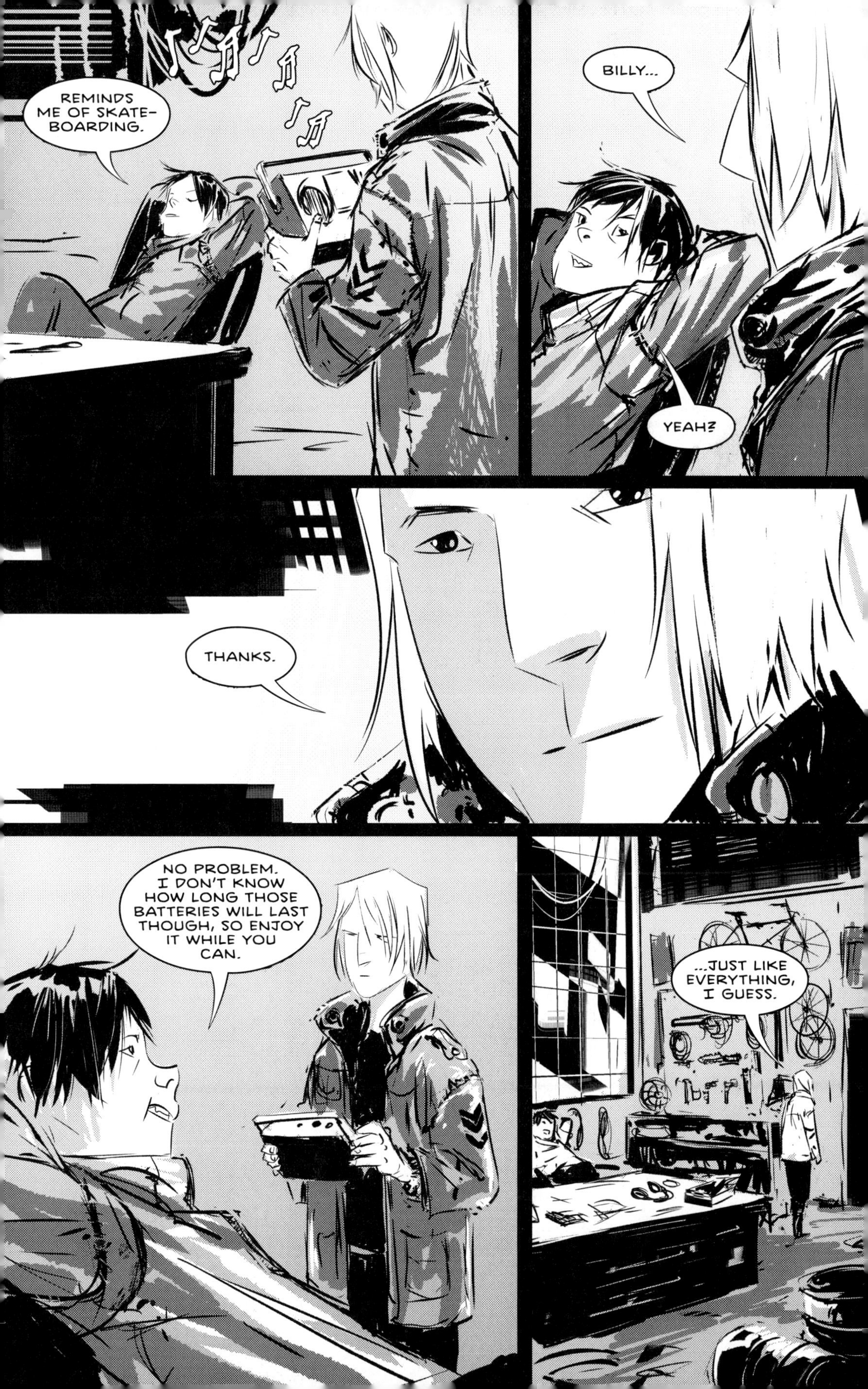
REMINDS ME OF SKATE-BOARDING.
BILLY...
YEAH?
THANKS.
NO PROBLEM. I DON'T KNOW HOW LONG THOSE BATTERIES WILL LAST THOUGH, SO ENJOY IT WHILE YOU CAN.
...JUST LIKE EVERYTHING, I GUESS.

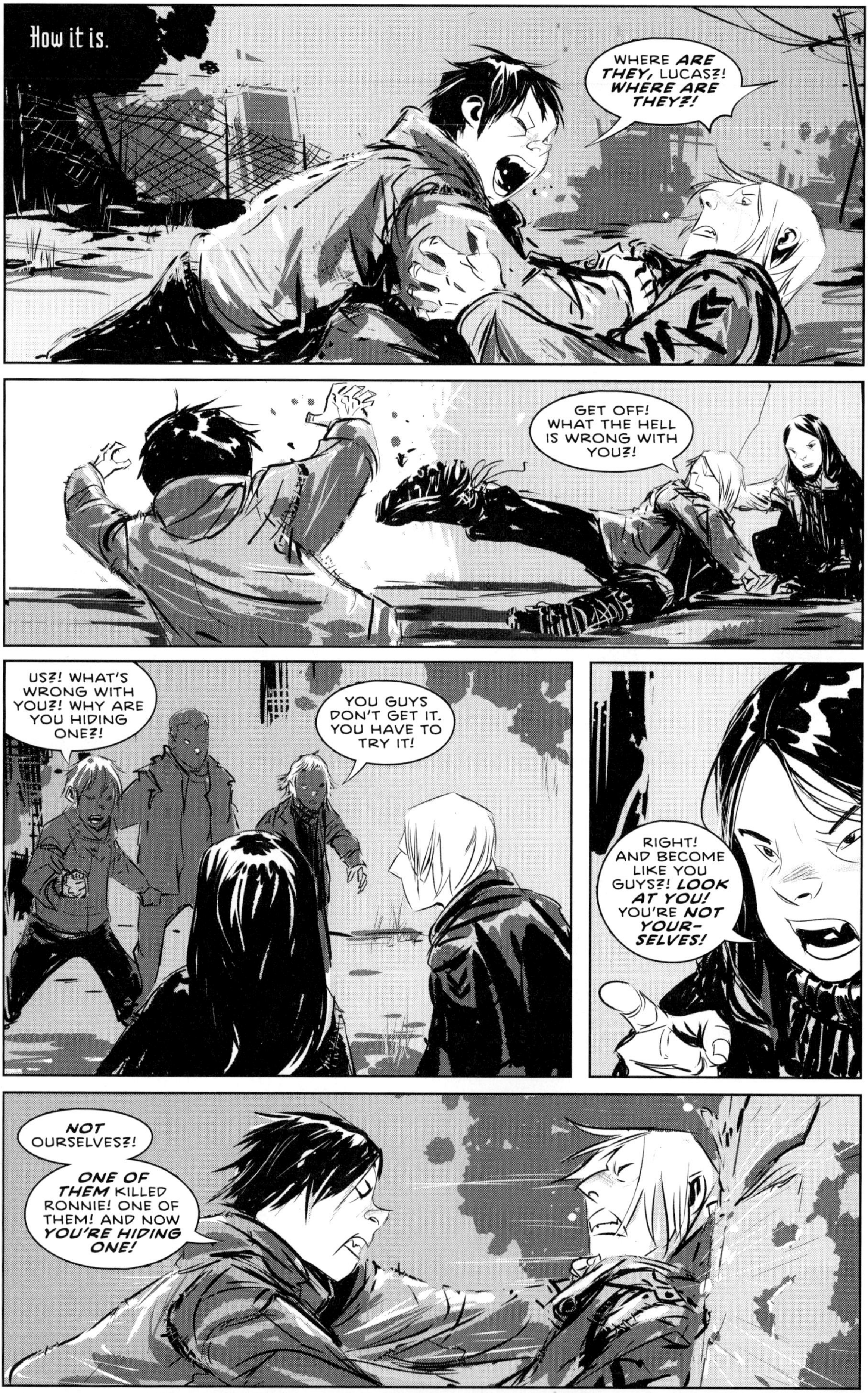
How it is.
WHERE ARE THEY, LUCAS?! WHERE ARE THEY?!
GET OFF! WHAT THE HELL IS WRONG WITH YOU?!
US?! WHAT'S WRONG WITH YOU?! WHY ARE YOU HIDING ONE?!
YOU GUYS DON'T GET IT. YOU HAVE TO TRY IT!
RIGHT! AND BECOME LIKE YOU GUYS?! LOOK AT YOU! YOU'RE NOT YOUR-SELVES!
NOT OURSELVES?!
ONE OF THEM KILLED RONNIE! ONE OF THEM! AND NOW YOU'RE HIDING ONE!

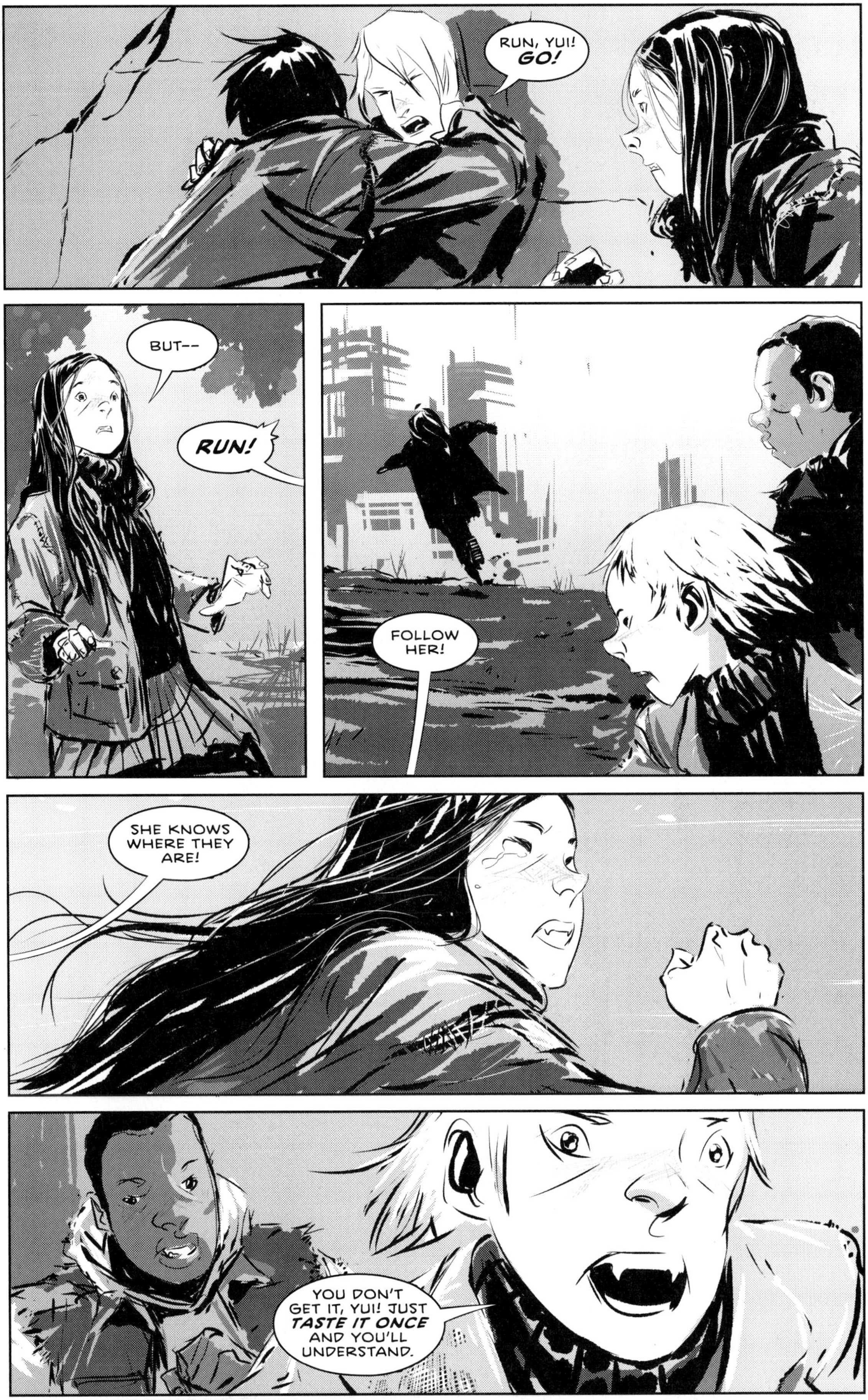

RUN, YUI! *GO!*
BUT--
RUN!
FOLLOW HER!
SHE KNOWS WHERE THEY ARE!
YOU DON'T GET IT, YUI! JUST *TASTE IT ONCE* AND YOU'LL UNDERSTAND.

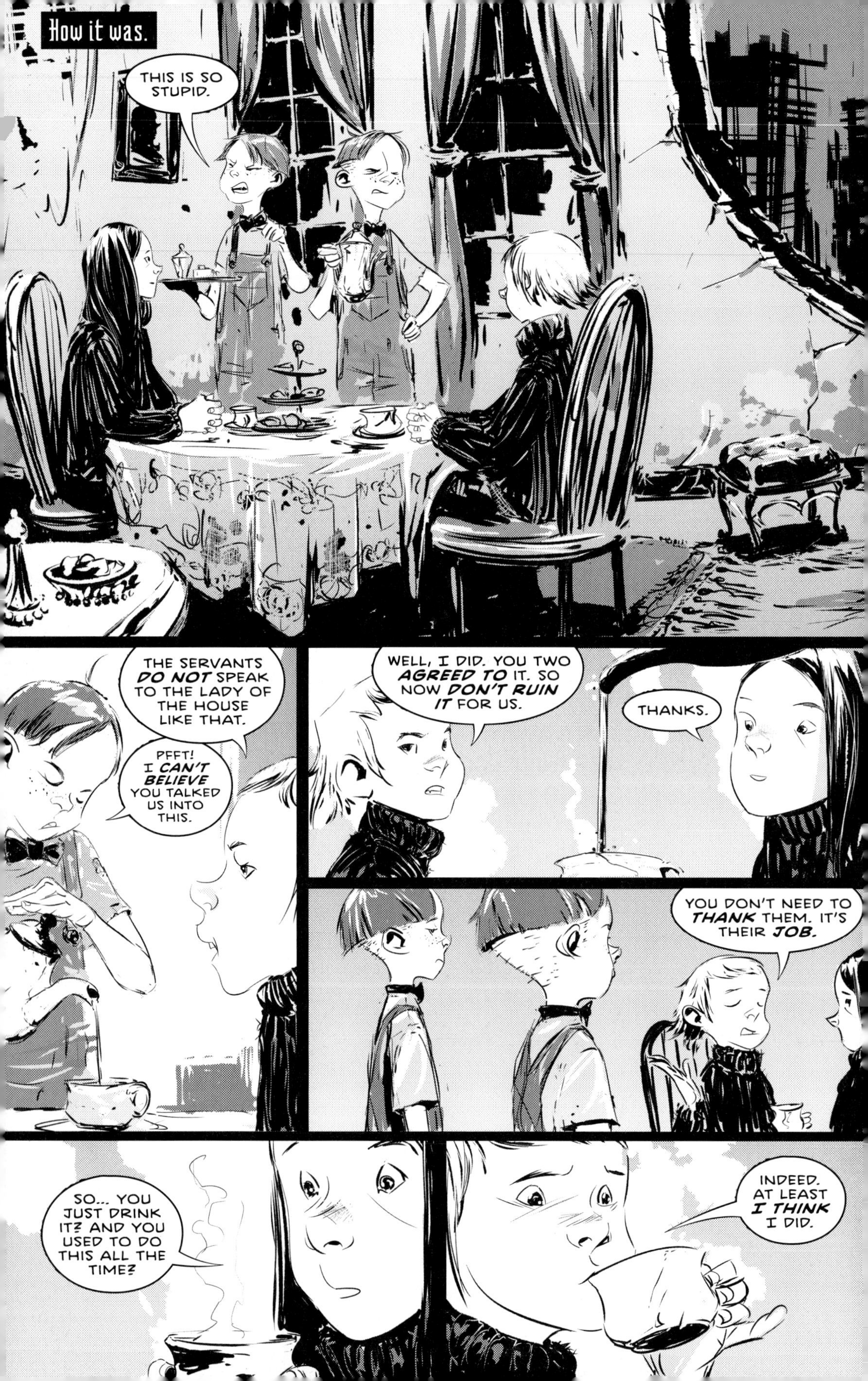
How it was.
THIS IS SO STUPID.
THE SERVANTS DO NOT SPEAK TO THE LADY OF THE HOUSE LIKE THAT.
PFFT! I CAN'T BELIEVE YOU TALKED US INTO THIS.
WELL, I DID. YOU TWO AGREED TO IT. SO NOW DON'T RUIN IT FOR US.
THANKS.
YOU DON'T NEED TO THANK THEM. IT'S THEIR JOB.
SO... YOU JUST DRINK IT? AND YOU USED TO DO THIS ALL THE TIME?
INDEED. AT LEAST I THINK I DID.

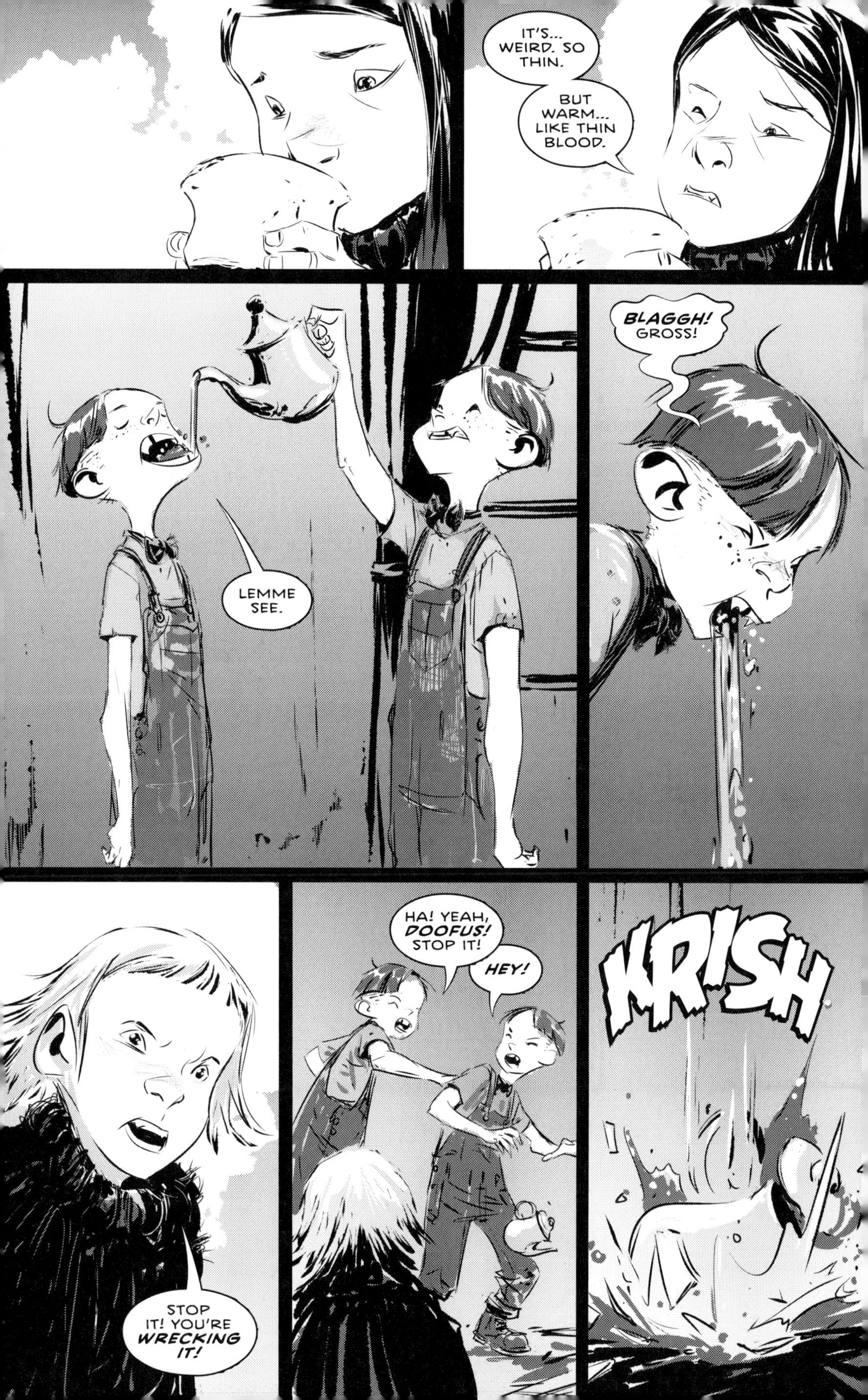

IT'S... WEIRD. SO THIN.
BUT WARM... LIKE THIN BLOOD.
LEMME SEE.
BLAGGH! GROSS!
STOP IT! YOU'RE WRECKING IT!
HA! YEAH, DOOFUS! STOP IT!
HEY!
KRISH

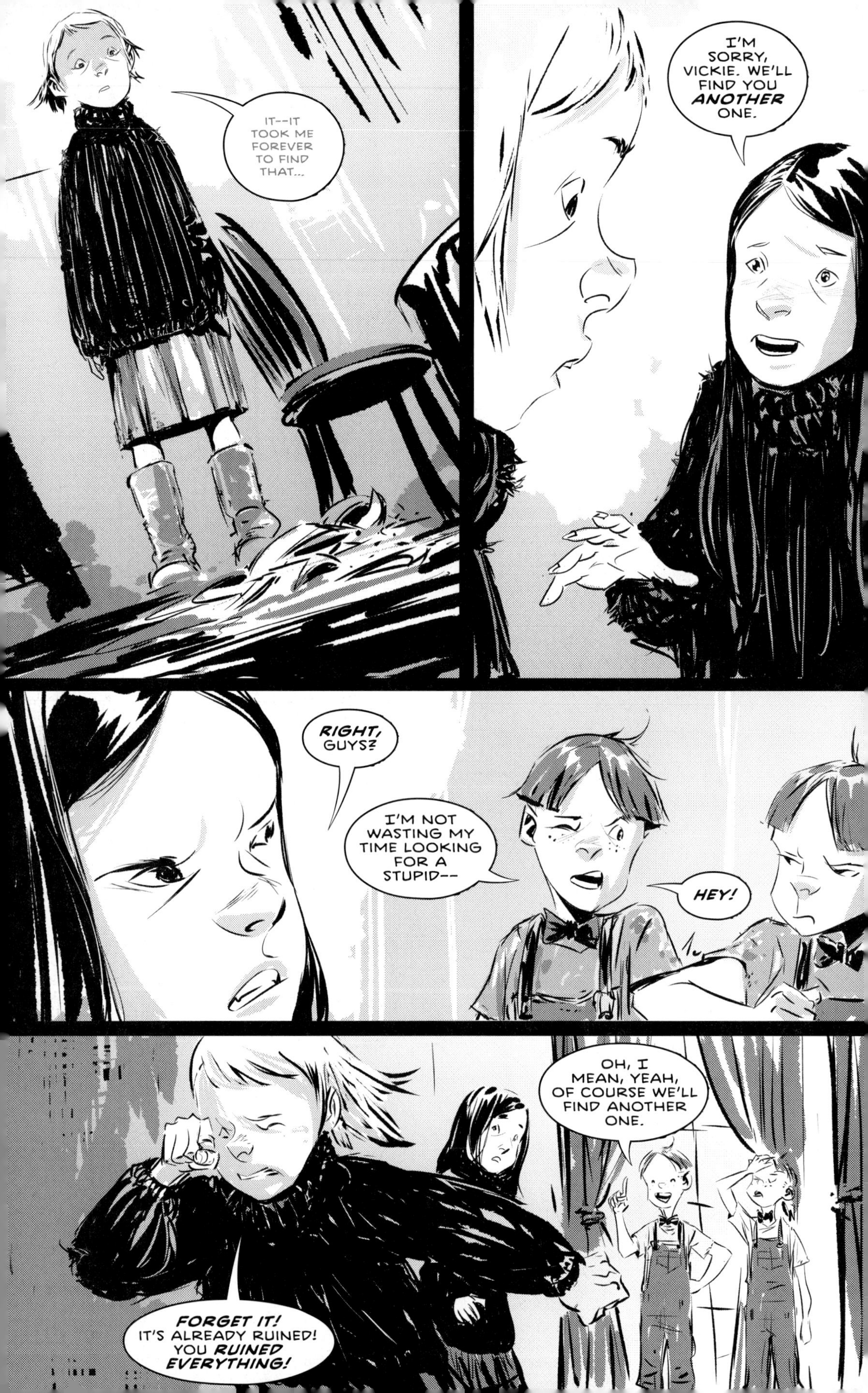
IT--IT TOOK ME FOREVER TO FIND THAT...
I'M SORRY, VICKIE. WE'LL FIND YOU ANOTHER ONE.
RIGHT, GUYS?
I'M NOT WASTING MY TIME LOOKING FOR A STUPID--
HEY!
OH, I MEAN, YEAH, OF COURSE WE'LL FIND ANOTHER ONE.
FORGET IT! IT'S ALREADY RUINED! YOU RUINED EVERYTHING!

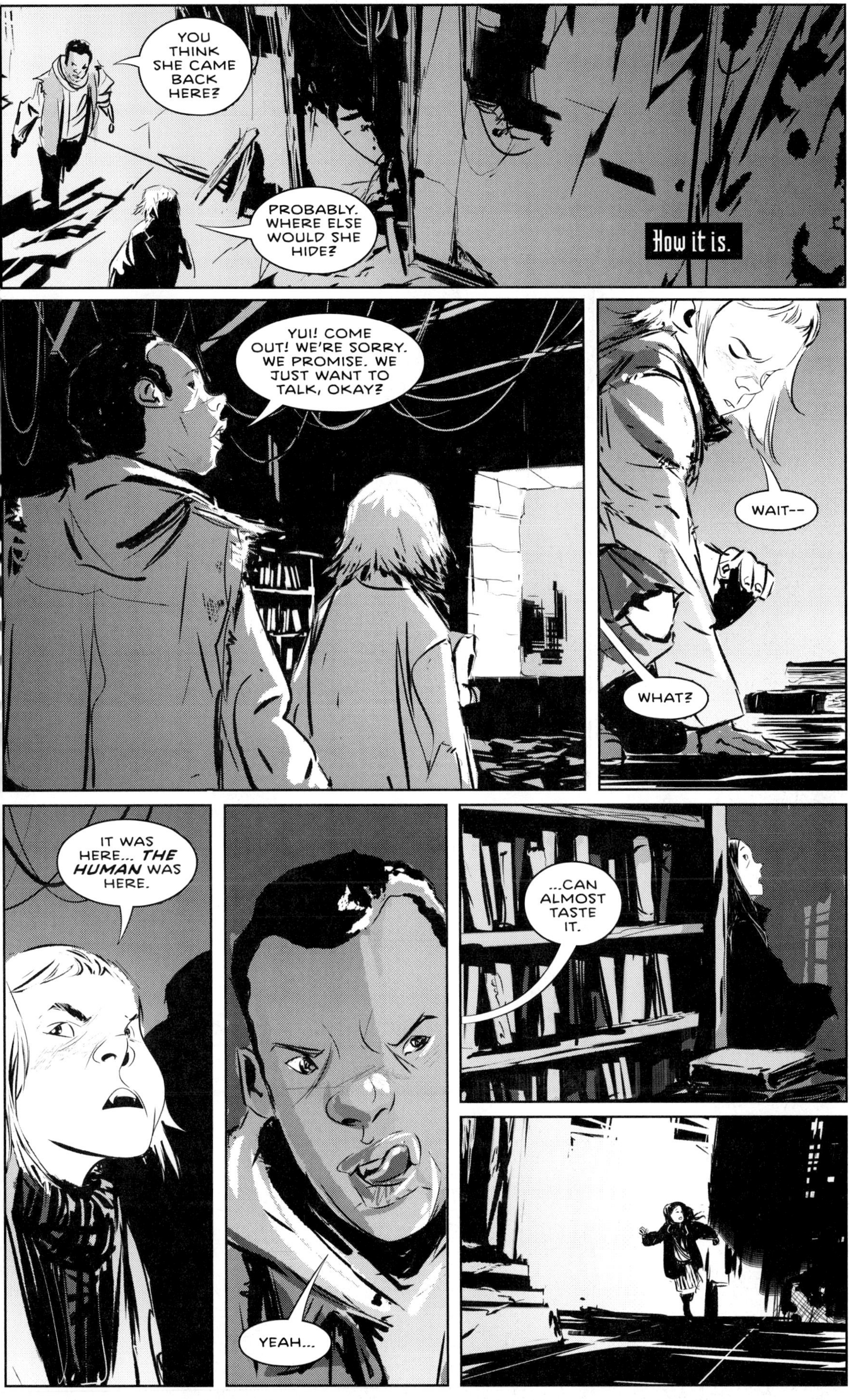
YOU THINK SHE CAME BACK HERE?
PROBABLY. WHERE ELSE WOULD SHE HIDE?
How it is.
YUI! COME OUT! WE'RE SORRY. WE PROMISE. WE JUST WANT TO TALK, OKAY?
WAIT--
WHAT?
IT WAS HERE... *THE HUMAN* WAS HERE.
YEAH...
...CAN ALMOST TASTE IT.

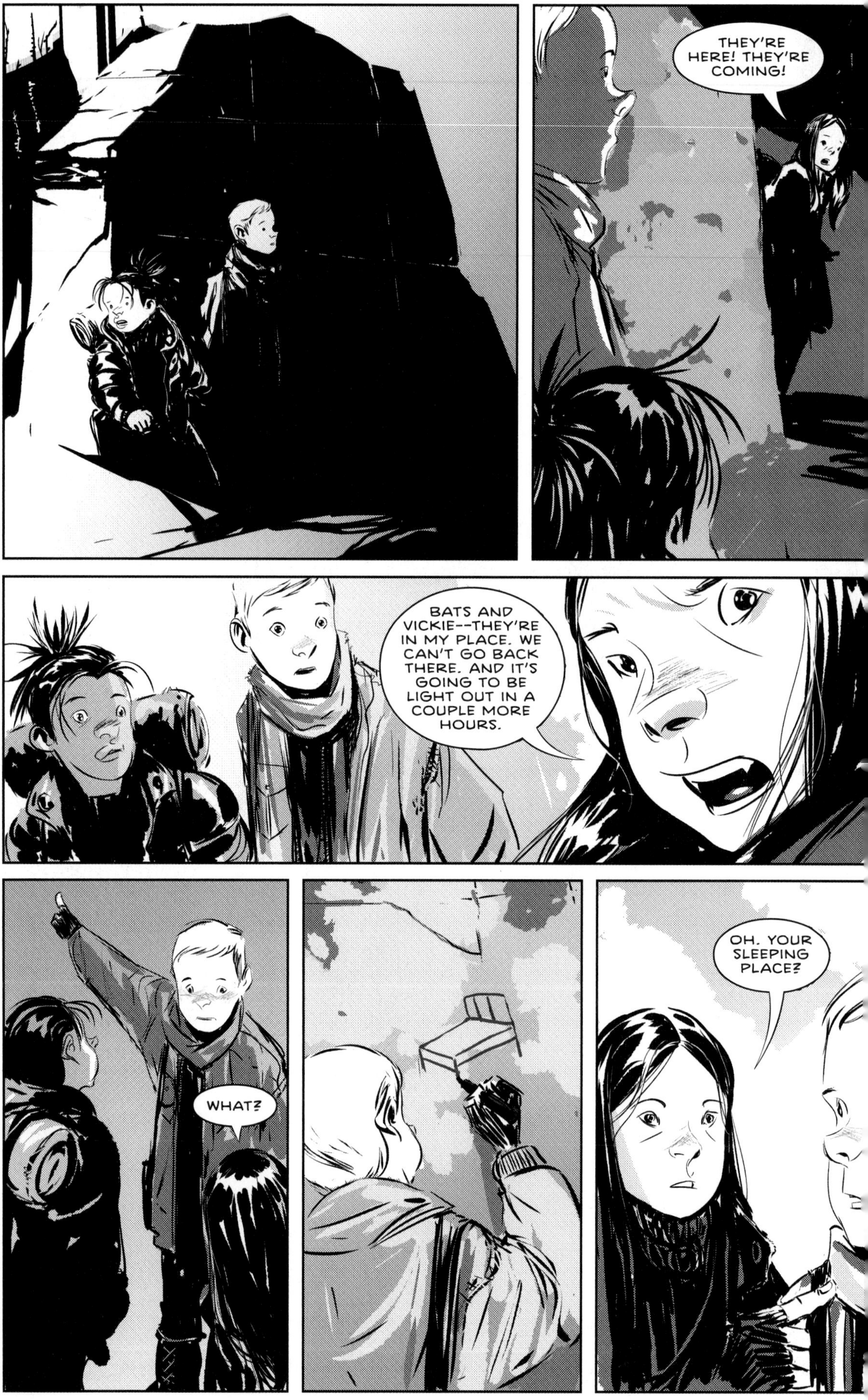
THEY'RE HERE! THEY'RE COMING!
BATS AND VICKIE--THEY'RE IN MY PLACE. WE CAN'T GO BACK THERE. AND IT'S GOING TO BE LIGHT OUT IN A COUPLE MORE HOURS.
WHAT?
OH. YOUR SLEEPING PLACE?

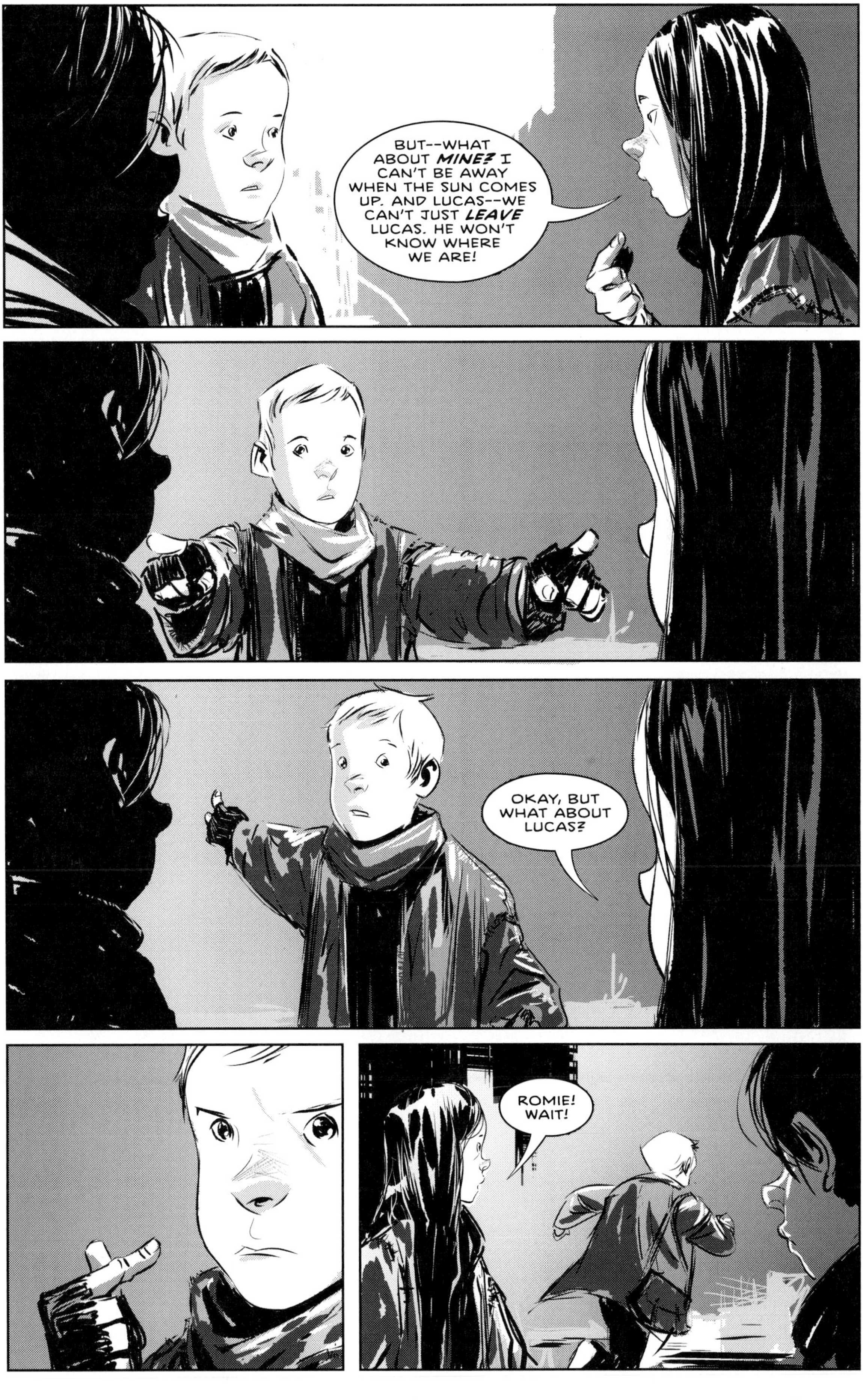
BUT--WHAT ABOUT *MINE?* I CAN'T BE AWAY WHEN THE SUN COMES UP. AND LUCAS--WE CAN'T JUST *LEAVE* LUCAS. HE WON'T KNOW WHERE WE ARE!
OKAY, BUT WHAT ABOUT LUCAS?
ROMIE! WAIT!

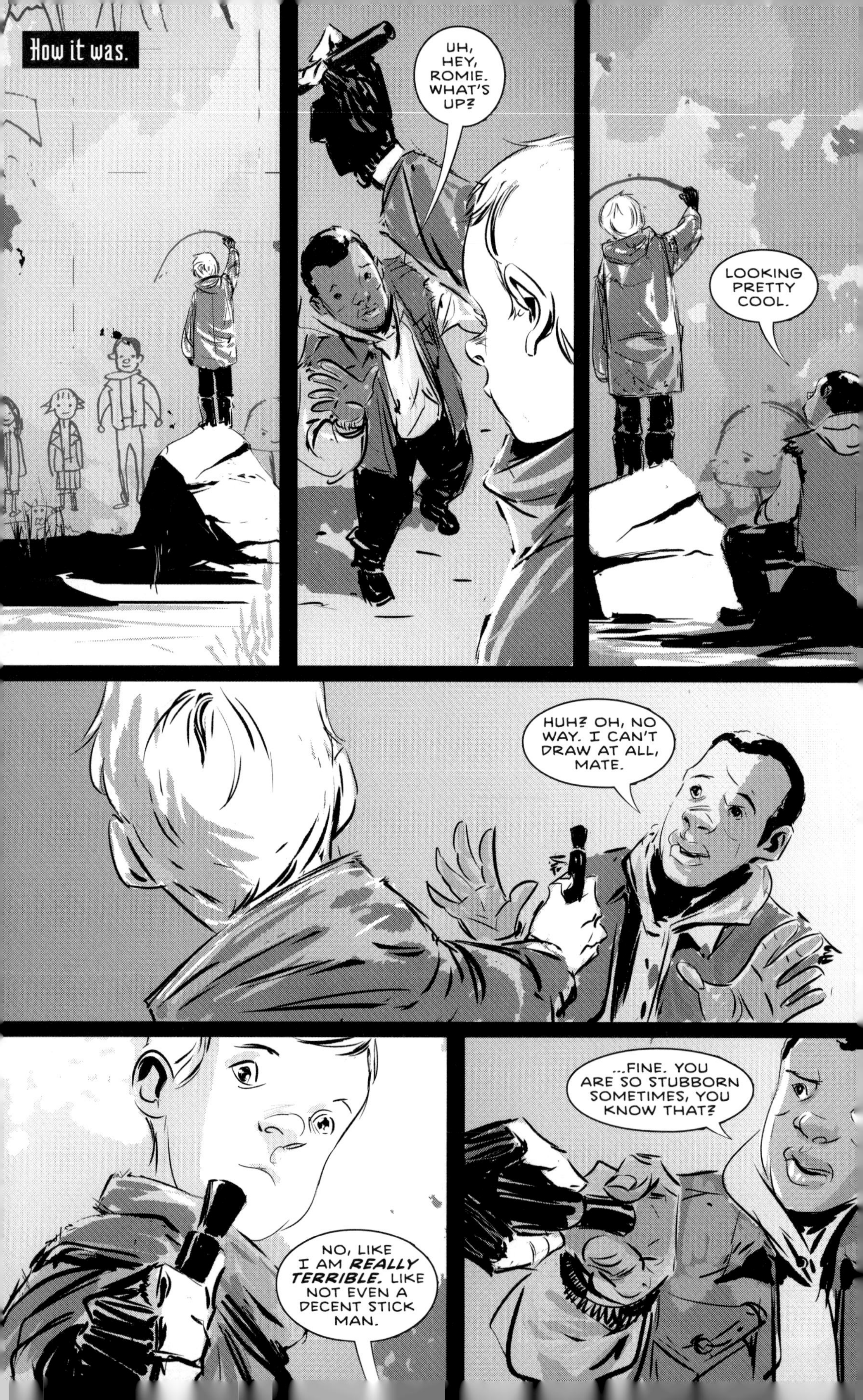
How it was.
UH, HEY, ROMIE. WHAT'S UP?
LOOKING PRETTY COOL.
HUH? OH, NO WAY. I CAN'T DRAW AT ALL, MATE.
NO, LIKE I AM *REALLY TERRIBLE.* LIKE NOT EVEN A DECENT STICK MAN.
...FINE. YOU ARE SO STUBBORN SOMETIMES, YOU KNOW THAT?

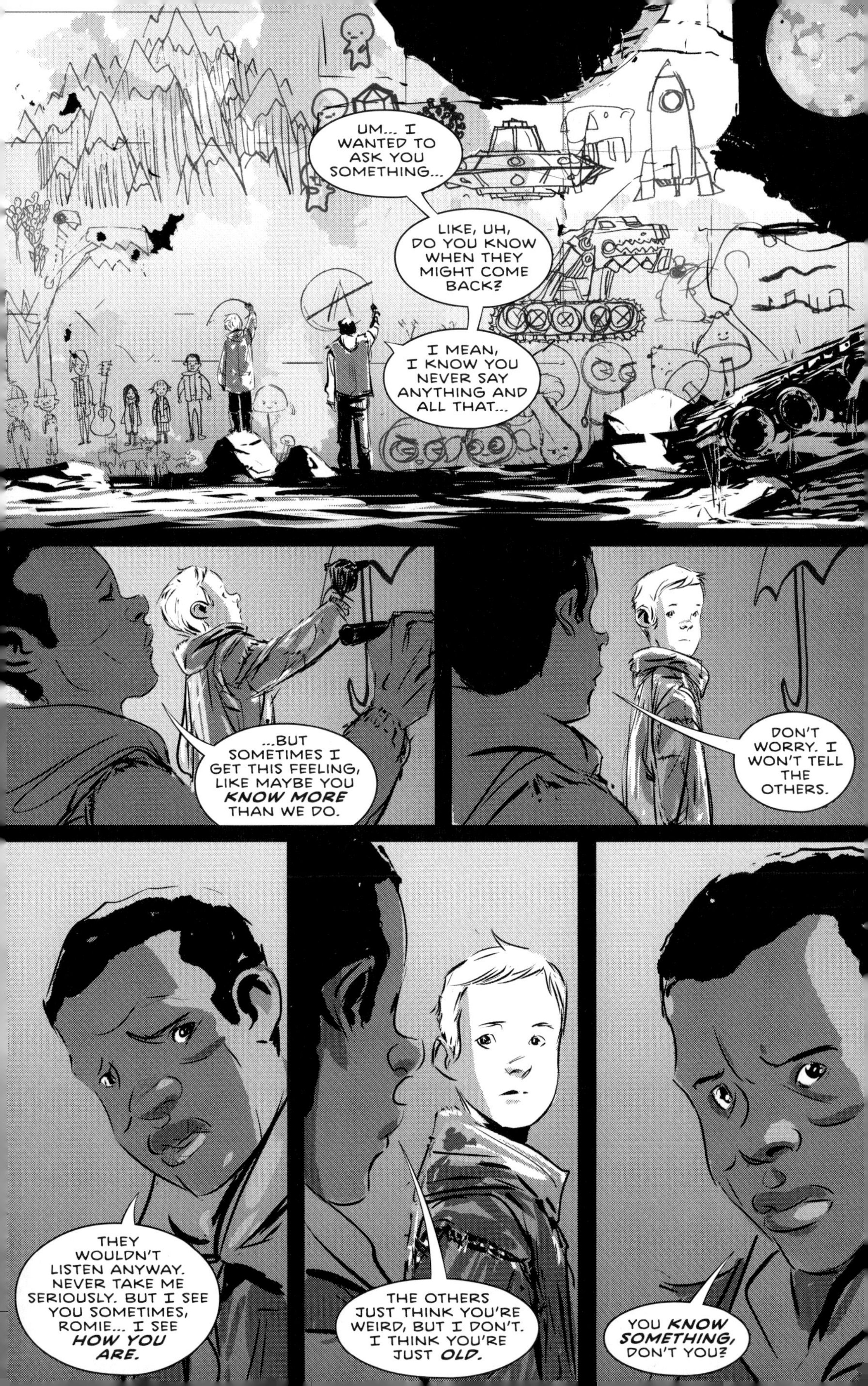
UM... I WANTED TO ASK YOU SOMETHING...
LIKE, UH, DO YOU KNOW WHEN THEY MIGHT COME BACK?
I MEAN, I KNOW YOU NEVER SAY ANYTHING AND ALL THAT...
...BUT SOMETIMES I GET THIS FEELING, LIKE MAYBE YOU KNOW MORE THAN WE DO.
DON'T WORRY. I WON'T TELL THE OTHERS.
THEY WOULDN'T LISTEN ANYWAY. NEVER TAKE ME SERIOUSLY. BUT I SEE YOU SOMETIMES, ROMIE... I SEE HOW YOU ARE.
THE OTHERS JUST THINK YOU'RE WEIRD, BUT I DON'T. I THINK YOU'RE JUST OLD.
YOU KNOW SOMETHING, DON'T YOU?

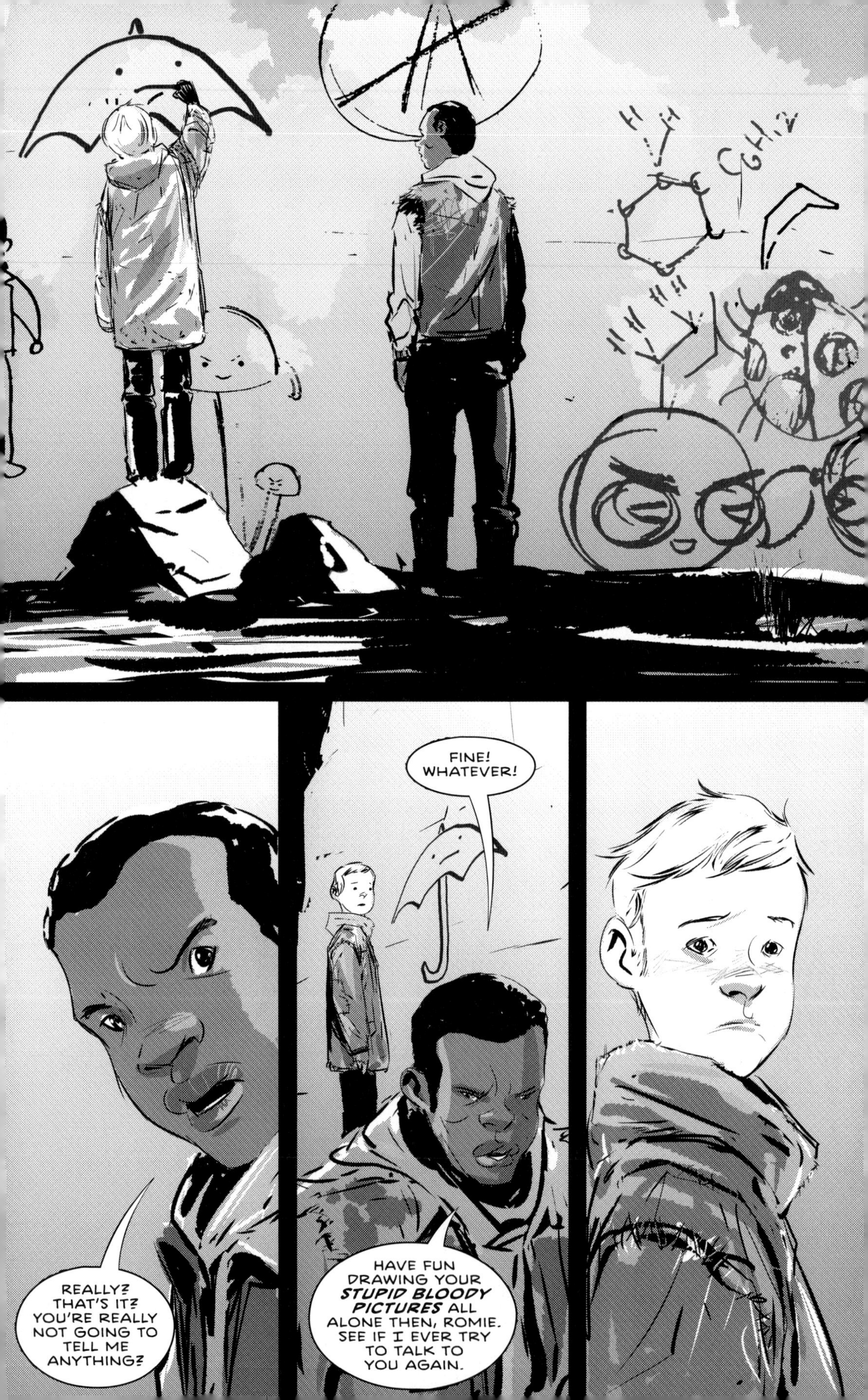
REALLY? THAT'S IT? YOU'RE REALLY NOT GOING TO TELL ME ANYTHING?
FINE! WHATEVER!
HAVE FUN DRAWING YOUR ***STUPID BLOODY PICTURES*** ALL ALONE THEN, ROMIE. SEE IF I EVER TRY TO TALK TO YOU AGAIN.

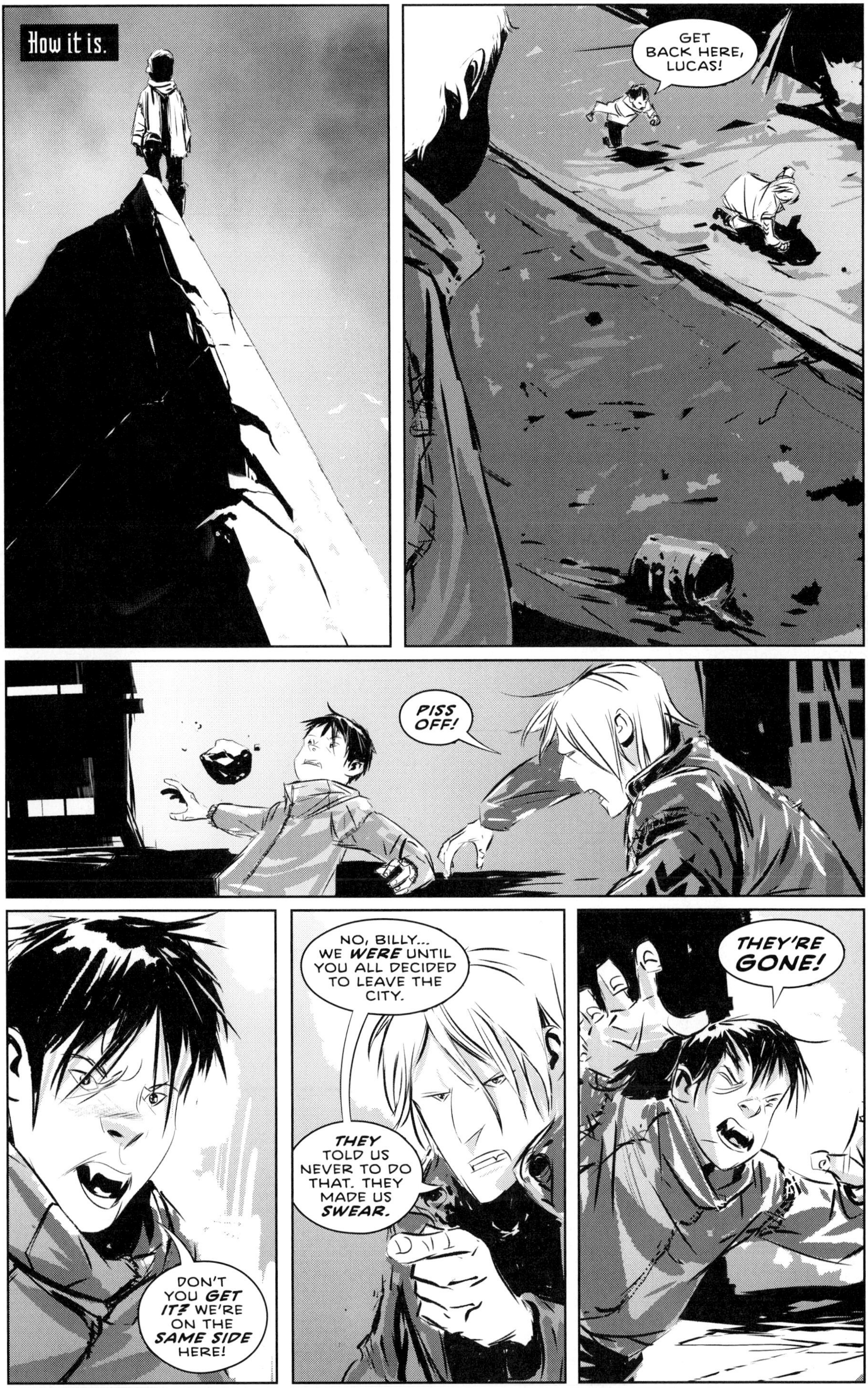
How it is.
GET BACK HERE, LUCAS!
PISS OFF!
DON'T YOU GET IT? WE'RE ON THE SAME SIDE HERE!
NO, BILLY... WE WERE UNTIL YOU ALL DECIDED TO LEAVE THE CITY.
THEY TOLD US NEVER TO DO THAT. THEY MADE US SWEAR.
THEY'RE GONE!

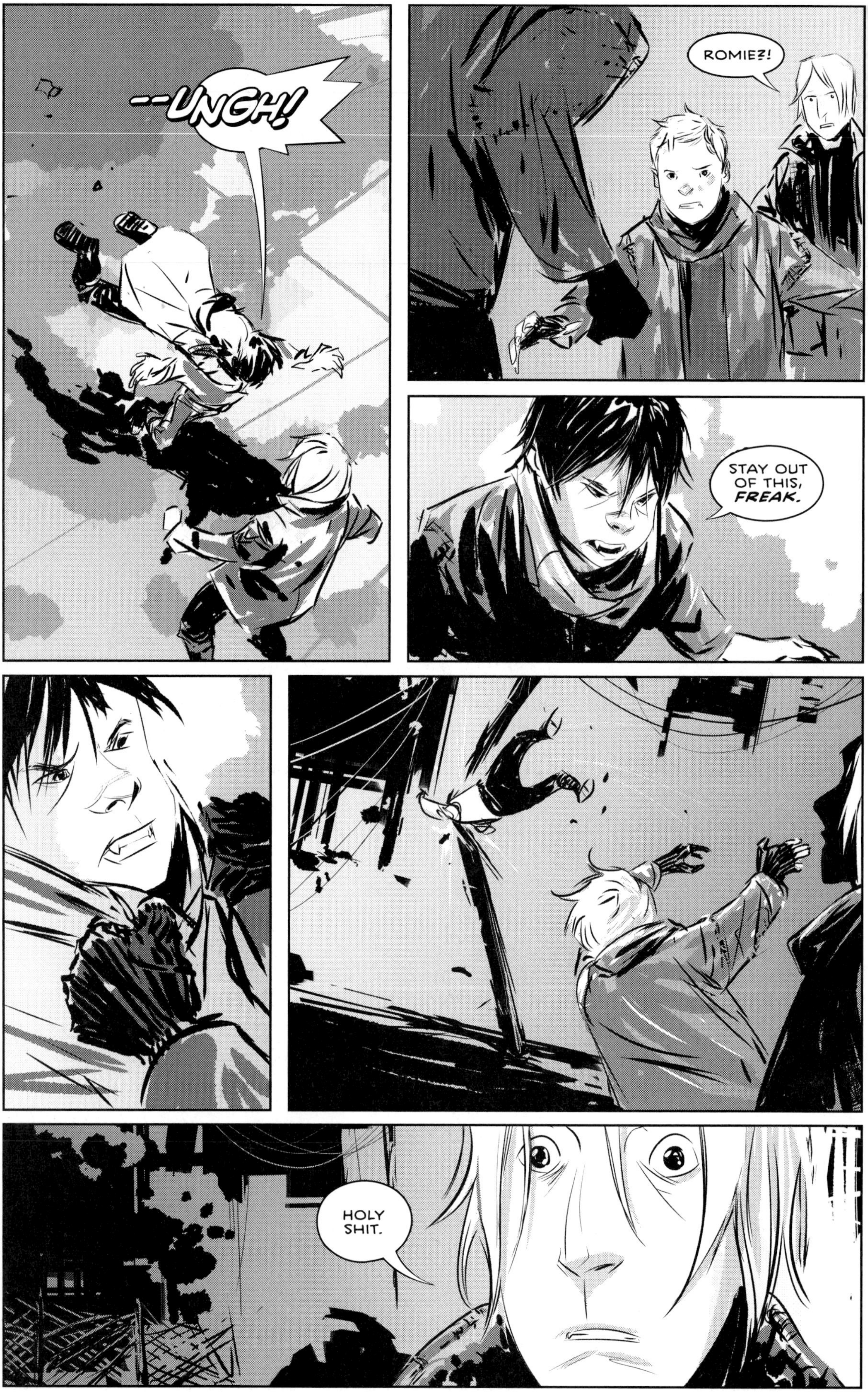
--UNGH!
ROMIEZ!
STAY OUT OF THIS, FREAK.
HOLY SHIT.

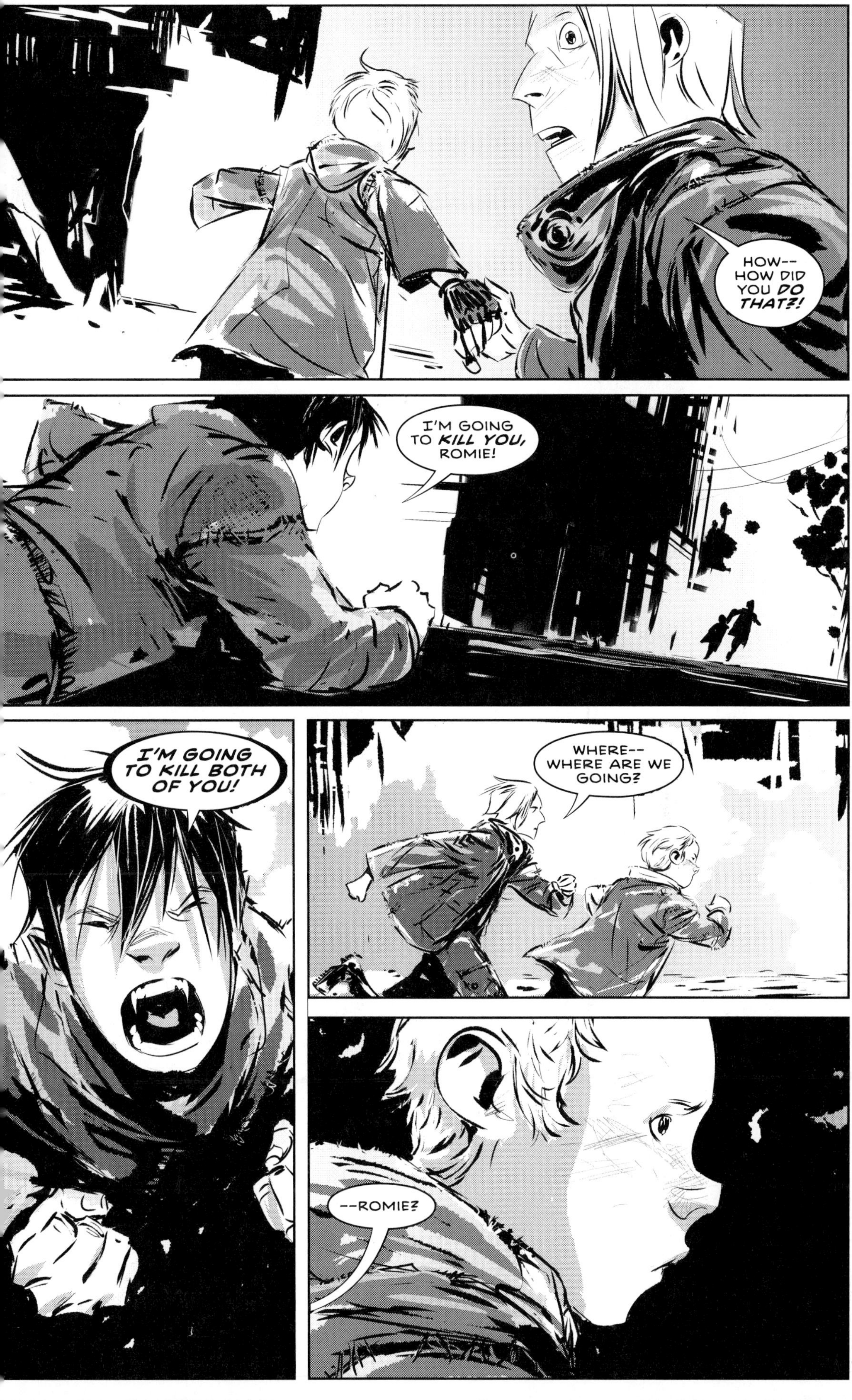

HOW-- HOW DID YOU DO THAT?!
I'M GOING TO KILL YOU, ROMIE!
I'M GOING TO KILL BOTH OF YOU!
WHERE-- WHERE ARE WE GOING?
--ROMIE?

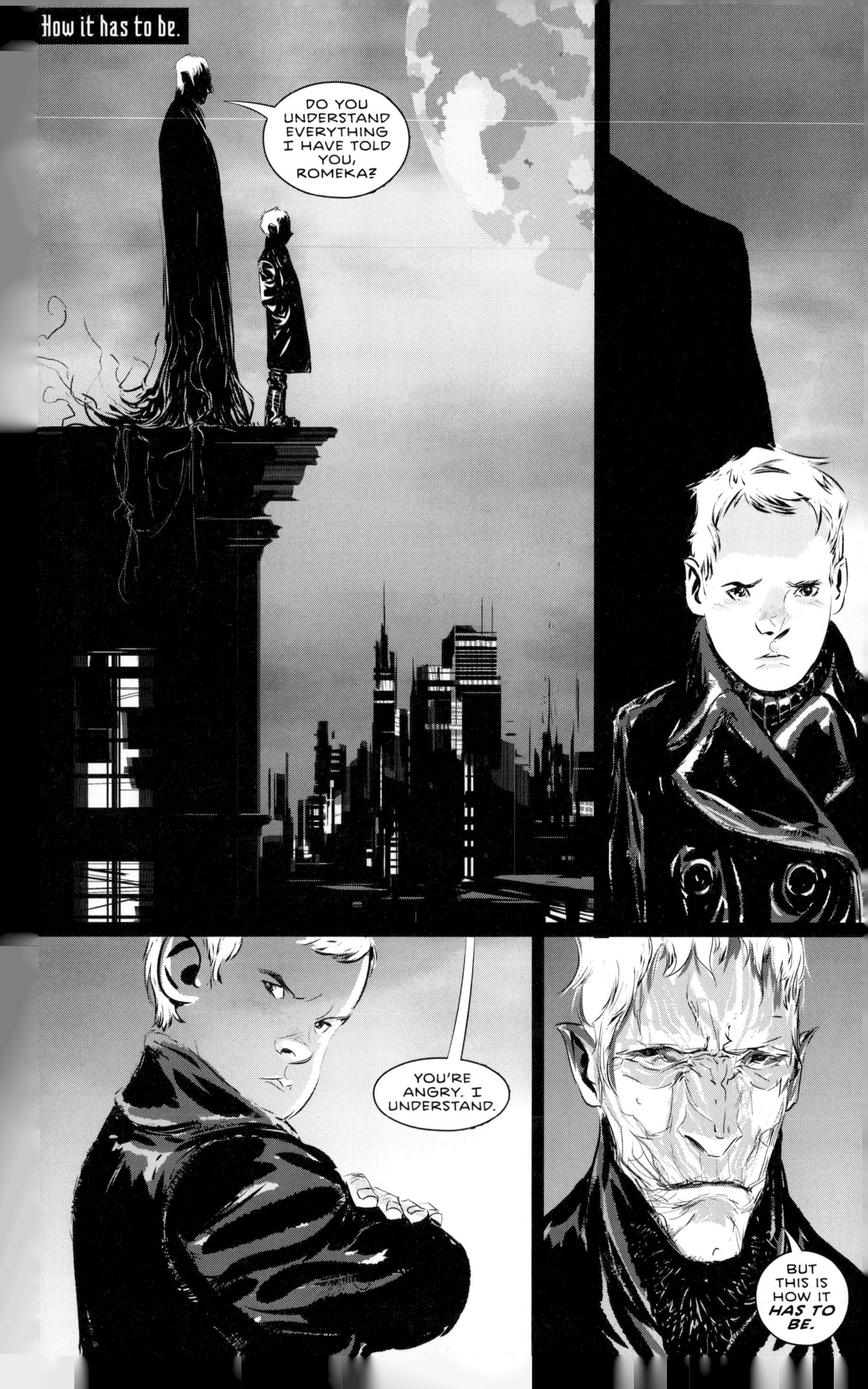
How it has to be.
DO YOU UNDERSTAND EVERYTHING I HAVE TOLD YOU, ROMEKA?
YOU'RE ANGRY. I UNDERSTAND.
BUT THIS IS HOW IT HAS TO BE.

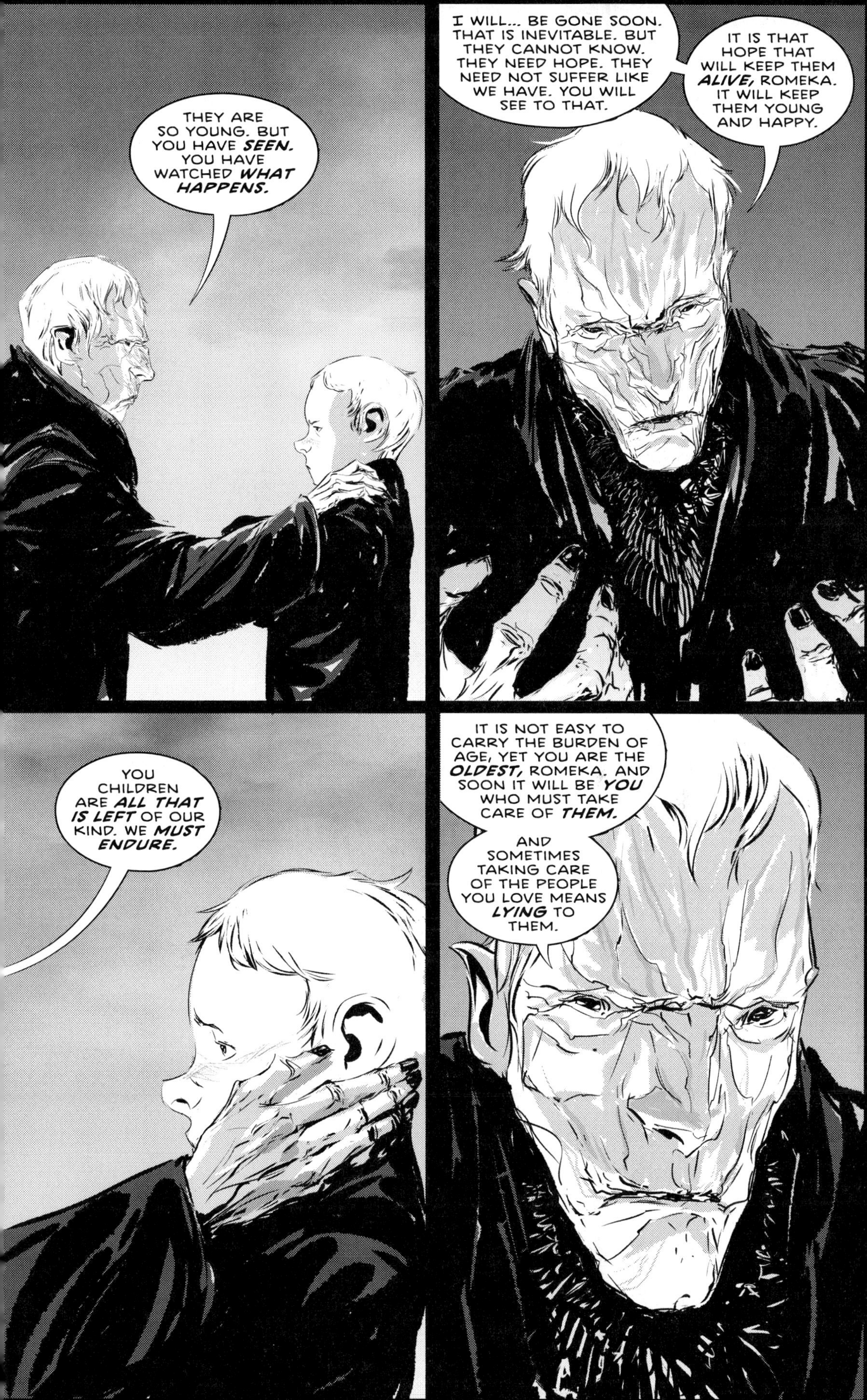
THEY ARE SO YOUNG. BUT YOU HAVE SEEN. YOU HAVE WATCHED WHAT HAPPENS.
I WILL... BE GONE SOON. THAT IS INEVITABLE. BUT THEY CANNOT KNOW. THEY NEED HOPE. THEY NEED NOT SUFFER LIKE WE HAVE. YOU WILL SEE TO THAT.
IT IS THAT HOPE THAT WILL KEEP THEM ALIVE, ROMEKA. IT WILL KEEP THEM YOUNG AND HAPPY.
YOU CHILDREN ARE ALL THAT IS LEFT OF OUR KIND. WE MUST ENDURE.
IT IS NOT EASY TO CARRY THE BURDEN OF AGE, YET YOU ARE THE OLDEST, ROMEKA. AND SOON IT WILL BE YOU WHO MUST TAKE CARE OF THEM.
AND SOMETIMES TAKING CARE OF THE PEOPLE YOU LOVE MEANS LYING TO THEM.

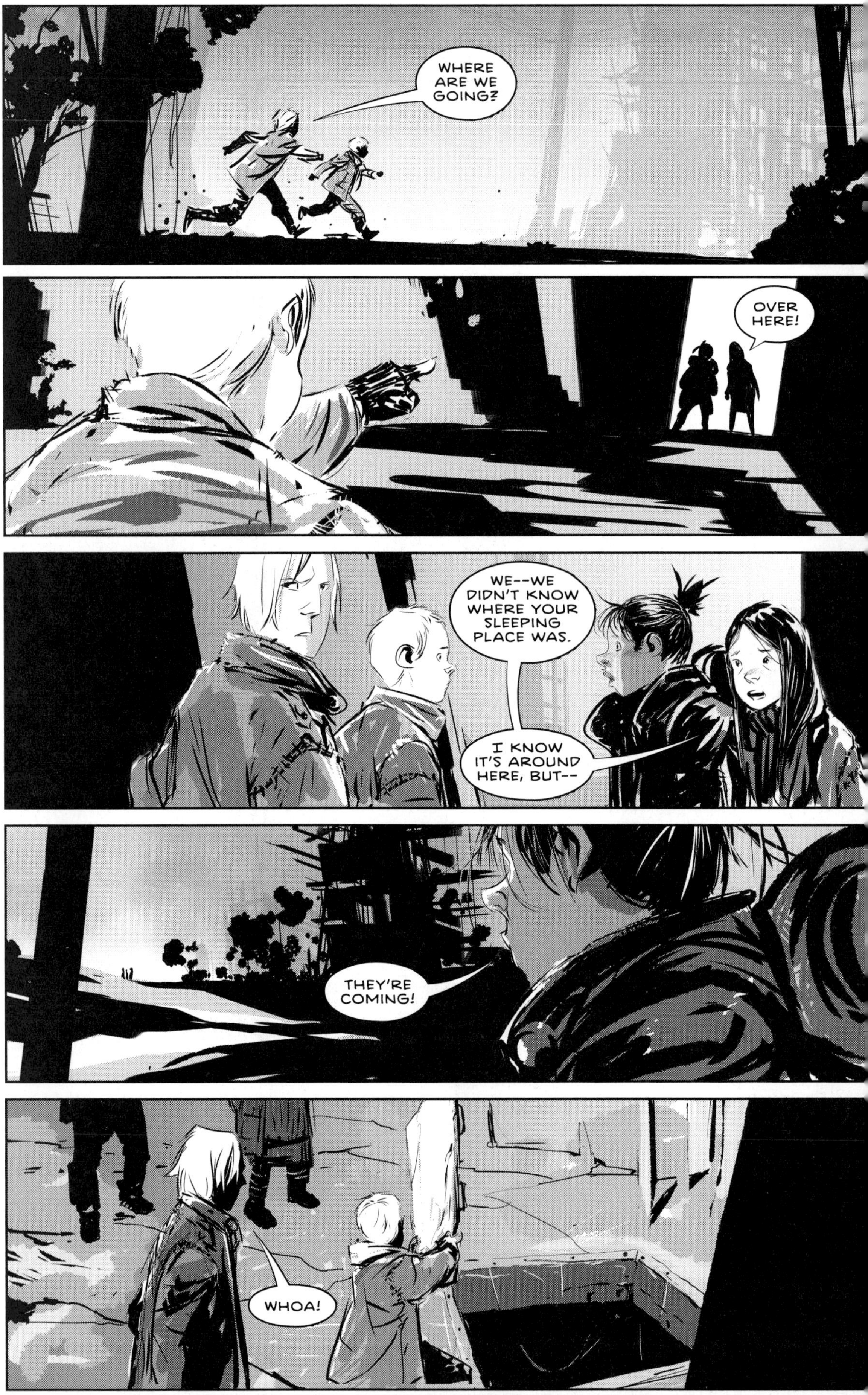
WHERE ARE WE GOING?
OVER HERE!
WE--WE DIDN'T KNOW WHERE YOUR SLEEPING PLACE WAS.
I KNOW IT'S AROUND HERE, BUT--
THEY'RE COMING!
WHOA!

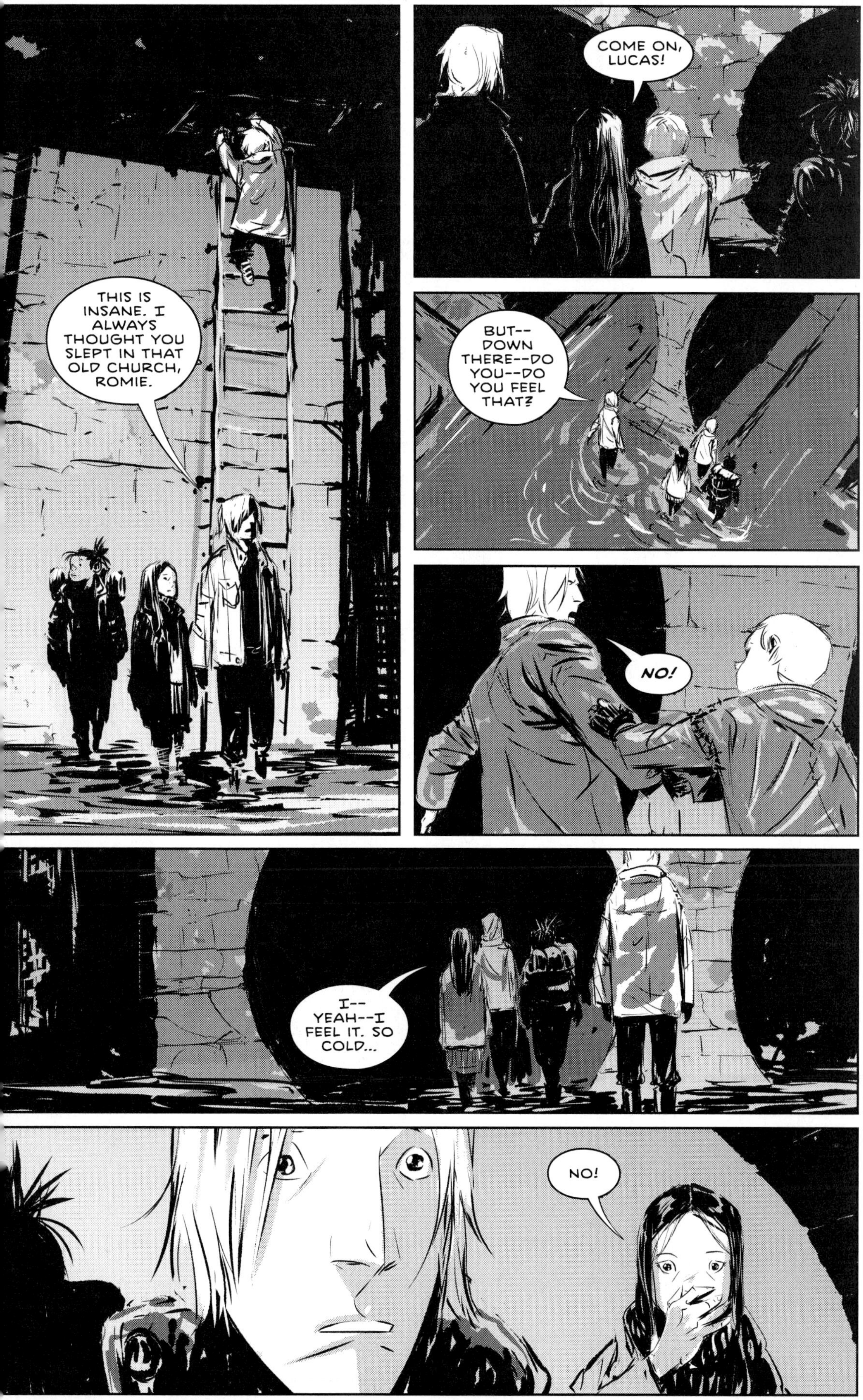
THIS IS INSANE. I ALWAYS THOUGHT YOU SLEPT IN THAT OLD CHURCH, ROMIE.
COME ON, LUCAS!
BUT--DOWN THERE--DO YOU--DO YOU FEEL THAT?
NO!
I--YEAH--I FEEL IT. SO COLD...
NO!

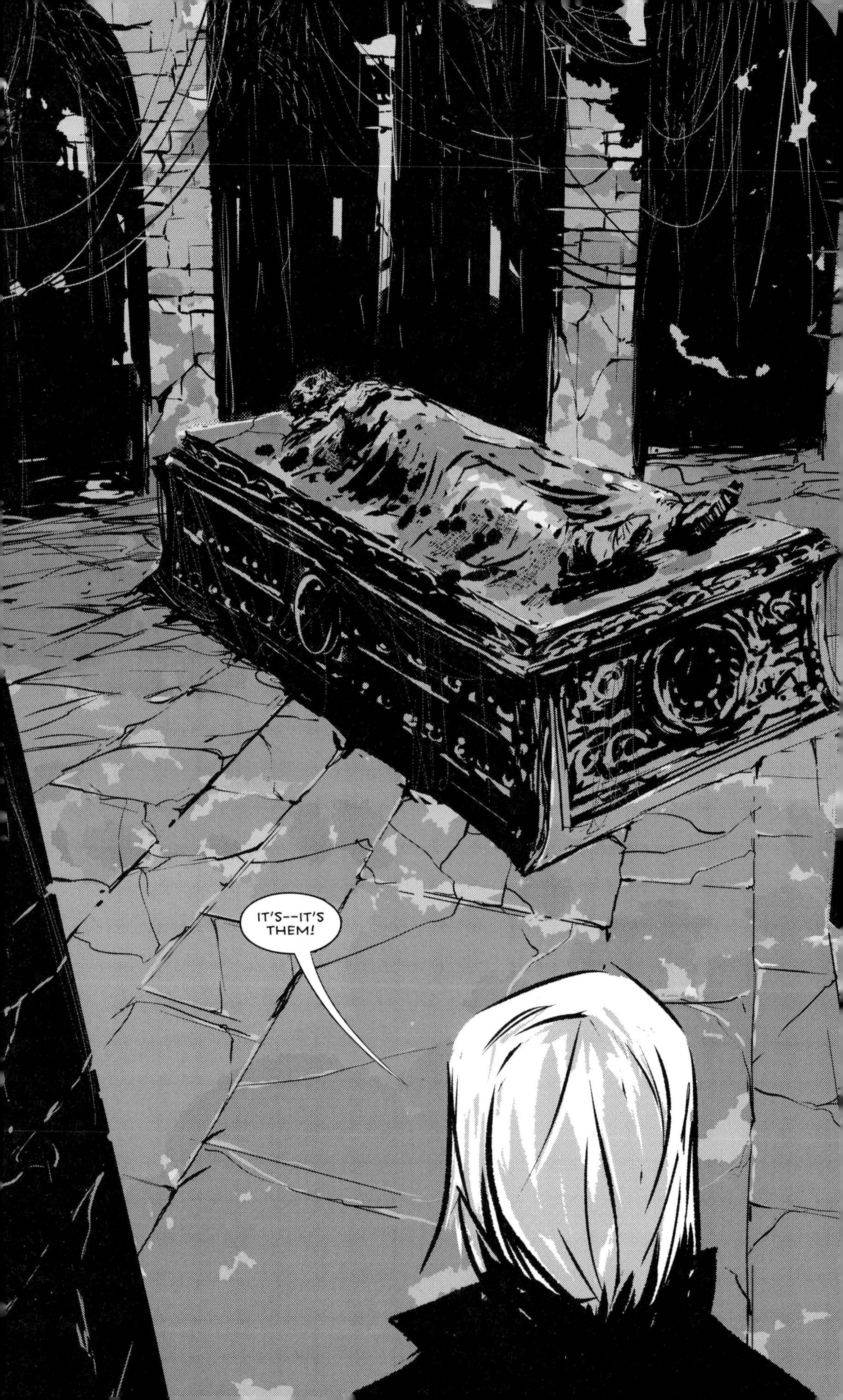
IT'S--IT'S THEM!

Little Monsters

An Illustrated Novel By
Jeff Lemire And Dustin Nguyen
·BOOK·
8

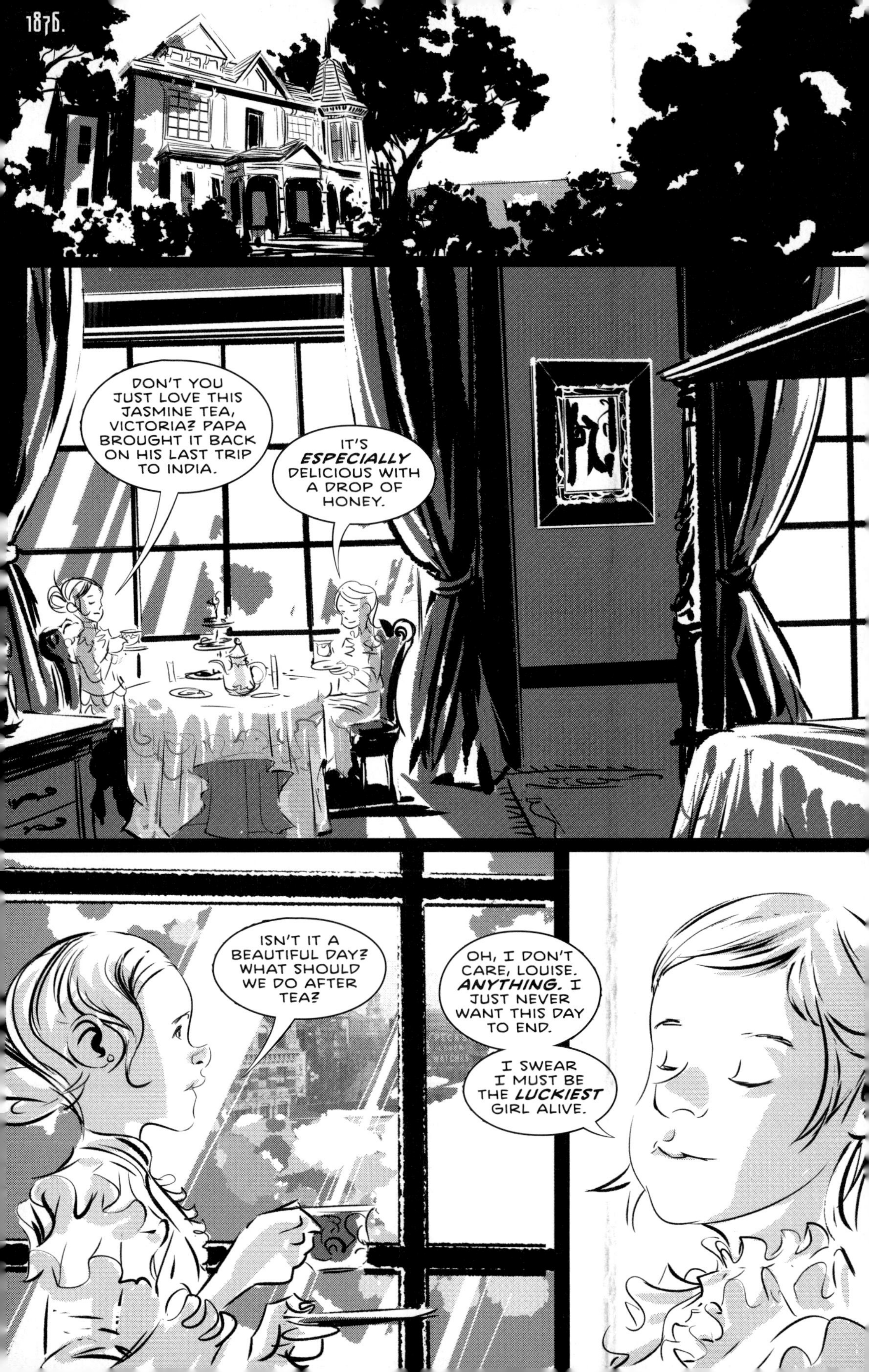
1876.
DON'T YOU JUST LOVE THIS JASMINE TEA, VICTORIA? PAPA BROUGHT IT BACK ON HIS LAST TRIP TO INDIA.
IT'S ESPECIALLY DELICIOUS WITH A DROP OF HONEY.
ISN'T IT A BEAUTIFUL DAY? WHAT SHOULD WE DO AFTER TEA?
OH, I DON'T CARE, LOUISE. ANYTHING. I JUST NEVER WANT THIS DAY TO END.
I SWEAR I MUST BE THE LUCKIEST GIRL ALIVE.

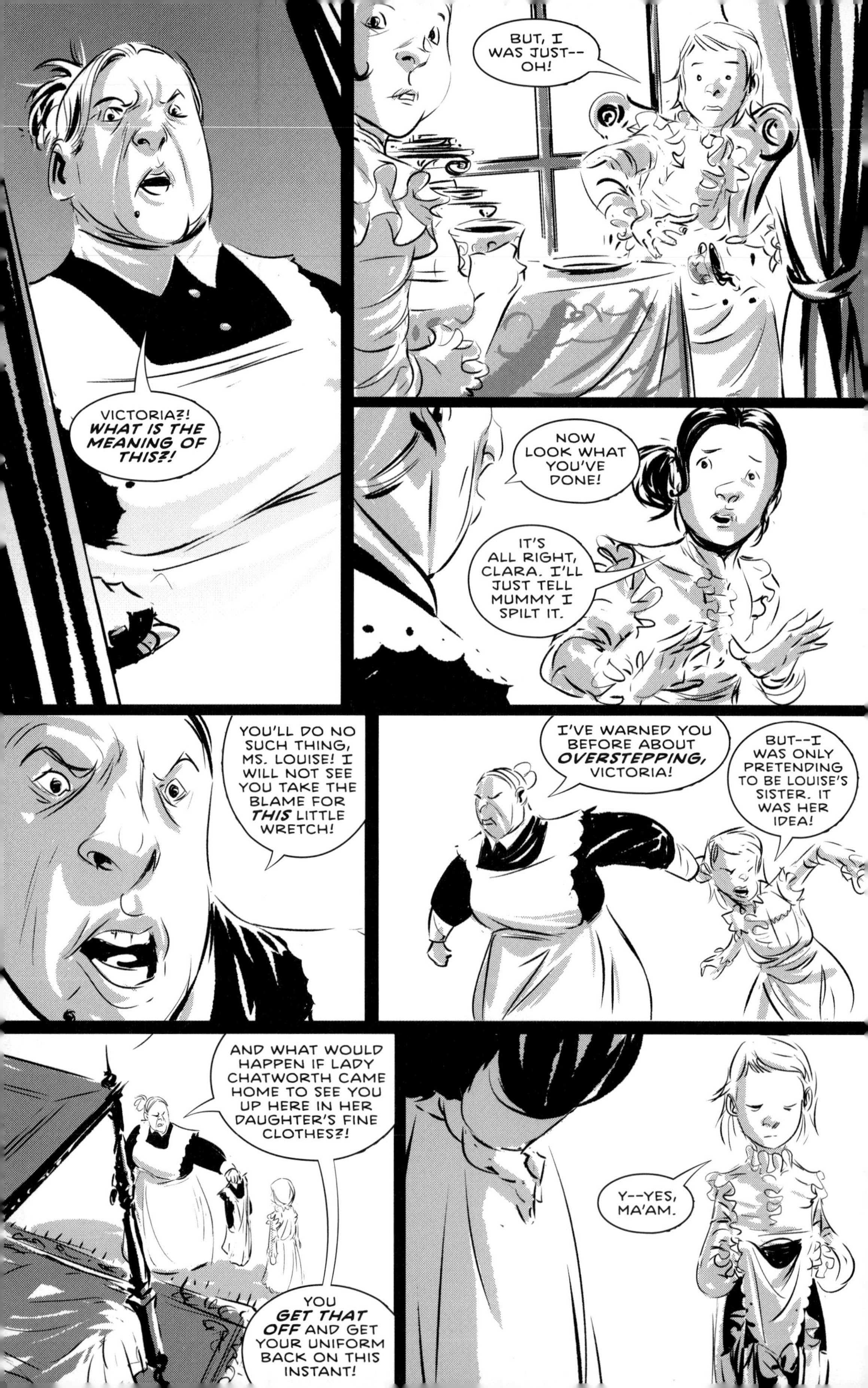
VICTORIA?! WHAT IS THE MEANING OF THIS?!
BUT, I WAS JUST-- OH!
NOW LOOK WHAT YOU'VE DONE!
IT'S ALL RIGHT, CLARA. I'LL JUST TELL MUMMY I SPILT IT.
YOU'LL DO NO SUCH THING, MS. LOUISE! I WILL NOT SEE YOU TAKE THE BLAME FOR THIS LITTLE WRETCH!
I'VE WARNED YOU BEFORE ABOUT OVERSTEPPING, VICTORIA!
BUT--I WAS ONLY PRETENDING TO BE LOUISE'S SISTER. IT WAS HER IDEA!
AND WHAT WOULD HAPPEN IF LADY CHATWORTH CAME HOME TO SEE YOU UP HERE IN HER DAUGHTER'S FINE CLOTHES?!
YOU GET THAT OFF AND GET YOUR UNIFORM BACK ON THIS INSTANT!
Y--YES, MA'AM.

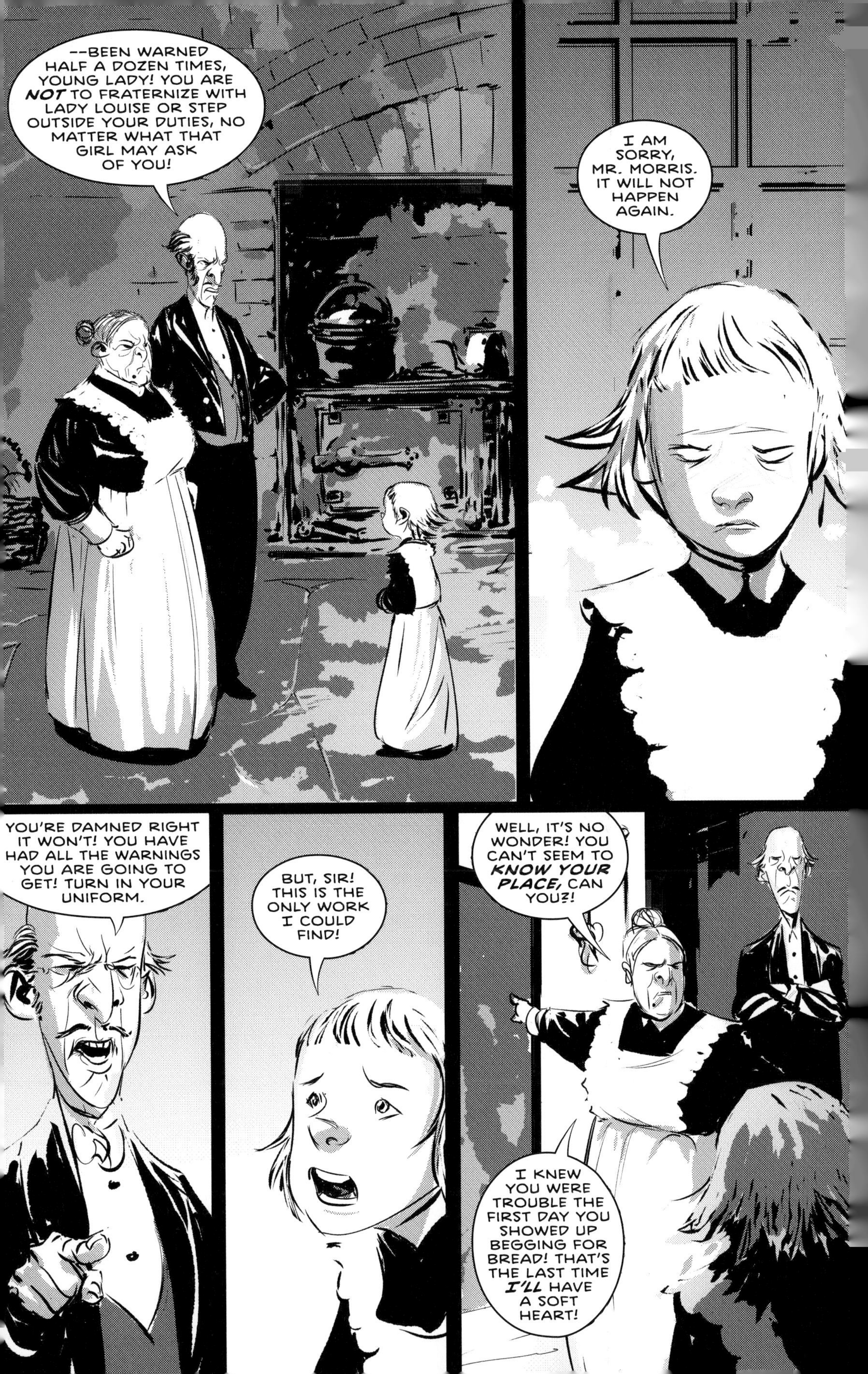
--BEEN WARNED HALF A DOZEN TIMES, YOUNG LADY! YOU ARE *NOT* TO FRATERNIZE WITH LADY LOUISE OR STEP OUTSIDE YOUR DUTIES, NO MATTER WHAT THAT GIRL MAY ASK OF YOU!
I AM SORRY, MR. MORRIS. IT WILL NOT HAPPEN AGAIN.
YOU'RE DAMNED RIGHT IT WON'T! YOU HAVE HAD ALL THE WARNINGS YOU ARE GOING TO GET! TURN IN YOUR UNIFORM.
BUT, SIR! THIS IS THE ONLY WORK I COULD FIND!
WELL, IT'S NO WONDER! YOU CAN'T SEEM TO *KNOW YOUR PLACE,* CAN YOU?!
I KNEW YOU WERE TROUBLE THE FIRST DAY YOU SHOWED UP BEGGING FOR BREAD! THAT'S THE LAST TIME *I'LL* HAVE A SOFT HEART!

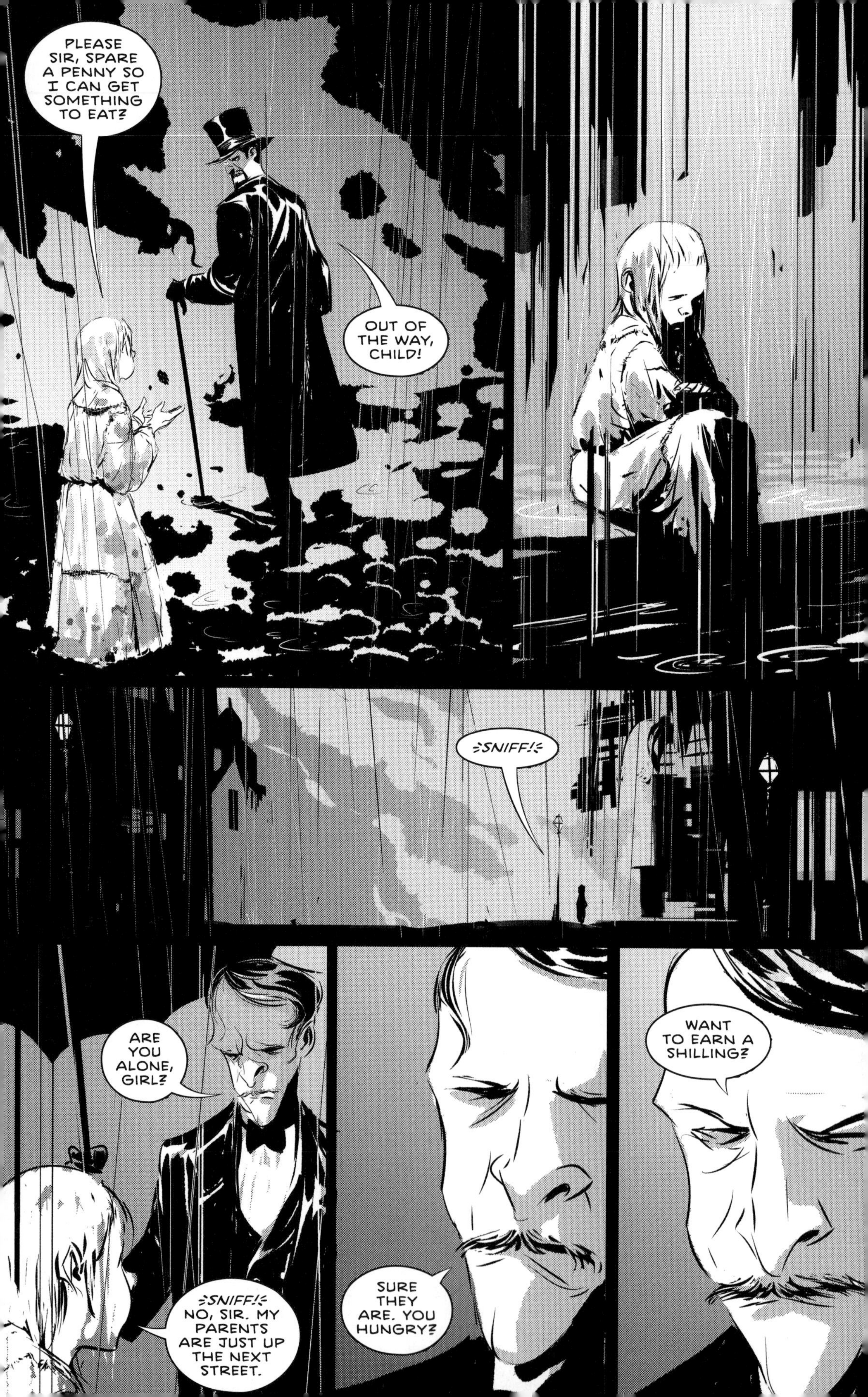
PLEASE SIR, SPARE A PENNY SO I CAN GET SOMETHING TO EAT?
OUT OF THE WAY, CHILD!
SNIFF!
ARE YOU ALONE, GIRL?
SNIFF! NO, SIR. MY PARENTS ARE JUST UP THE NEXT STREET.
SURE THEY ARE. YOU HUNGRY?
WANT TO EARN A SHILLING?

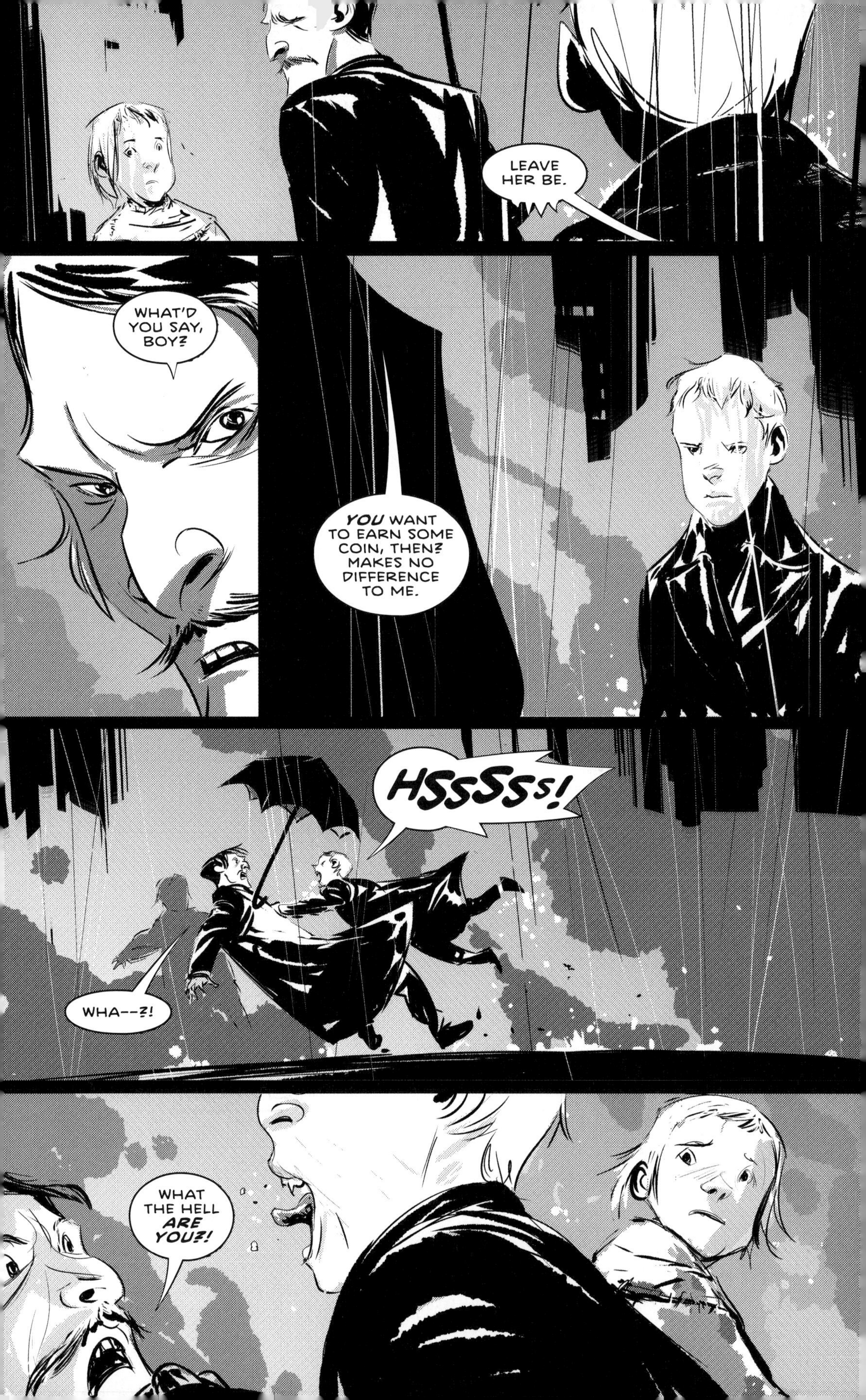
LEAVE HER BE.
WHAT'D YOU SAY, BOY?
YOU WANT TO EARN SOME COIN, THEN? MAKES NO DIFFERENCE TO ME.
HSSSSs!
WHA--?!
WHAT THE HELL ARE YOU?!

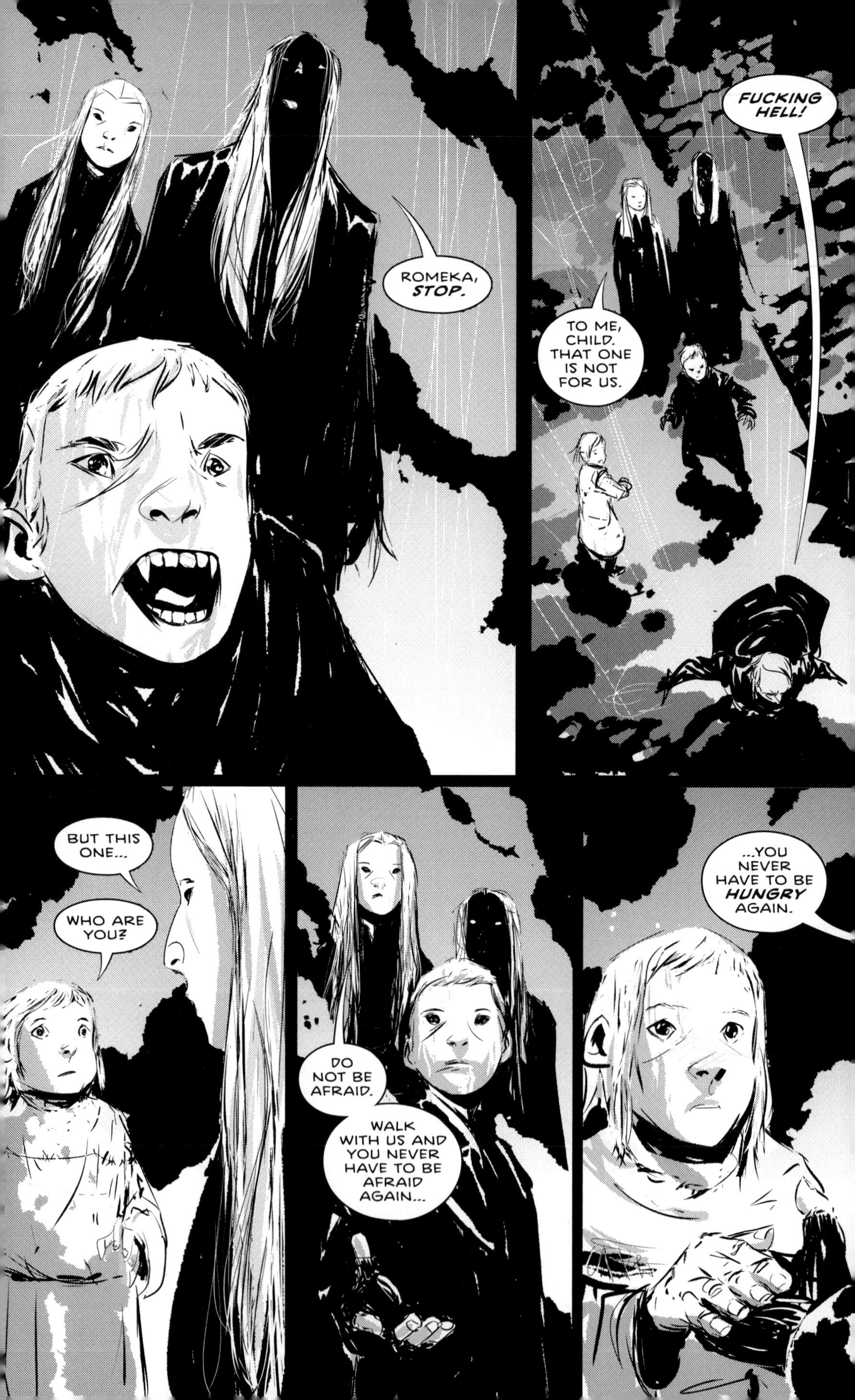
ROMEKA, STOP.
FUCKING HELL!
TO ME, CHILD. THAT ONE IS NOT FOR US.
BUT THIS ONE...
WHO ARE YOU?
DO NOT BE AFRAID.
WALK WITH US AND YOU NEVER HAVE TO BE AFRAID AGAIN...
...YOU NEVER HAVE TO BE HUNGRY AGAIN.

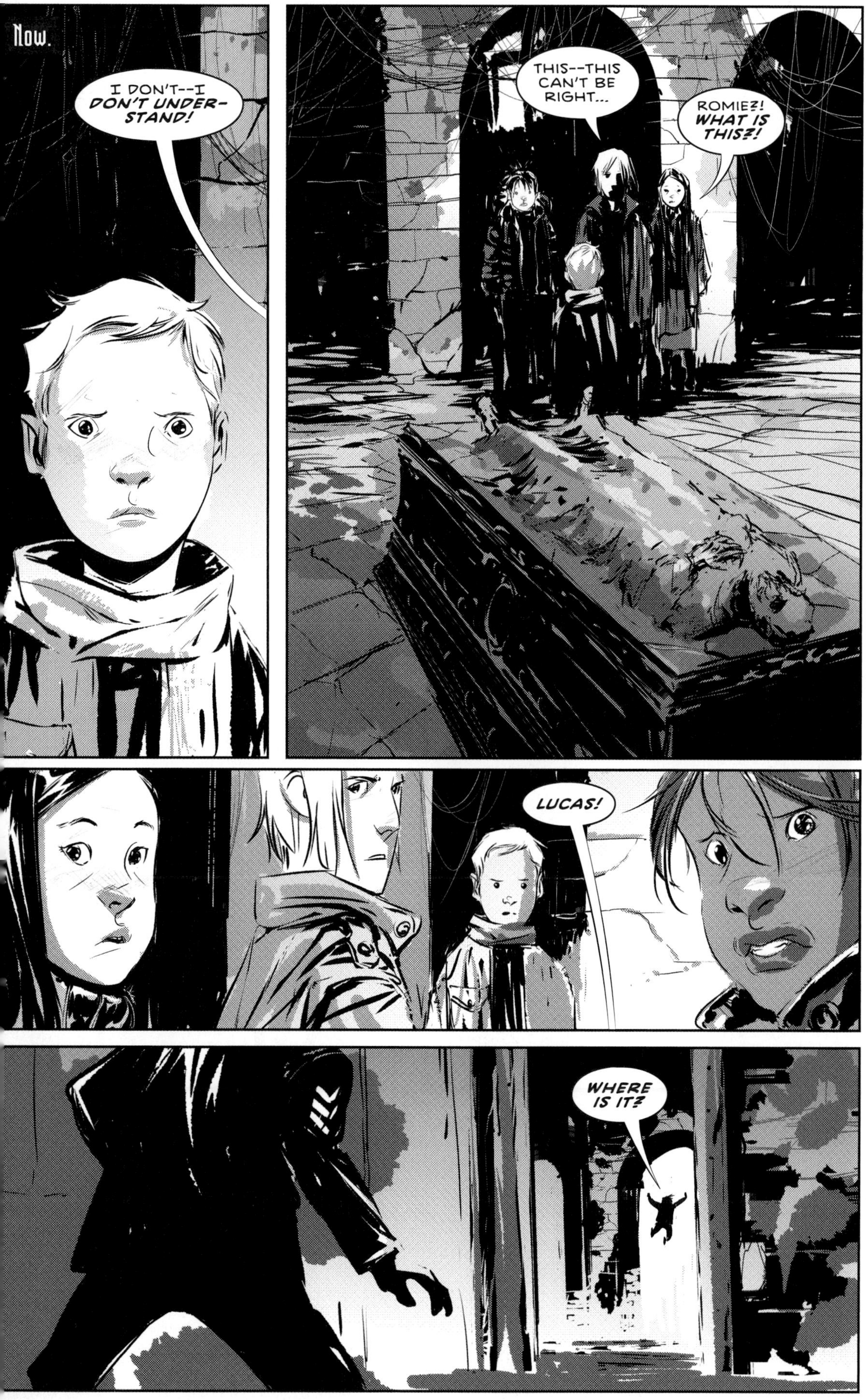
Now.
I DON'T--I DON'T UNDER-STAND!
THIS--THIS CAN'T BE RIGHT...
ROMIE?! WHAT IS THIS?!
LUCAS!
WHERE IS IT?

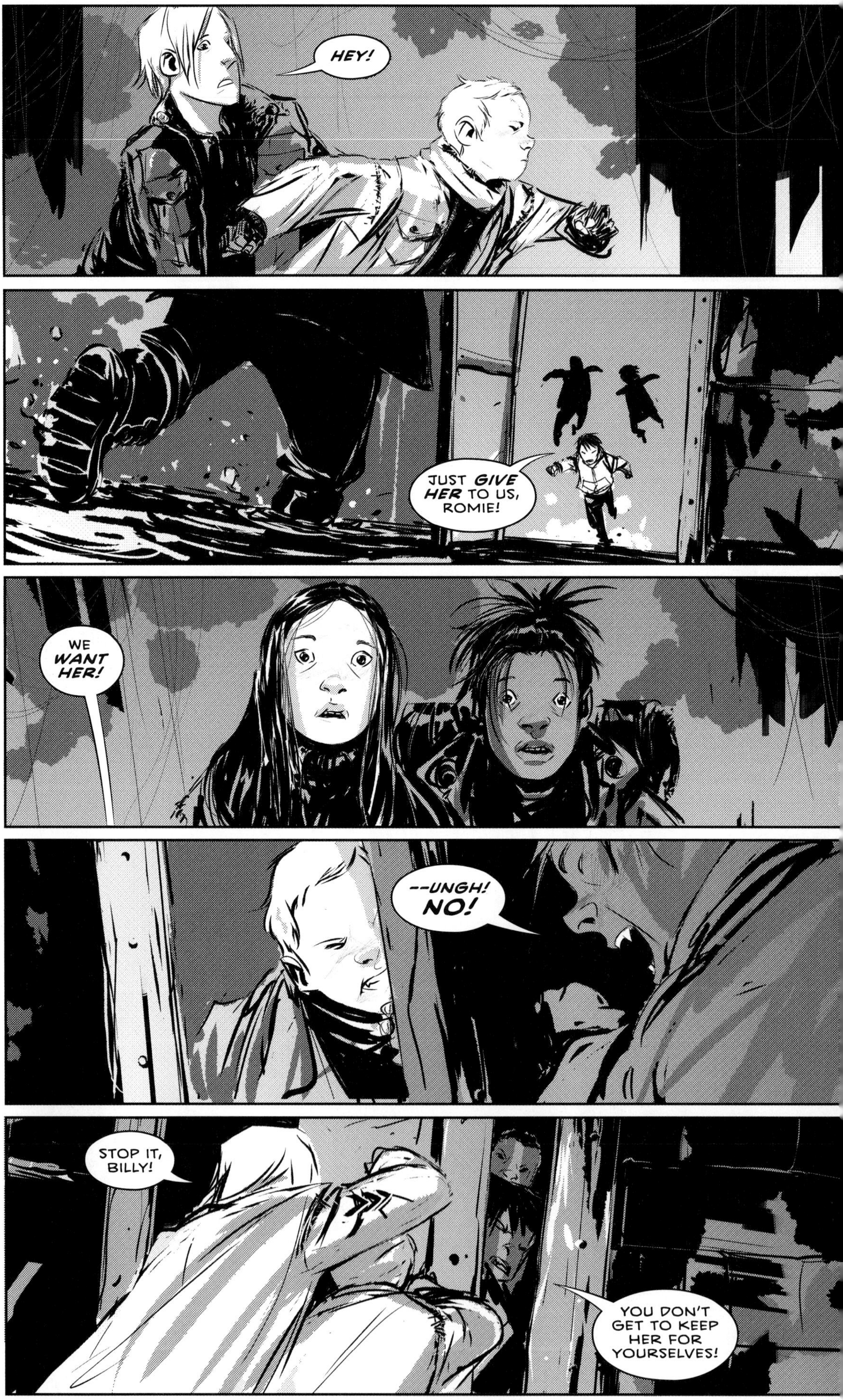
HEY!
JUST GIVE HER TO US, ROMIE!
WE WANT HER!
--UNGH! NO!
STOP IT, BILLY!
YOU DON'T GET TO KEEP HER FOR YOURSELVES!

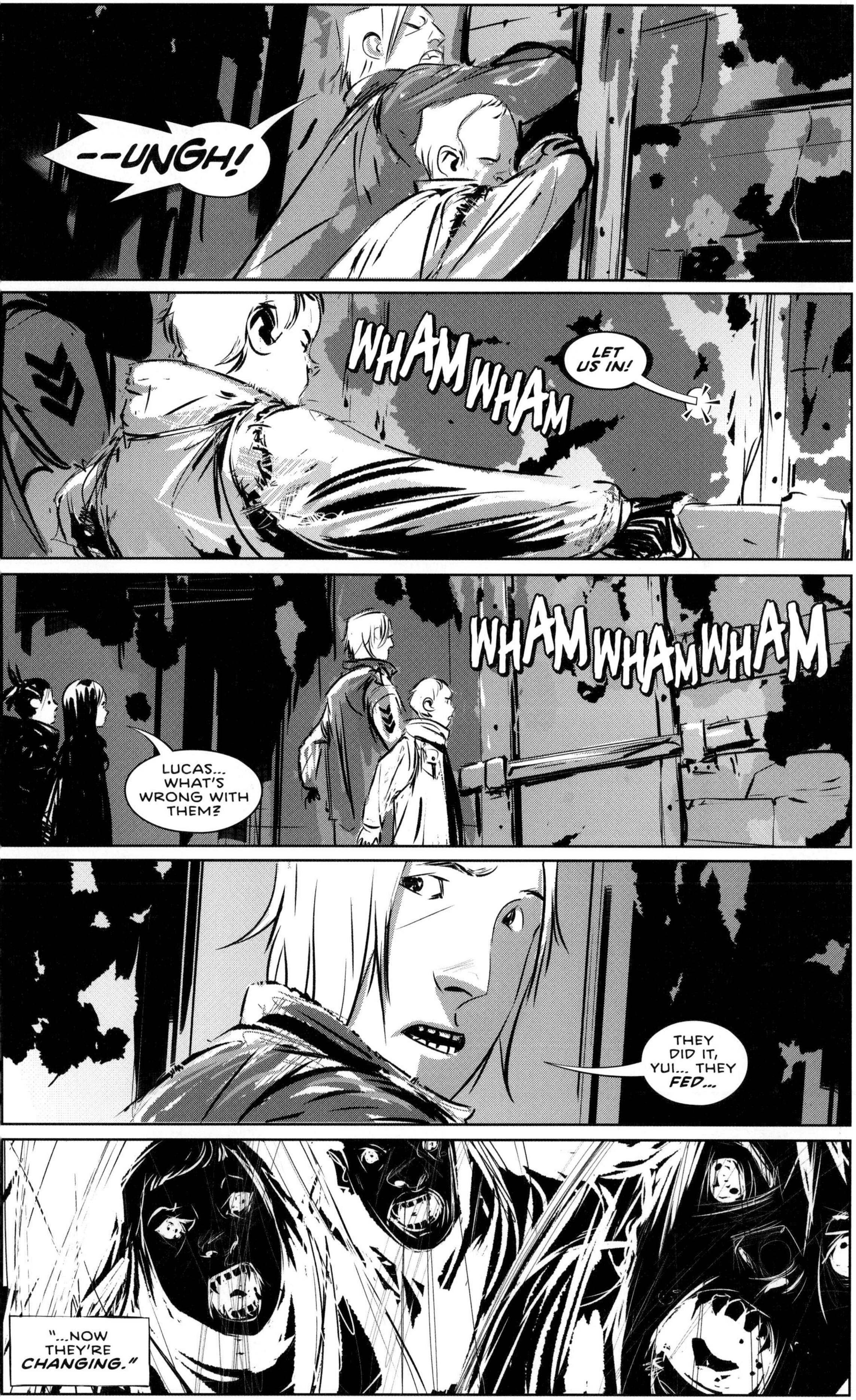
--UNGH!
WHAM WHAM
LET US IN!
WHAM WHAM WHAM
LUCAS... WHAT'S WRONG WITH THEM?
THEY DID IT, YUI... THEY *FED*...
"...NOW THEY'RE *CHANGING*."

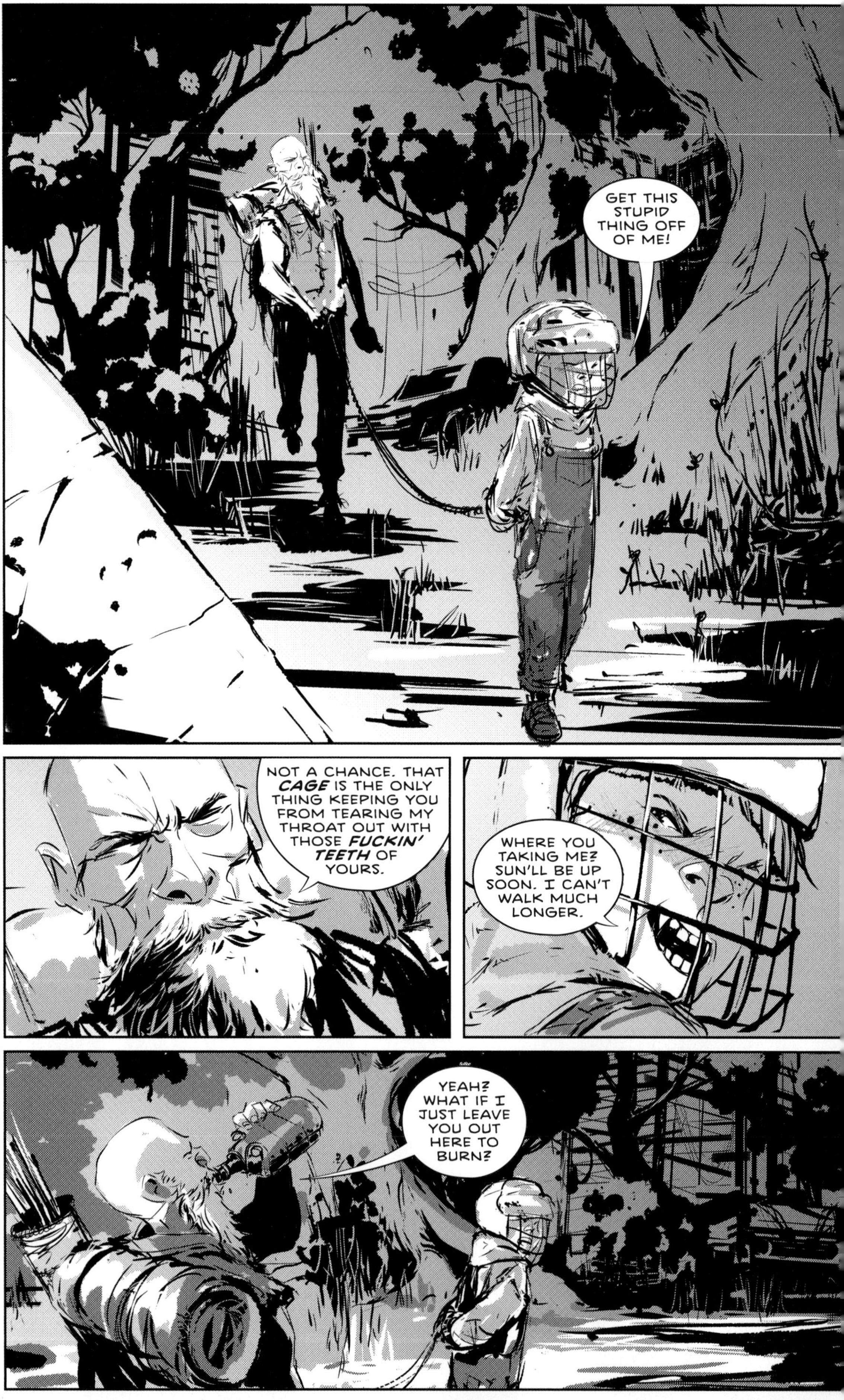
GET THIS STUPID THING OFF OF ME!
NOT A CHANCE. THAT CAGE IS THE ONLY THING KEEPING YOU FROM TEARING MY THROAT OUT WITH THOSE FUCKIN' TEETH OF YOURS.
WHERE YOU TAKING ME? SUN'LL BE UP SOON. I CAN'T WALK MUCH LONGER.
YEAH? WHAT IF I JUST LEAVE YOU OUT HERE TO BURN?

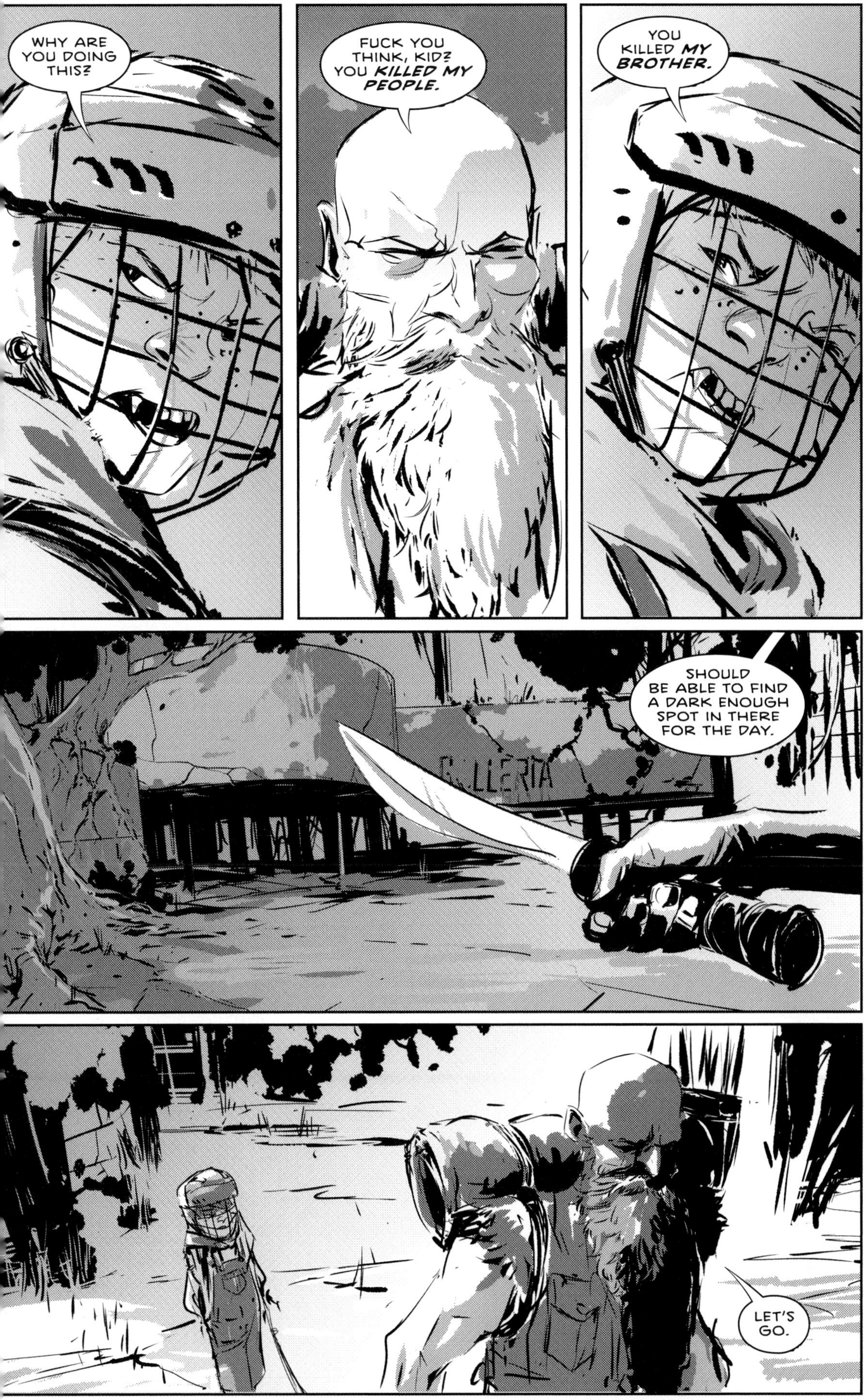
WHY ARE YOU DOING THIS?
FUCK YOU THINK, KID? YOU KILLED MY PEOPLE.
YOU KILLED MY BROTHER.
SHOULD BE ABLE TO FIND A DARK ENOUGH SPOT IN THERE FOR THE DAY.
LET'S GO.

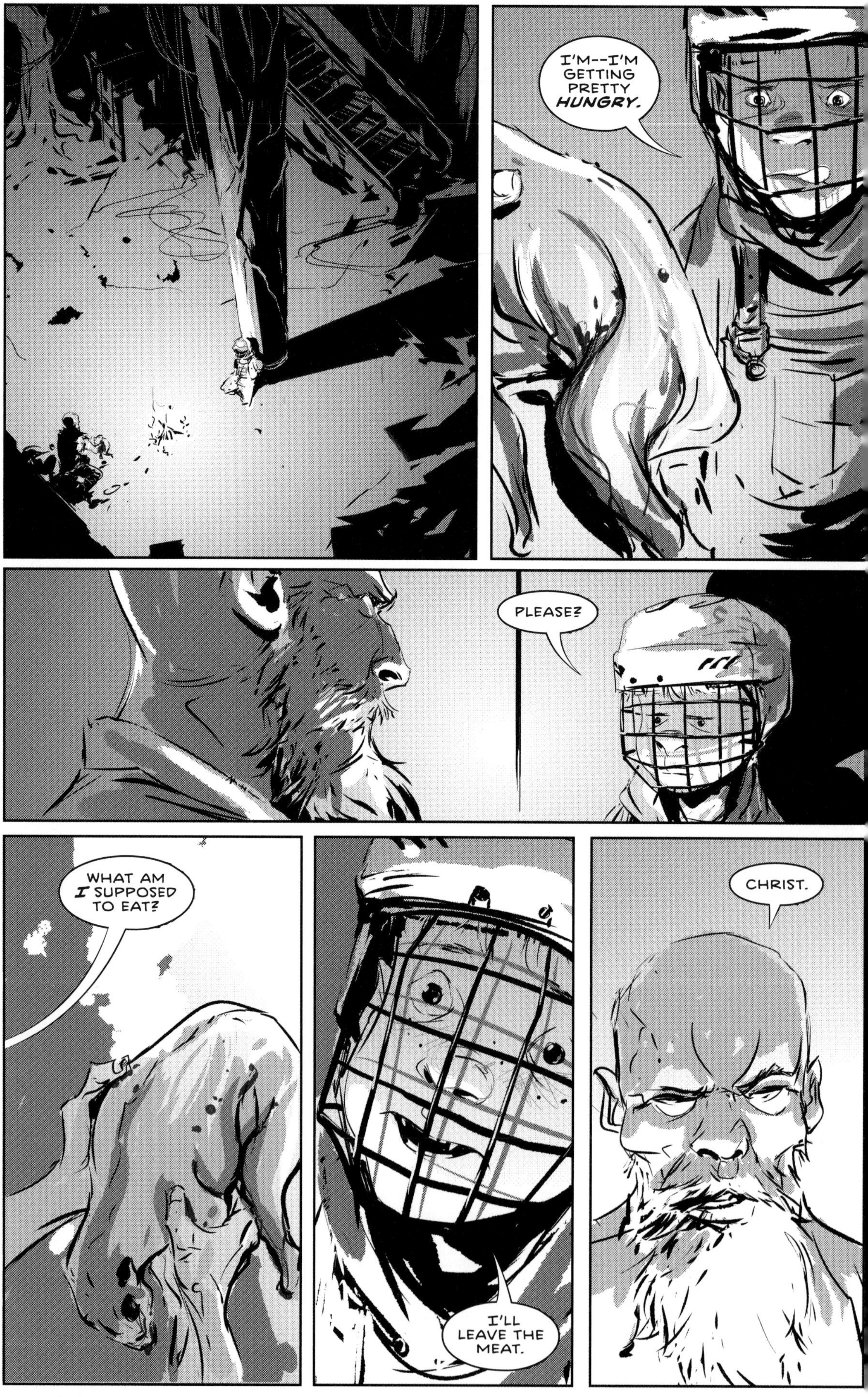
I'M--I'M GETTING PRETTY HUNGRY.
PLEASE?
WHAT AM I SUPPOSED TO EAT?
I'LL LEAVE THE MEAT.
CHRIST.

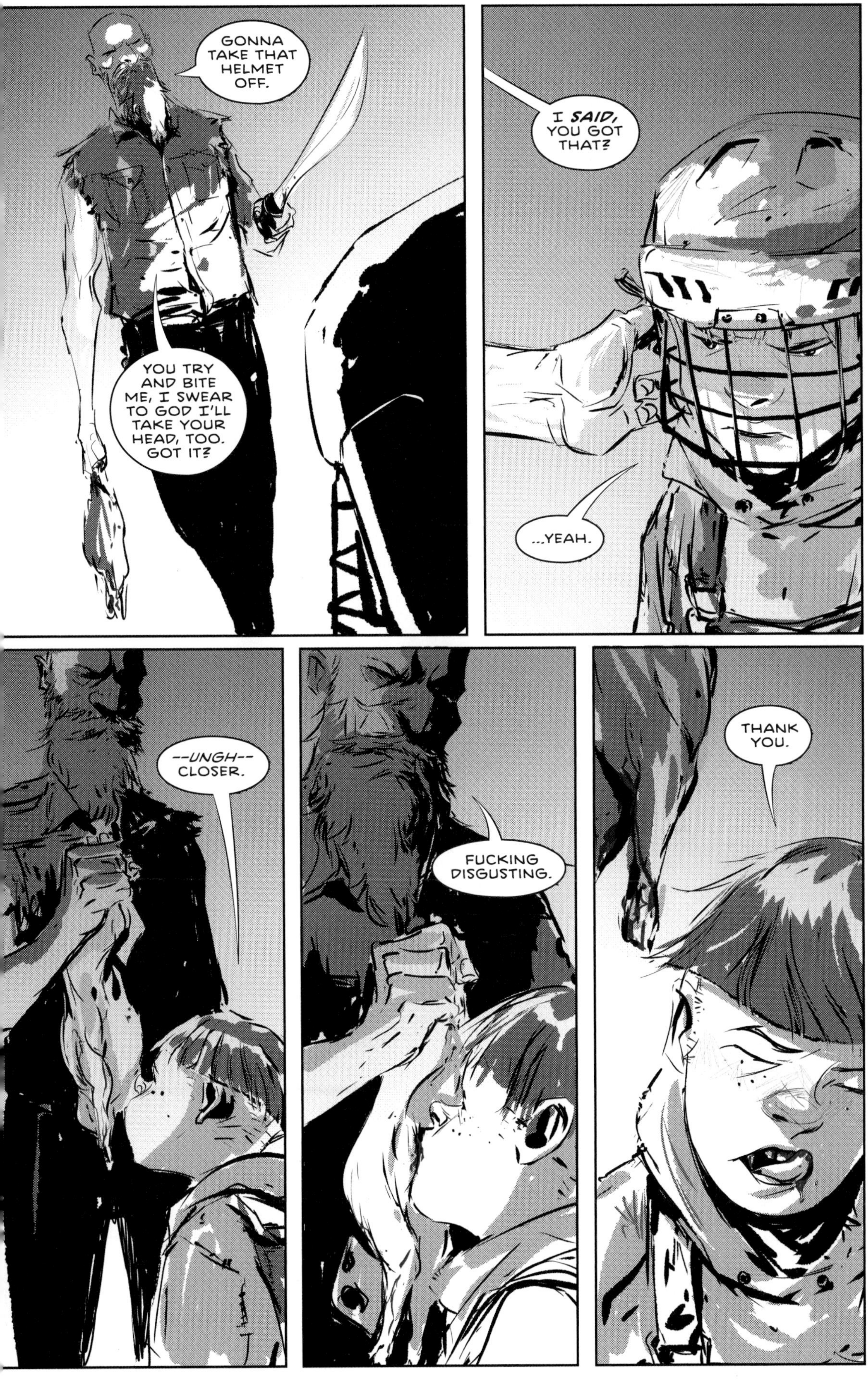
GONNA TAKE THAT HELMET OFF.
YOU TRY AND BITE ME, I SWEAR TO GOD I'LL TAKE YOUR HEAD, TOO. GOT IT?
I *SAID*, YOU GOT THAT?
...YEAH.
--UNGH-- CLOSER.
FUCKING DISGUSTING.
THANK YOU.

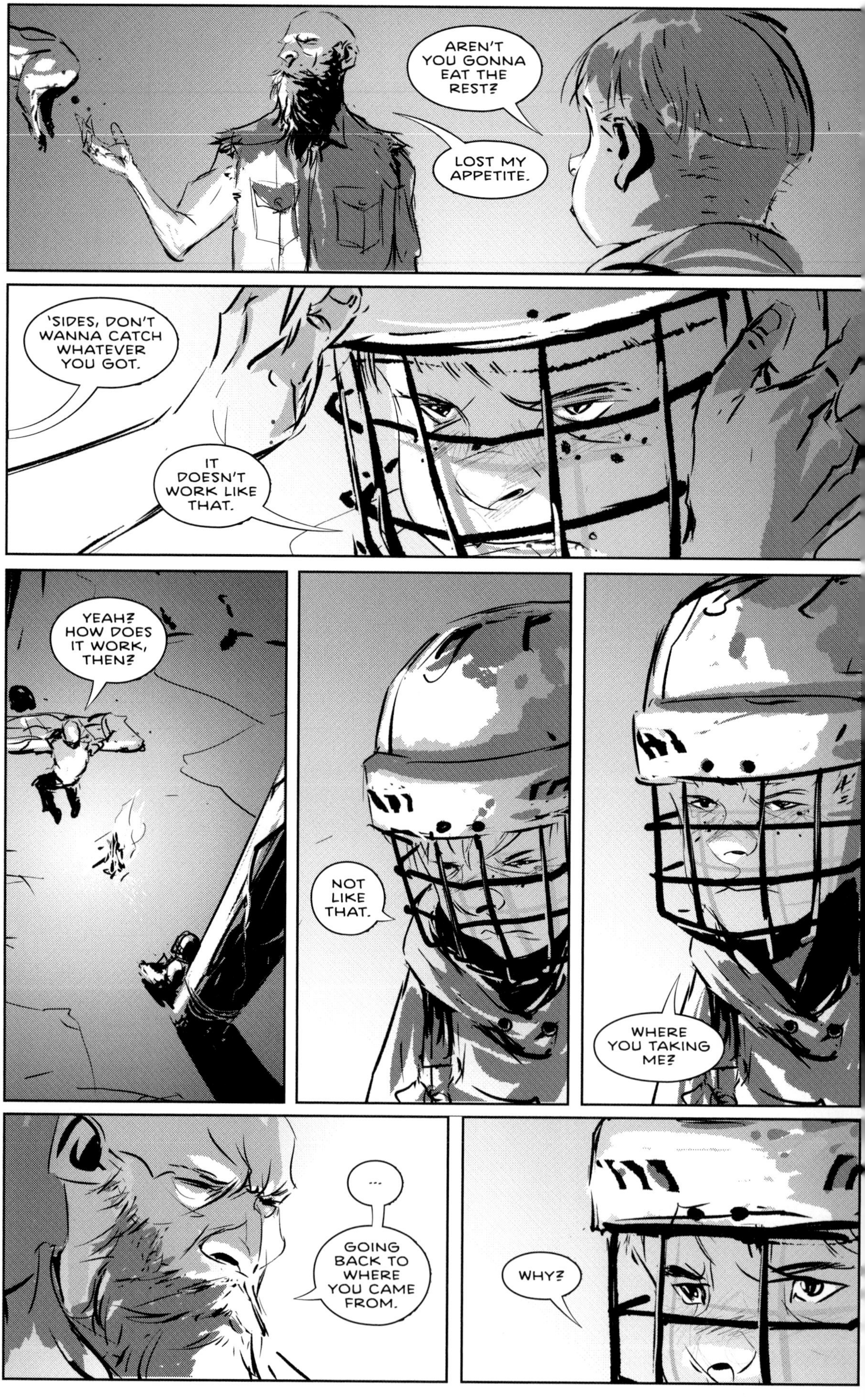
AREN'T YOU GONNA EAT THE REST?
LOST MY APPETITE.
'SIDES, DON'T WANNA CATCH WHATEVER YOU GOT.
IT DOESN'T WORK LIKE THAT.
YEAH? HOW DOES IT WORK, THEN?
NOT LIKE THAT.
WHERE YOU TAKING ME?
...
GOING BACK TO WHERE YOU CAME FROM.
WHY?

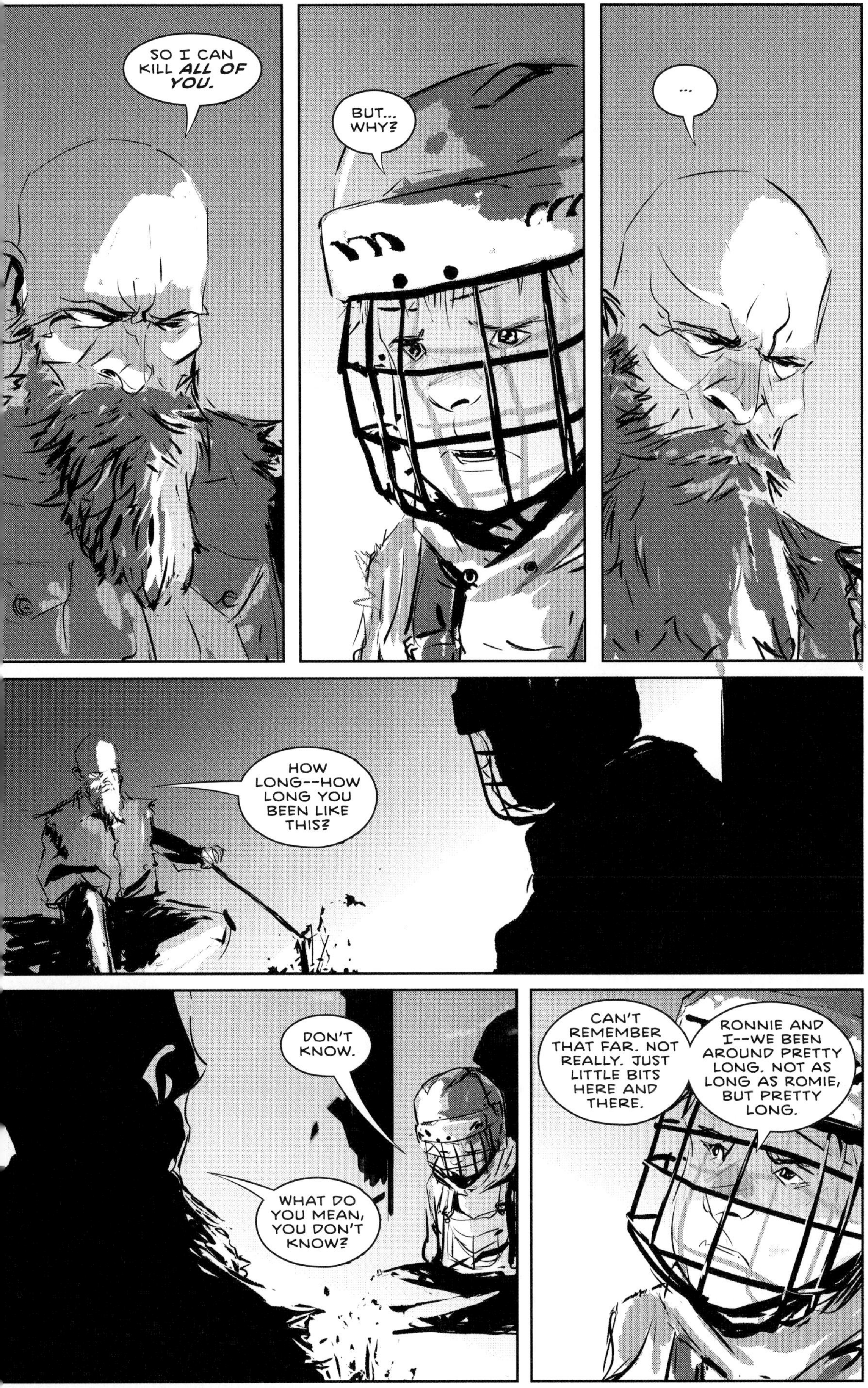
SO I CAN KILL ALL OF YOU.
BUT... WHY?
...
HOW LONG--HOW LONG YOU BEEN LIKE THIS?
DON'T KNOW.
WHAT DO YOU MEAN, YOU DON'T KNOW?
CAN'T REMEMBER THAT FAR. NOT REALLY. JUST LITTLE BITS HERE AND THERE.
RONNIE AND I--WE BEEN AROUND PRETTY LONG. NOT AS LONG AS ROMIE, BUT PRETTY LONG.

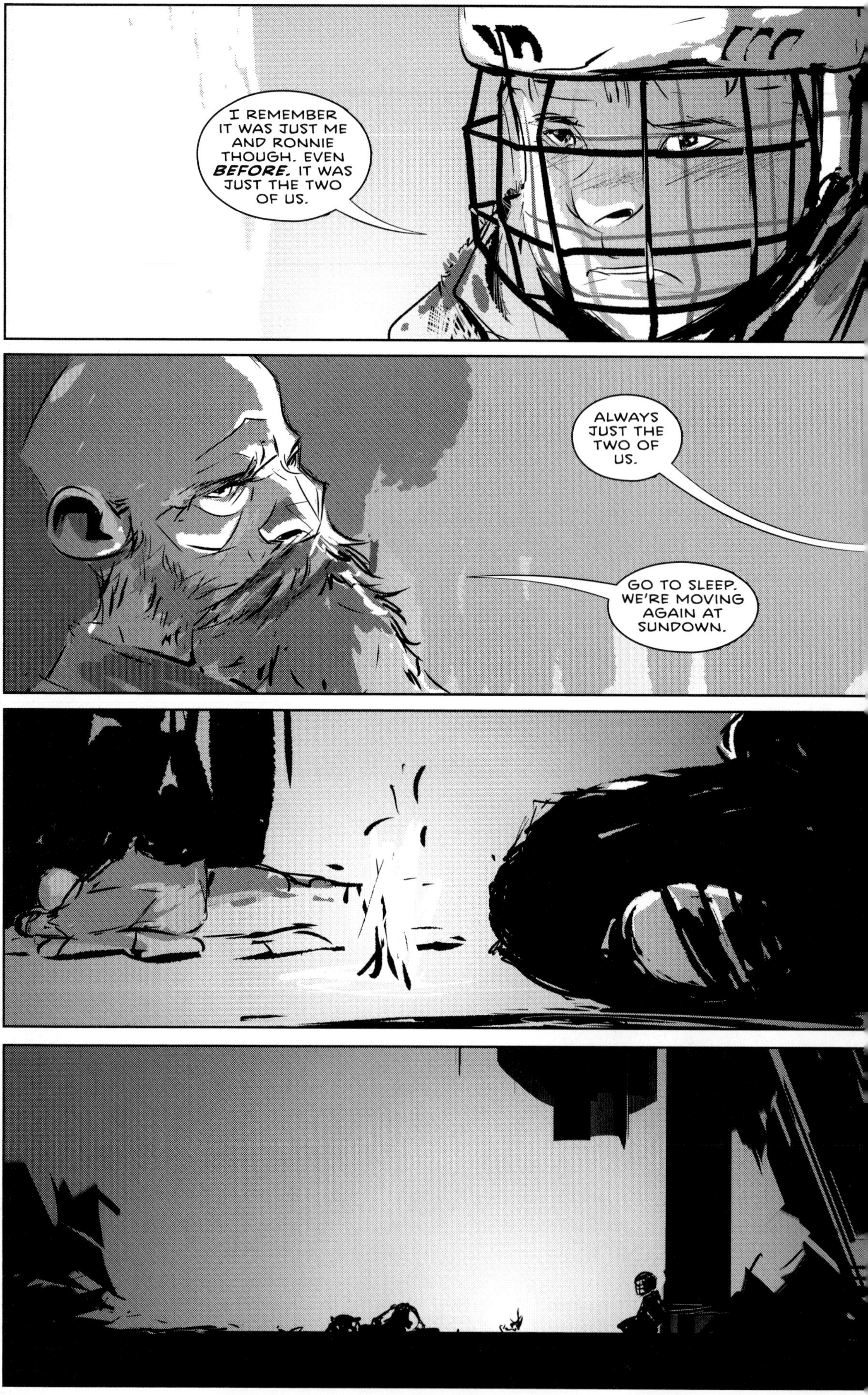
I REMEMBER IT WAS JUST ME AND RONNIE THOUGH. EVEN *BEFORE.* IT WAS JUST THE TWO OF US.
ALWAYS JUST THE TWO OF US.
GO TO SLEEP. WE'RE MOVING AGAIN AT SUNDOWN.

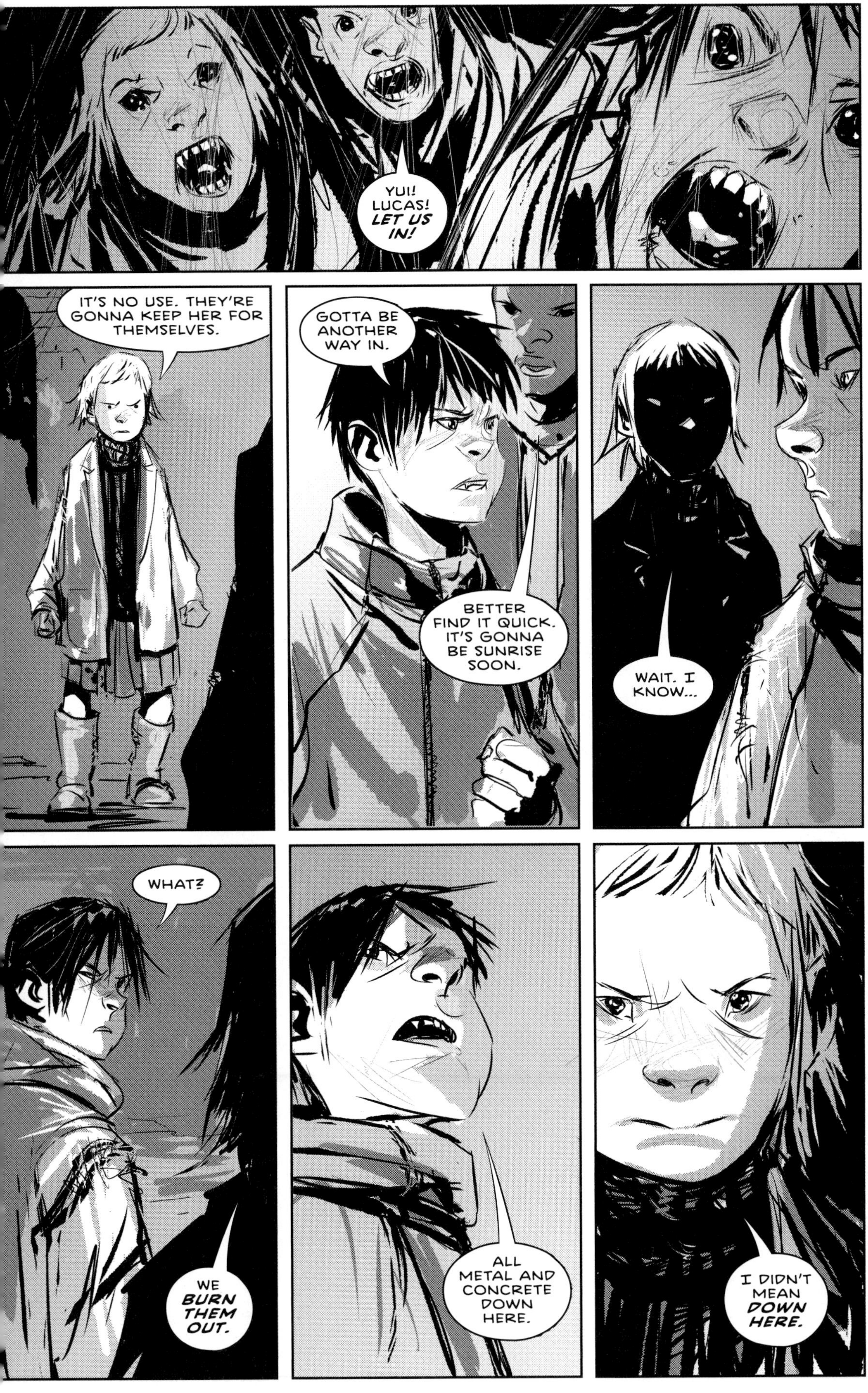
YUI! LUCAS! LET US IN!
IT'S NO USE. THEY'RE GONNA KEEP HER FOR THEMSELVES.
GOTTA BE ANOTHER WAY IN.
BETTER FIND IT QUICK. IT'S GONNA BE SUNRISE SOON.
WAIT. I KNOW...
WHAT?
WE BURN THEM OUT.
ALL METAL AND CONCRETE DOWN HERE.
I DIDN'T MEAN DOWN HERE.

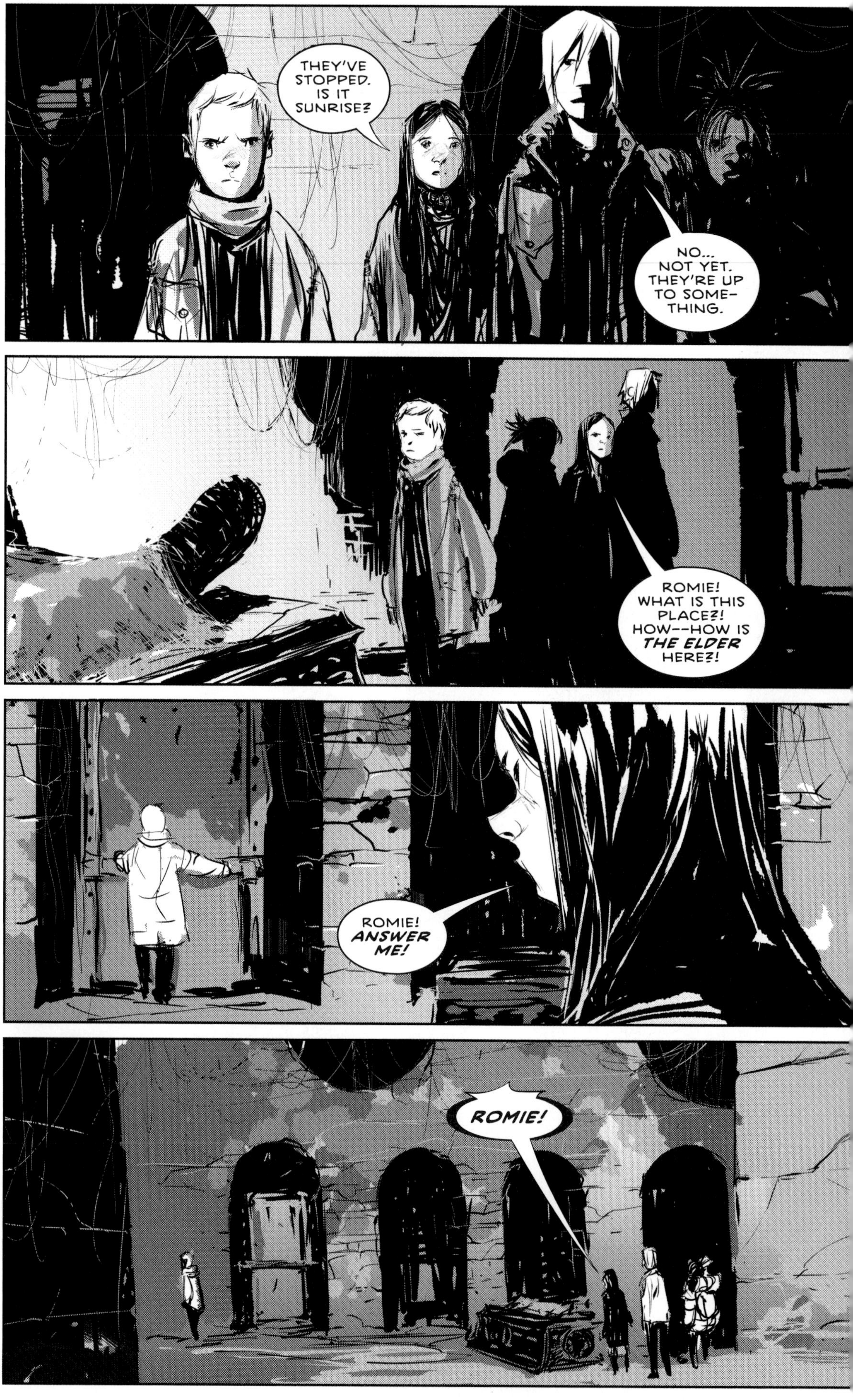
THEY'VE STOPPED. IS IT SUNRISE?
NO... NOT YET. THEY'RE UP TO SOME-THING.
ROMIE! WHAT IS THIS PLACE?! HOW--HOW IS THE ELDER HERE?!
ROMIE! ANSWER ME!
ROMIE!

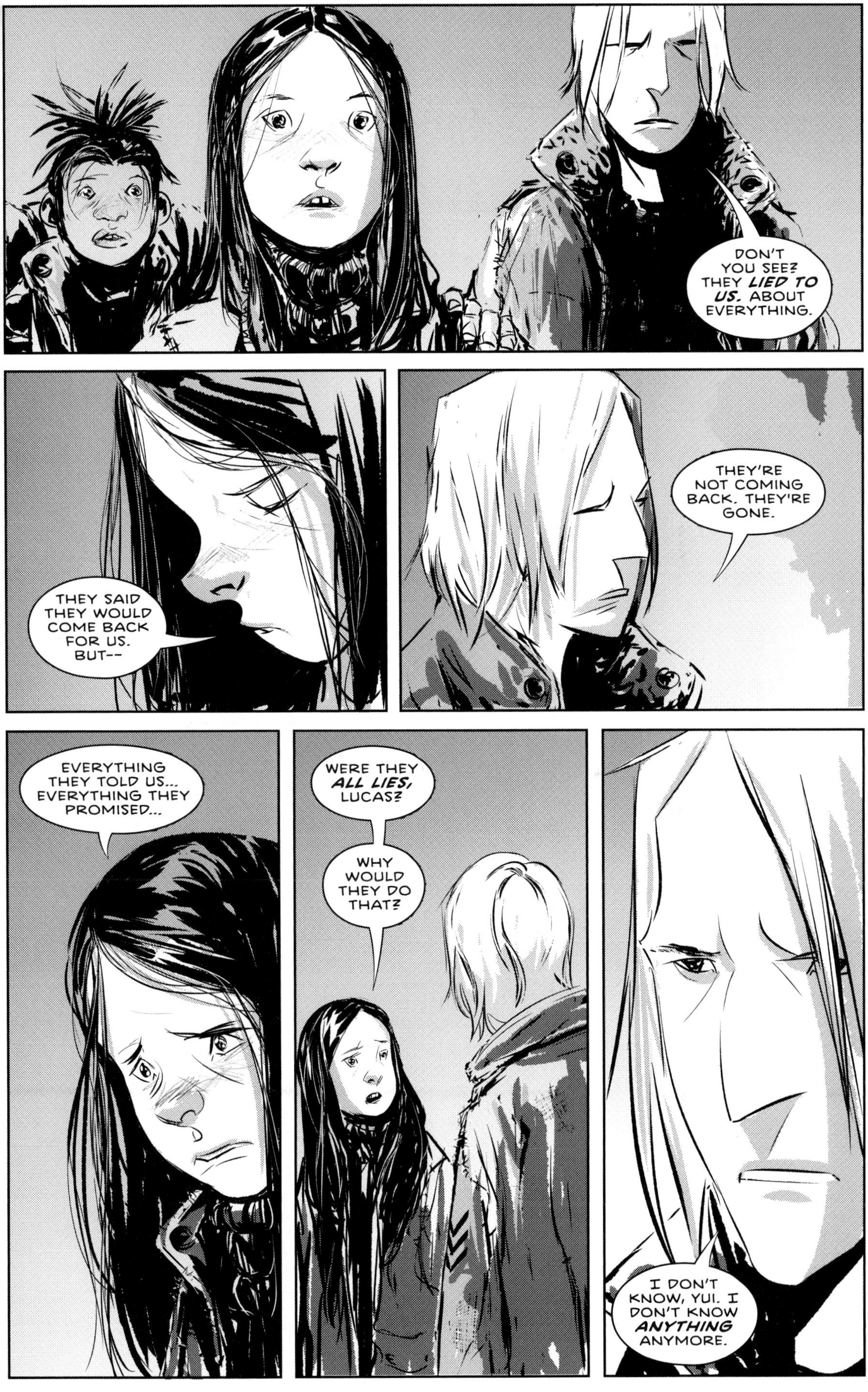
DON'T YOU SEE? THEY LIED TO US. ABOUT EVERYTHING.
THEY SAID THEY WOULD COME BACK FOR US. BUT--
THEY'RE NOT COMING BACK. THEY'RE GONE.
EVERYTHING THEY TOLD US... EVERYTHING THEY PROMISED...
WERE THEY ALL LIES, LUCAS?
WHY WOULD THEY DO THAT?
I DON'T KNOW, YUI. I DON'T KNOW ANYTHING ANYMORE.

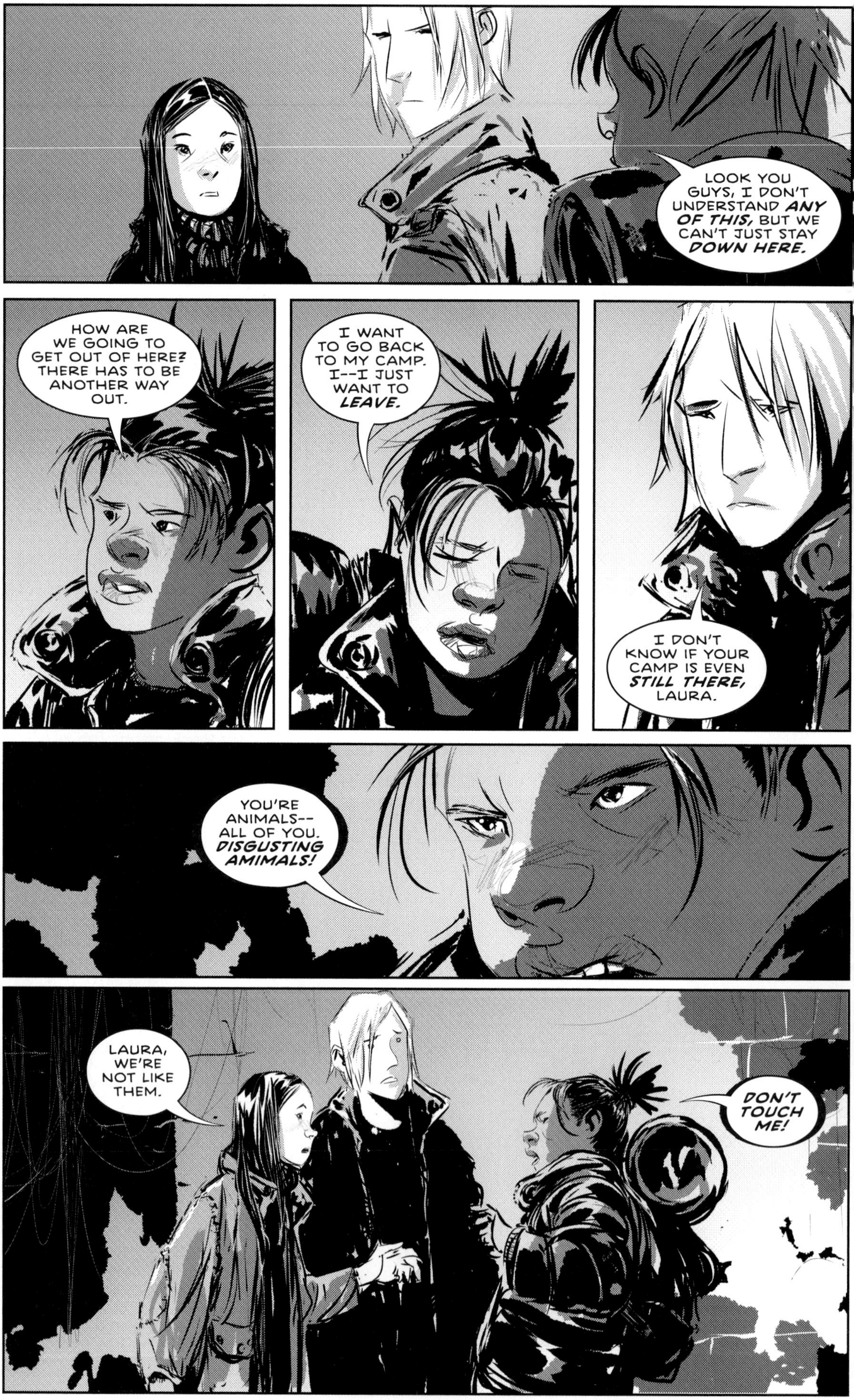
LOOK YOU GUYS, I DON'T UNDERSTAND ANY OF THIS, BUT WE CAN'T JUST STAY DOWN HERE.
HOW ARE WE GOING TO GET OUT OF HERE? THERE HAS TO BE ANOTHER WAY OUT.
I WANT TO GO BACK TO MY CAMP. I--I JUST WANT TO LEAVE.
I DON'T KNOW IF YOUR CAMP IS EVEN STILL THERE, LAURA.
YOU'RE ANIMALS--ALL OF YOU. DISGUSTING ANIMALS!
LAURA, WE'RE NOT LIKE THEM.
DON'T TOUCH ME!

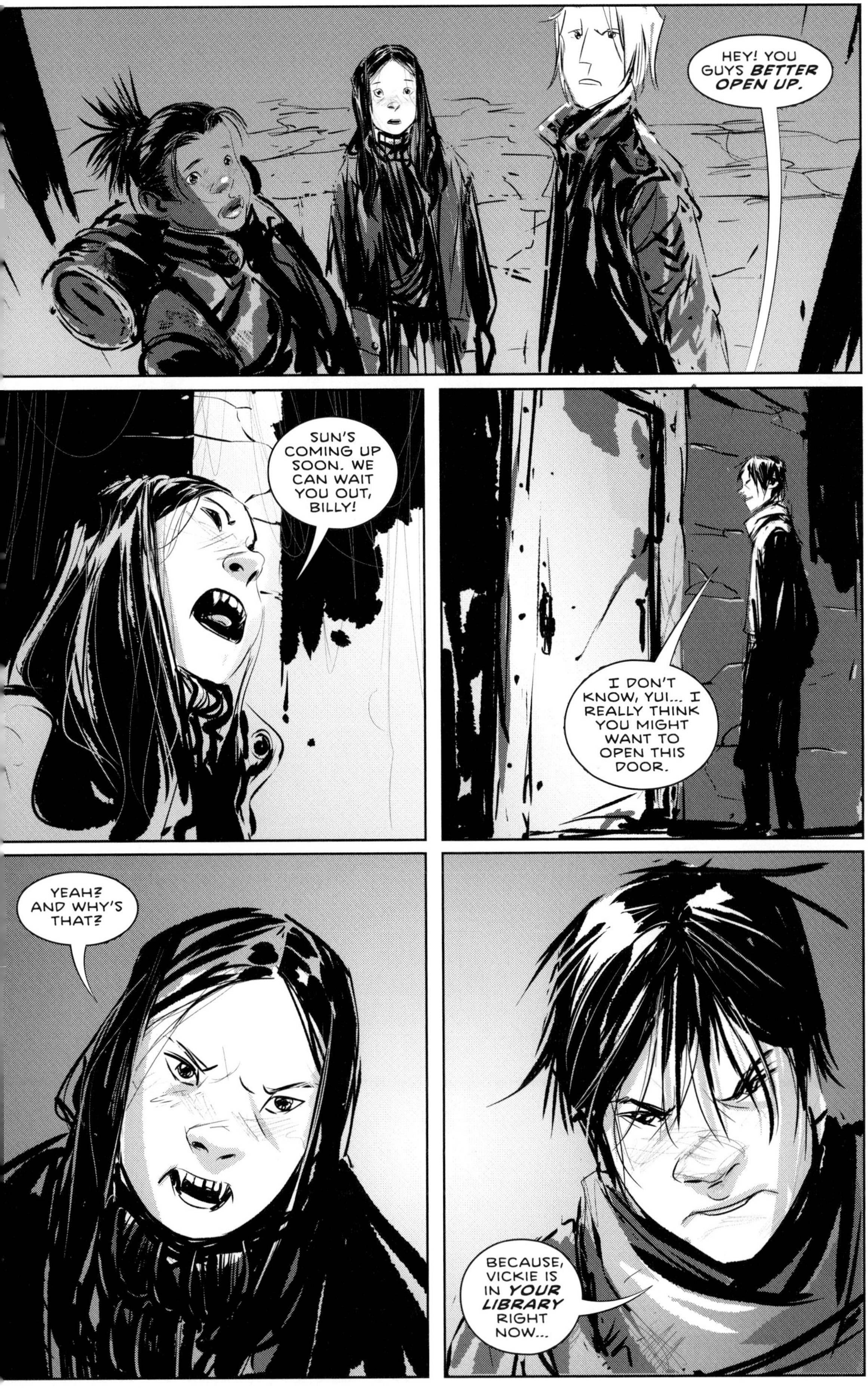
HEY! YOU GUYS BETTER OPEN UP.
SUN'S COMING UP SOON. WE CAN WAIT YOU OUT, BILLY!
I DON'T KNOW, YUI... I REALLY THINK YOU MIGHT WANT TO OPEN THIS DOOR.
YEAH? AND WHY'S THAT?
BECAUSE, VICKIE IS IN YOUR LIBRARY RIGHT NOW...

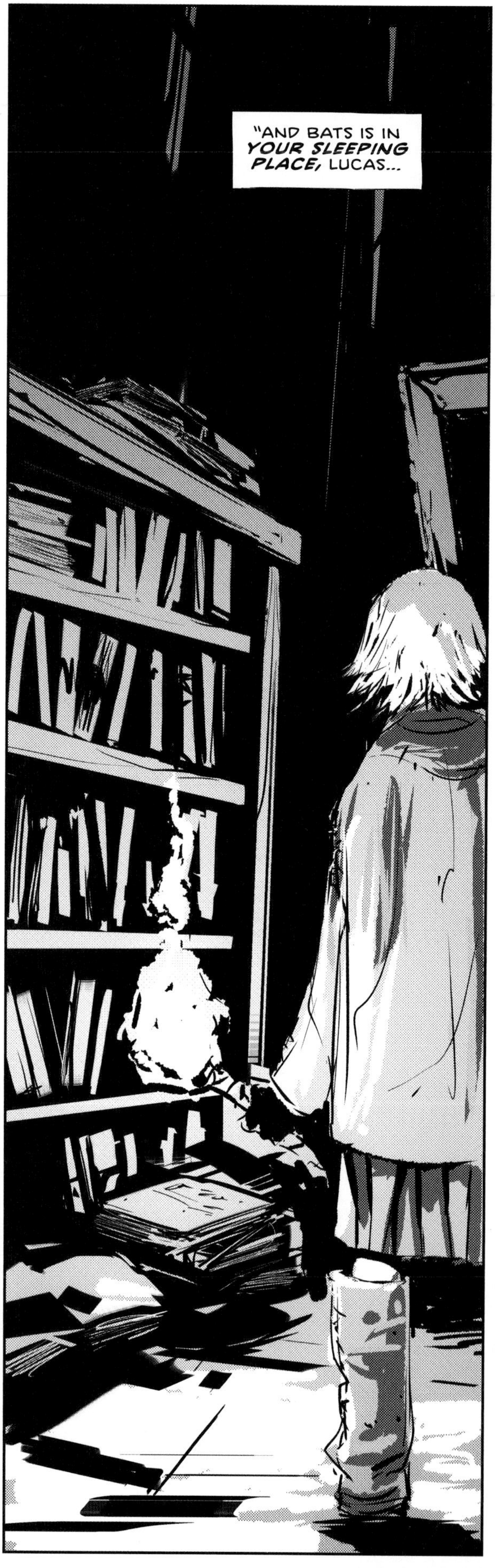
"AND BATS IS IN YOUR SLEEPING PLACE, LUCAS...

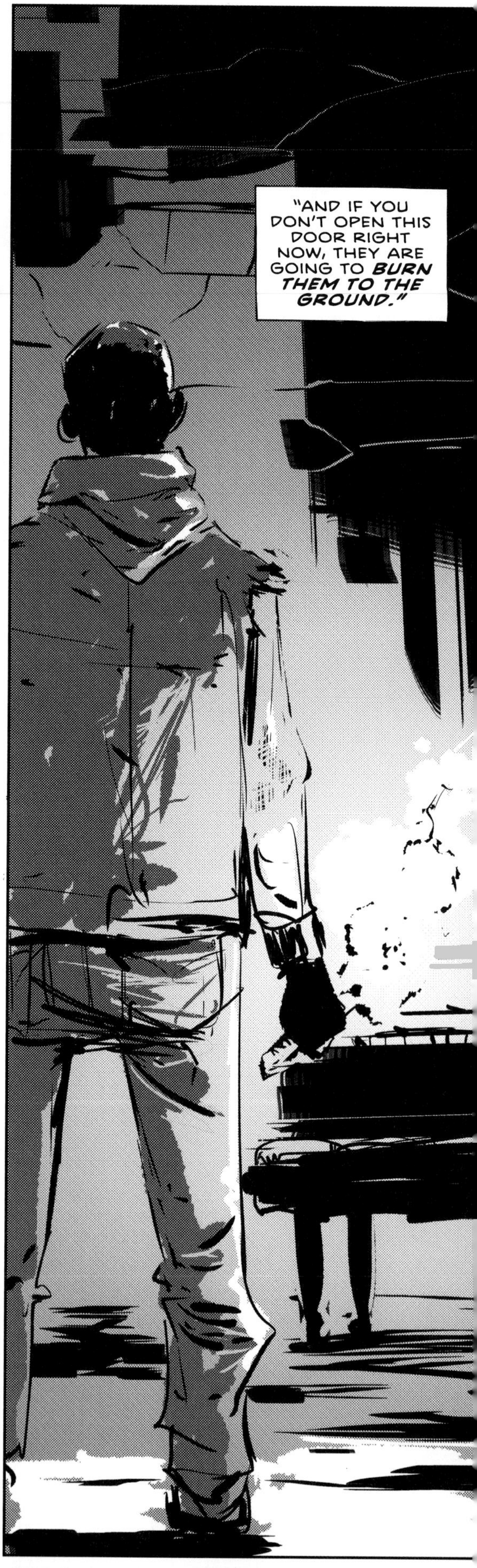
"AND IF YOU DON'T OPEN THIS DOOR RIGHT NOW, THEY ARE GOING TO BURN THEM TO THE GROUND."

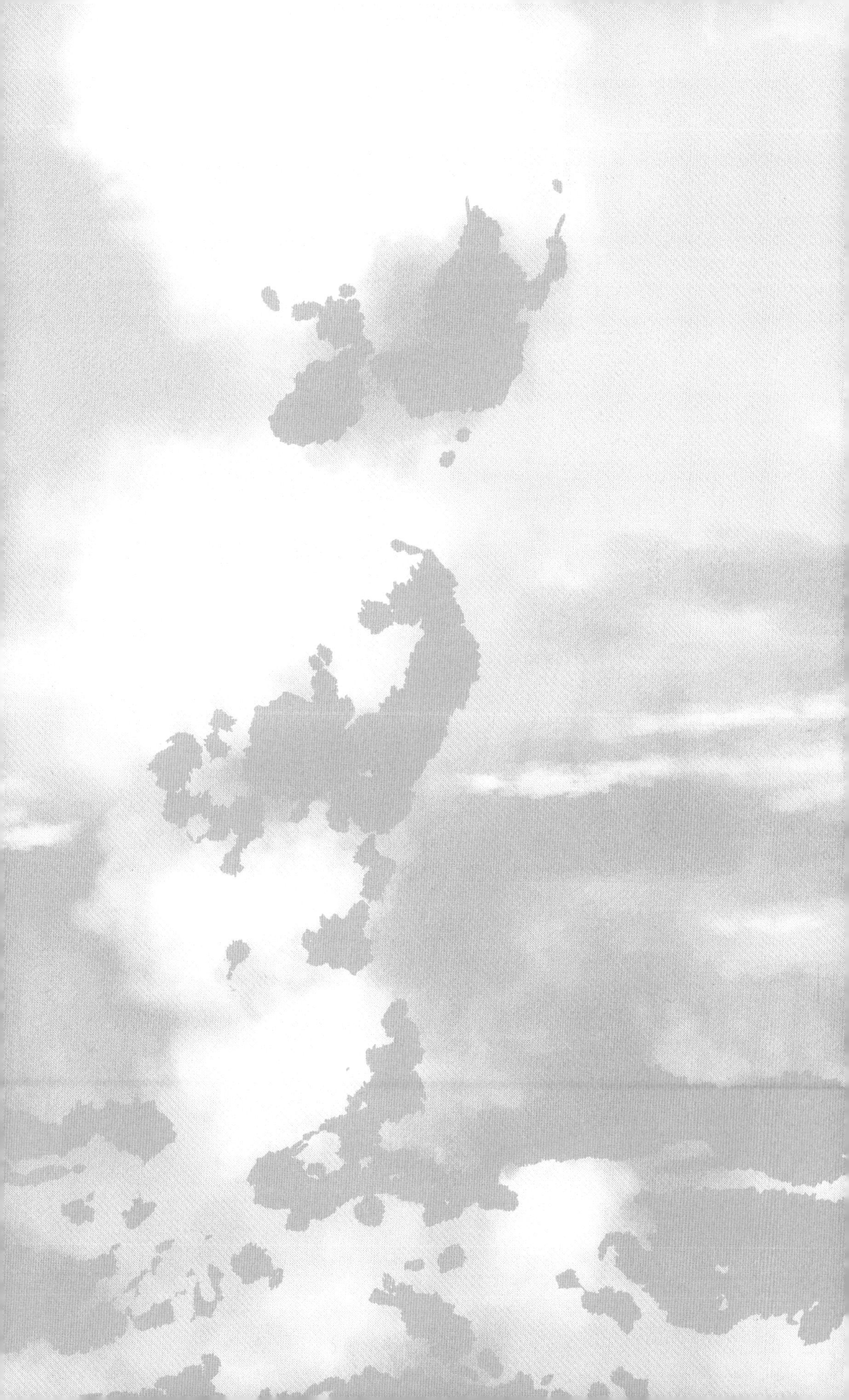

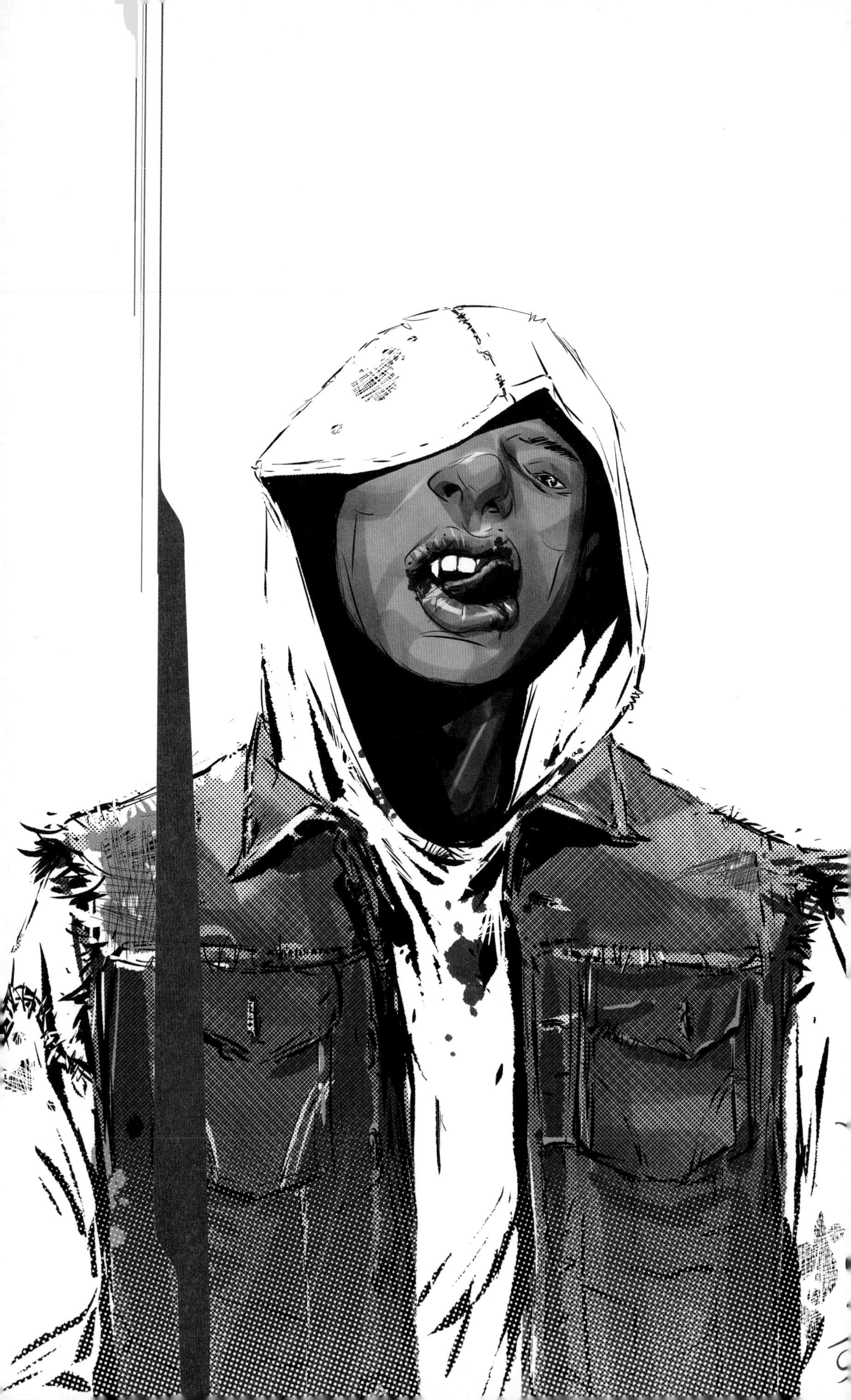

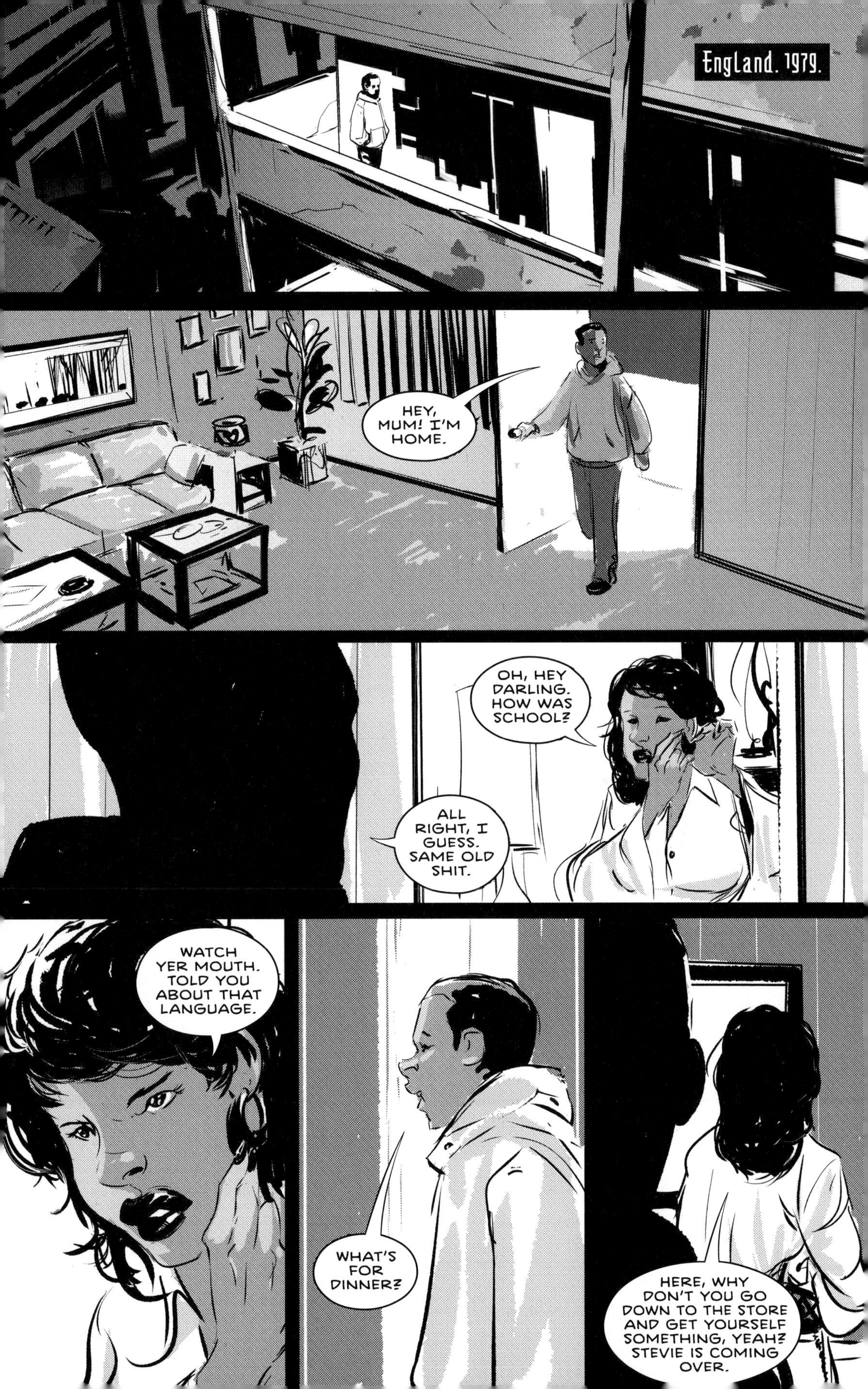
England. 1979.
HEY, MUM! I'M HOME.
OH, HEY DARLING. HOW WAS SCHOOL?
ALL RIGHT, I GUESS. SAME OLD SHIT.
WATCH YER MOUTH. TOLD YOU ABOUT THAT LANGUAGE.
WHAT'S FOR DINNER?
HERE, WHY DON'T YOU GO DOWN TO THE STORE AND GET YOURSELF SOMETHING, YEAH? STEVIE IS COMING OVER.

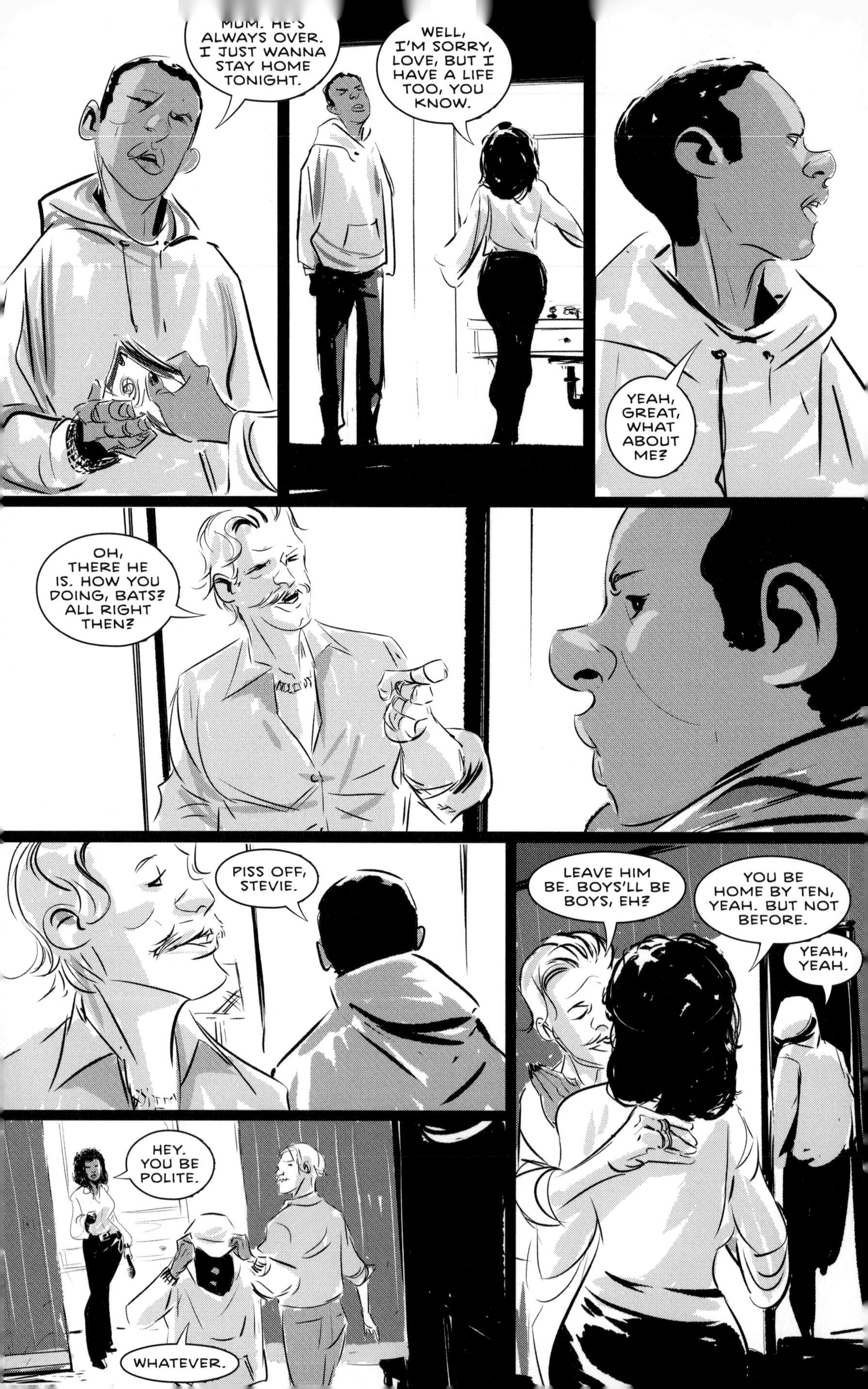
MUM. HE'S ALWAYS OVER. I JUST WANNA STAY HOME TONIGHT.
WELL, I'M SORRY, LOVE, BUT I HAVE A LIFE TOO, YOU KNOW.
YEAH, GREAT, WHAT ABOUT ME?
OH, THERE HE IS. HOW YOU DOING, BATS? ALL RIGHT THEN?
PISS OFF, STEVIE.
HEY. YOU BE POLITE.
WHATEVER.
LEAVE HIM BE. BOYS'LL BE BOYS, EH?
YOU BE HOME BY TEN, YEAH. BUT NOT BEFORE.
YEAH, YEAH.

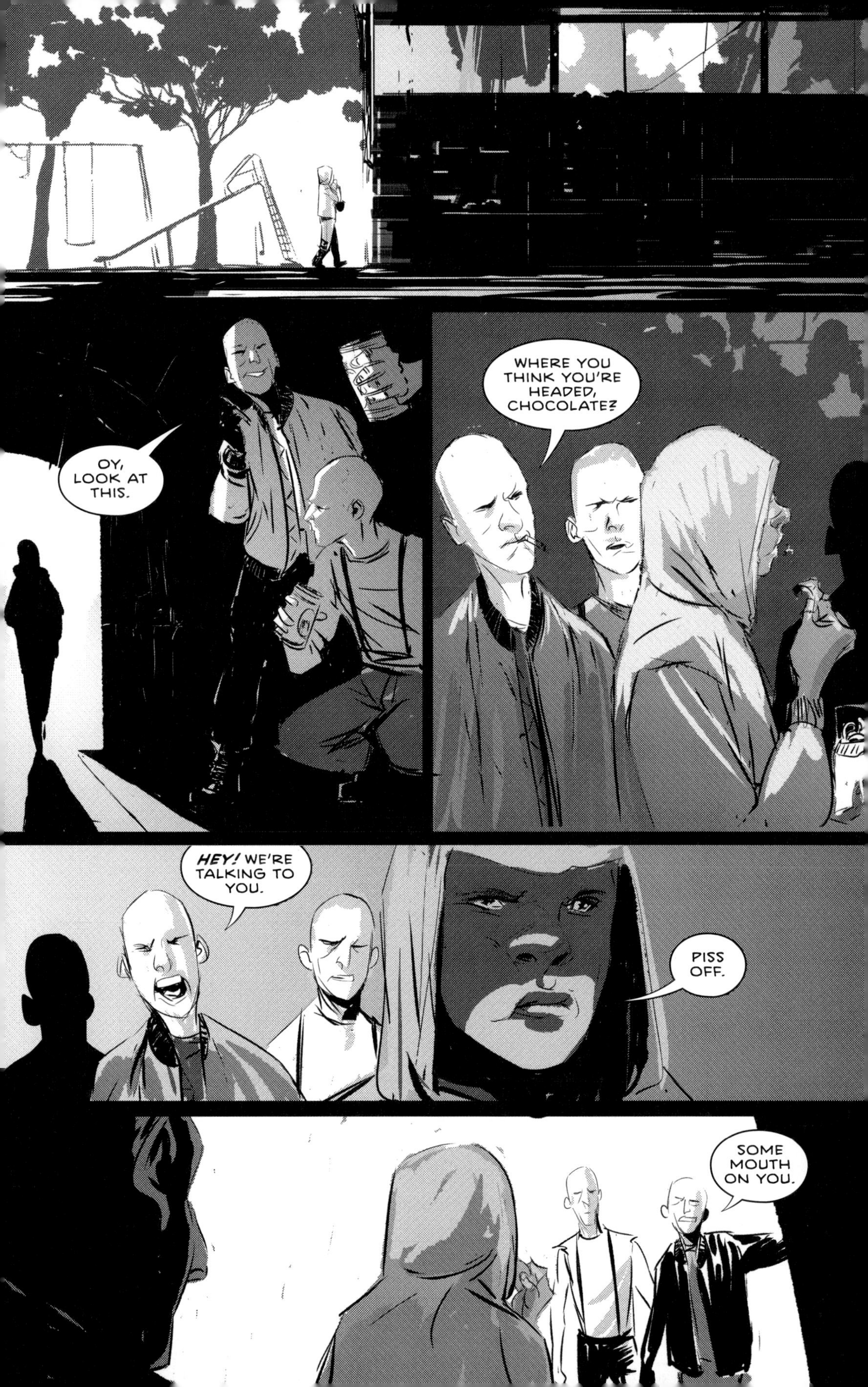
OY, LOOK AT THIS.
WHERE YOU THINK YOU'RE HEADED, CHOCOLATE?
HEY! WE'RE TALKING TO YOU.
PISS OFF.
SOME MOUTH ON YOU.

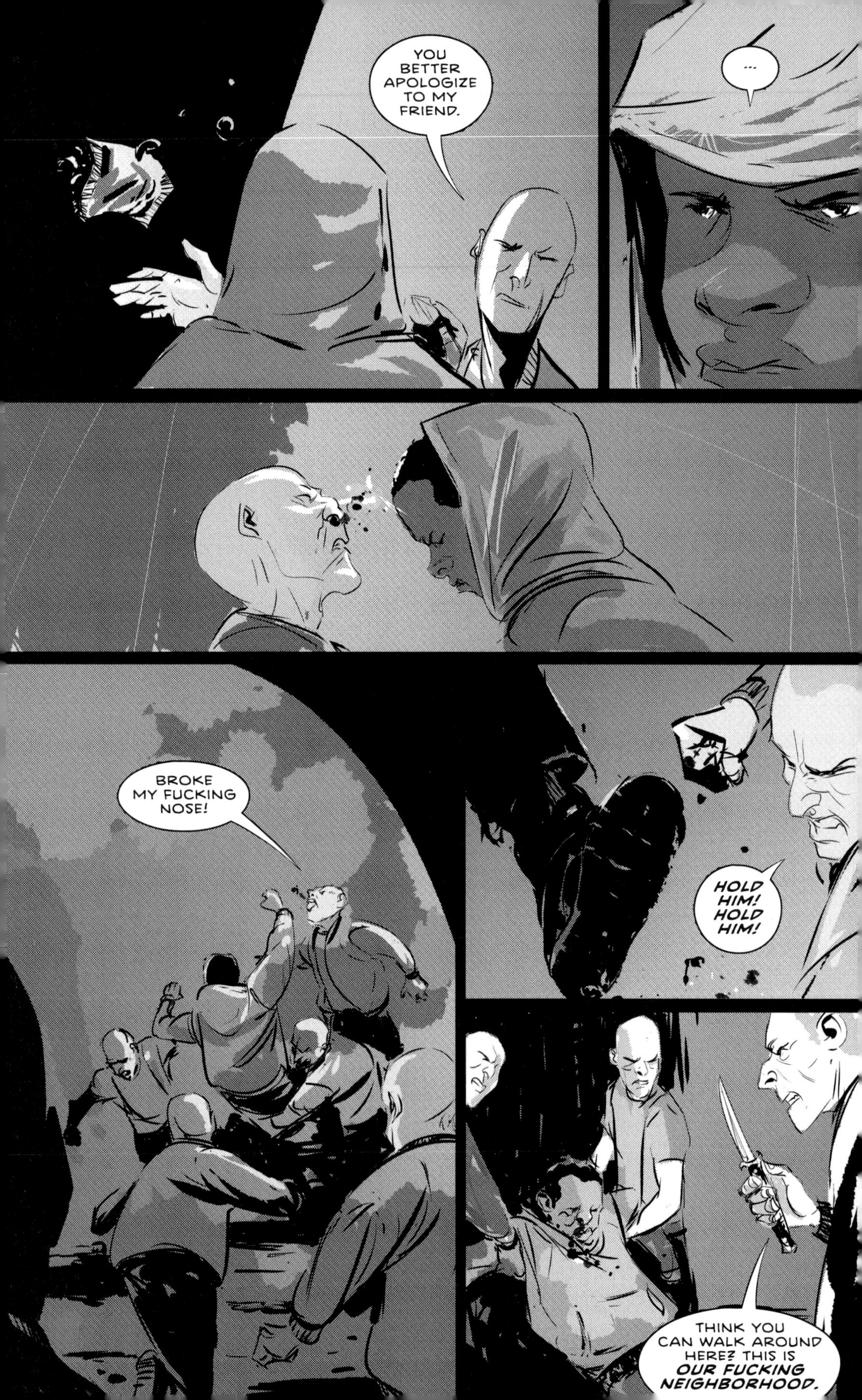
YOU BETTER APOLOGIZE TO MY FRIEND.
...
BROKE MY FUCKING NOSE!
HOLD HIM! HOLD HIM!
THINK YOU CAN WALK AROUND HERE? THIS IS OUR FUCKING NEIGHBORHOOD.

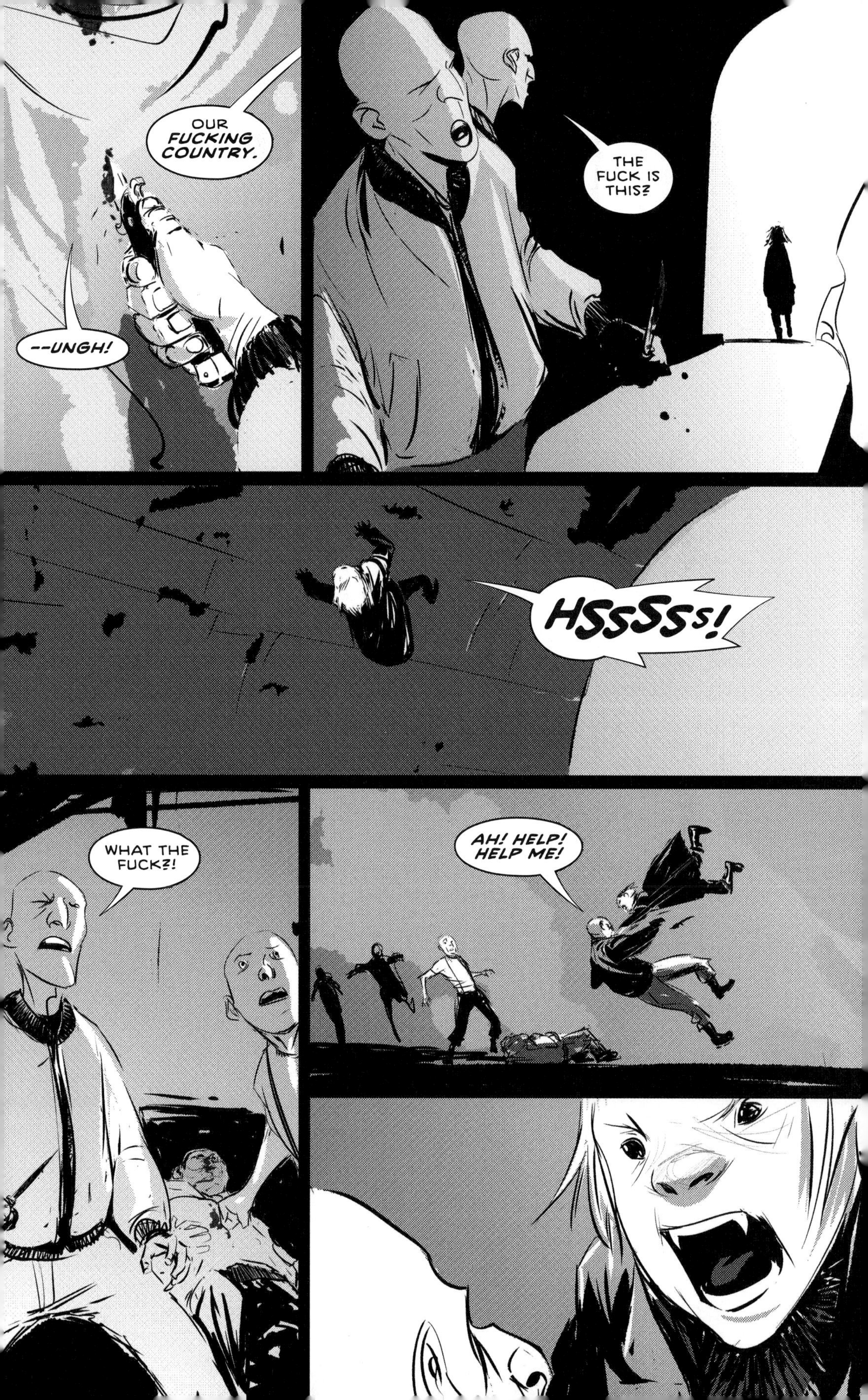
OUR FUCKING COUNTRY.
--UNGH!
THE FUCK IS THIS?
HSSSSS!
WHAT THE FUCK?!
AH! HELP! HELP ME!

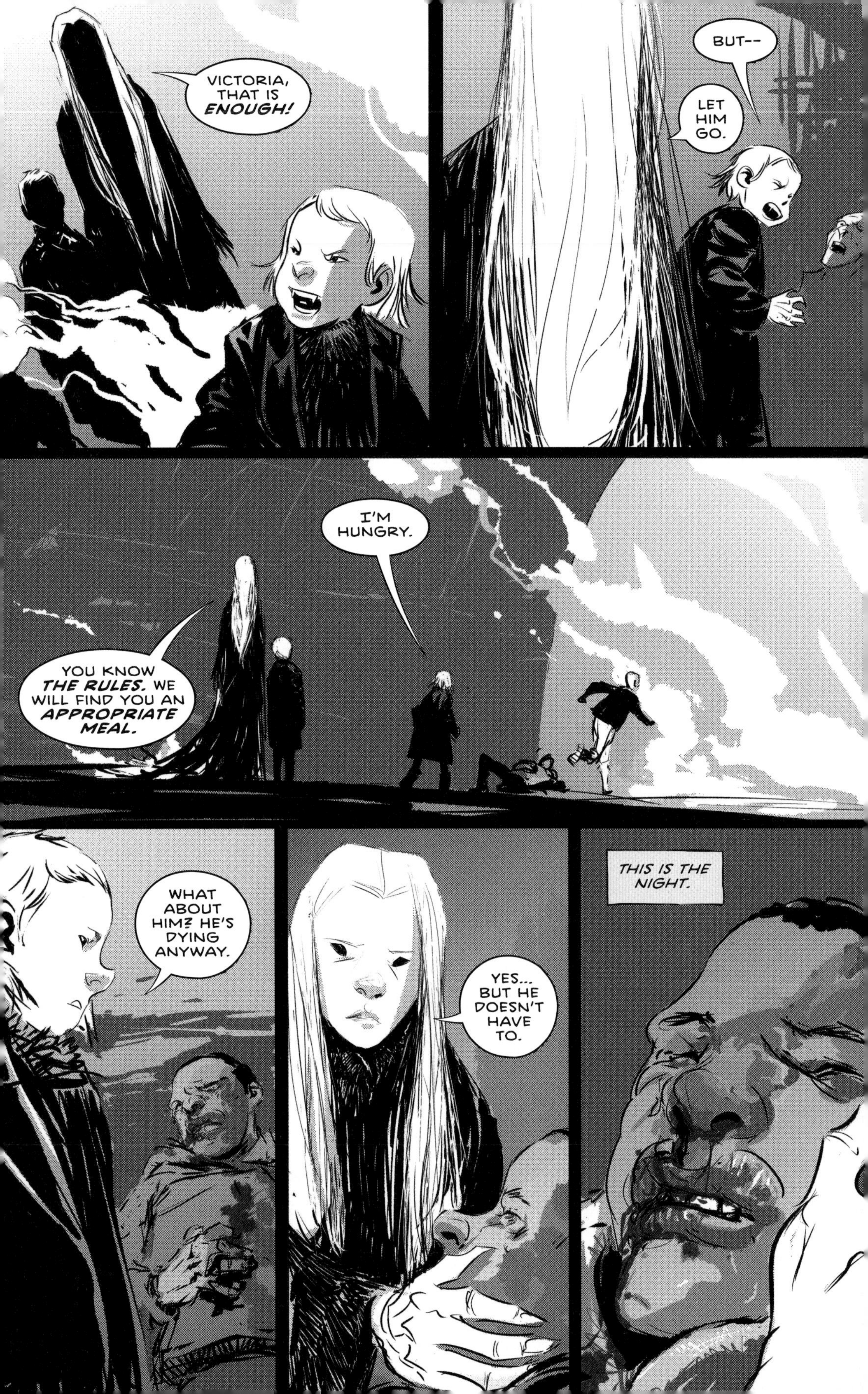
VICTORIA, THAT IS ENOUGH!
BUT--
LET HIM GO.
I'M HUNGRY.
YOU KNOW THE RULES. WE WILL FIND YOU AN APPROPRIATE MEAL.
WHAT ABOUT HIM? HE'S DYING ANYWAY.
YES... BUT HE DOESN'T HAVE TO.
THIS IS THE NIGHT.

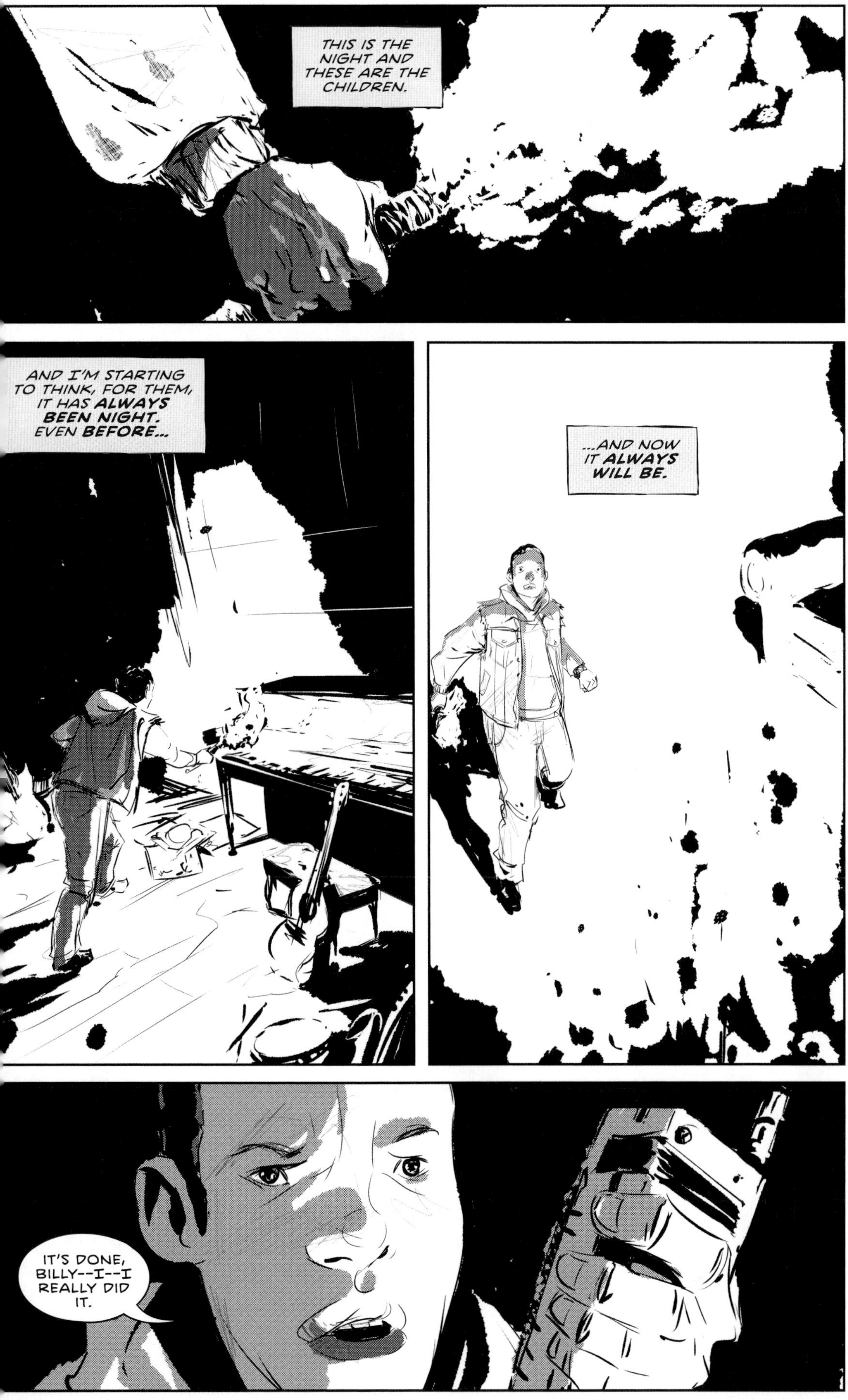
THIS IS THE NIGHT AND THESE ARE THE CHILDREN.
AND I'M STARTING TO THINK, FOR THEM, IT HAS ALWAYS BEEN NIGHT. EVEN BEFORE...
...AND NOW IT ALWAYS WILL BE.
IT'S DONE, BILLY--I--I REALLY DID IT.

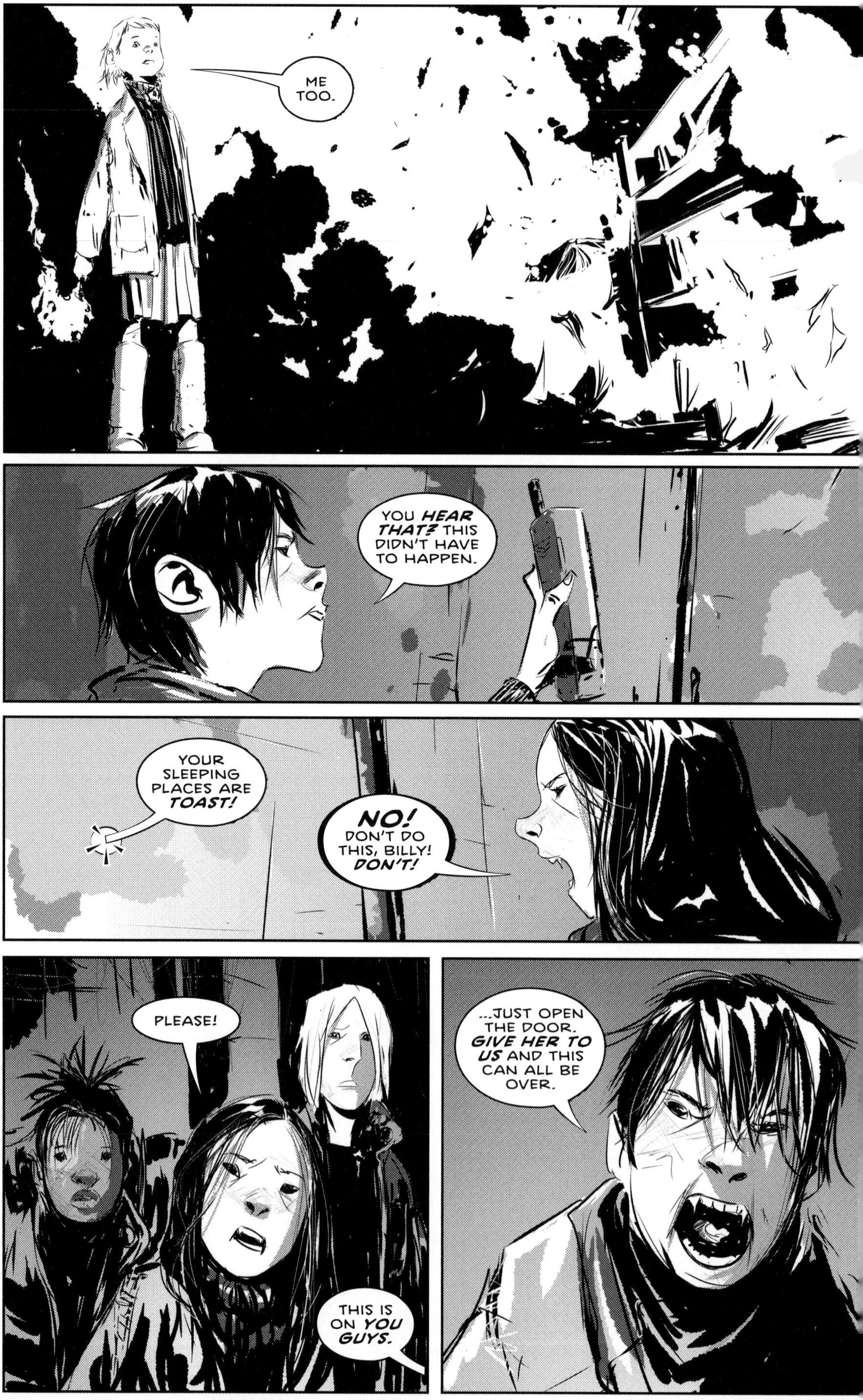
ME TOO.
YOU HEAR THAT? THIS DIDN'T HAVE TO HAPPEN.
YOUR SLEEPING PLACES ARE TOAST!
NO! DON'T DO THIS, BILLY! DON'T!
PLEASE!
THIS IS ON YOU GUYS.
...JUST OPEN THE DOOR. GIVE HER TO US AND THIS CAN ALL BE OVER.

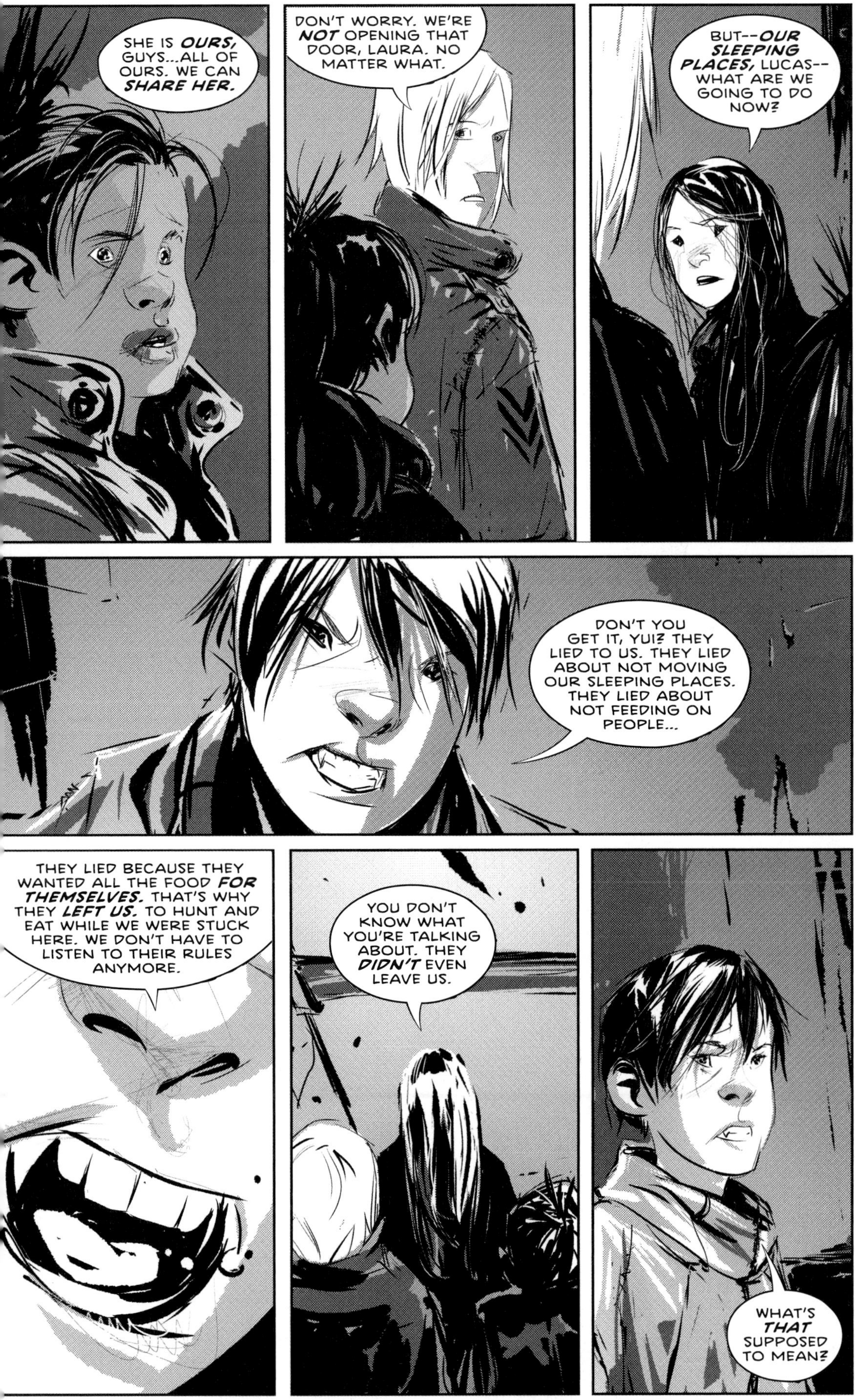
SHE IS OURS, GUYS...ALL OF OURS. WE CAN SHARE HER.
DON'T WORRY. WE'RE NOT OPENING THAT DOOR, LAURA. NO MATTER WHAT.
BUT--OUR SLEEPING PLACES, LUCAS--WHAT ARE WE GOING TO DO NOW?
DON'T YOU GET IT, YUI? THEY LIED TO US. THEY LIED ABOUT NOT MOVING OUR SLEEPING PLACES. THEY LIED ABOUT NOT FEEDING ON PEOPLE...
THEY LIED BECAUSE THEY WANTED ALL THE FOOD FOR THEMSELVES. THAT'S WHY THEY LEFT US. TO HUNT AND EAT WHILE WE WERE STUCK HERE. WE DON'T HAVE TO LISTEN TO THEIR RULES ANYMORE.
YOU DON'T KNOW WHAT YOU'RE TALKING ABOUT. THEY DIDN'T EVEN LEAVE US.
WHAT'S THAT SUPPOSED TO MEAN?

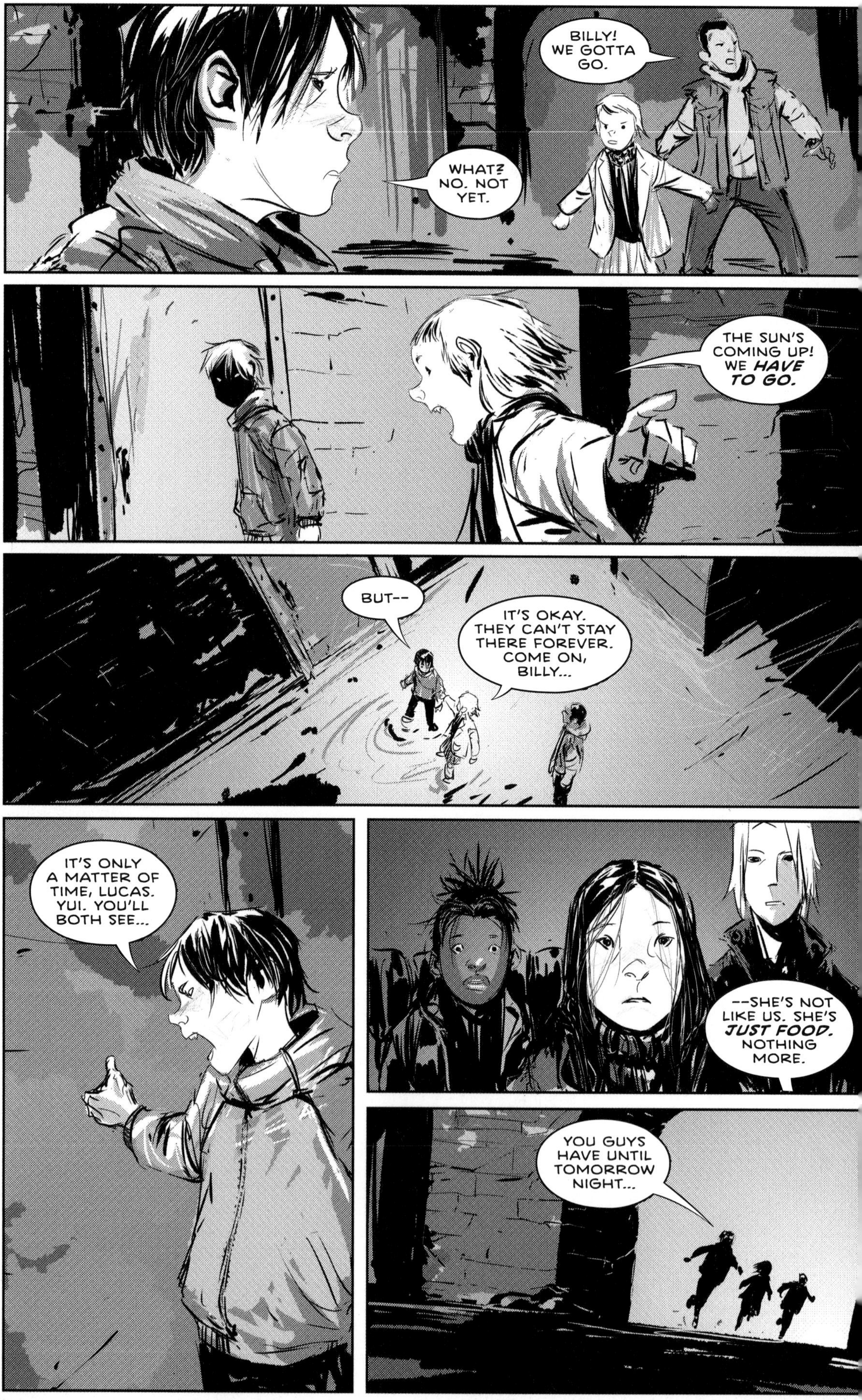
BILLY! WE GOTTA GO.
WHAT? NO. NOT YET.
THE SUN'S COMING UP! WE *HAVE TO GO.*
BUT--
IT'S OKAY. THEY CAN'T STAY THERE FOREVER. COME ON, BILLY...
IT'S ONLY A MATTER OF TIME, LUCAS. YUI. YOU'LL BOTH SEE...
--SHE'S NOT LIKE US. SHE'S *JUST FOOD.* NOTHING MORE.
YOU GUYS HAVE UNTIL TOMORROW NIGHT...

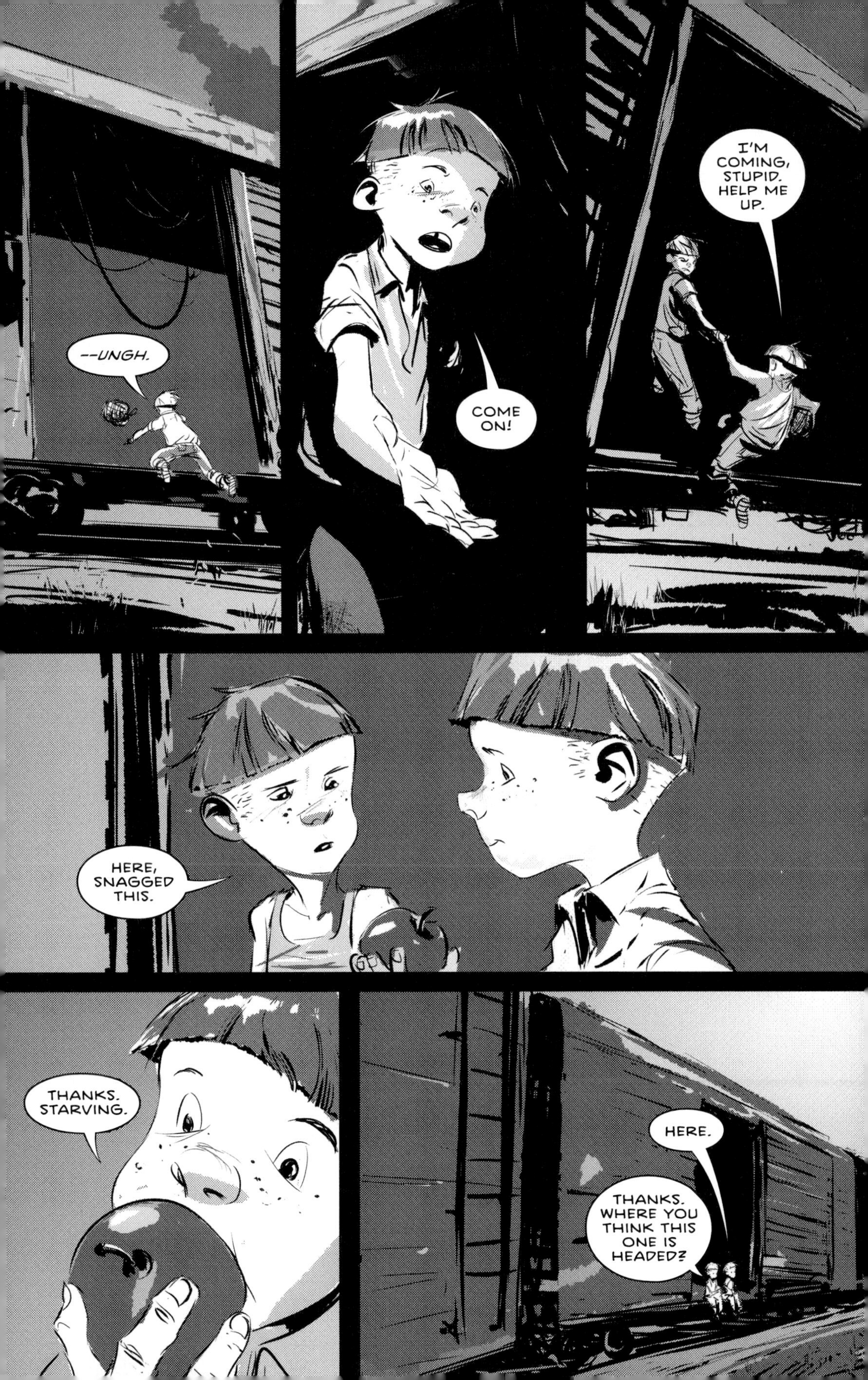
--UNGH.
COME ON!
I'M COMING, STUPID. HELP ME UP.
HERE, SNAGGED THIS.
THANKS. STARVING.
HERE.
THANKS. WHERE YOU THINK THIS ONE IS HEADED?

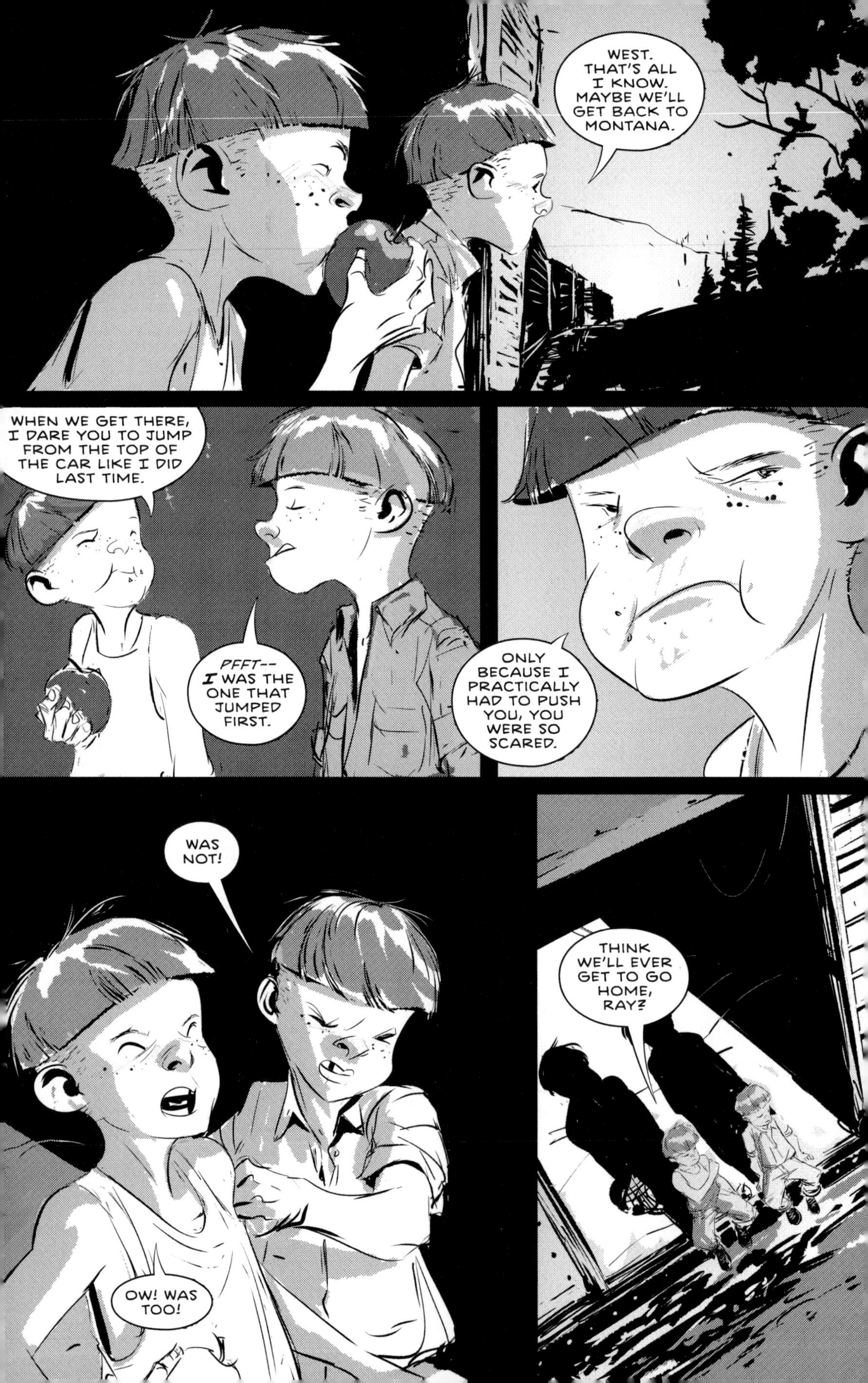
WEST. THAT'S ALL I KNOW. MAYBE WE'LL GET BACK TO MONTANA.
WHEN WE GET THERE, I DARE YOU TO JUMP FROM THE TOP OF THE CAR LIKE I DID LAST TIME.
PFFT-- I WAS THE ONE THAT JUMPED FIRST.
ONLY BECAUSE I PRACTICALLY HAD TO PUSH YOU, YOU WERE SO SCARED.
WAS NOT!
OW! WAS TOO!
THINK WE'LL EVER GET TO GO HOME, RAY?

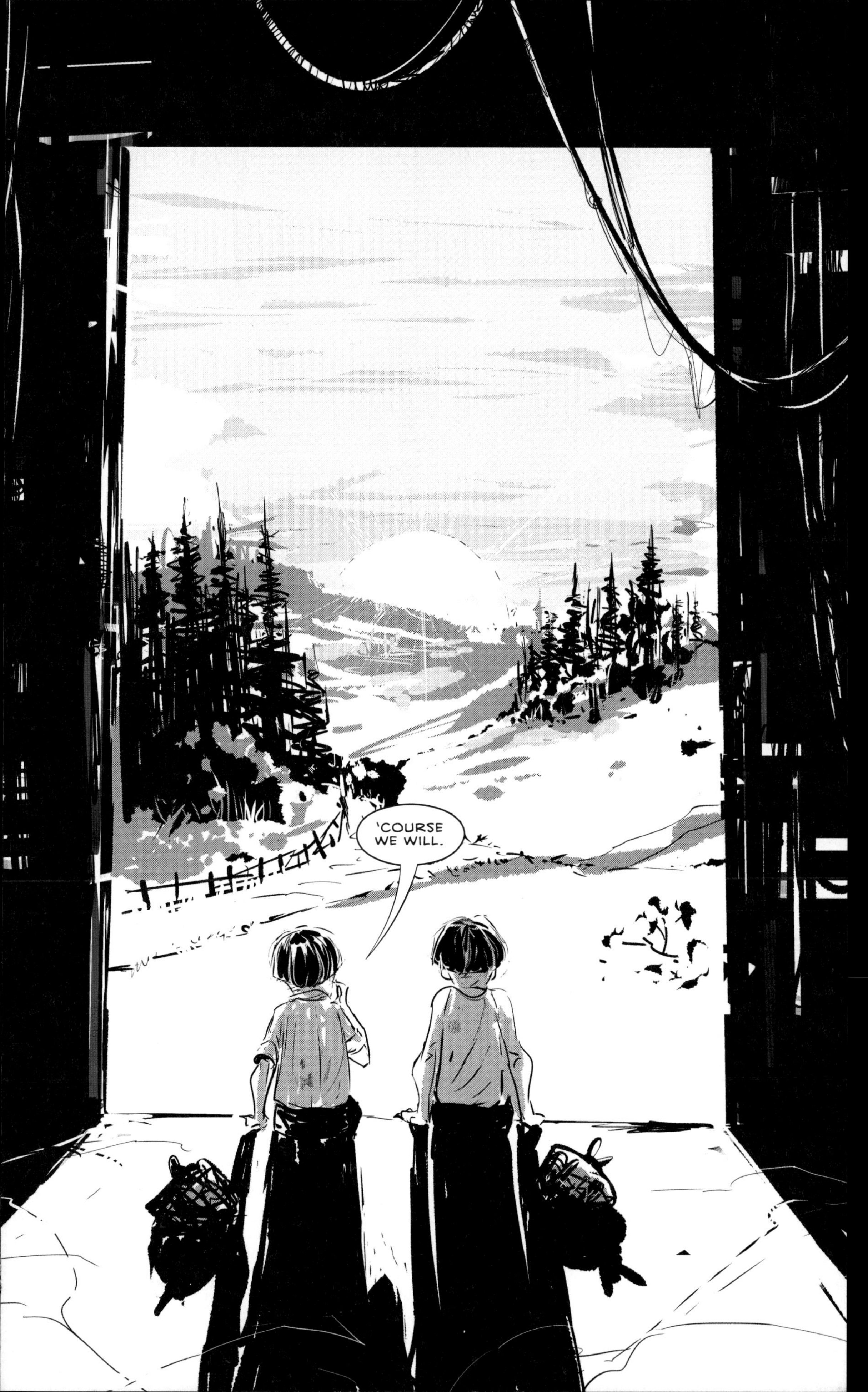
'COURSE WE WILL.

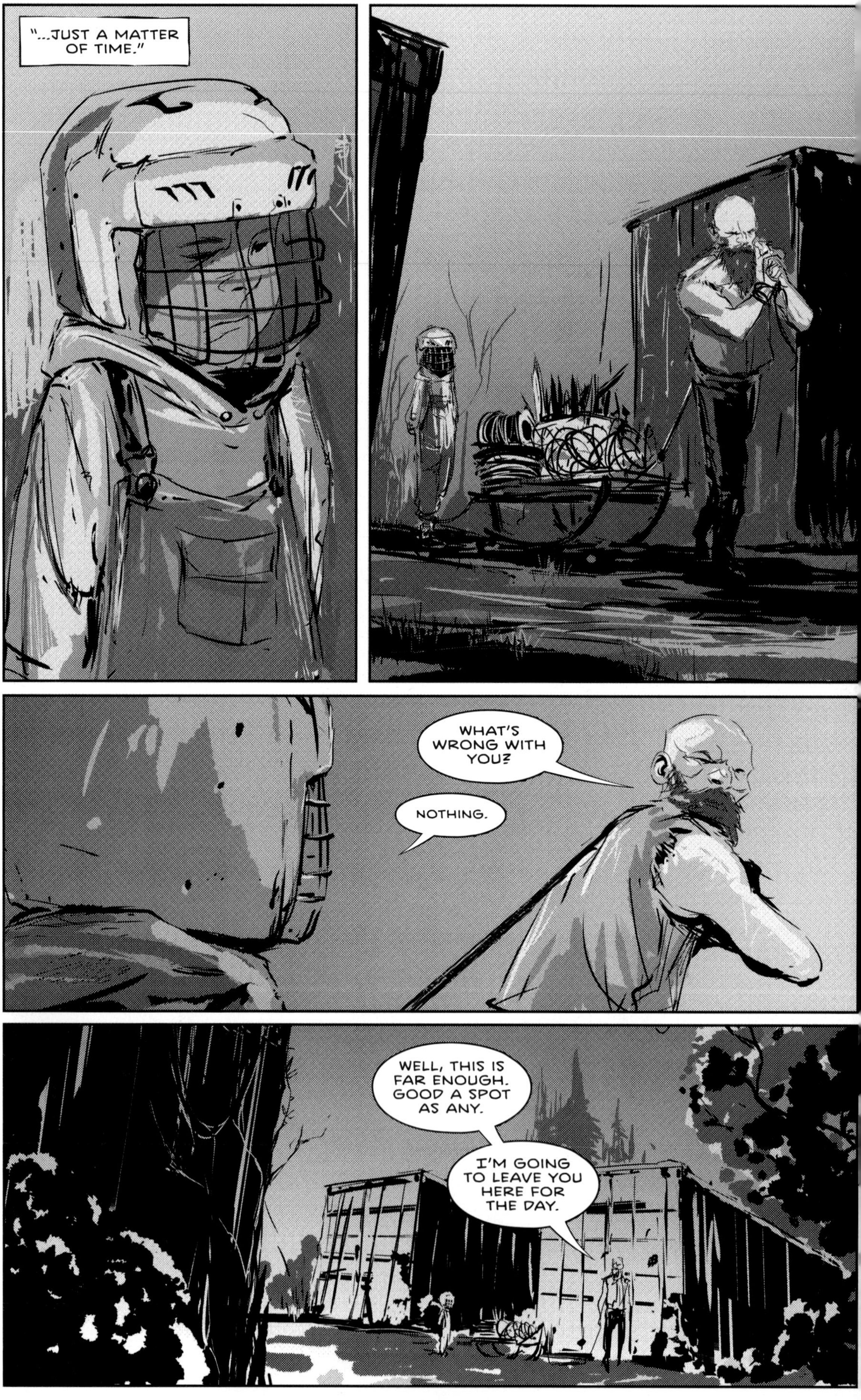
"...JUST A MATTER OF TIME."
WHAT'S WRONG WITH YOU?
NOTHING.
WELL, THIS IS FAR ENOUGH. GOOD A SPOT AS ANY.
I'M GOING TO LEAVE YOU HERE FOR THE DAY.

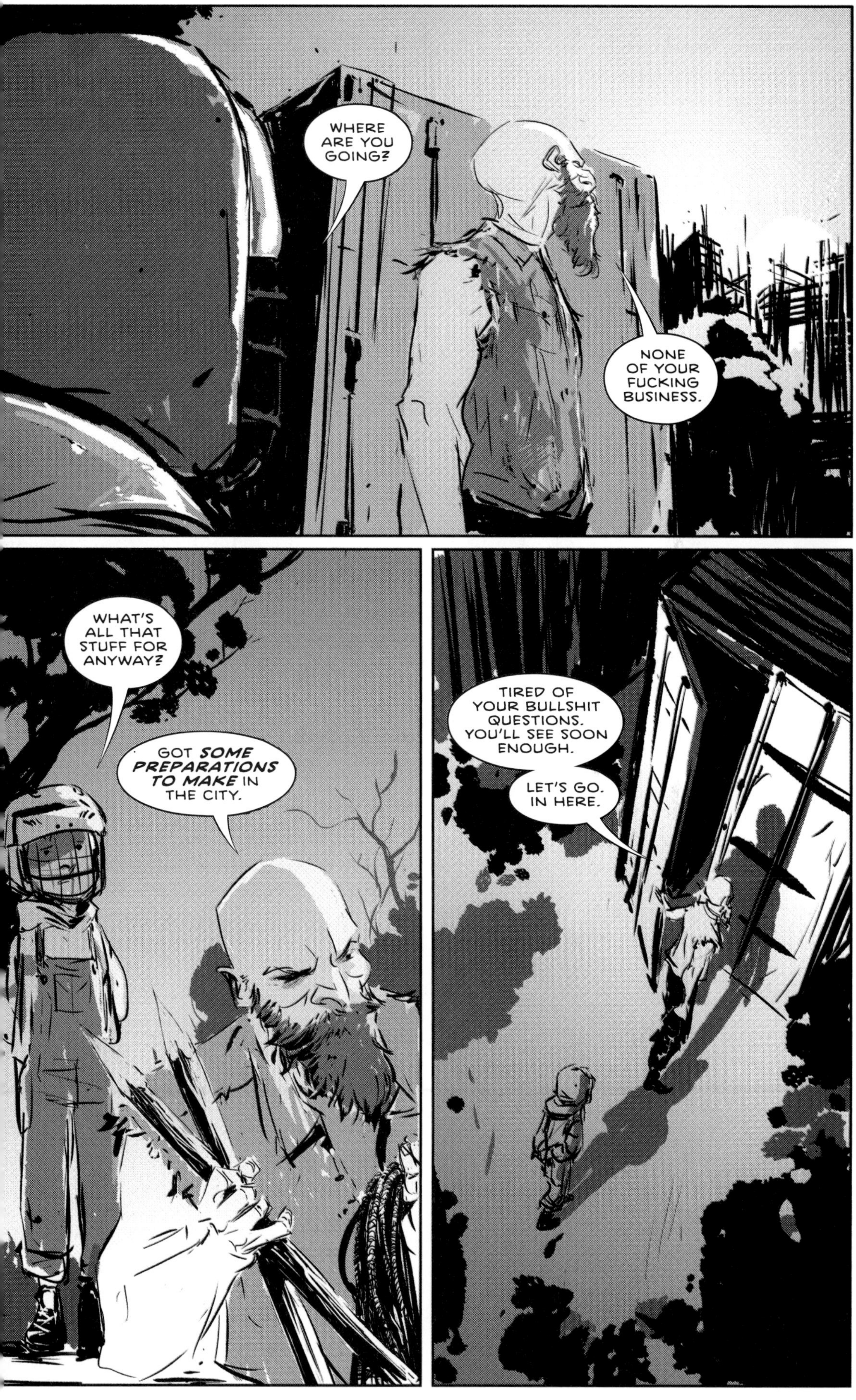
WHERE ARE YOU GOING?
NONE OF YOUR FUCKING BUSINESS.
WHAT'S ALL THAT STUFF FOR ANYWAY?
GOT *SOME PREPARATIONS TO MAKE* IN THE CITY.
TIRED OF YOUR BULLSHIT QUESTIONS. YOU'LL SEE SOON ENOUGH.
LET'S GO. IN HERE.

YOU SHOULD GET SOME SLEEP. YOU'RE GONNA NEED IT.

CAN'T SLEEP. NEVER HAVE WITHOUT MY BROTHER.

THAT SUPPOSED TO MAKE ME FEEL GUILTY OR SOMETHING? MAYBE YOU AND YOUR BROTHER SHOULDN'T HAVE KILLED ALL MY FRIENDS, HUH?

WHATEVER THE FUCK YOU ARE, *YOU AIN'T NATURAL.* DON'T YOU SEE THAT?

...

WHAT AM I, THEN?

SLEEP OR DON'T SLEEP. I DON'T REALLY CARE. I'LL BE BACK AT SUN-DOWN. THEN *WE FINISH THIS.*

SLAM

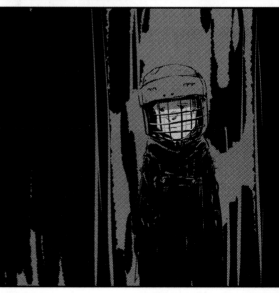

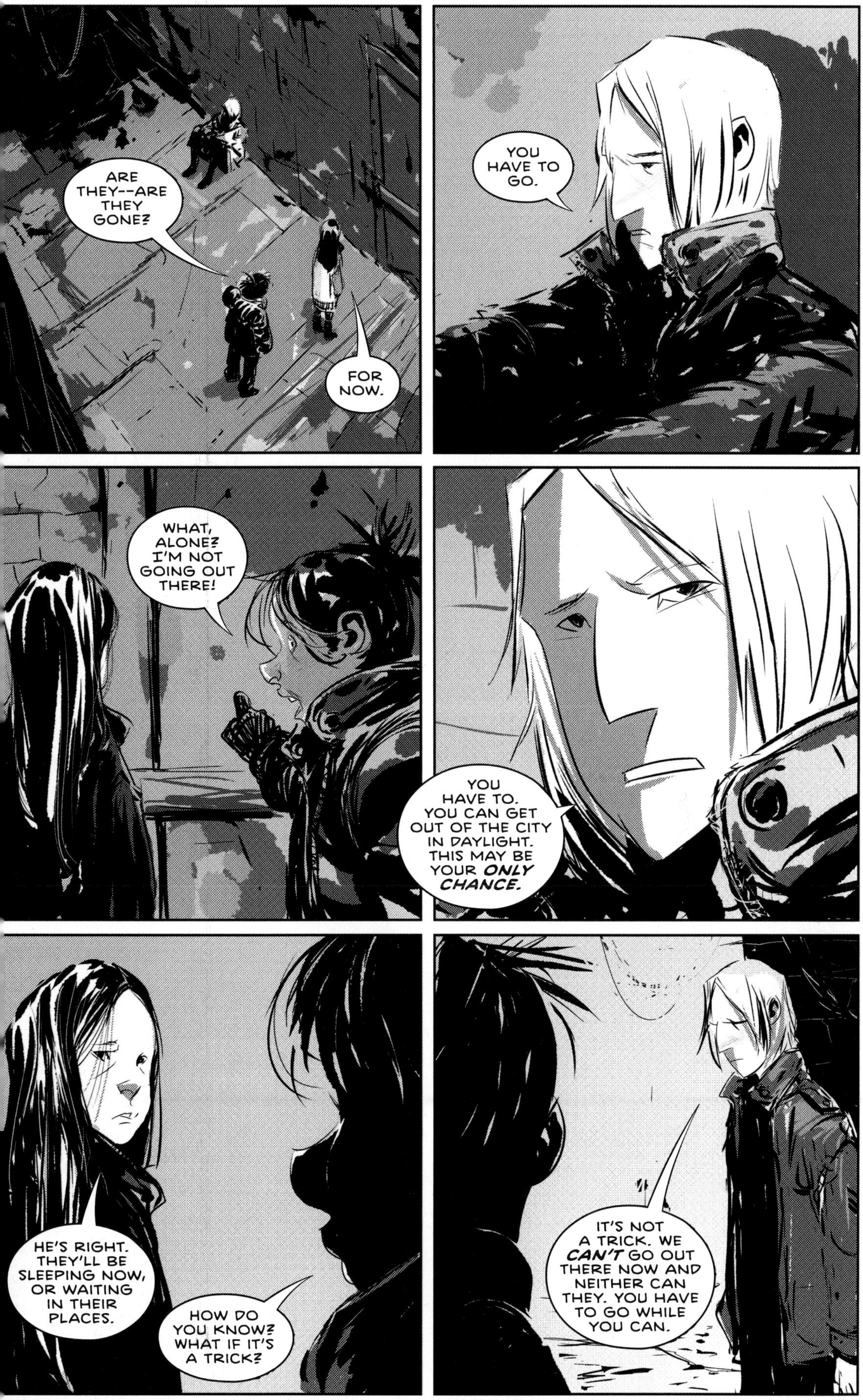
ARE THEY--ARE THEY GONE?
FOR NOW.
YOU HAVE TO GO.
WHAT, ALONE? I'M NOT GOING OUT THERE!
YOU HAVE TO. YOU CAN GET OUT OF THE CITY IN DAYLIGHT. THIS MAY BE YOUR ONLY CHANCE.
HE'S RIGHT. THEY'LL BE SLEEPING NOW, OR WAITING IN THEIR PLACES.
HOW DO YOU KNOW? WHAT IF IT'S A TRICK?
IT'S NOT A TRICK. WE CAN'T GO OUT THERE NOW AND NEITHER CAN THEY. YOU HAVE TO GO WHILE YOU CAN.

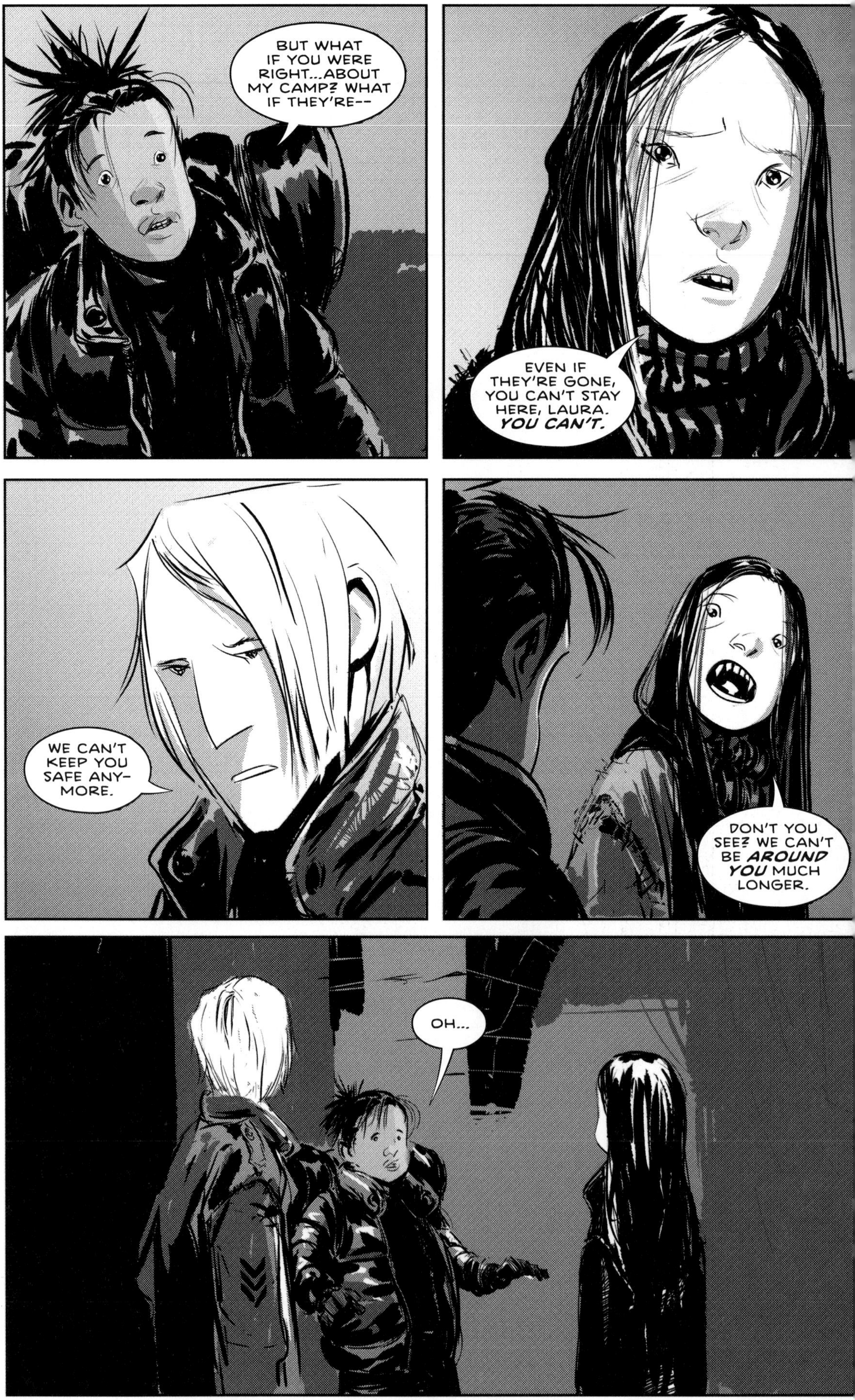
BUT WHAT IF YOU WERE RIGHT...ABOUT MY CAMP? WHAT IF THEY'RE--
EVEN IF THEY'RE GONE, YOU CAN'T STAY HERE, LAURA. *YOU CAN'T.*
WE CAN'T KEEP YOU SAFE ANY-MORE.
DON'T YOU SEE? WE CAN'T BE *AROUND YOU* MUCH LONGER.
OH...

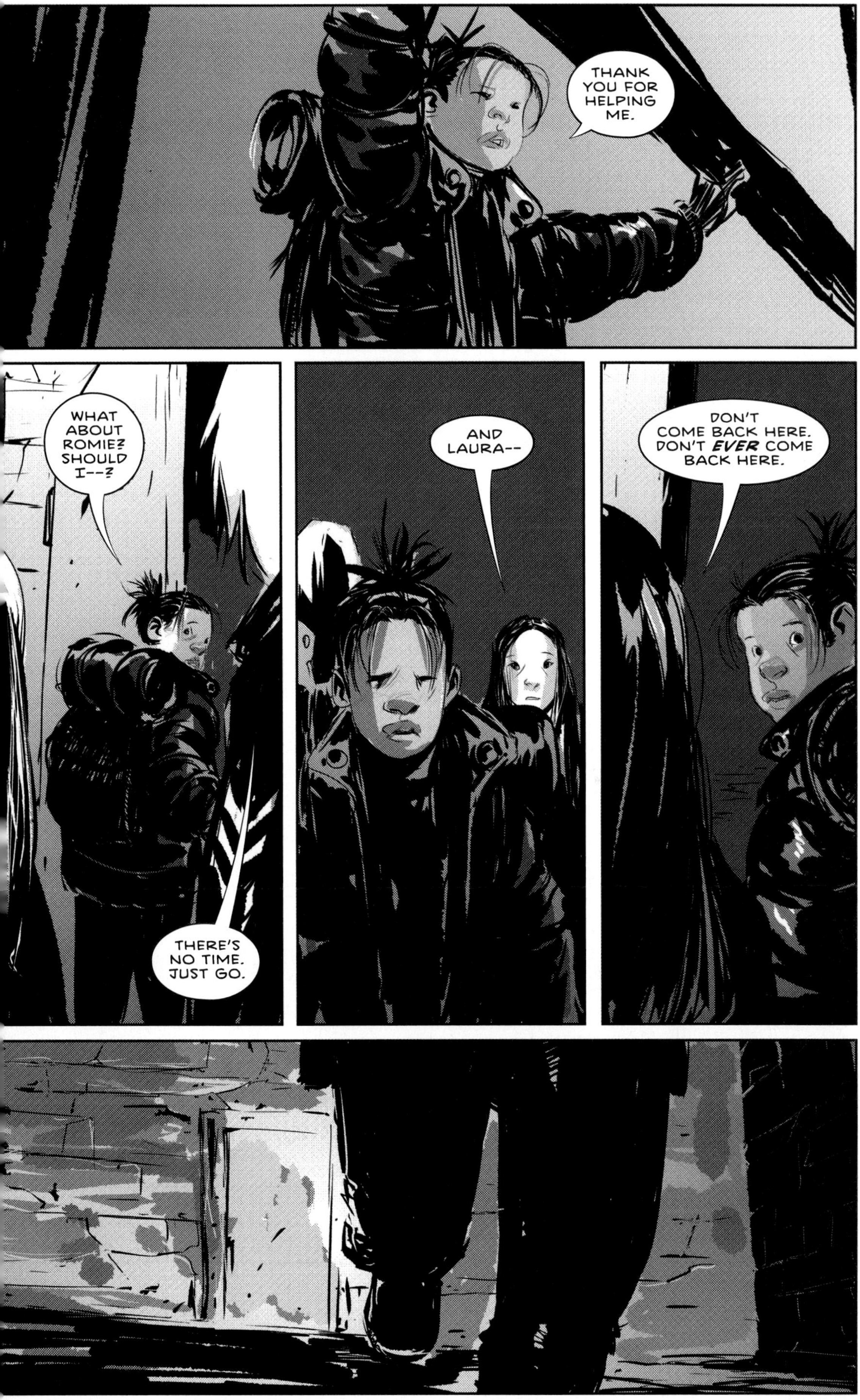
THANK YOU FOR HELPING ME.
WHAT ABOUT ROMIE? SHOULD I--?
THERE'S NO TIME. JUST GO.
AND LAURA--
DON'T COME BACK HERE. DON'T *EVER* COME BACK HERE.

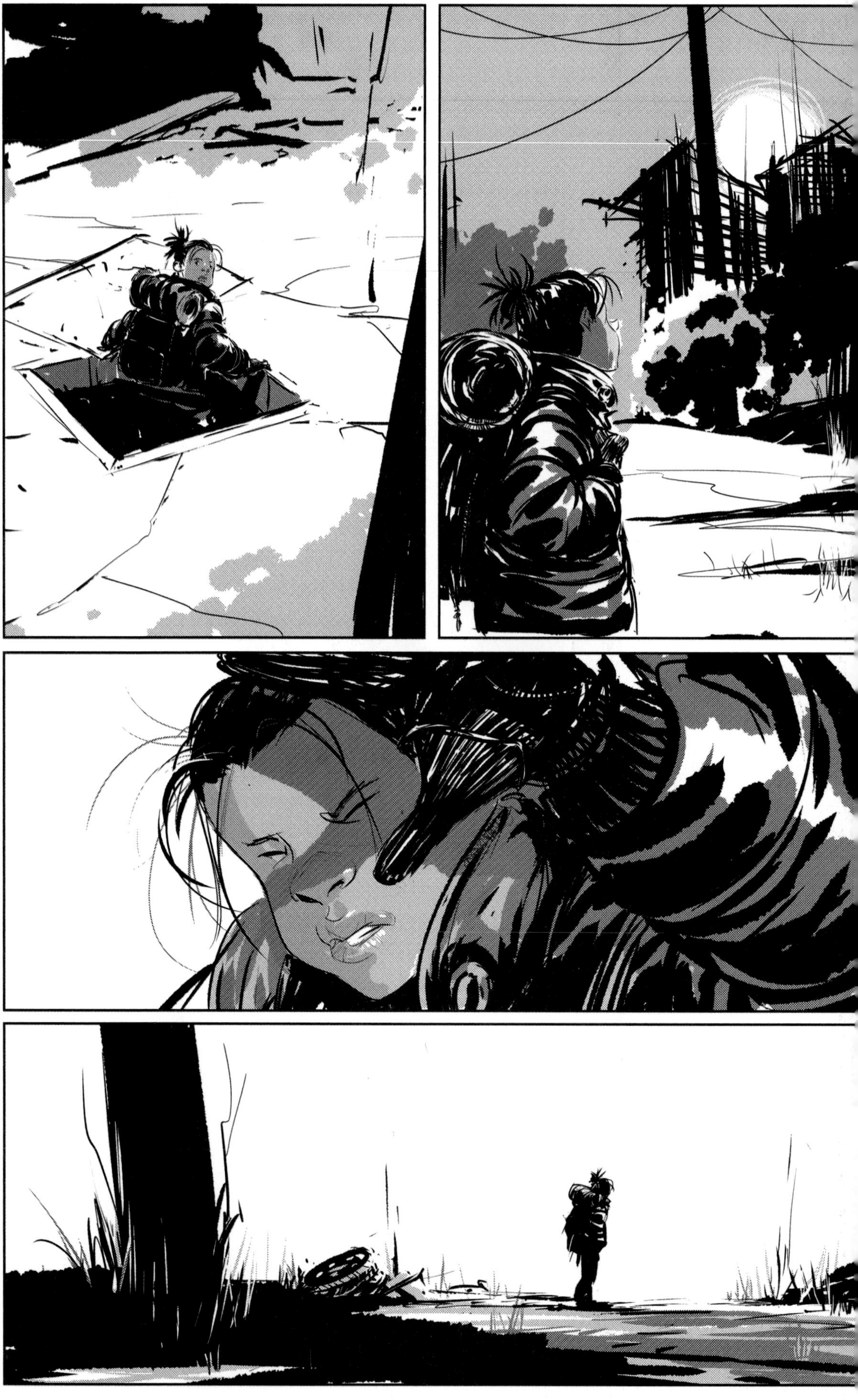

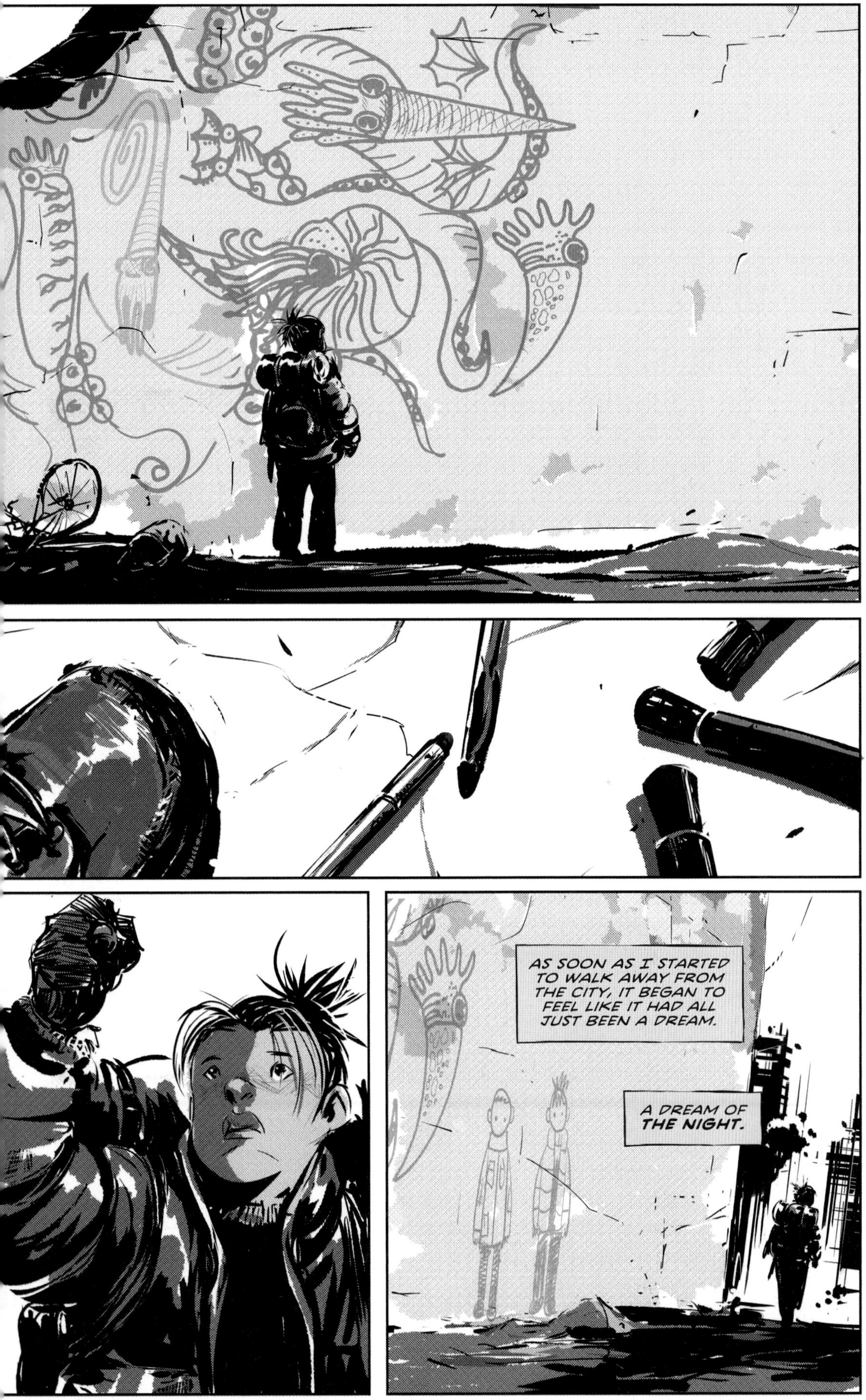
AS SOON AS I STARTED TO WALK AWAY FROM THE CITY, IT BEGAN TO FEEL LIKE IT HAD ALL JUST BEEN A DREAM.
A DREAM OF **THE NIGHT.**

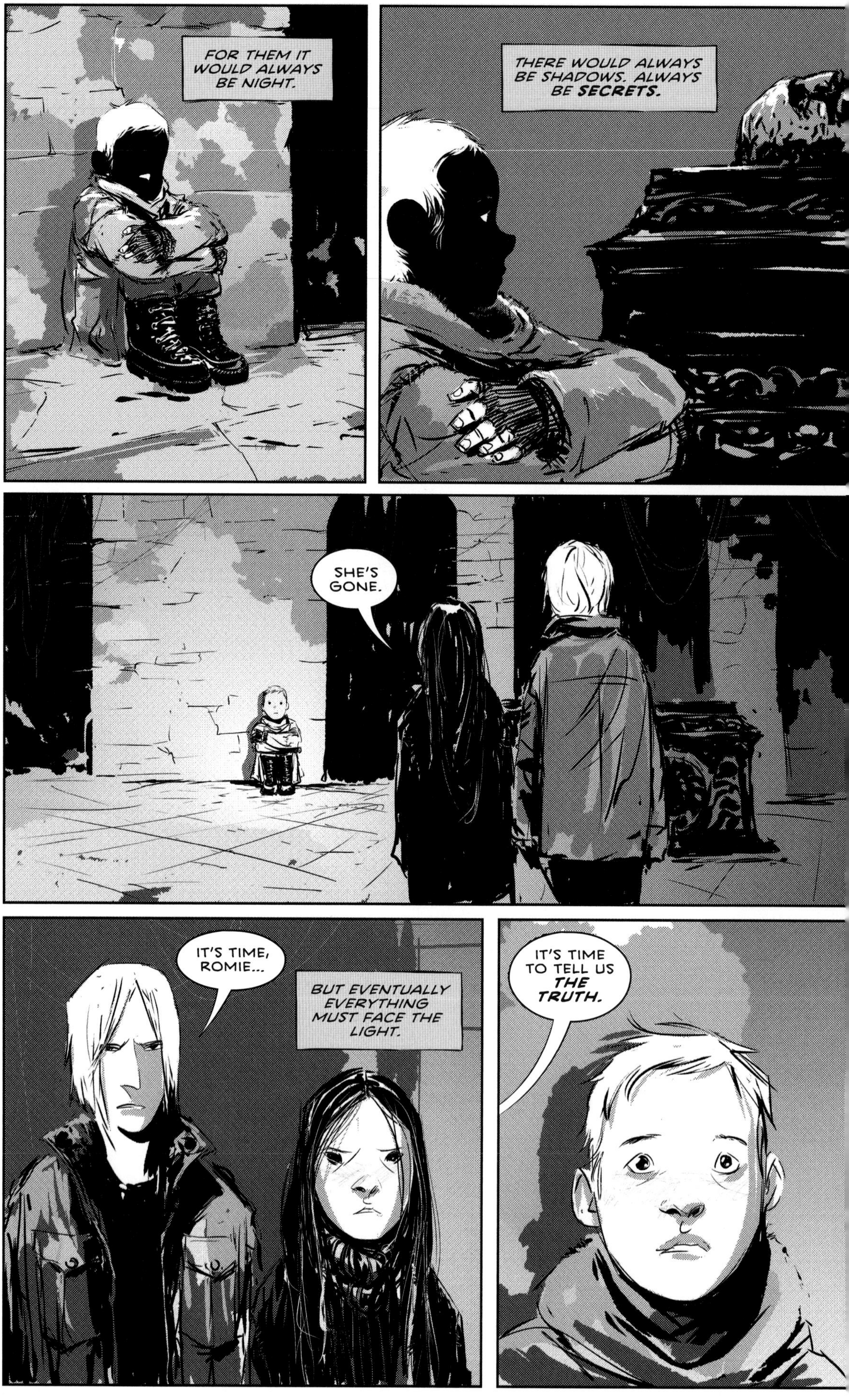
FOR THEM IT WOULD ALWAYS BE NIGHT.
THERE WOULD ALWAYS BE SHADOWS. ALWAYS BE SECRETS.
SHE'S GONE.
IT'S TIME, ROMIE...
BUT EVENTUALLY EVERYTHING MUST FACE THE LIGHT.
IT'S TIME TO TELL US THE TRUTH.

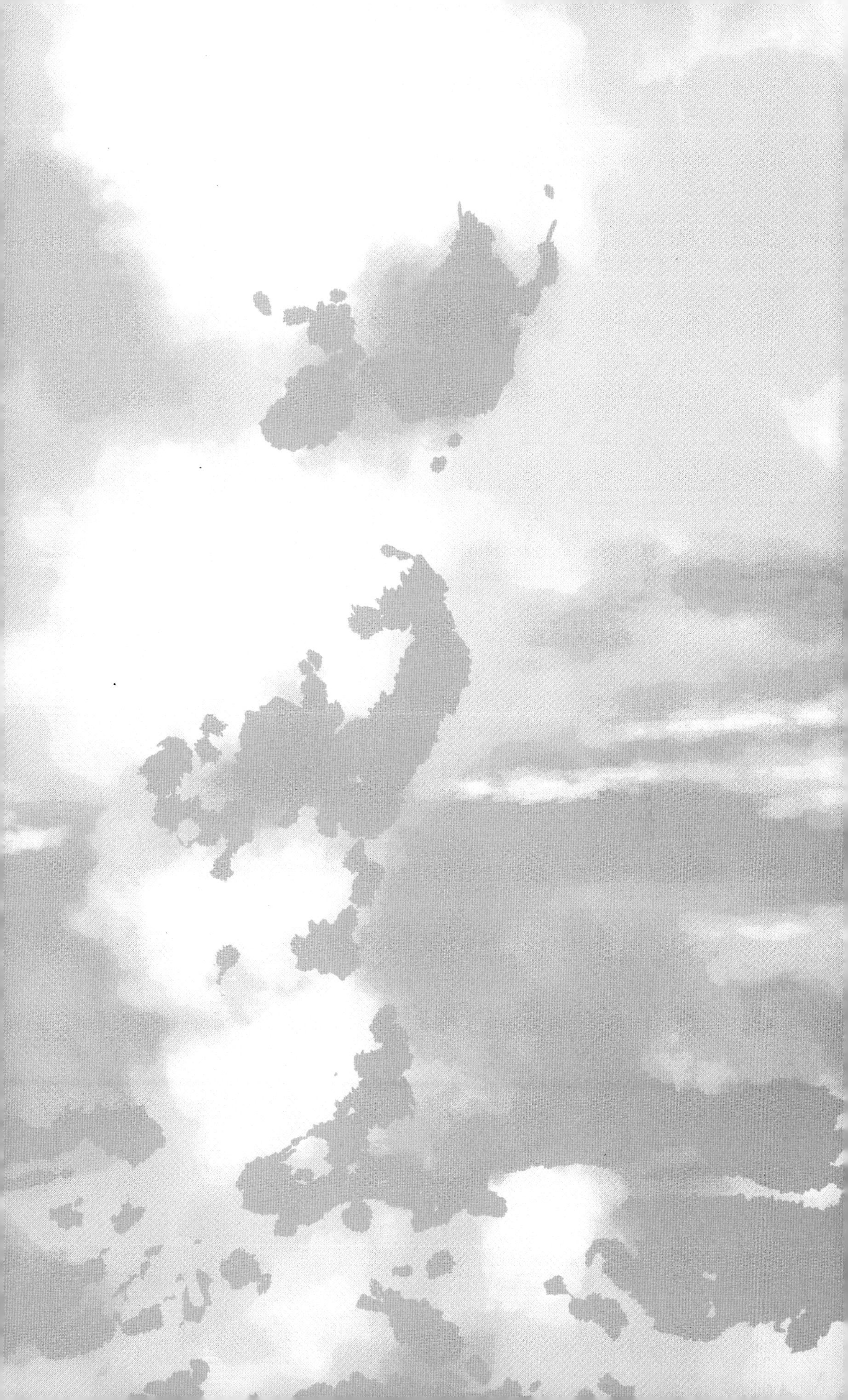

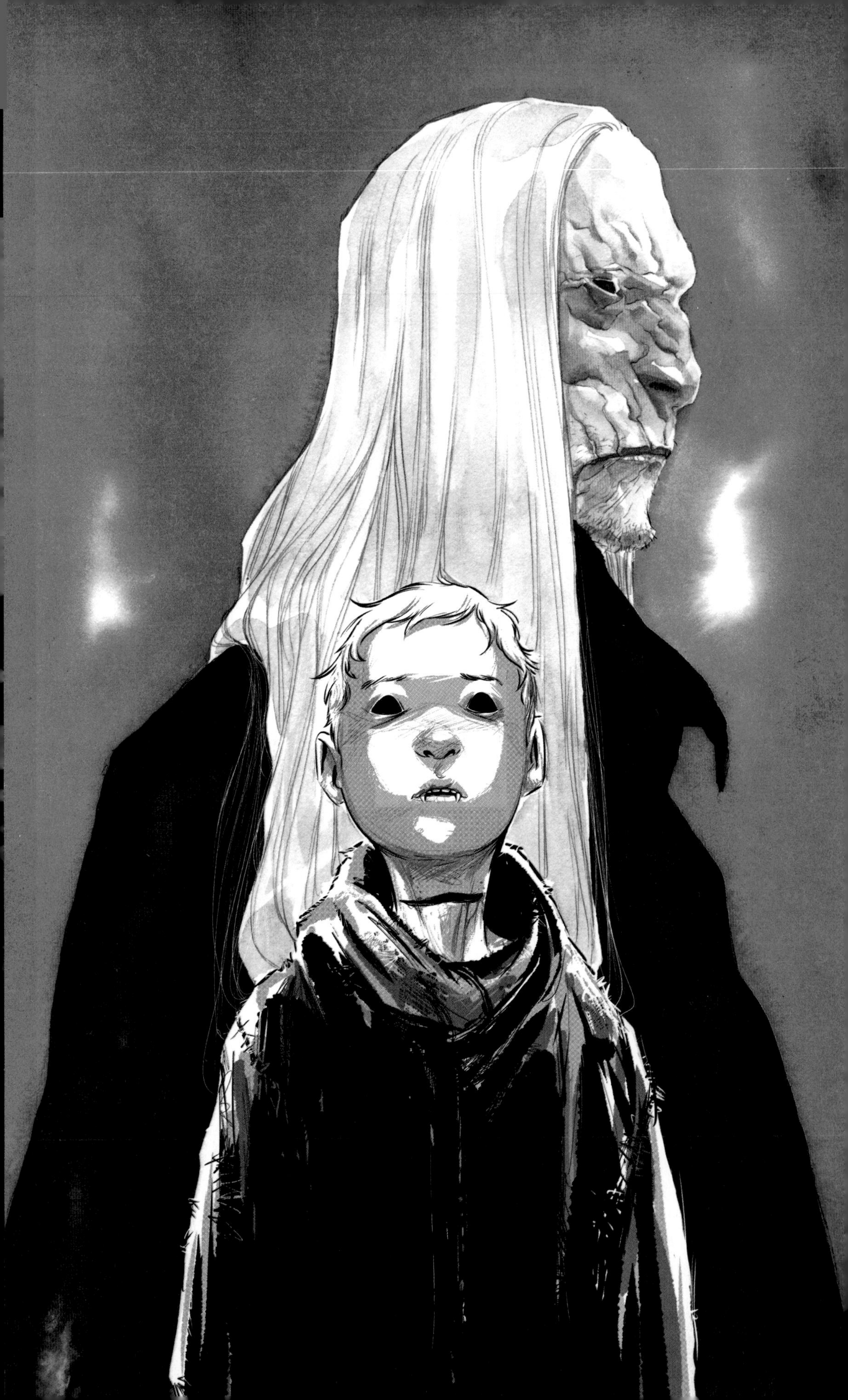

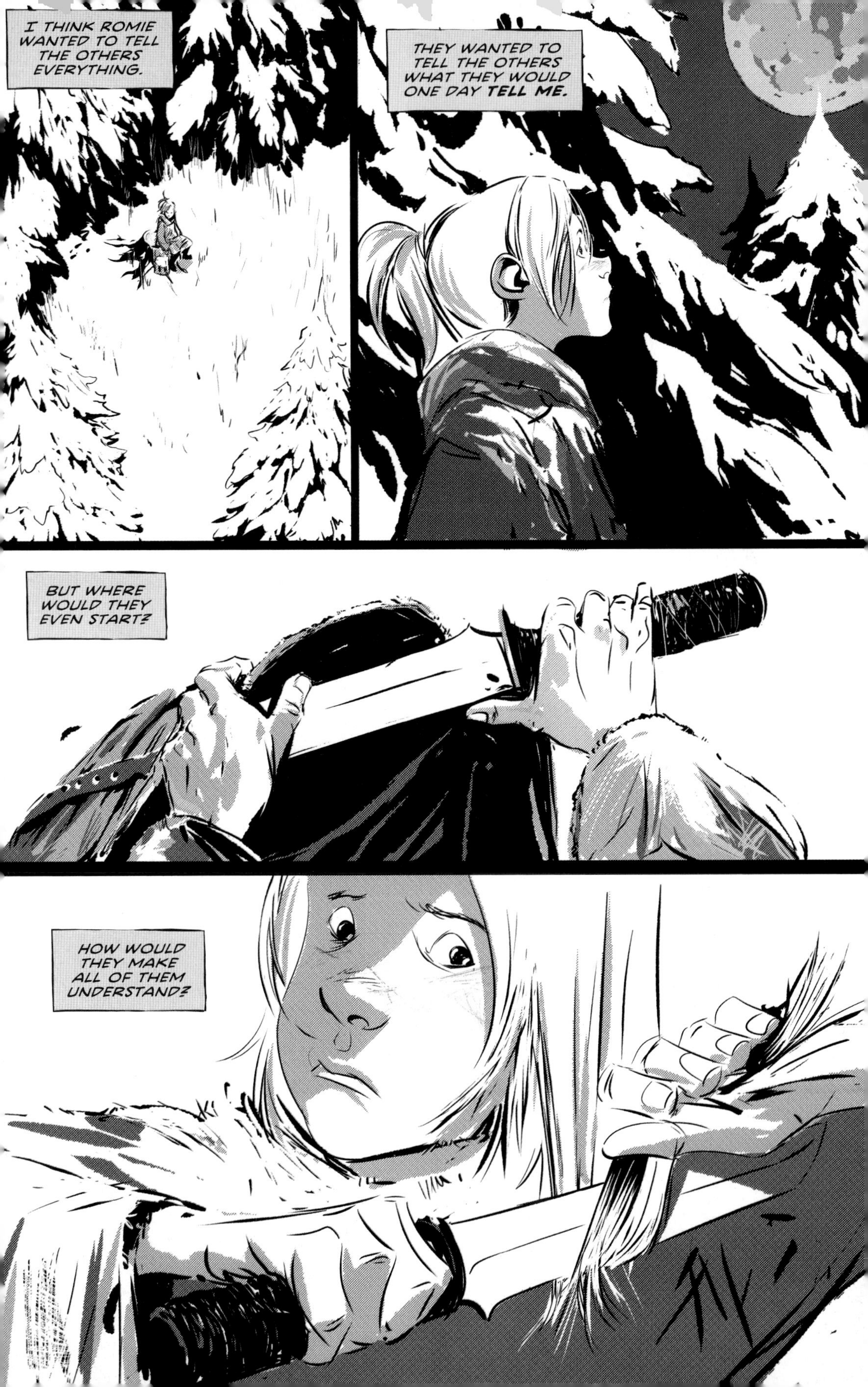
I THINK ROMIE WANTED TO TELL THE OTHERS EVERYTHING.
THEY WANTED TO TELL THE OTHERS WHAT THEY WOULD ONE DAY TELL ME.
BUT WHERE WOULD THEY EVEN START?
HOW WOULD THEY MAKE ALL OF THEM UNDERSTAND?

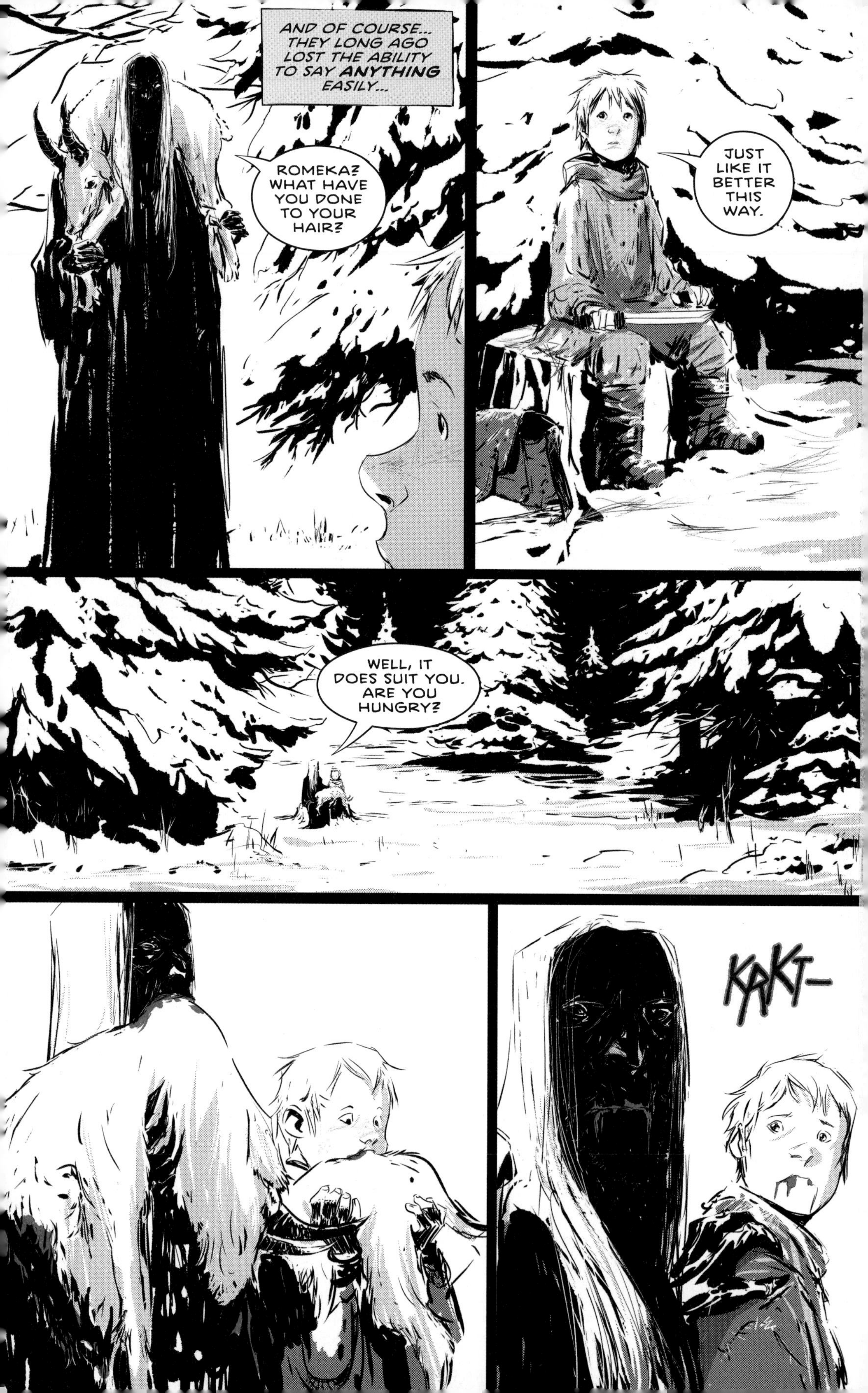
AND OF COURSE... THEY LONG AGO LOST THE ABILITY TO SAY ANYTHING EASILY...
ROMEKA? WHAT HAVE YOU DONE TO YOUR HAIR?
JUST LIKE IT BETTER THIS WAY.
WELL, IT DOES SUIT YOU. ARE YOU HUNGRY?
KRKT—

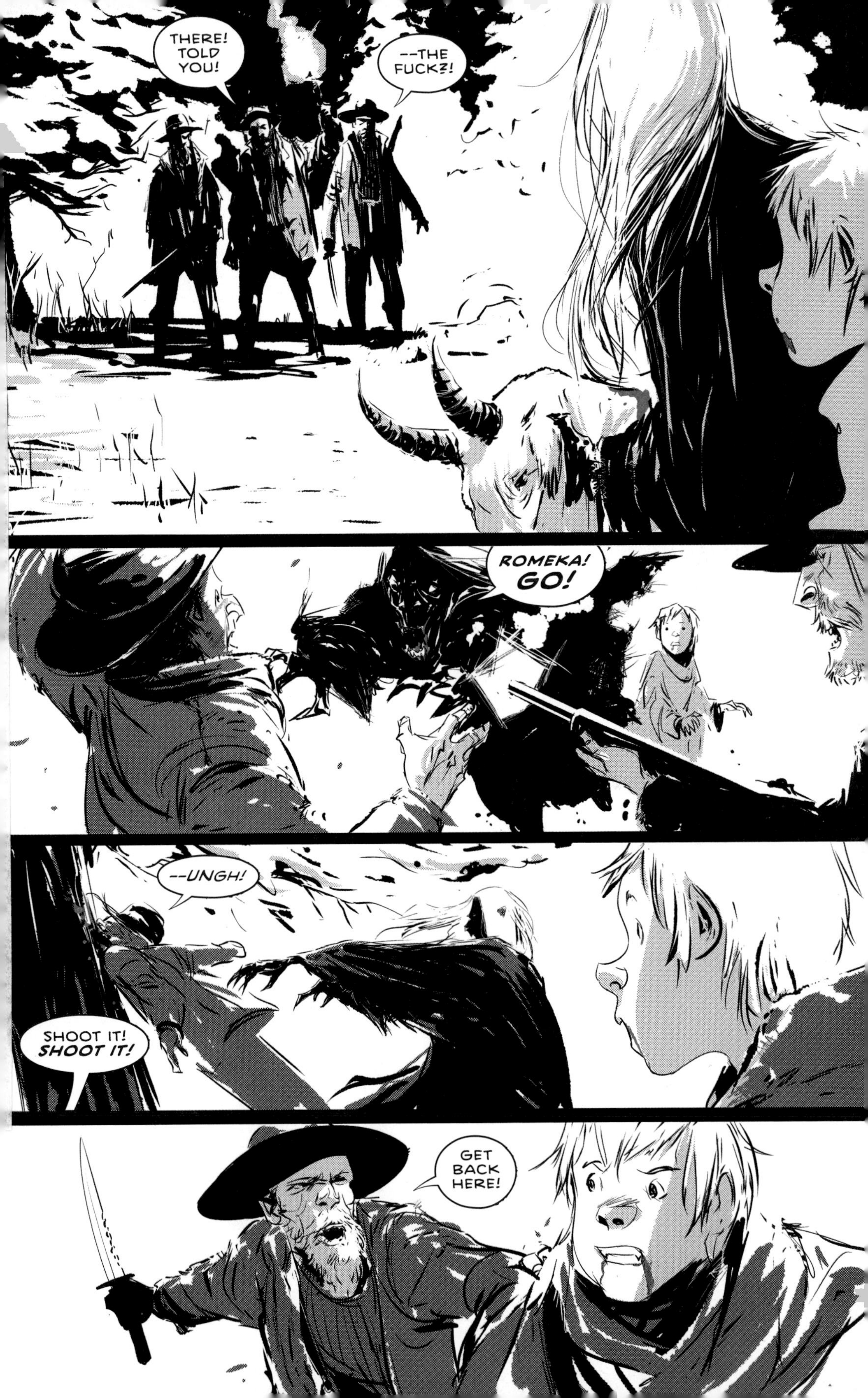
THERE! TOLD YOU!
--THE FUCK?!
ROMEKA! GO!
--UNGH!
SHOOT IT! SHOOT IT!
GET BACK HERE!

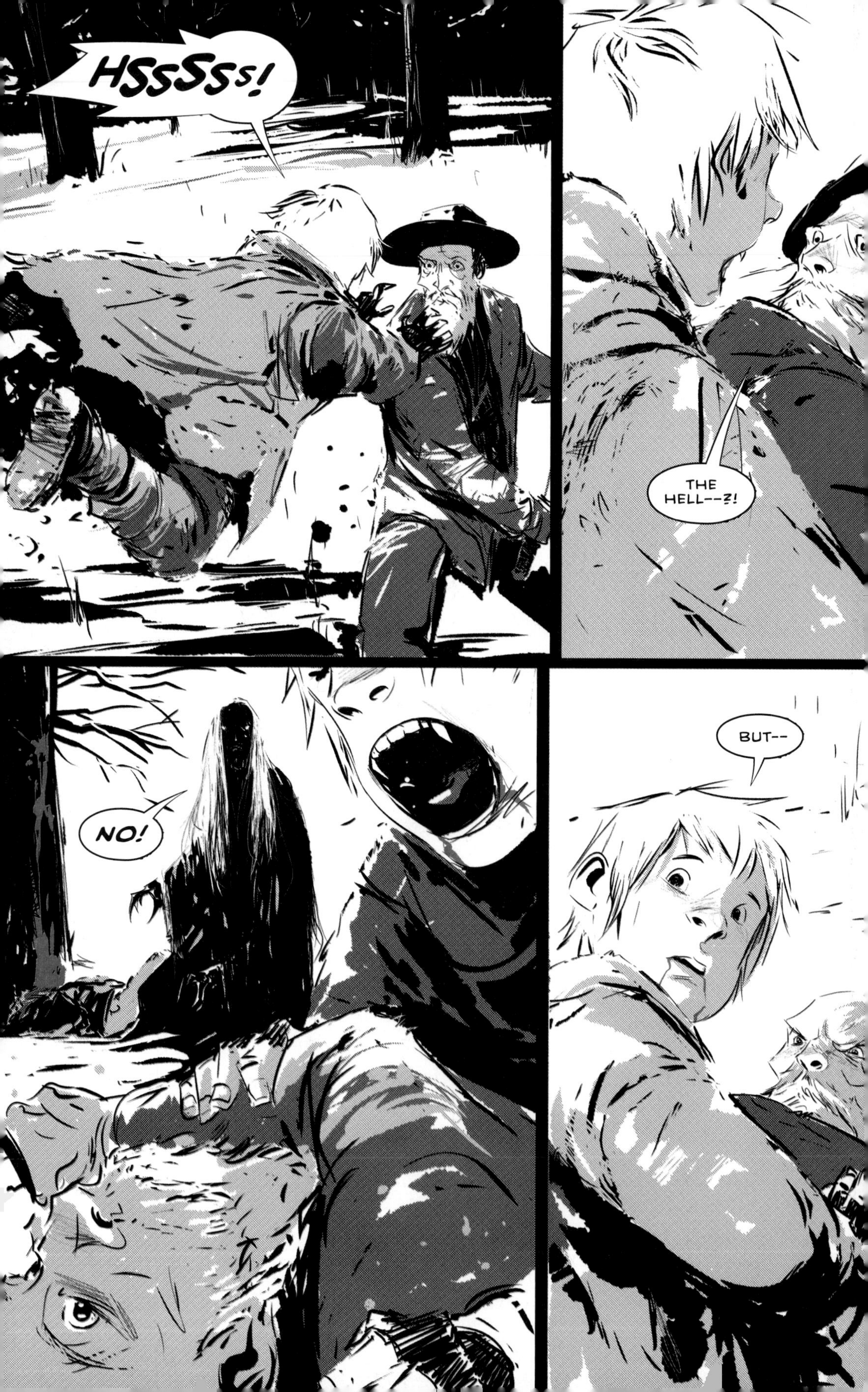
HSsSSs!
THE HELL--?!
NO!
BUT--

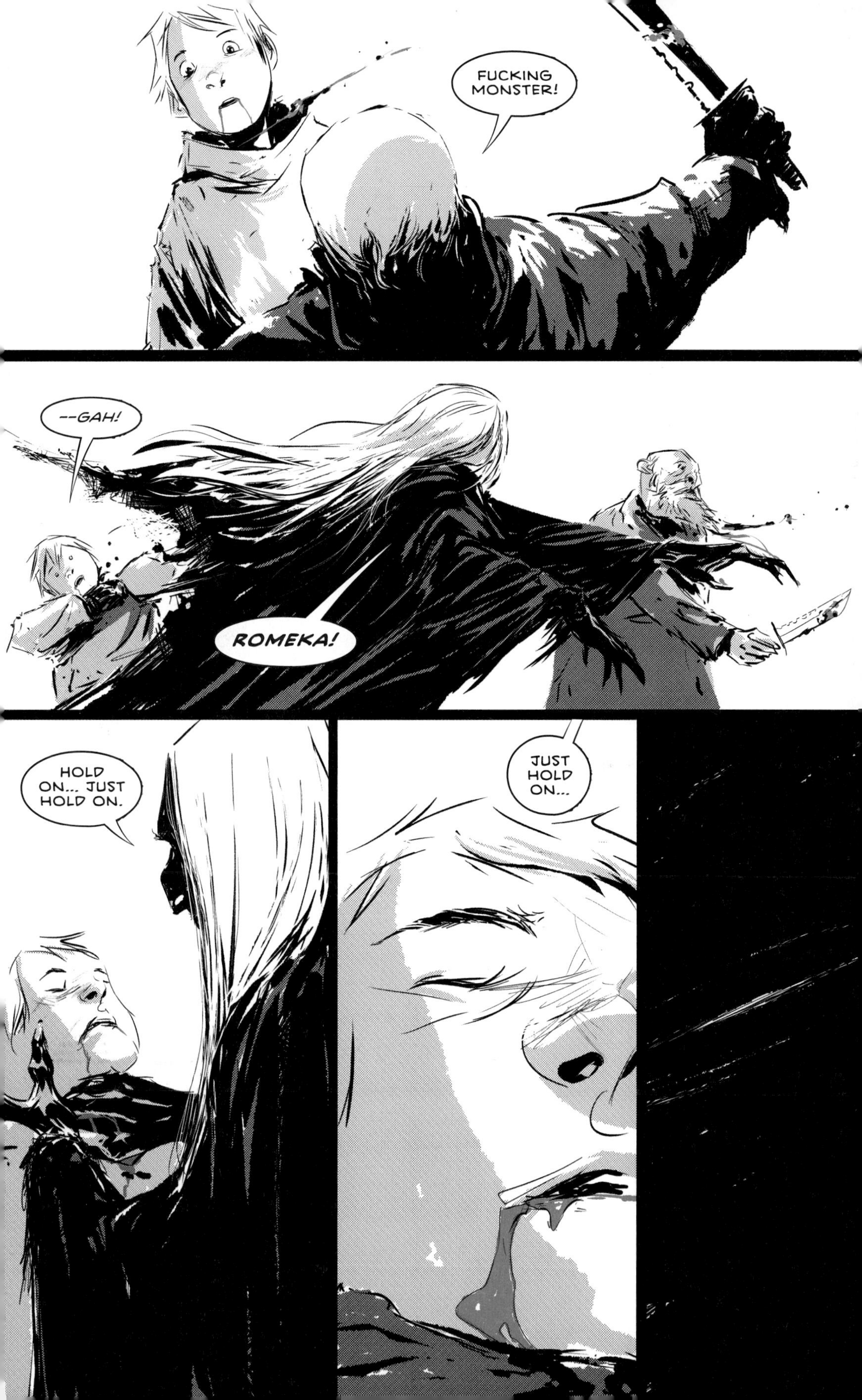
FUCKING MONSTER!
--GAH!
ROMEKA!
HOLD ON... JUST HOLD ON.
JUST HOLD ON...

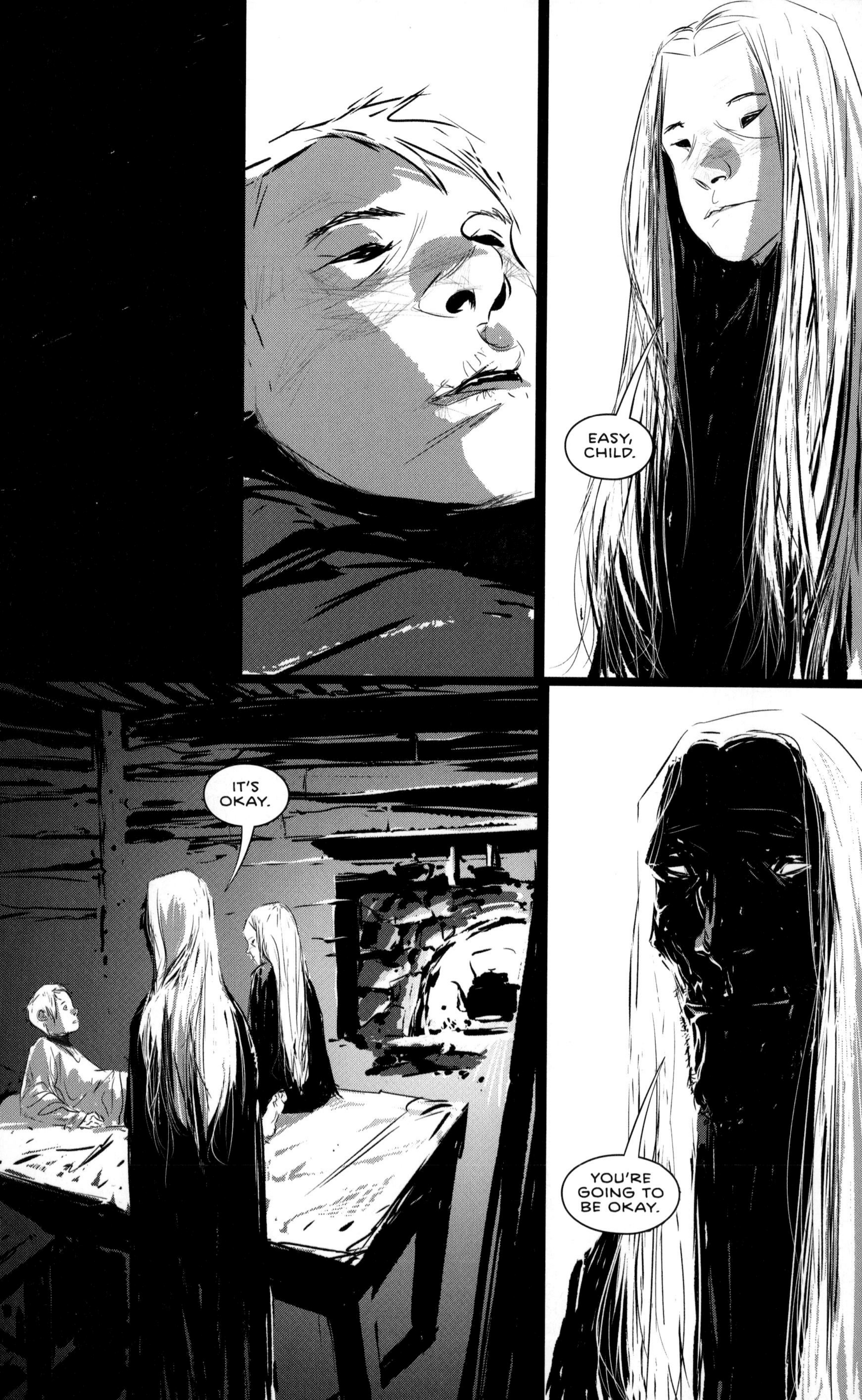
EASY, CHILD.
IT'S OKAY.
YOU'RE GOING TO BE OKAY.

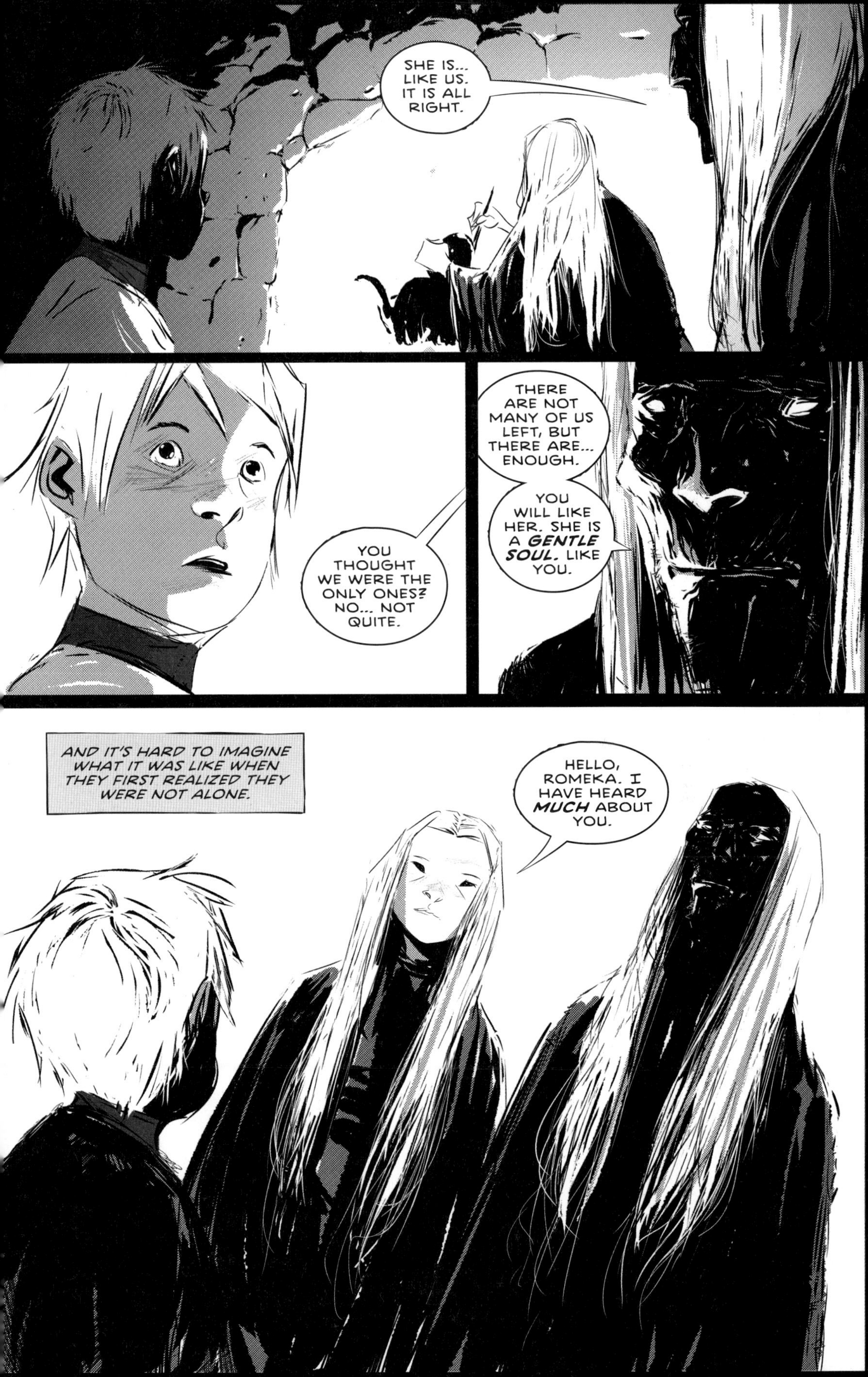
SHE IS... LIKE US. IT IS ALL RIGHT.
YOU THOUGHT WE WERE THE ONLY ONES? NO... NOT QUITE.
THERE ARE NOT MANY OF US LEFT, BUT THERE ARE... ENOUGH.
YOU WILL LIKE HER. SHE IS A GENTLE SOUL. LIKE YOU.
AND IT'S HARD TO IMAGINE WHAT IT WAS LIKE WHEN THEY FIRST REALIZED THEY WERE NOT ALONE.
HELLO, ROMEKA. I HAVE HEARD MUCH ABOUT YOU.

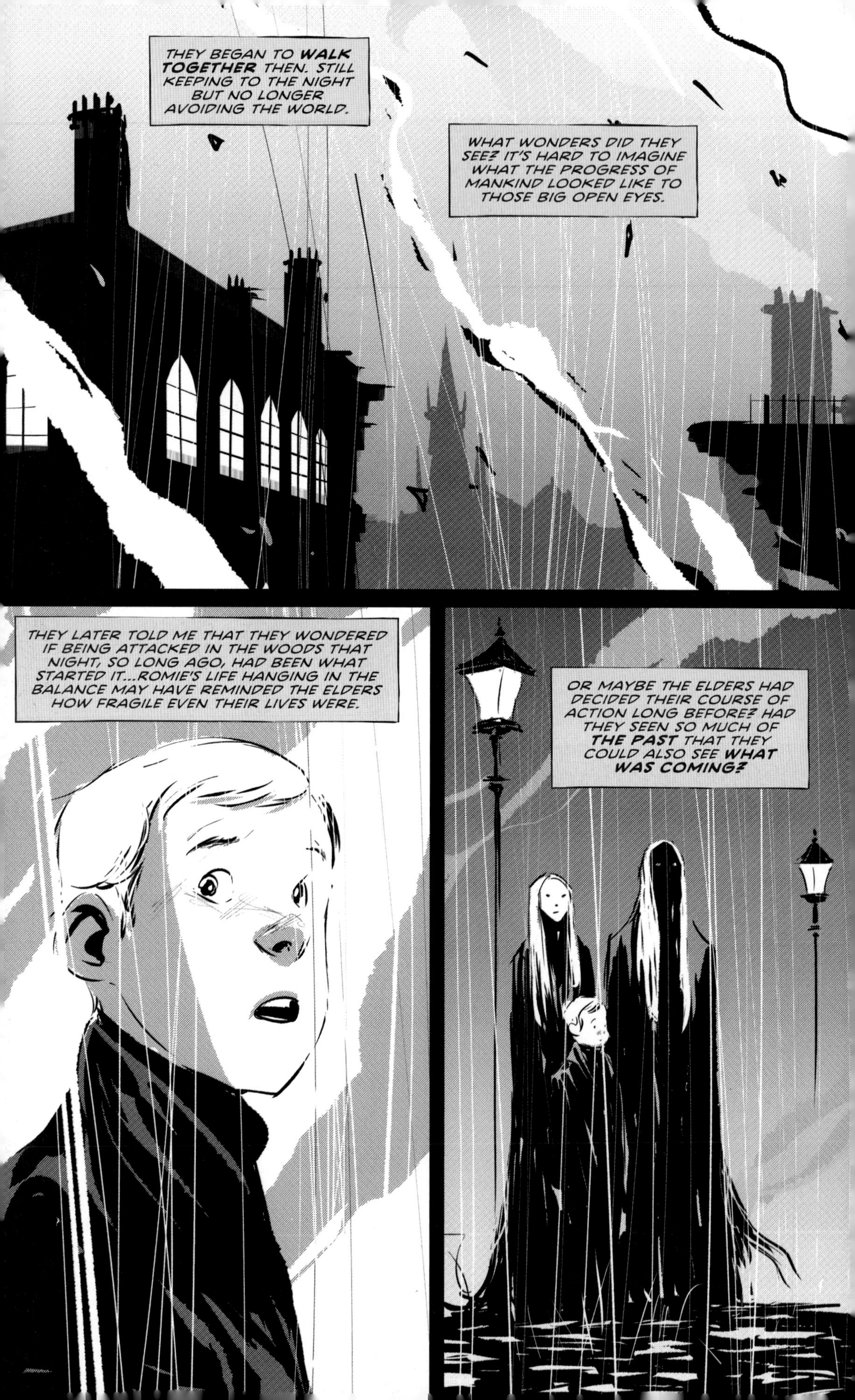
THEY BEGAN TO **WALK TOGETHER** THEN. STILL KEEPING TO THE NIGHT BUT NO LONGER AVOIDING THE WORLD.
WHAT WONDERS DID THEY SEE? IT'S HARD TO IMAGINE WHAT THE PROGRESS OF MANKIND LOOKED LIKE TO THOSE BIG OPEN EYES.
THEY LATER TOLD ME THAT THEY WONDERED IF BEING ATTACKED IN THE WOODS THAT NIGHT, SO LONG AGO, HAD BEEN WHAT STARTED IT...ROMIE'S LIFE HANGING IN THE BALANCE MAY HAVE REMINDED THE ELDERS HOW FRAGILE EVEN THEIR LIVES WERE.
OR MAYBE THE ELDERS HAD DECIDED THEIR COURSE OF ACTION LONG BEFORE? HAD THEY SEEN SO MUCH OF **THE PAST** THAT THEY COULD ALSO SEE **WHAT WAS COMING?**

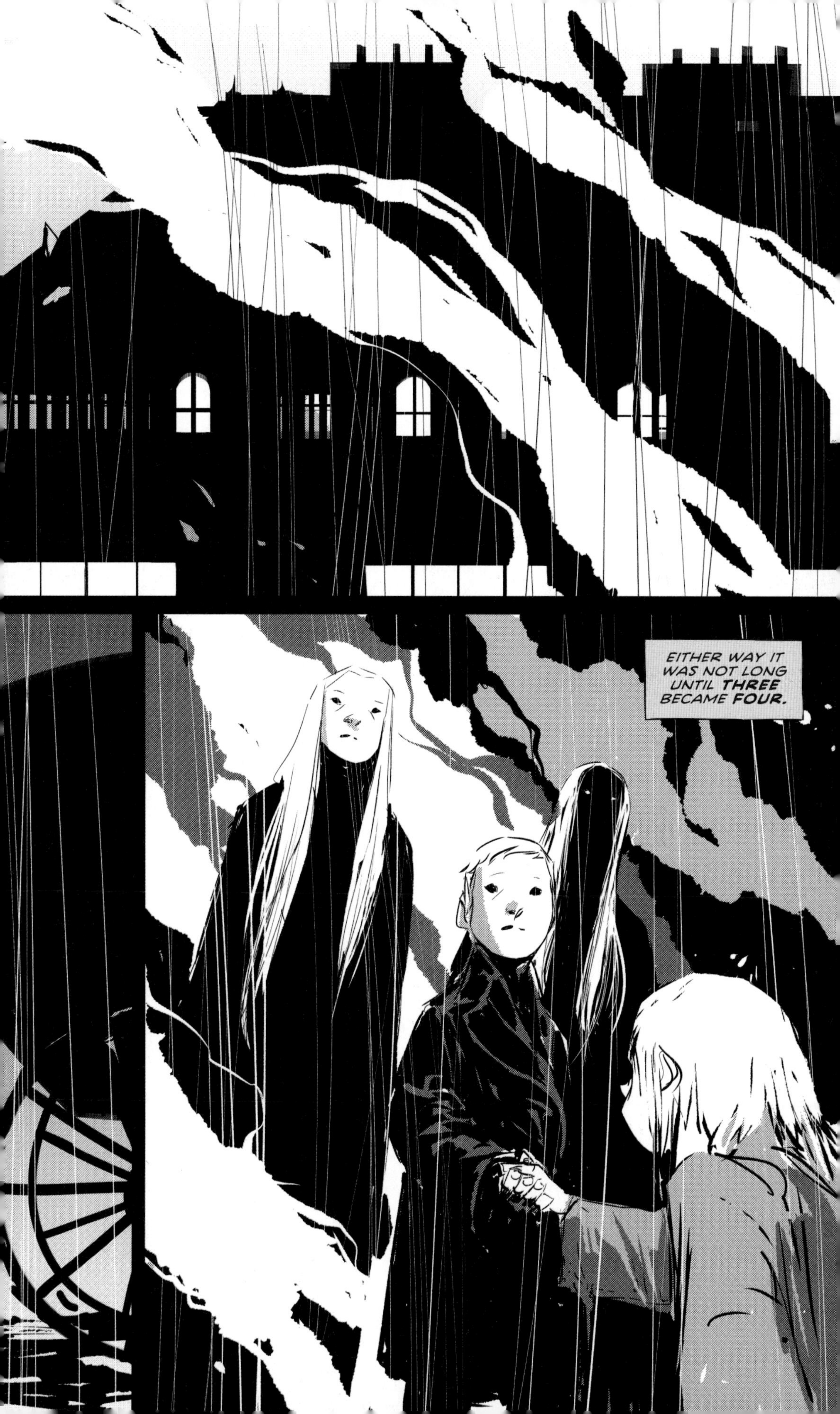
EITHER WAY IT WAS NOT LONG UNTIL THREE BECAME FOUR.

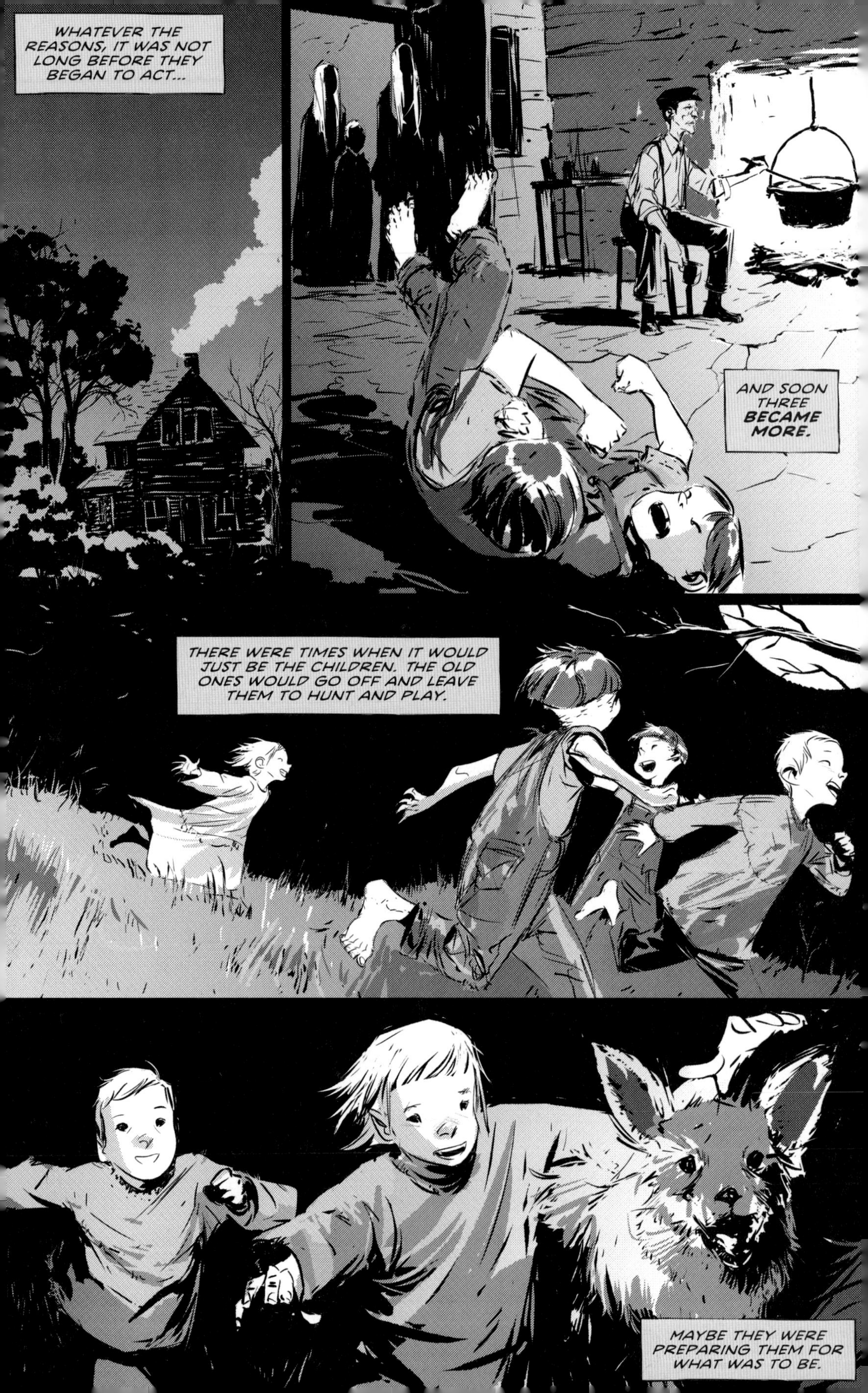
WHATEVER THE REASONS, IT WAS NOT LONG BEFORE THEY BEGAN TO ACT...
AND SOON THREE BECAME MORE.
THERE WERE TIMES WHEN IT WOULD JUST BE THE CHILDREN. THE OLD ONES WOULD GO OFF AND LEAVE THEM TO HUNT AND PLAY.
MAYBE THEY WERE PREPARING THEM FOR WHAT WAS TO BE.

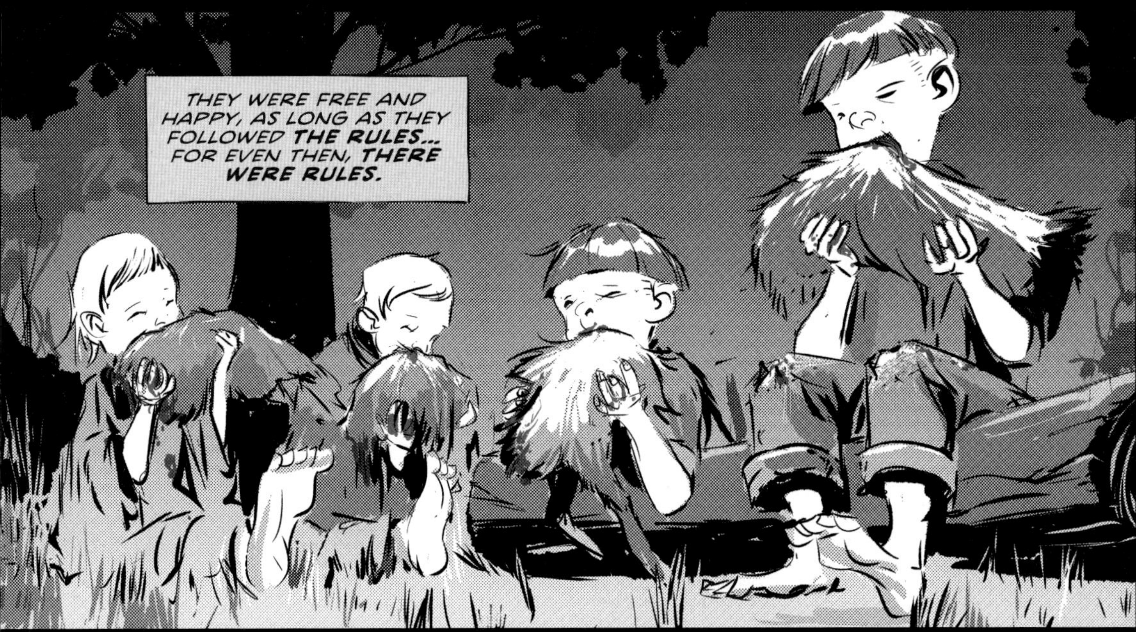
THEY WERE FREE AND HAPPY, AS LONG AS THEY FOLLOWED THE RULES... FOR EVEN THEN, THERE WERE RULES.

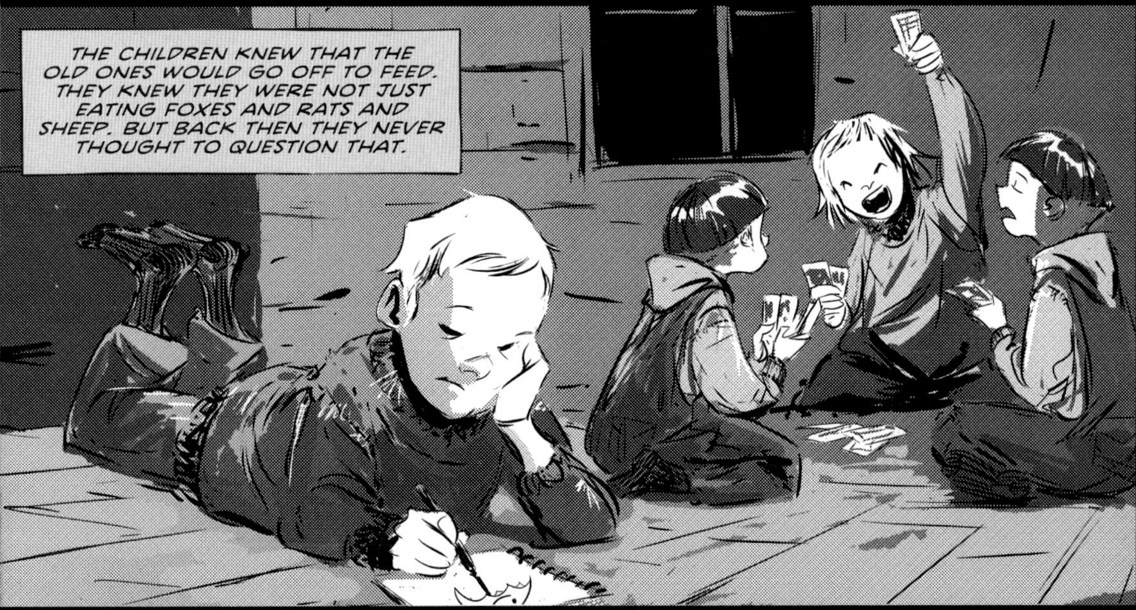
THE CHILDREN KNEW THAT THE OLD ONES WOULD GO OFF TO FEED. THEY KNEW THEY WERE NOT JUST EATING FOXES AND RATS AND SHEEP. BUT BACK THEN THEY NEVER THOUGHT TO QUESTION THAT.

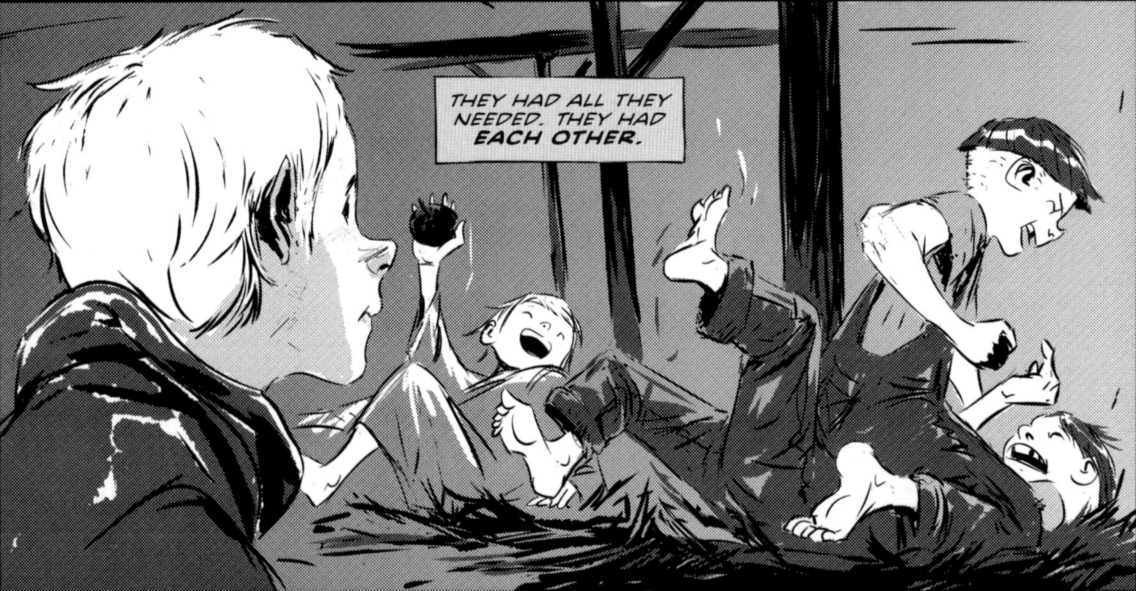
THEY HAD ALL THEY NEEDED. THEY HAD EACH OTHER.

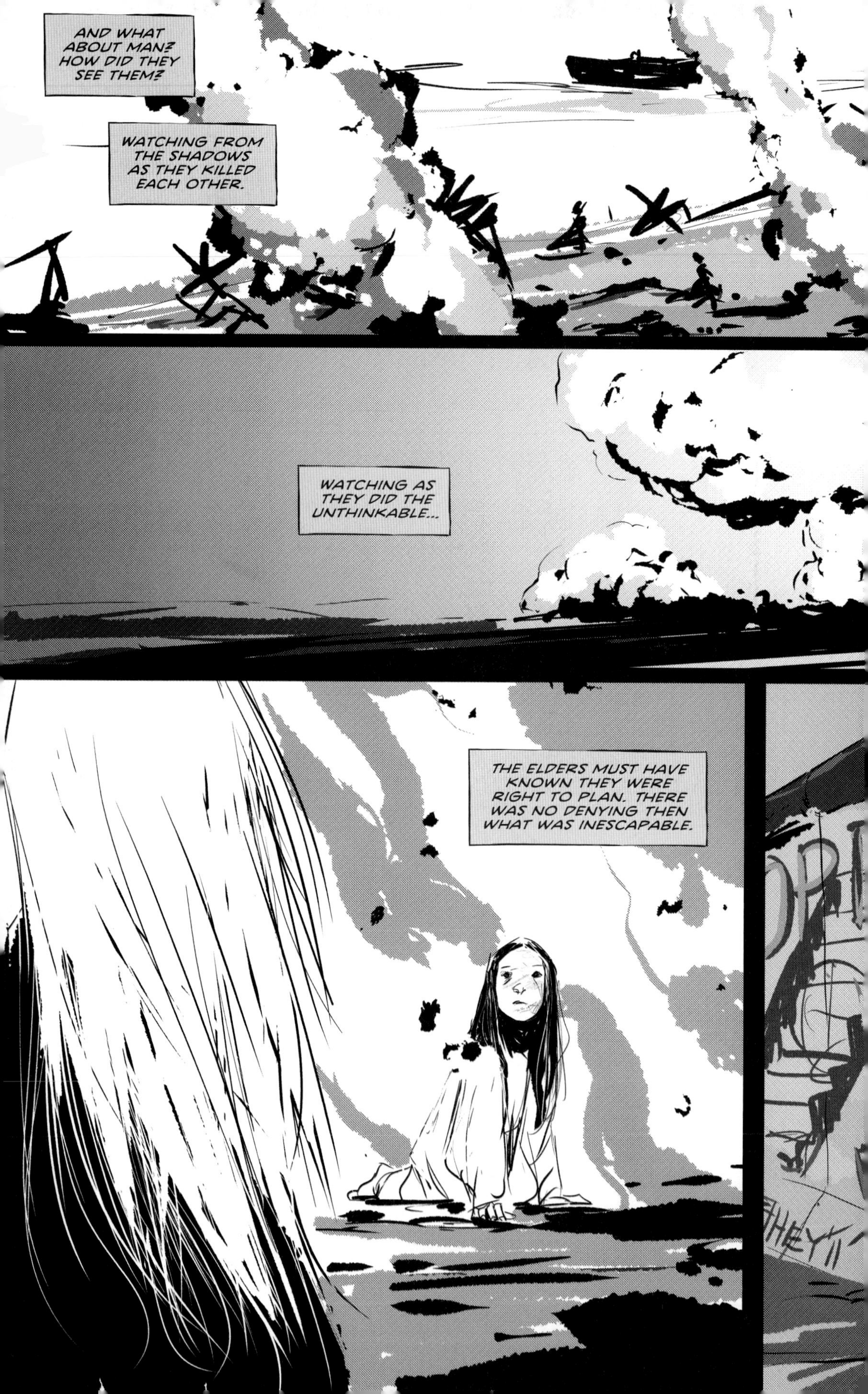
AND WHAT ABOUT MAN? HOW DID THEY SEE THEM?
WATCHING FROM THE SHADOWS AS THEY KILLED EACH OTHER.
WATCHING AS THEY DID THE UNTHINKABLE...
THE ELDERS MUST HAVE KNOWN THEY WERE RIGHT TO PLAN. THERE WAS NO DENYING THEN WHAT WAS INESCAPABLE.

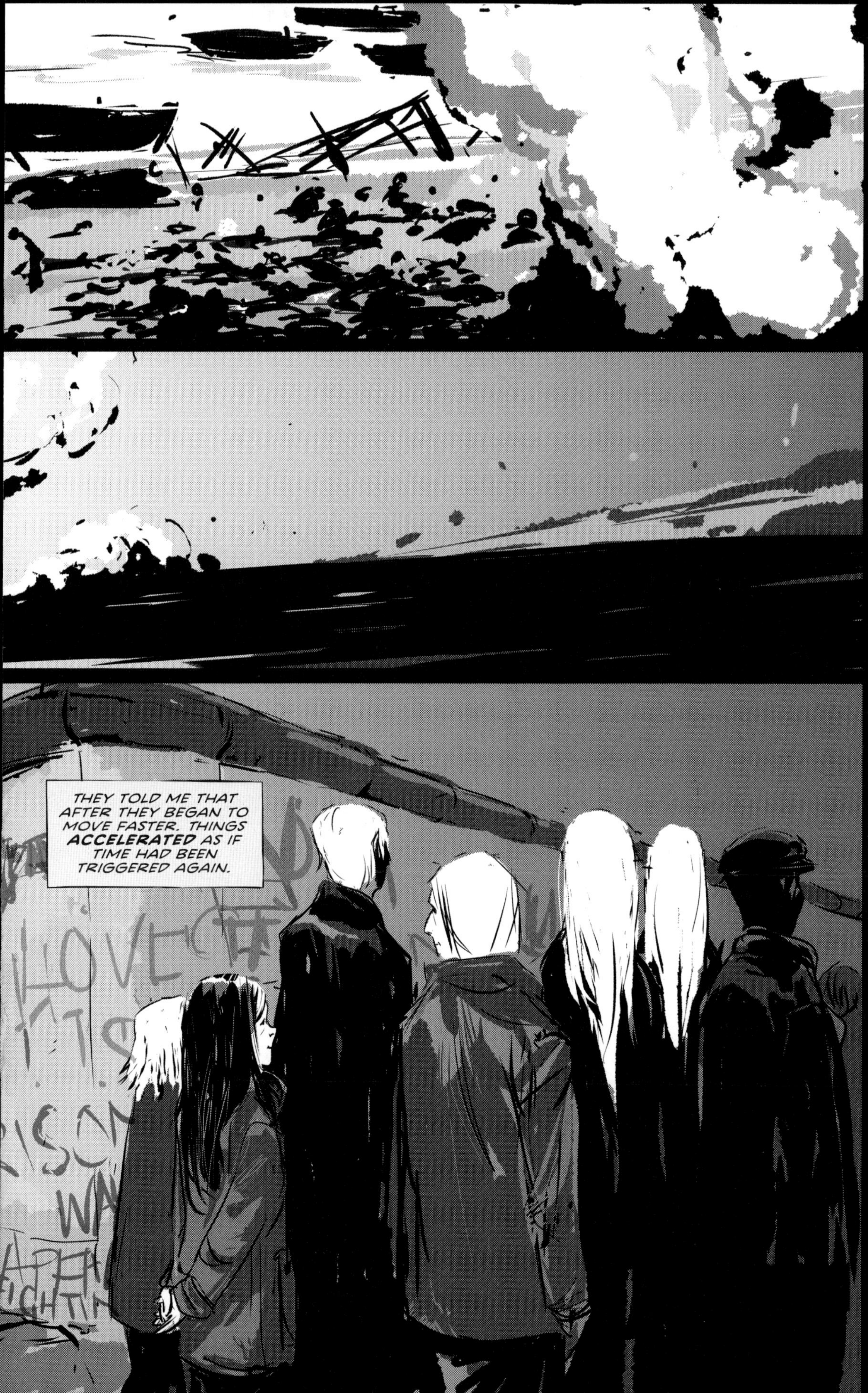
THEY TOLD ME THAT AFTER THEY BEGAN TO MOVE FASTER. THINGS **ACCELERATED** AS IF TIME HAD BEEN TRIGGERED AGAIN.

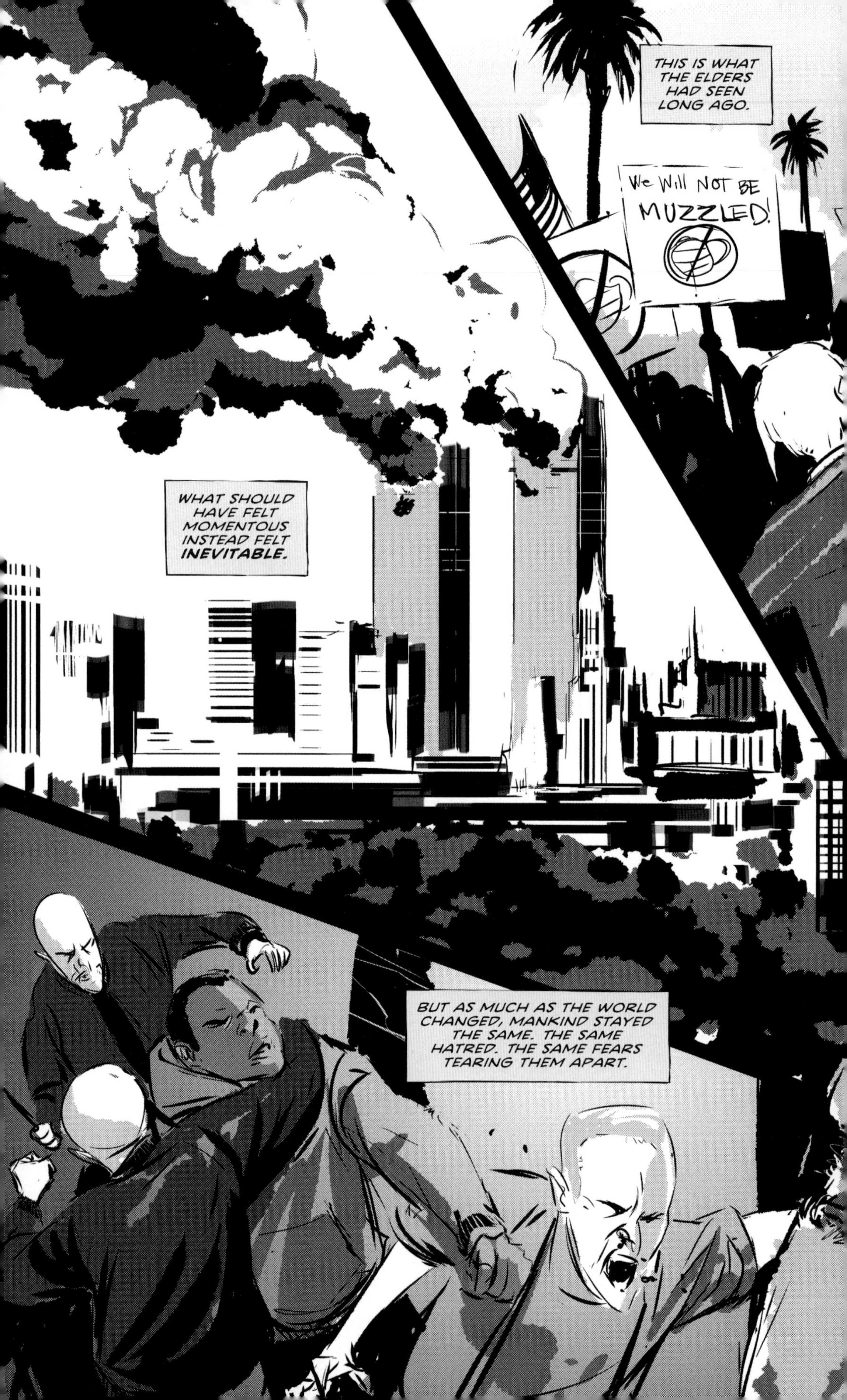
THIS IS WHAT THE ELDERS HAD SEEN LONG AGO.
We Will NOT BE MUZZLED!
WHAT SHOULD HAVE FELT MOMENTOUS INSTEAD FELT INEVITABLE.
BUT AS MUCH AS THE WORLD CHANGED, MANKIND STAYED THE SAME. THE SAME HATRED. THE SAME FEARS TEARING THEM APART.

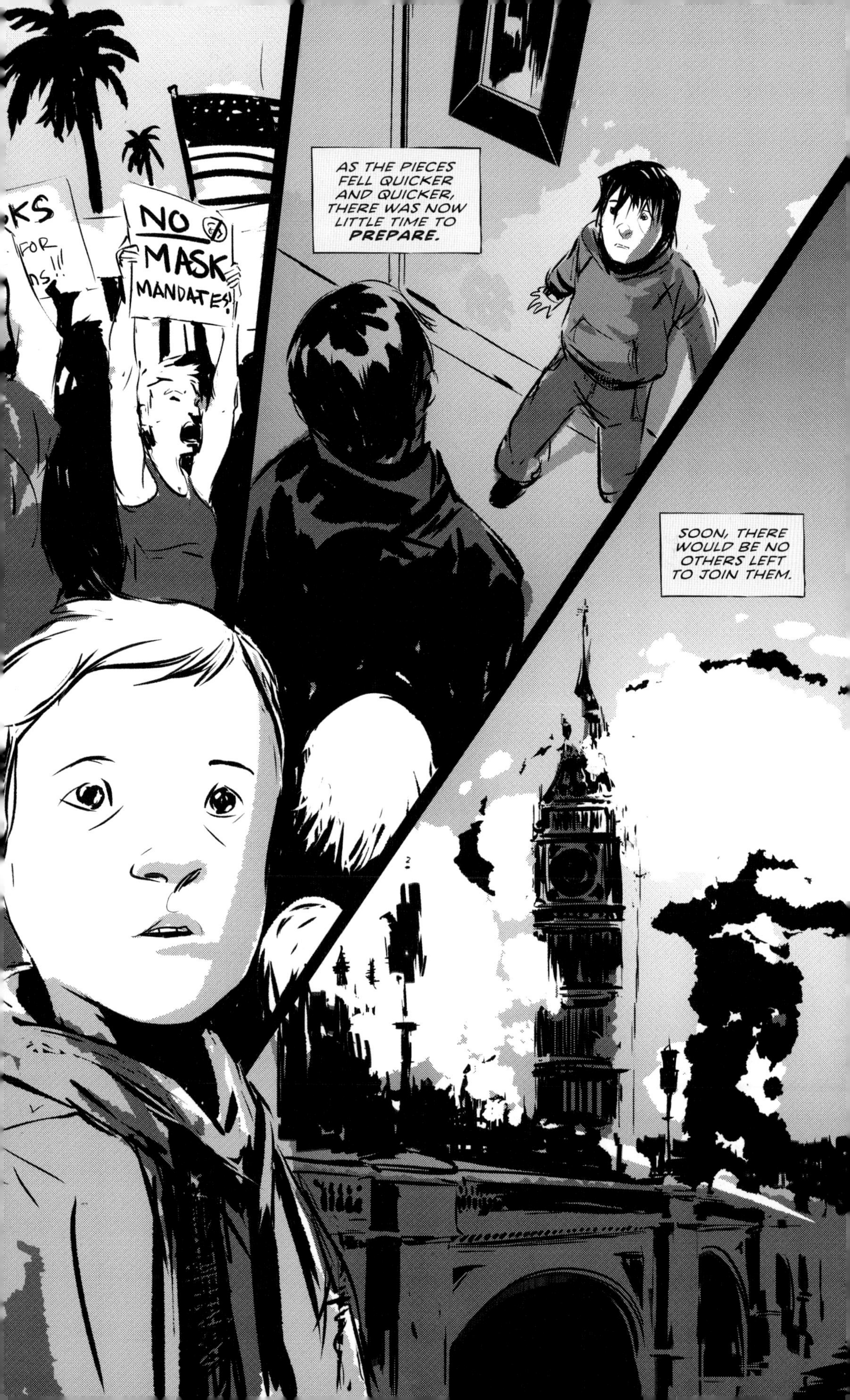
NO MASK MANDATES!
AS THE PIECES FELL QUICKER AND QUICKER, THERE WAS NOW LITTLE TIME TO PREPARE.
SOON, THERE WOULD BE NO OTHERS LEFT TO JOIN THEM.

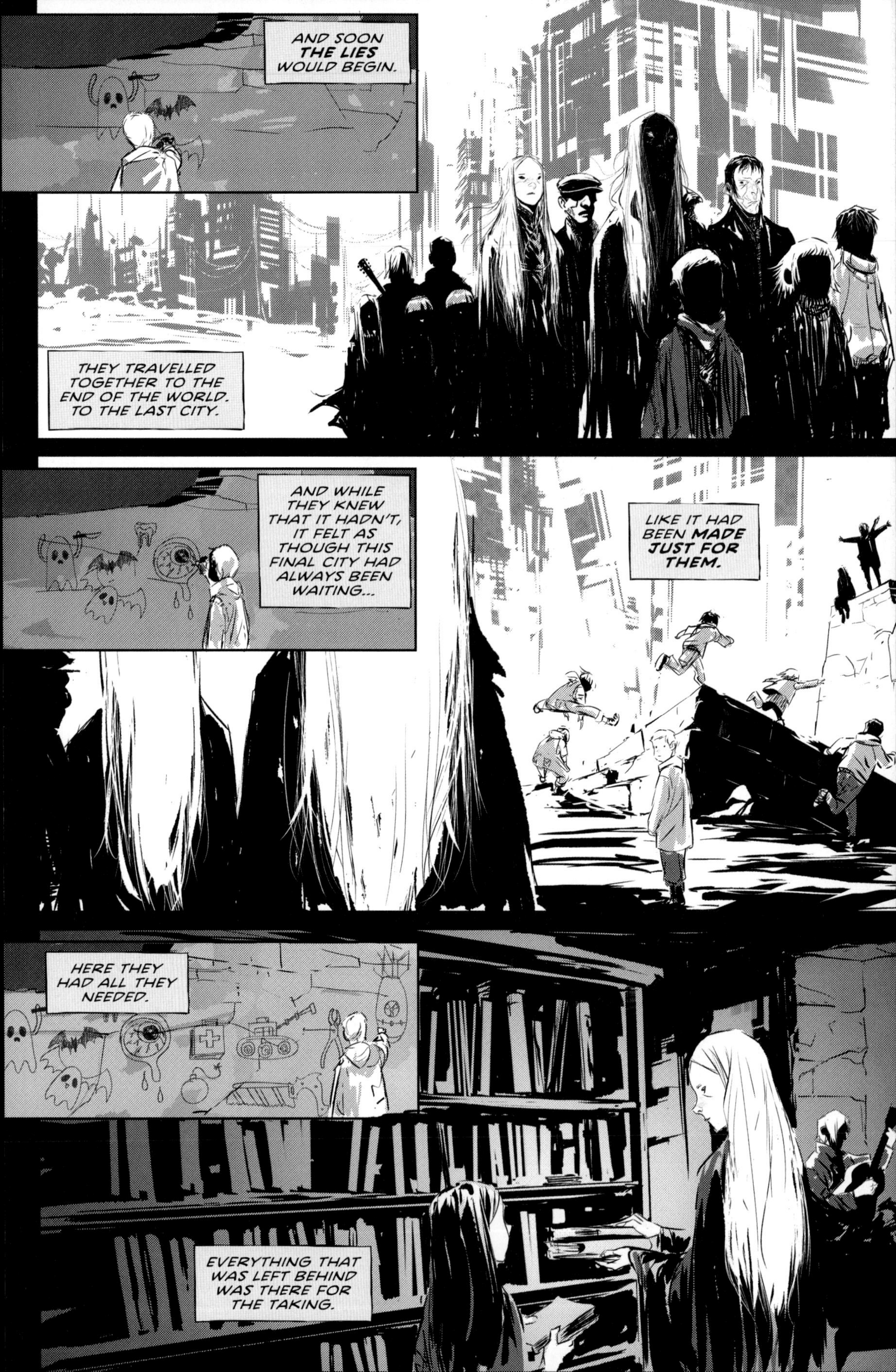
AND SOON THE LIES WOULD BEGIN.
THEY TRAVELLED TOGETHER TO THE END OF THE WORLD. TO THE LAST CITY.
AND WHILE THEY KNEW THAT IT HADN'T, IT FELT AS THOUGH THIS FINAL CITY HAD ALWAYS BEEN WAITING...
LIKE IT HAD BEEN MADE JUST FOR THEM.
HERE THEY HAD ALL THEY NEEDED.
EVERYTHING THAT WAS LEFT BEHIND WAS THERE FOR THE TAKING.

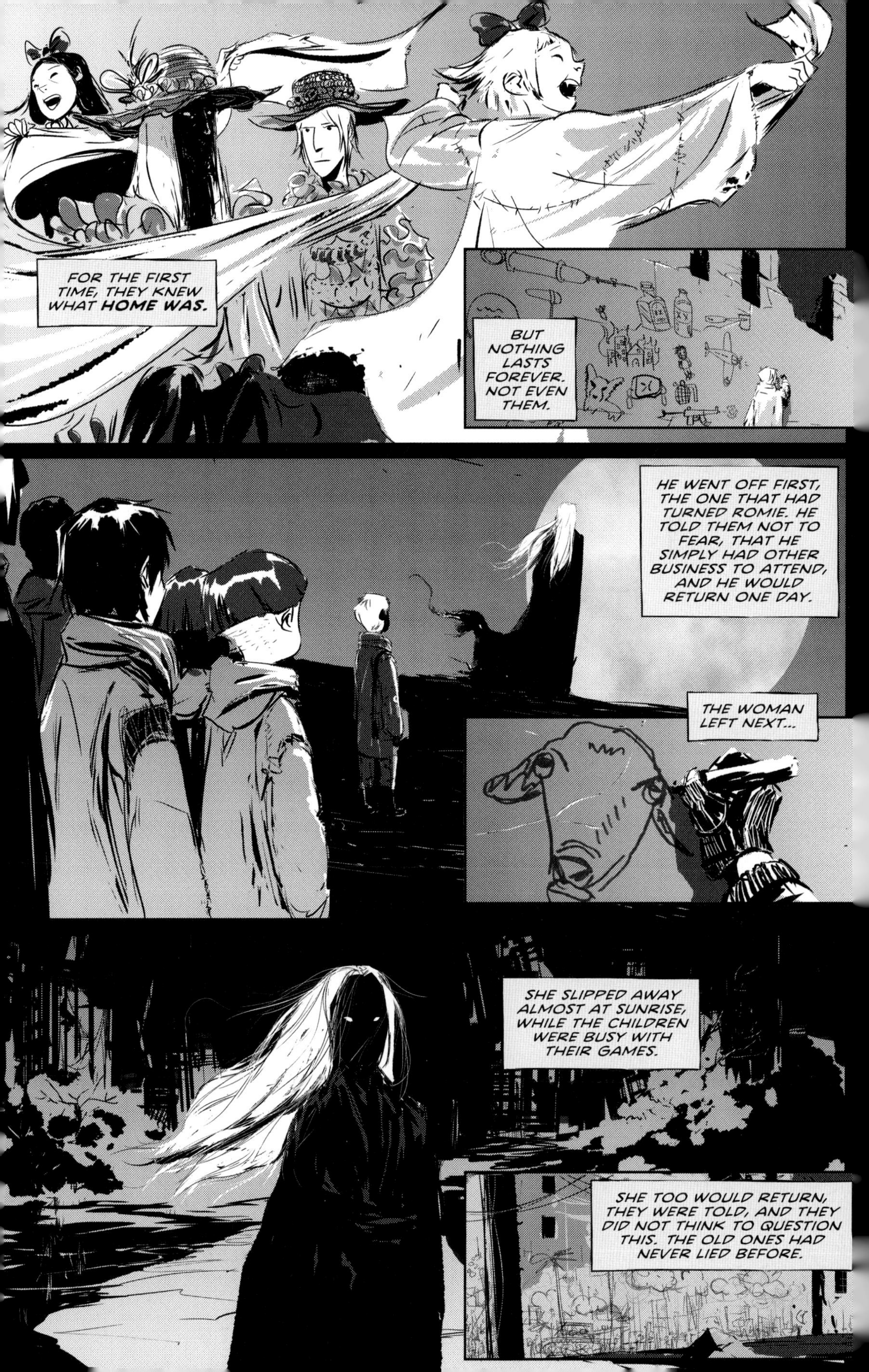
FOR THE FIRST TIME, THEY KNEW WHAT HOME WAS.
BUT NOTHING LASTS FOREVER. NOT EVEN THEM.
HE WENT OFF FIRST, THE ONE THAT HAD TURNED ROMIE. HE TOLD THEM NOT TO FEAR, THAT HE SIMPLY HAD OTHER BUSINESS TO ATTEND, AND HE WOULD RETURN ONE DAY.
THE WOMAN LEFT NEXT...
SHE SLIPPED AWAY ALMOST AT SUNRISE, WHILE THE CHILDREN WERE BUSY WITH THEIR GAMES.
SHE TOO WOULD RETURN, THEY WERE TOLD, AND THEY DID NOT THINK TO QUESTION THIS. THE OLD ONES HAD NEVER LIED BEFORE.

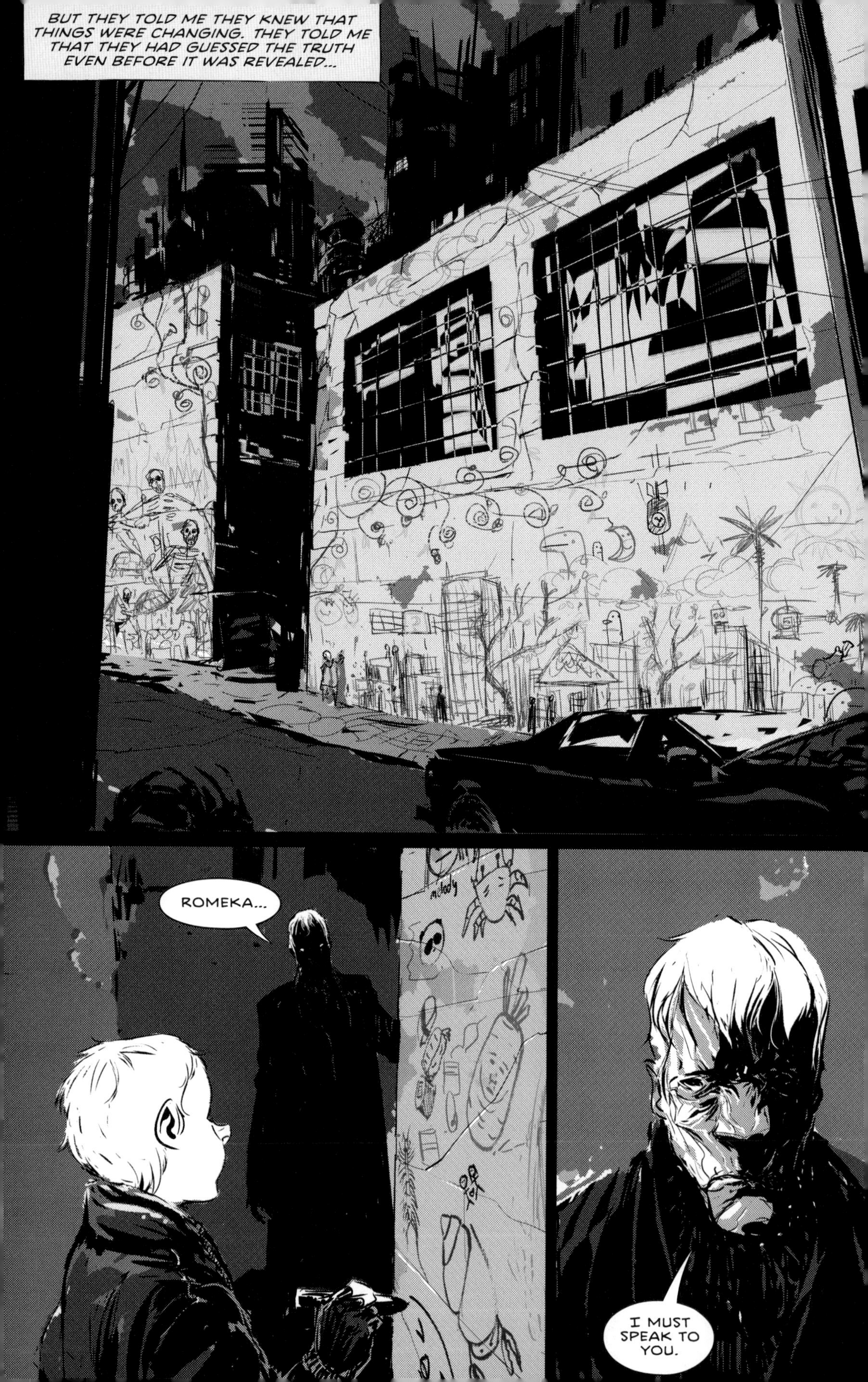
BUT THEY TOLD ME THEY KNEW THAT THINGS WERE CHANGING. THEY TOLD ME THAT THEY HAD GUESSED THE TRUTH EVEN BEFORE IT WAS REVEALED...
ROMEKA...
I MUST SPEAK TO YOU.

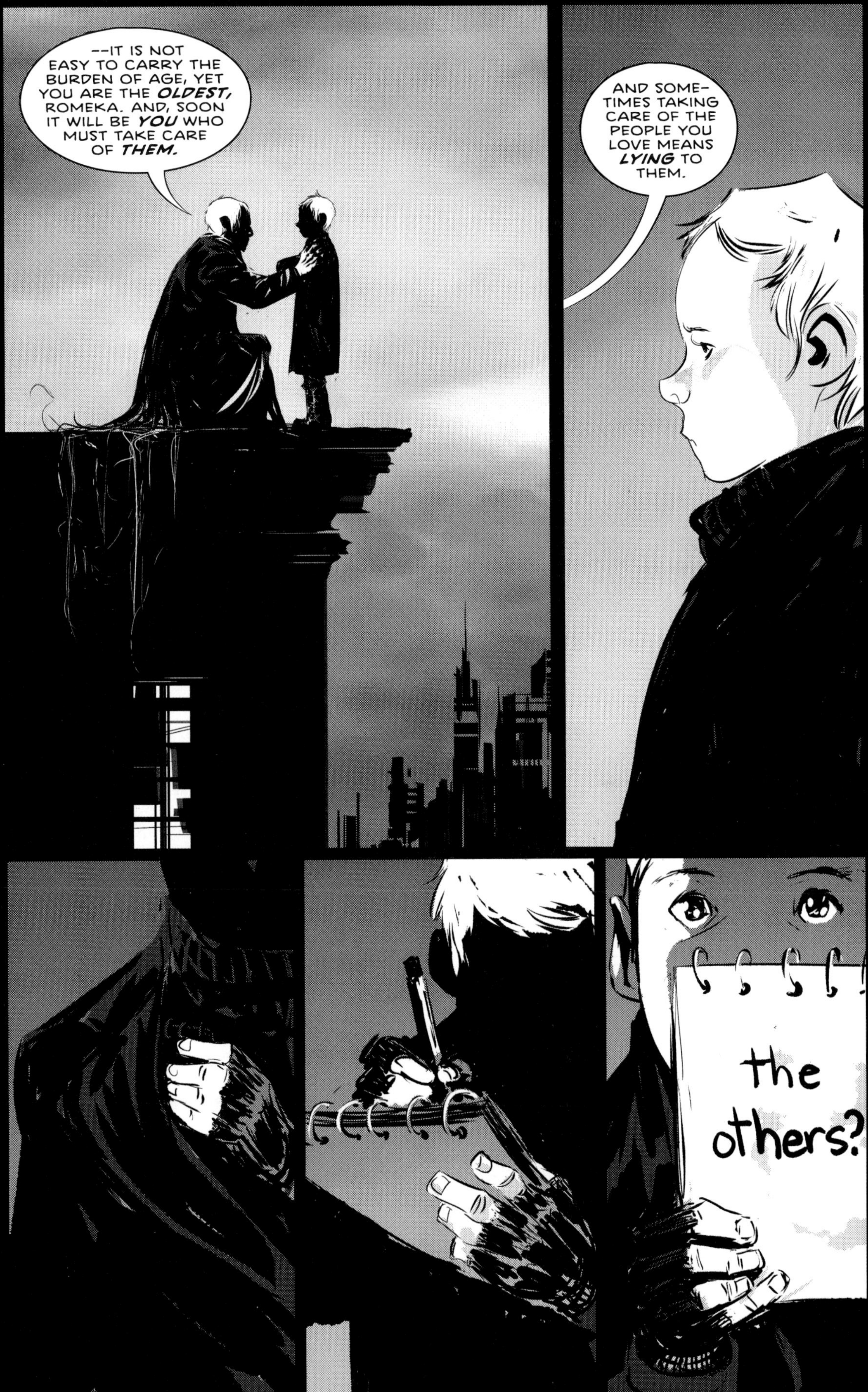
--IT IS NOT EASY TO CARRY THE BURDEN OF AGE, YET YOU ARE THE OLDEST, ROMEKA. AND, SOON IT WILL BE YOU WHO MUST TAKE CARE OF THEM.
AND SOME-TIMES TAKING CARE OF THE PEOPLE YOU LOVE MEANS LYING TO THEM.
the others?

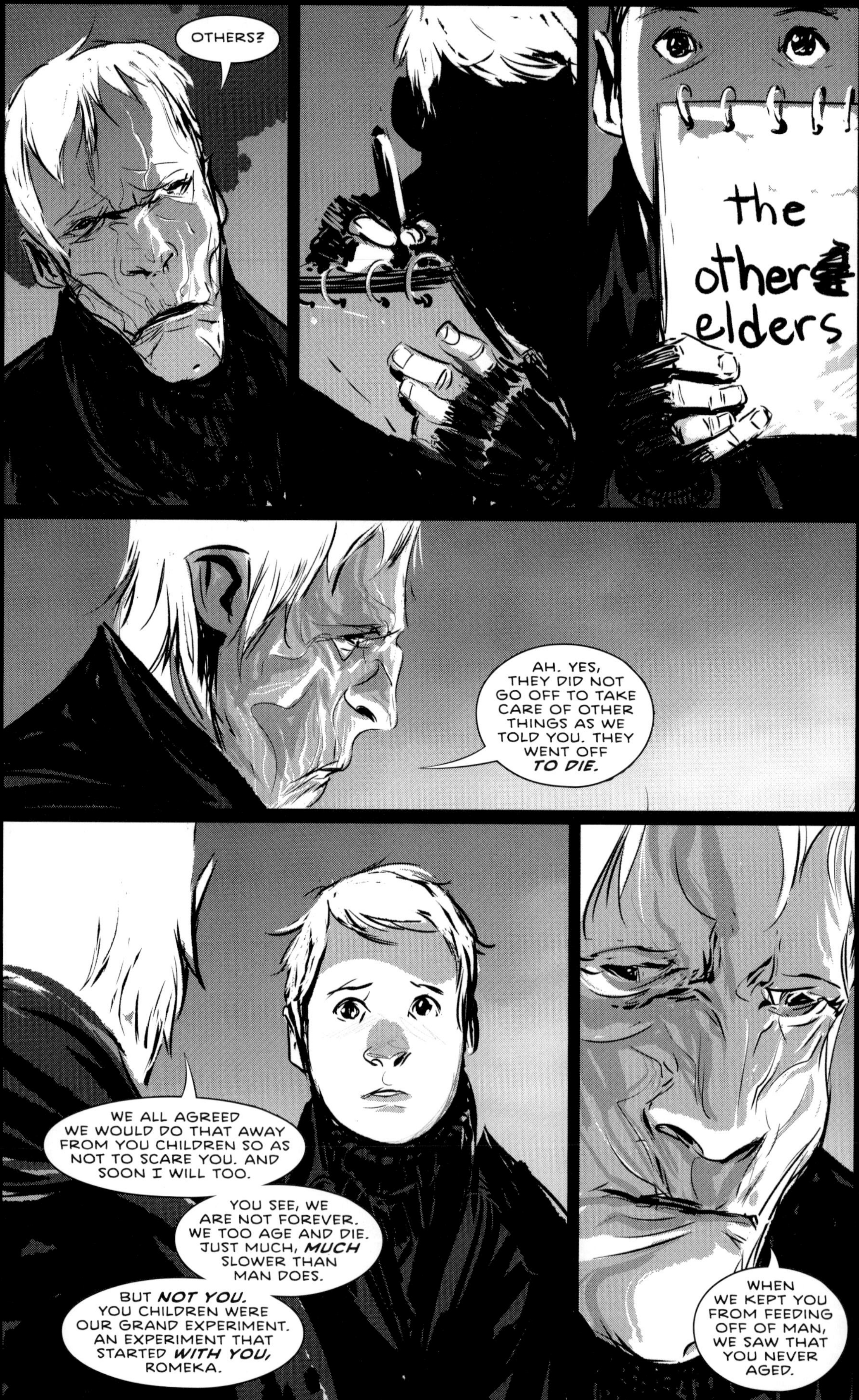
OTHERS?
the other elders
AH. YES, THEY DID NOT GO OFF TO TAKE CARE OF OTHER THINGS AS WE TOLD YOU. THEY WENT OFF TO DIE.
WE ALL AGREED WE WOULD DO THAT AWAY FROM YOU CHILDREN SO AS NOT TO SCARE YOU. AND SOON I WILL TOO.
YOU SEE, WE ARE NOT FOREVER. WE TOO AGE AND DIE. JUST MUCH, MUCH SLOWER THAN MAN DOES.
BUT NOT YOU. YOU CHILDREN WERE OUR GRAND EXPERIMENT. AN EXPERIMENT THAT STARTED WITH YOU, ROMEKA.
WHEN WE KEPT YOU FROM FEEDING OFF OF MAN, WE SAW THAT YOU NEVER AGED.

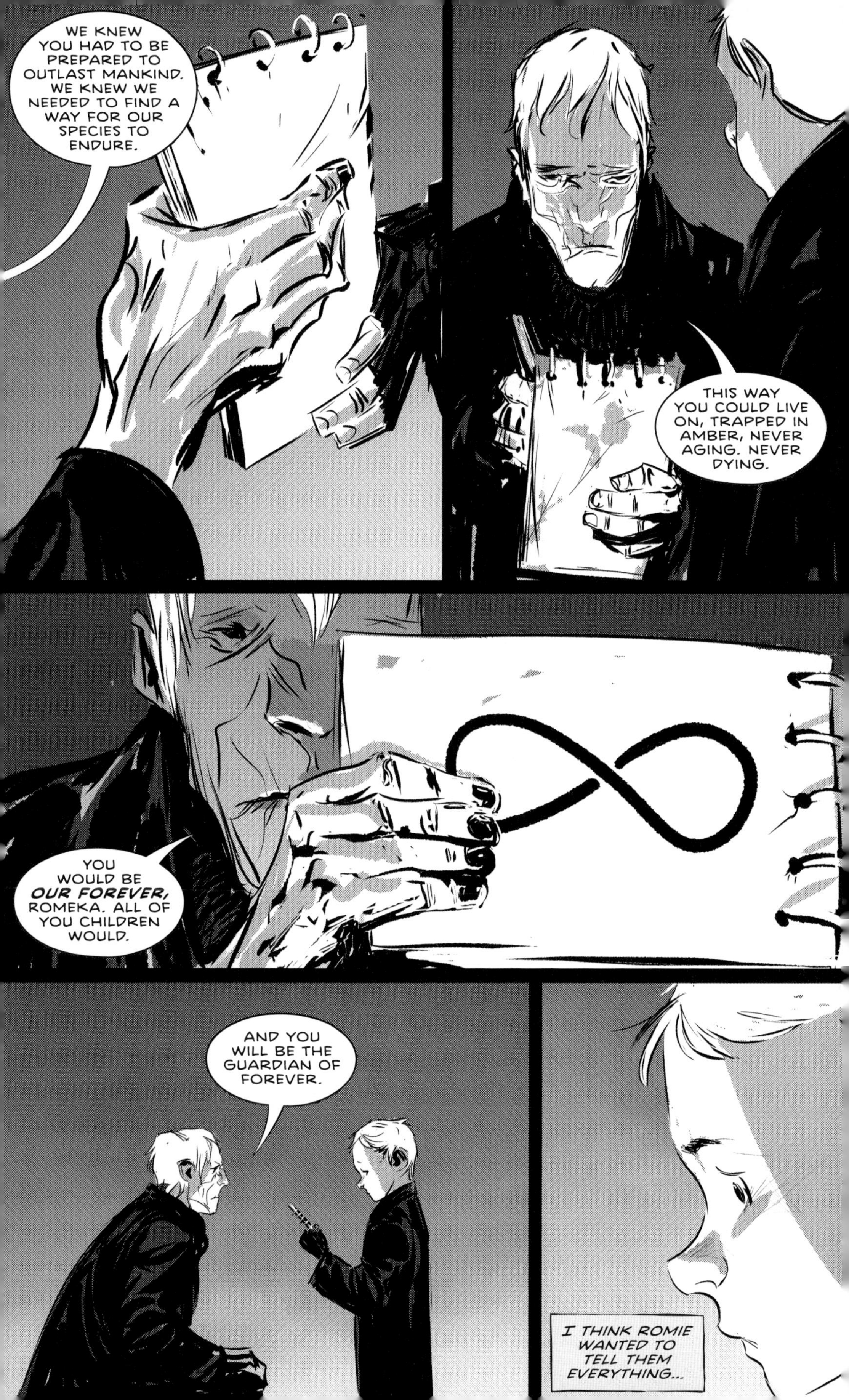
WE KNEW YOU HAD TO BE PREPARED TO OUTLAST MANKIND. WE KNEW WE NEEDED TO FIND A WAY FOR OUR SPECIES TO ENDURE.
THIS WAY YOU COULD LIVE ON, TRAPPED IN AMBER, NEVER AGING. NEVER DYING.
YOU WOULD BE ***OUR FOREVER,*** ROMEKA. ALL OF YOU CHILDREN WOULD.
AND YOU WILL BE THE GUARDIAN OF FOREVER.
I THINK ROMIE WANTED TO TELL THEM EVERYTHING...

...ALL THAT THEY WOULD ONE DAY TELL ME.

BUT WHERE WOULD ROMIE EVEN START?

HOW WOULD THEY MAKE THEM UNDERSTAND?

--TELL US, ROMIE. WHY DID THEY DO THIS TO US? TELL US THE TRUTH.

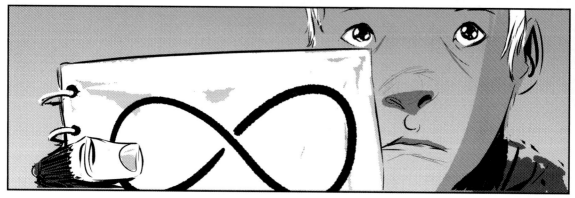

ROMIE?

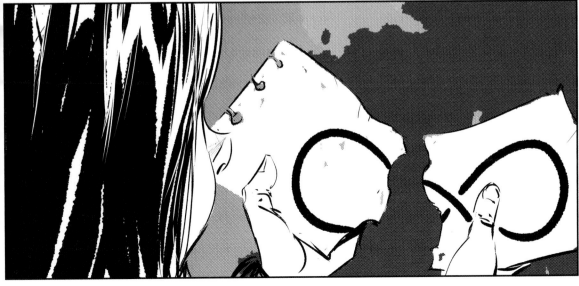

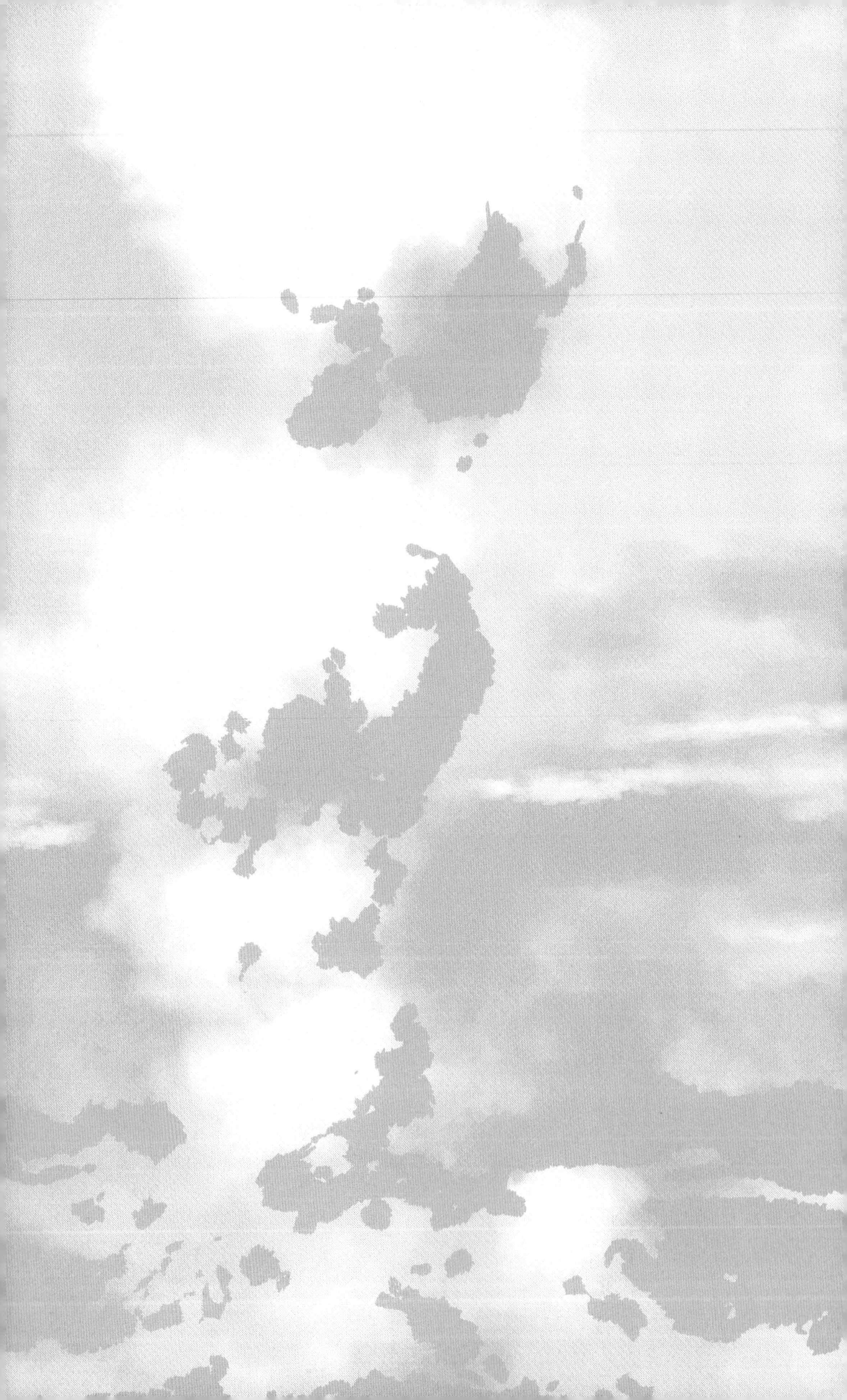

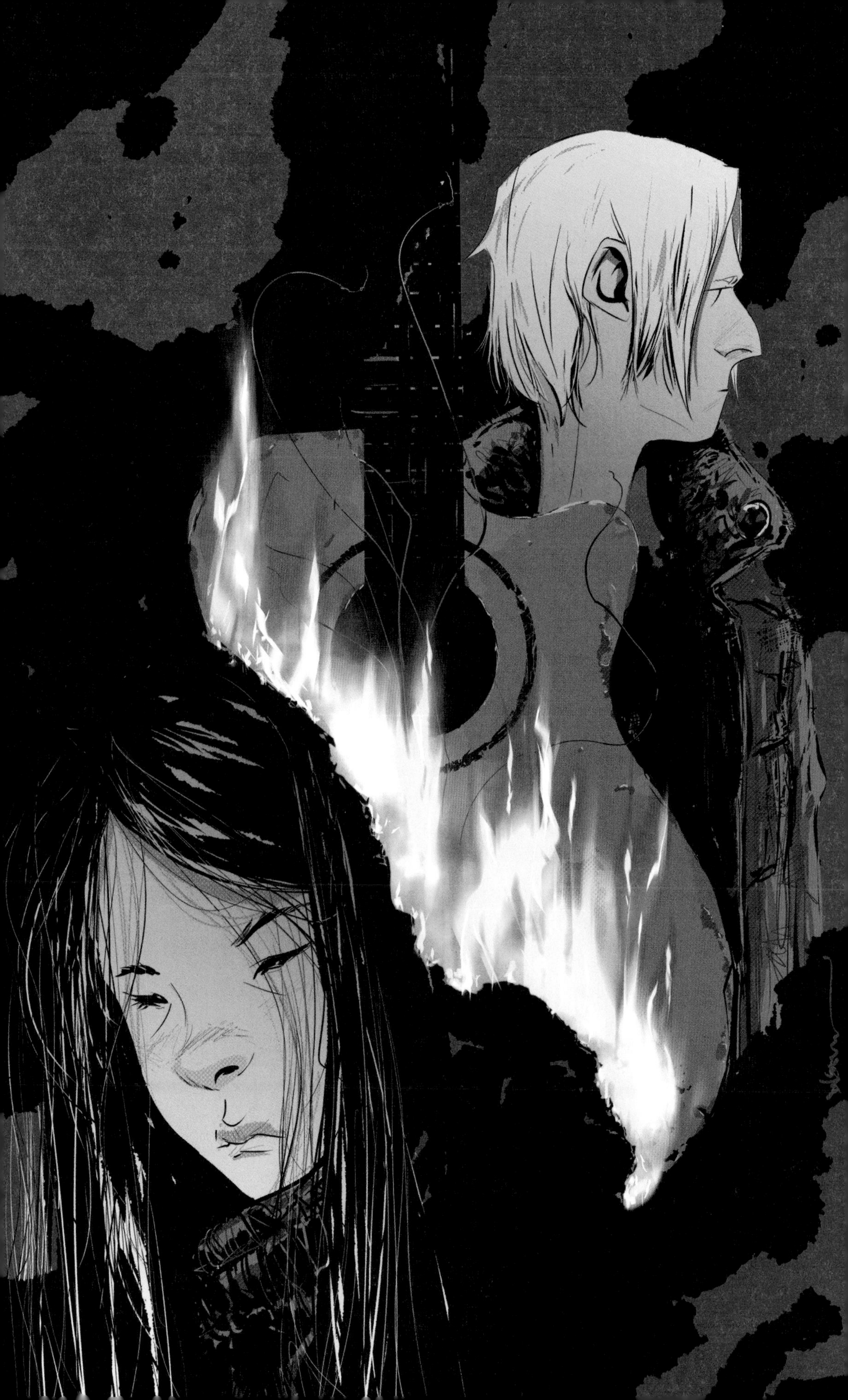

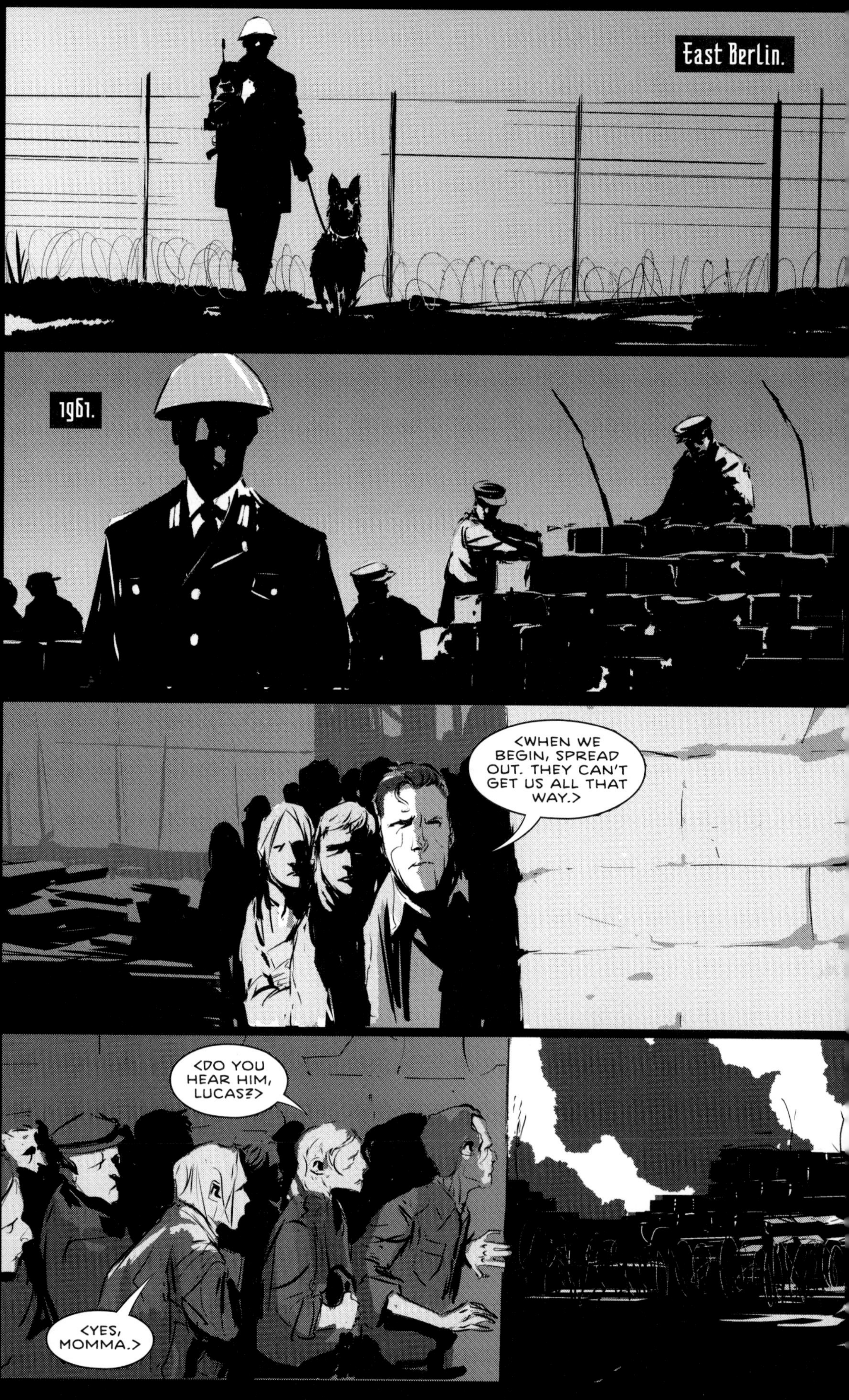
East Berlin.
1961.
<WHEN WE BEGIN, SPREAD OUT. THEY CAN'T GET US ALL THAT WAY.>
<DO YOU HEAR HIM, LUCAS?>
<YES, MOMMA.>

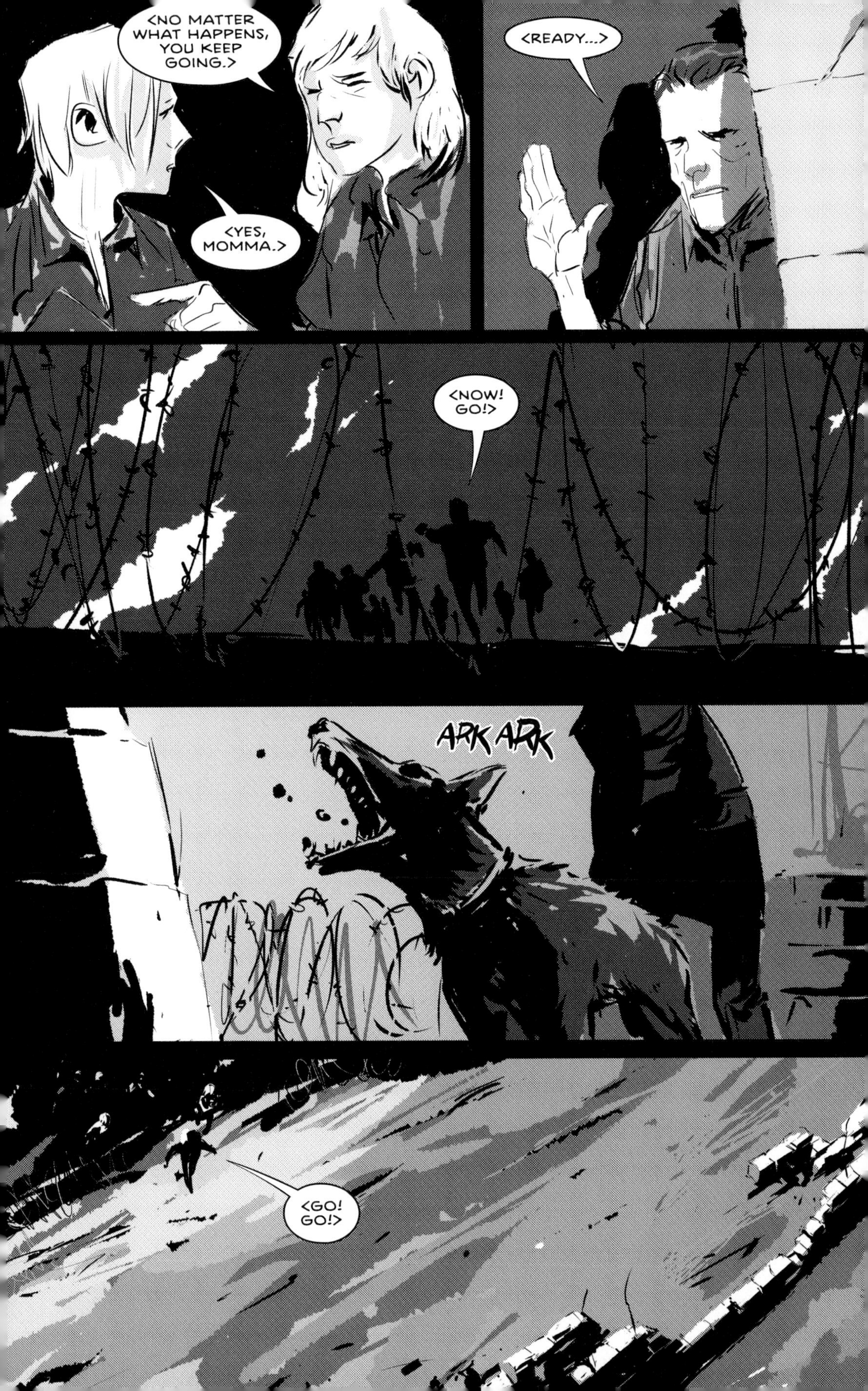
<NO MATTER WHAT HAPPENS, YOU KEEP GOING.>
<YES, MOMMA.>
<READY...>
<NOW! GO!>
ARK ARK
<GO! GO!>

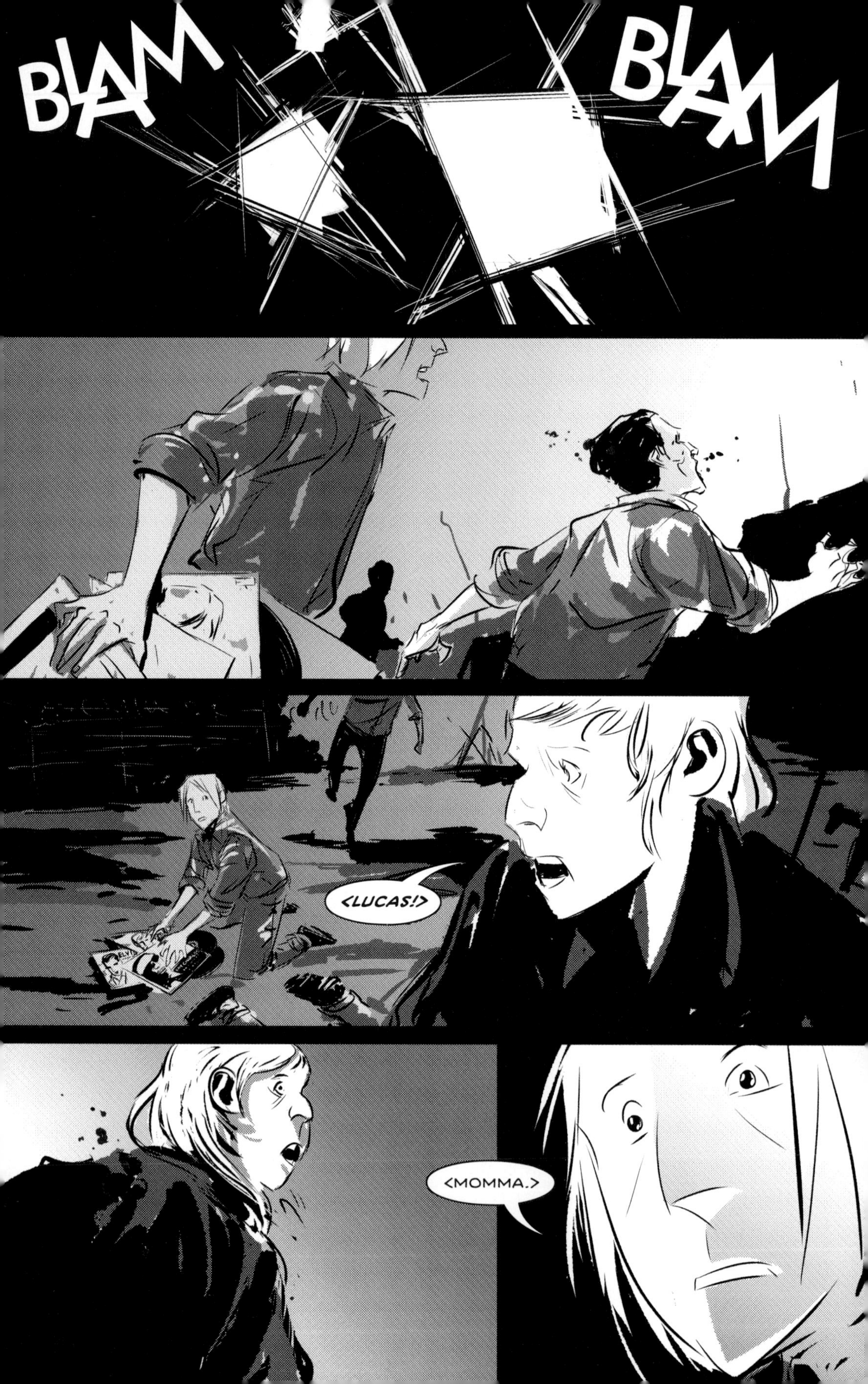
BLAM
BLAM
<LUCAS!>
<MOMMA.>

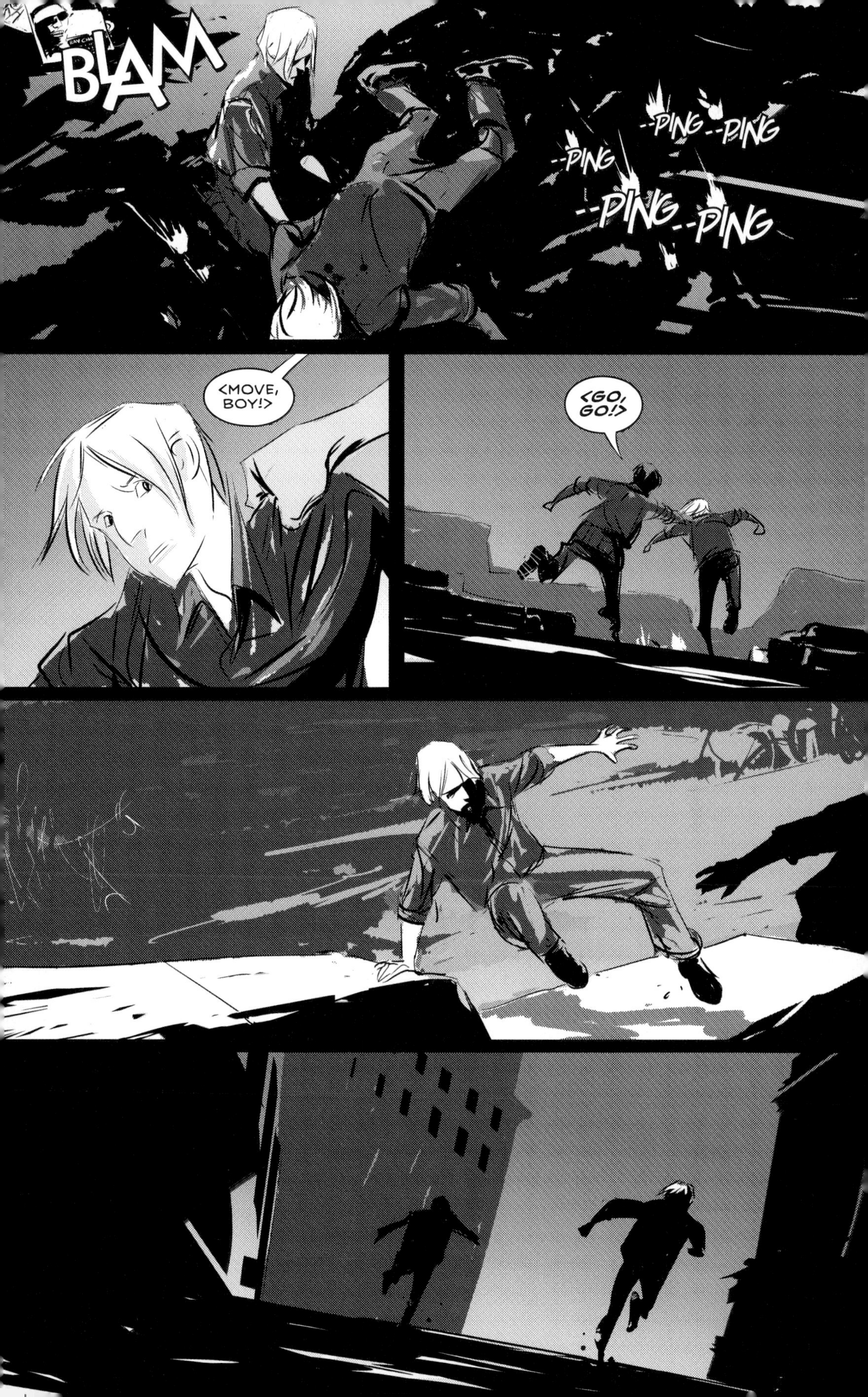
BLAM
--PING --PING
--PING
--PING --PING
<MOVE, BOY!>
<GO, GO!>

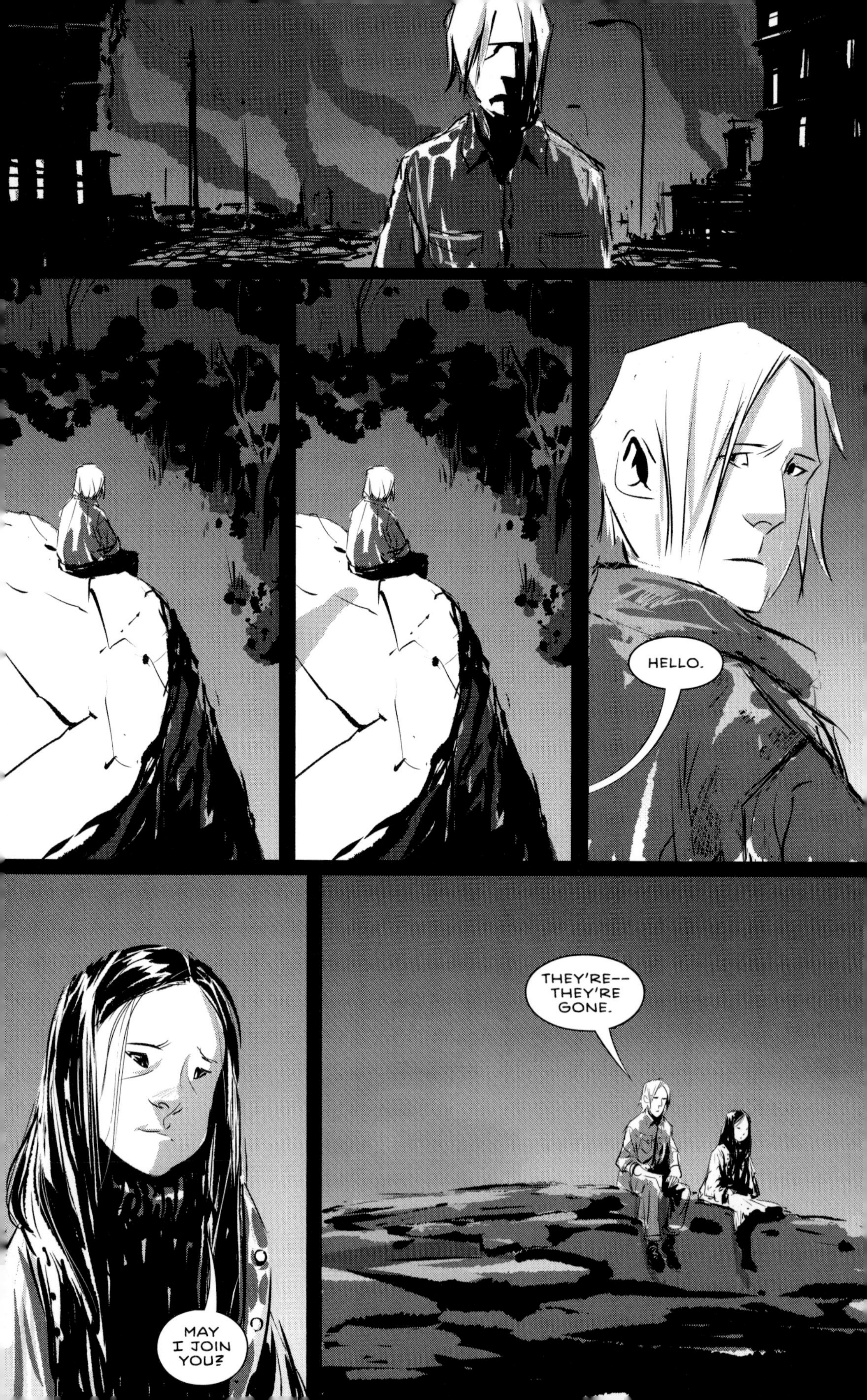
HELLO.
MAY I JOIN YOU?
THEY'RE-- THEY'RE GONE.

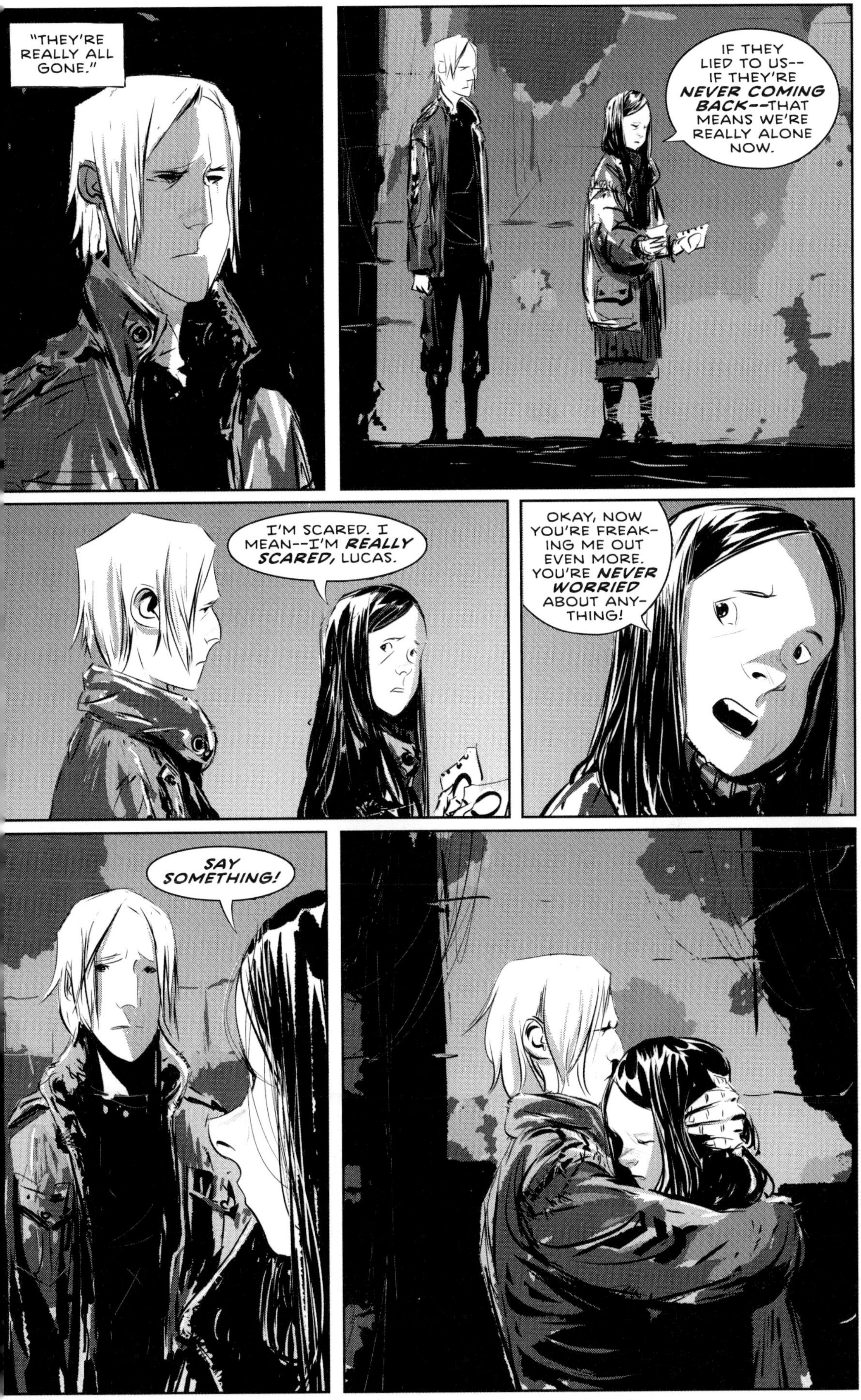
"THEY'RE REALLY ALL GONE."
IF THEY LIED TO US-- IF THEY'RE *NEVER COMING BACK*--THAT MEANS WE'RE REALLY ALONE NOW.
I'M SCARED. I MEAN--I'M *REALLY SCARED,* LUCAS.
OKAY, NOW YOU'RE FREAKING ME OUT EVEN MORE. YOU'RE *NEVER WORRIED* ABOUT ANYTHING!
SAY SOMETHING!

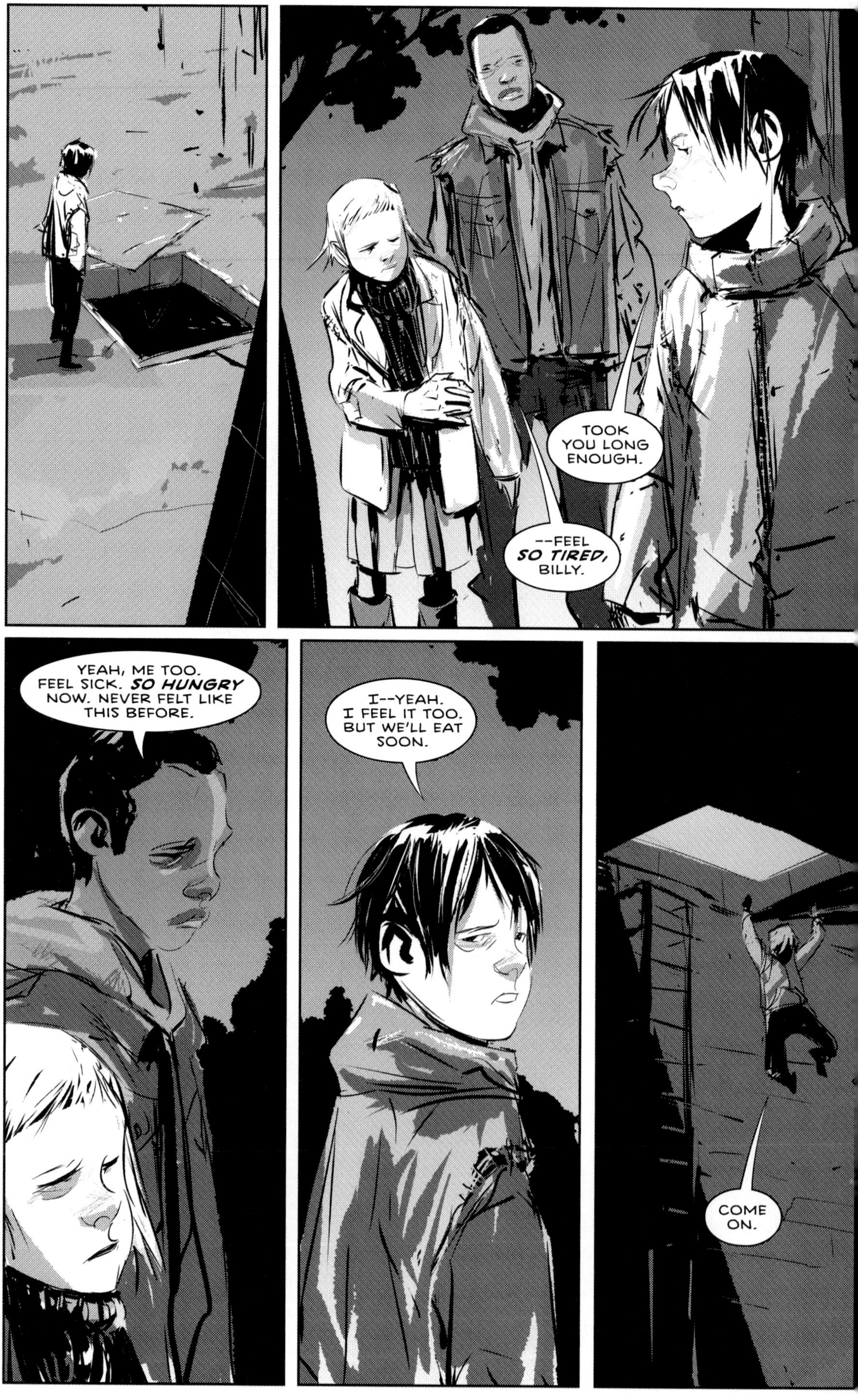
TOOK YOU LONG ENOUGH.
--FEEL SO TIRED, BILLY.
YEAH, ME TOO. FEEL SICK. SO HUNGRY NOW. NEVER FELT LIKE THIS BEFORE.
I--YEAH. I FEEL IT TOO. BUT WE'LL EAT SOON.
COME ON.

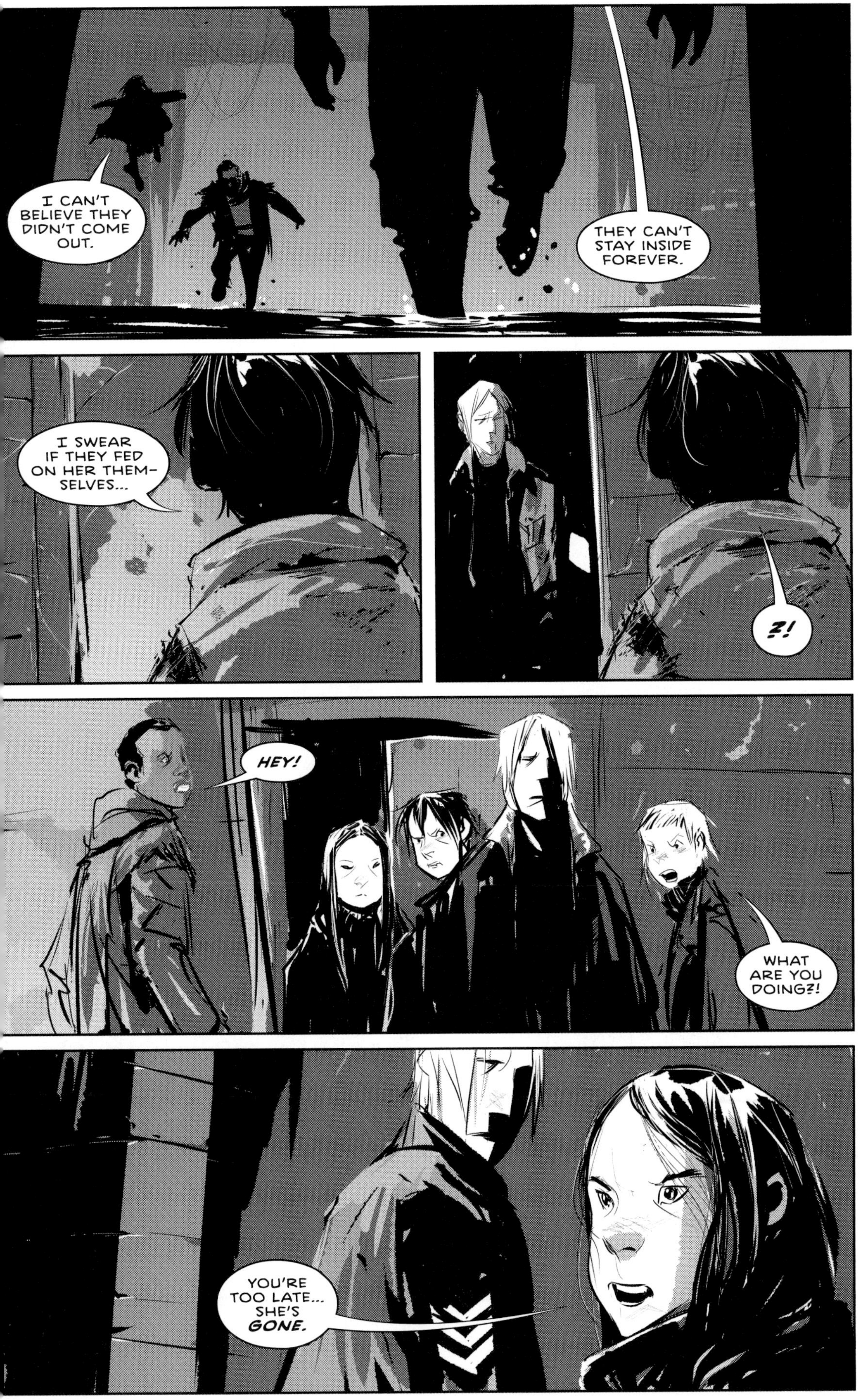
I CAN'T BELIEVE THEY DIDN'T COME OUT.
THEY CAN'T STAY INSIDE FOREVER.
I SWEAR IF THEY FED ON HER THEM-SELVES...
?!
HEY!
WHAT ARE YOU DOING?!
YOU'RE TOO LATE... SHE'S *GONE.*

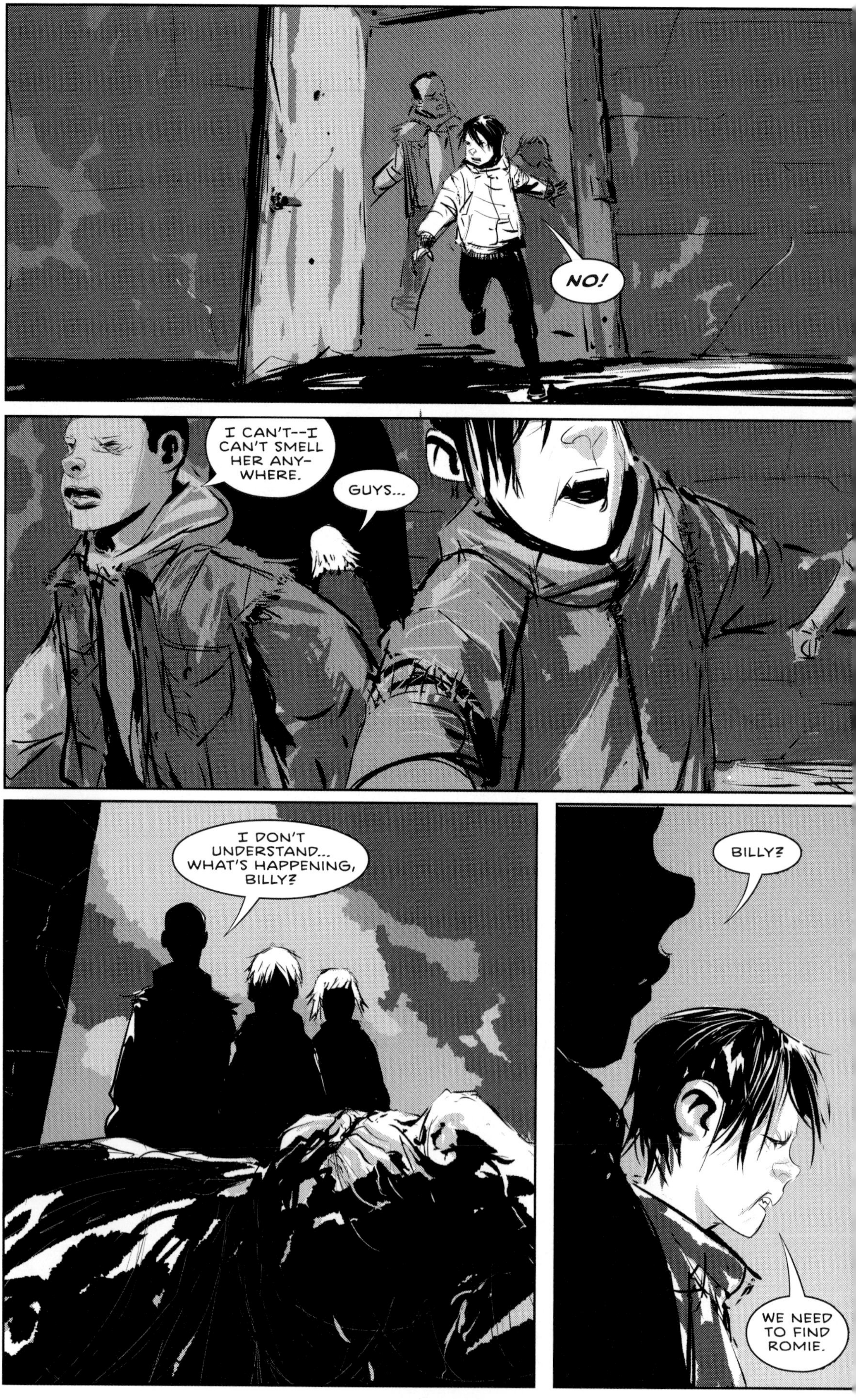
NO!
I CAN'T--I CAN'T SMELL HER ANYWHERE.
GUYS...
I DON'T UNDERSTAND... WHAT'S HAPPENING, BILLY?
BILLY?
WE NEED TO FIND ROMIE.

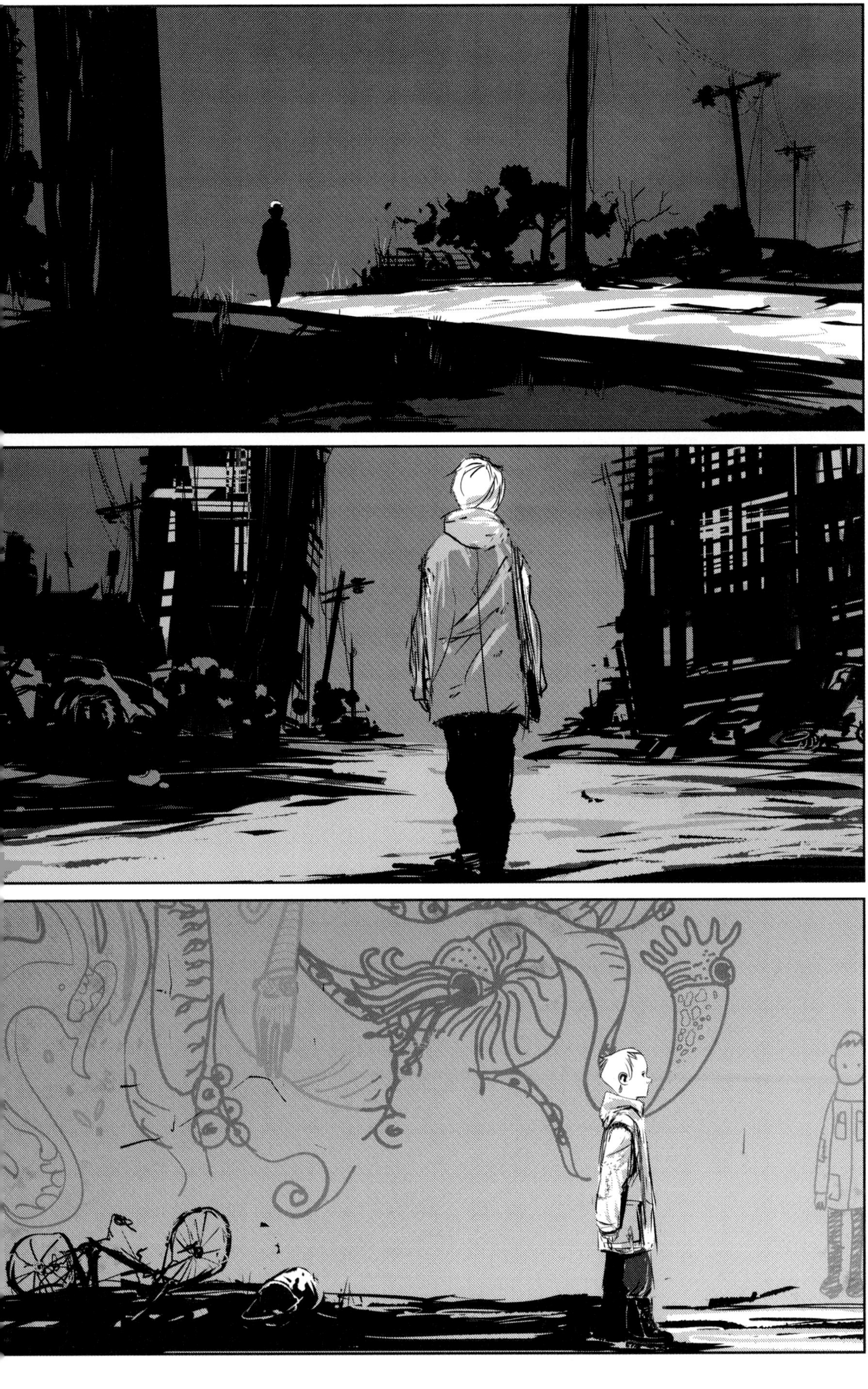

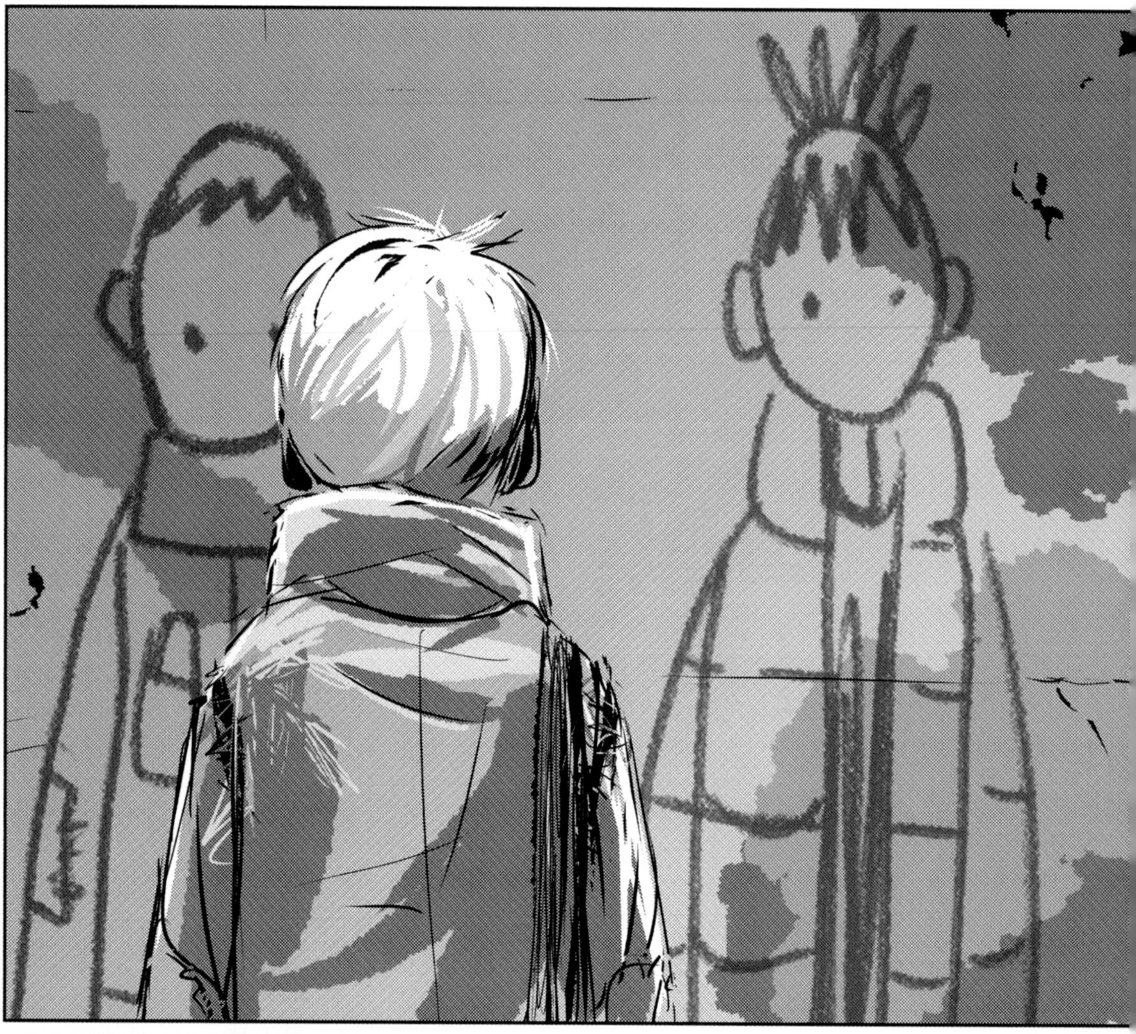

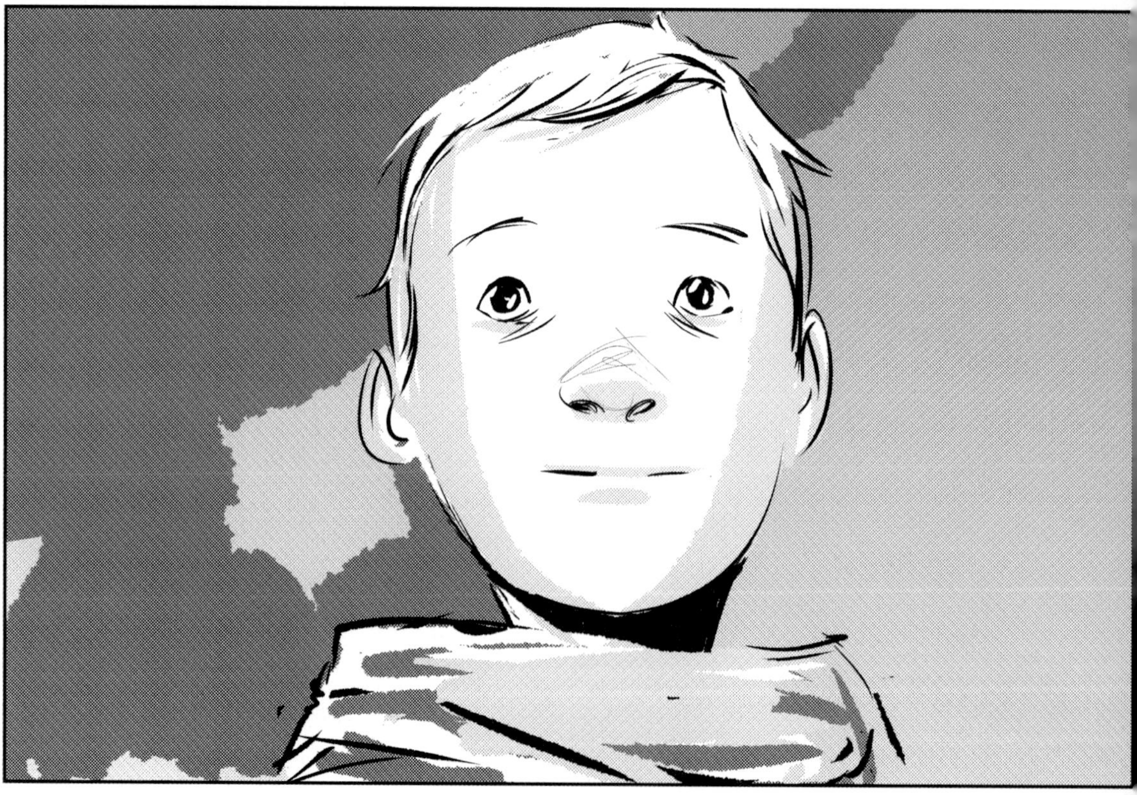

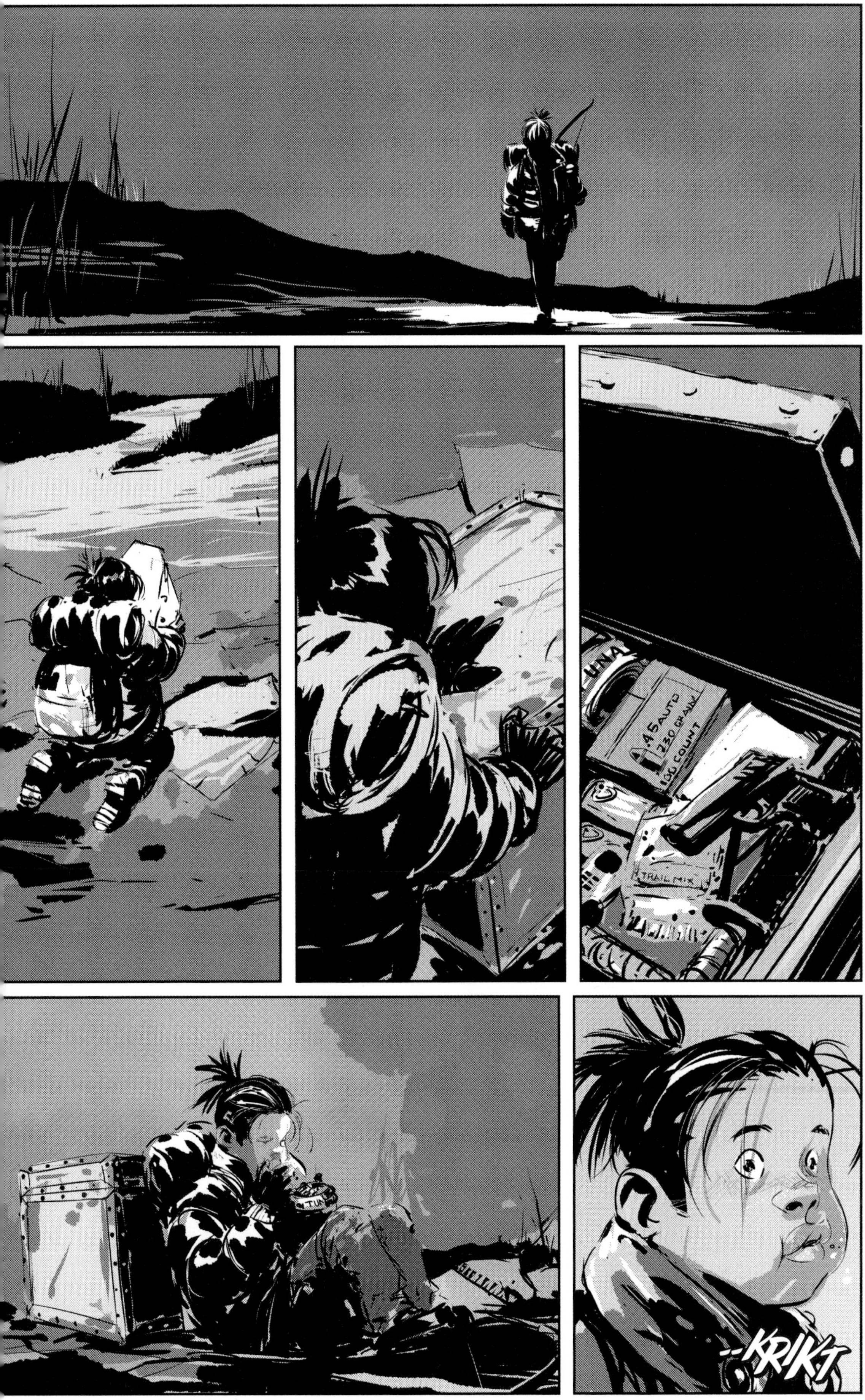
UNA
.45 AUTO
230 GRAIN
100 COUNT
TRAIL MIX
--KRIKT

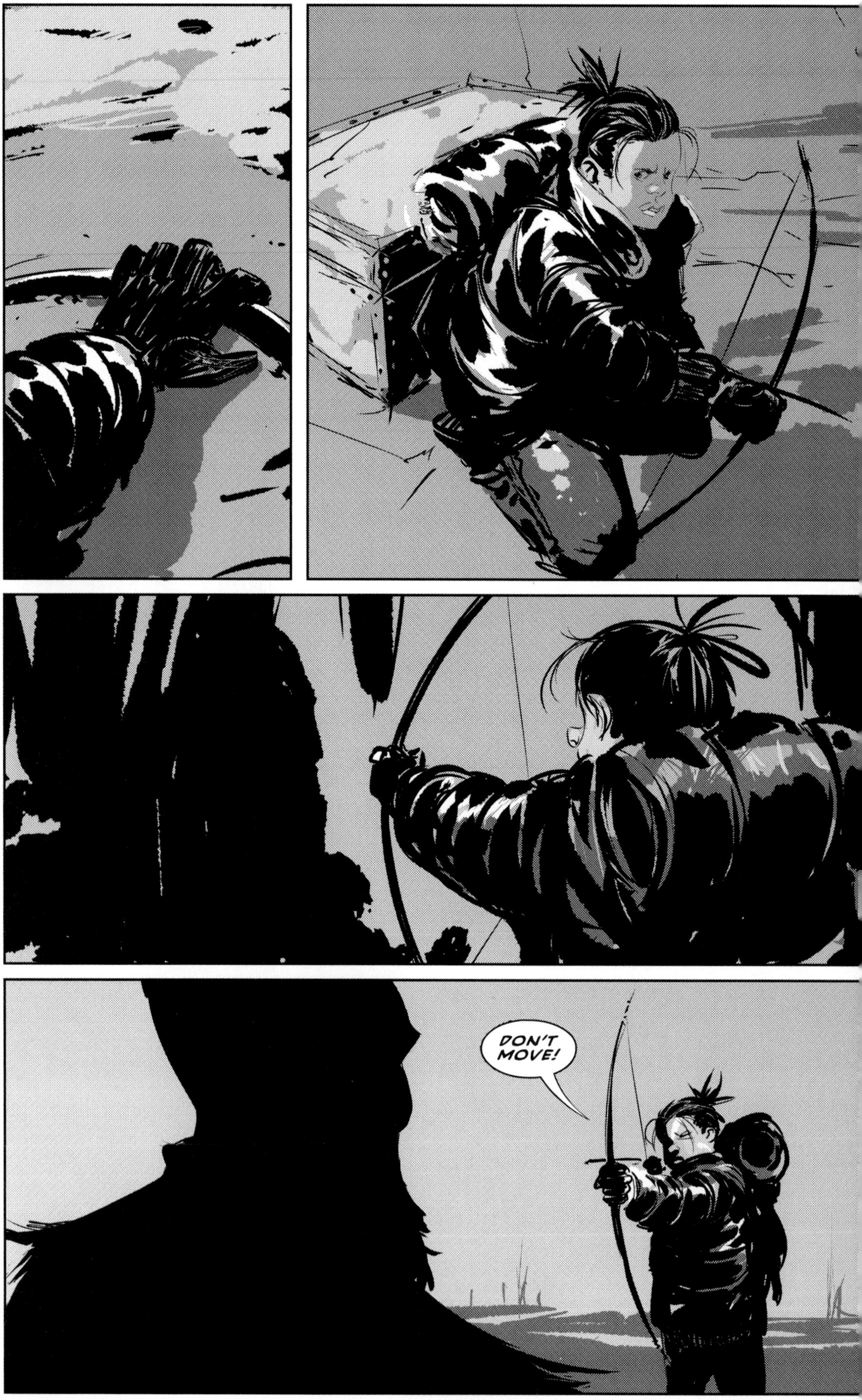
DON'T MOVE!

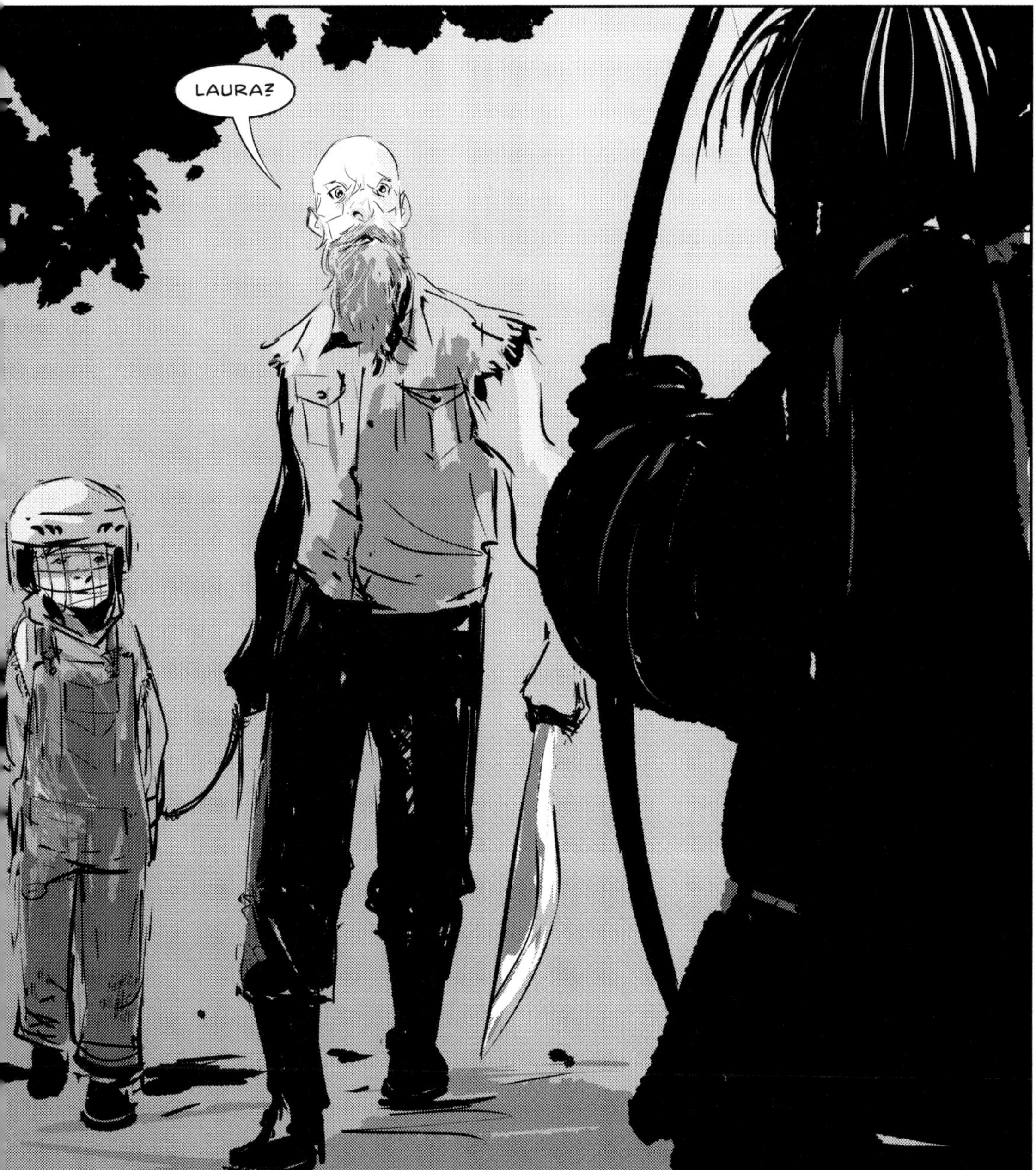
LAURA?

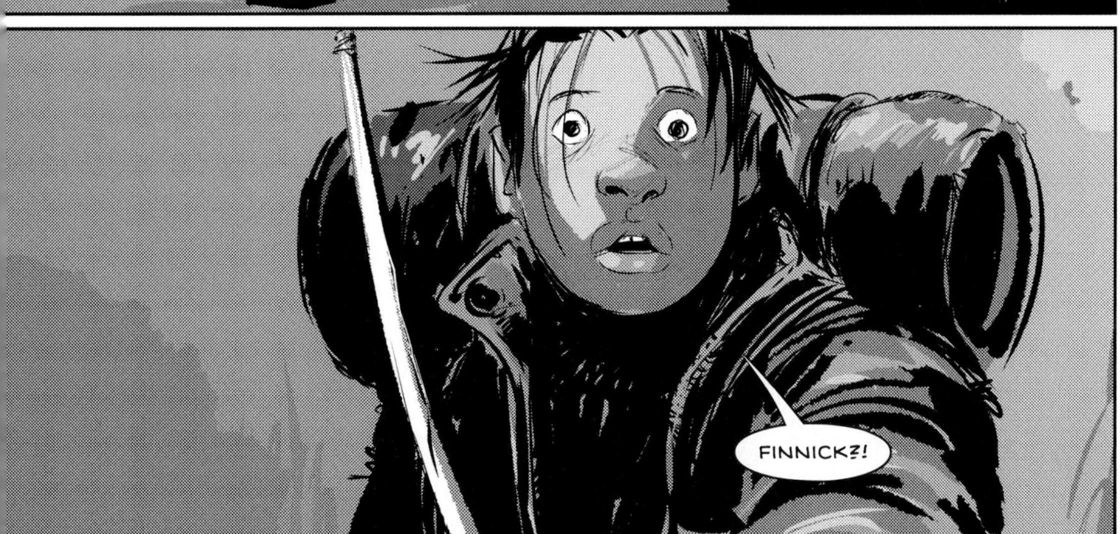
FINNICK?!

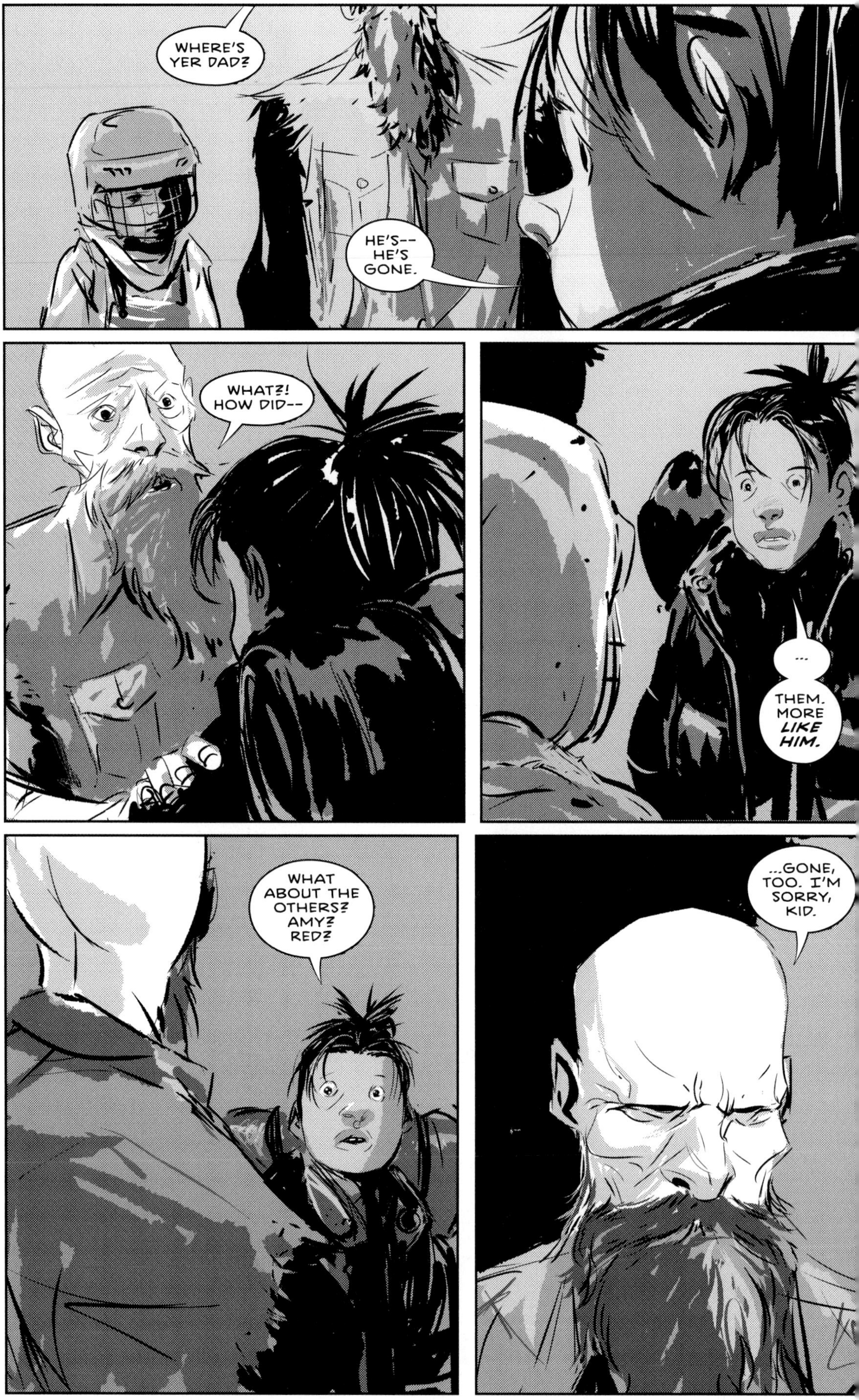
WHERE'S YER DAD?
HE'S-- HE'S GONE.
WHAT?! HOW DID--
...
THEM. MORE *LIKE HIM.*
WHAT ABOUT THE OTHERS? AMY? RED?
...GONE, TOO. I'M SORRY, KID.

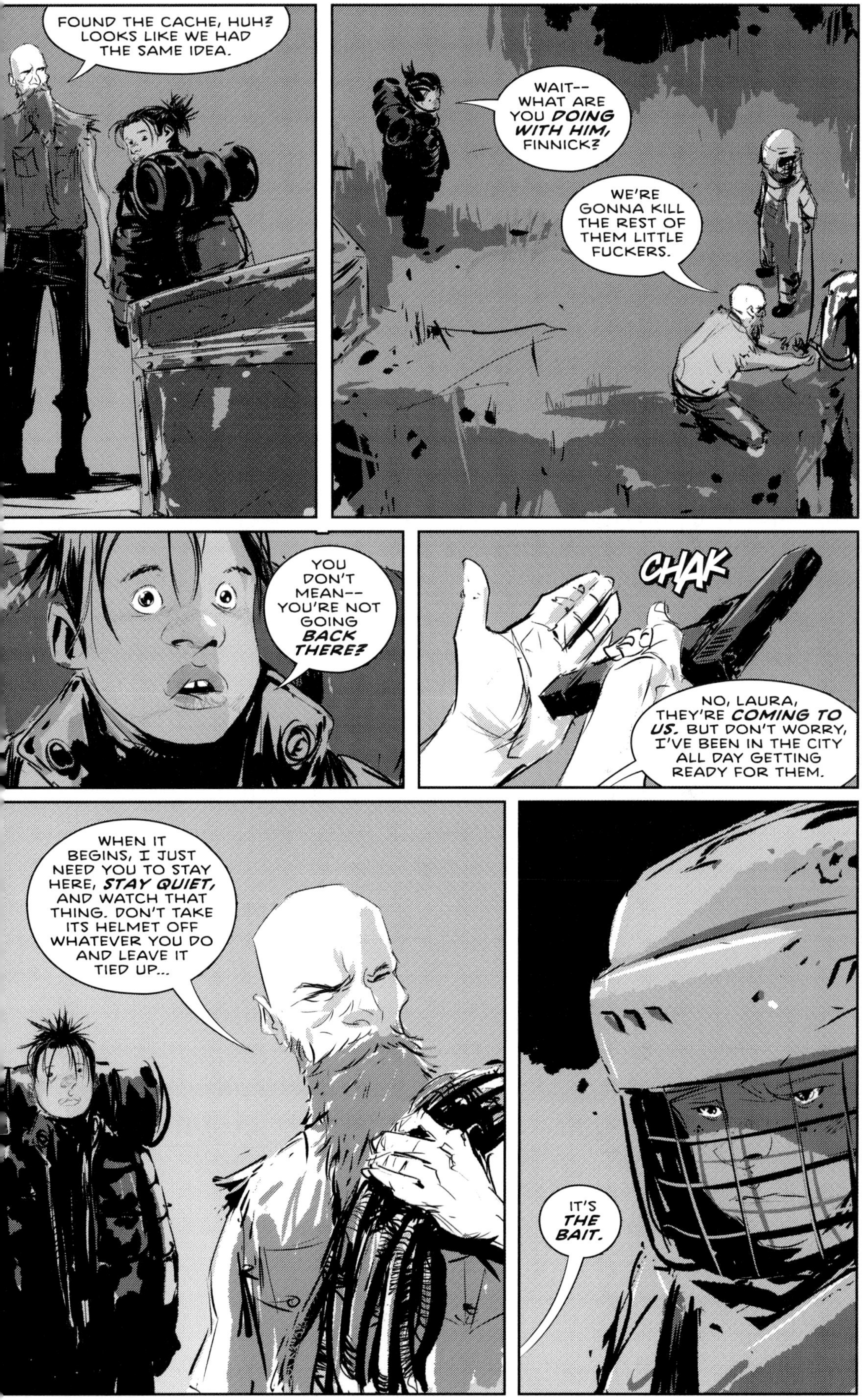
FOUND THE CACHE, HUH? LOOKS LIKE WE HAD THE SAME IDEA.
WAIT-- WHAT ARE YOU **DOING WITH HIM,** FINNICK?
WE'RE GONNA KILL THE REST OF THEM LITTLE FUCKERS.
YOU DON'T MEAN-- YOU'RE NOT GOING **BACK THERE?**
CHAK
NO, LAURA, THEY'RE **COMING TO US.** BUT DON'T WORRY, I'VE BEEN IN THE CITY ALL DAY GETTING READY FOR THEM.
WHEN IT BEGINS, I JUST NEED YOU TO STAY HERE, **STAY QUIET,** AND WATCH THAT THING. DON'T TAKE ITS HELMET OFF WHATEVER YOU DO AND LEAVE IT TIED UP...
IT'S **THE BAIT.**

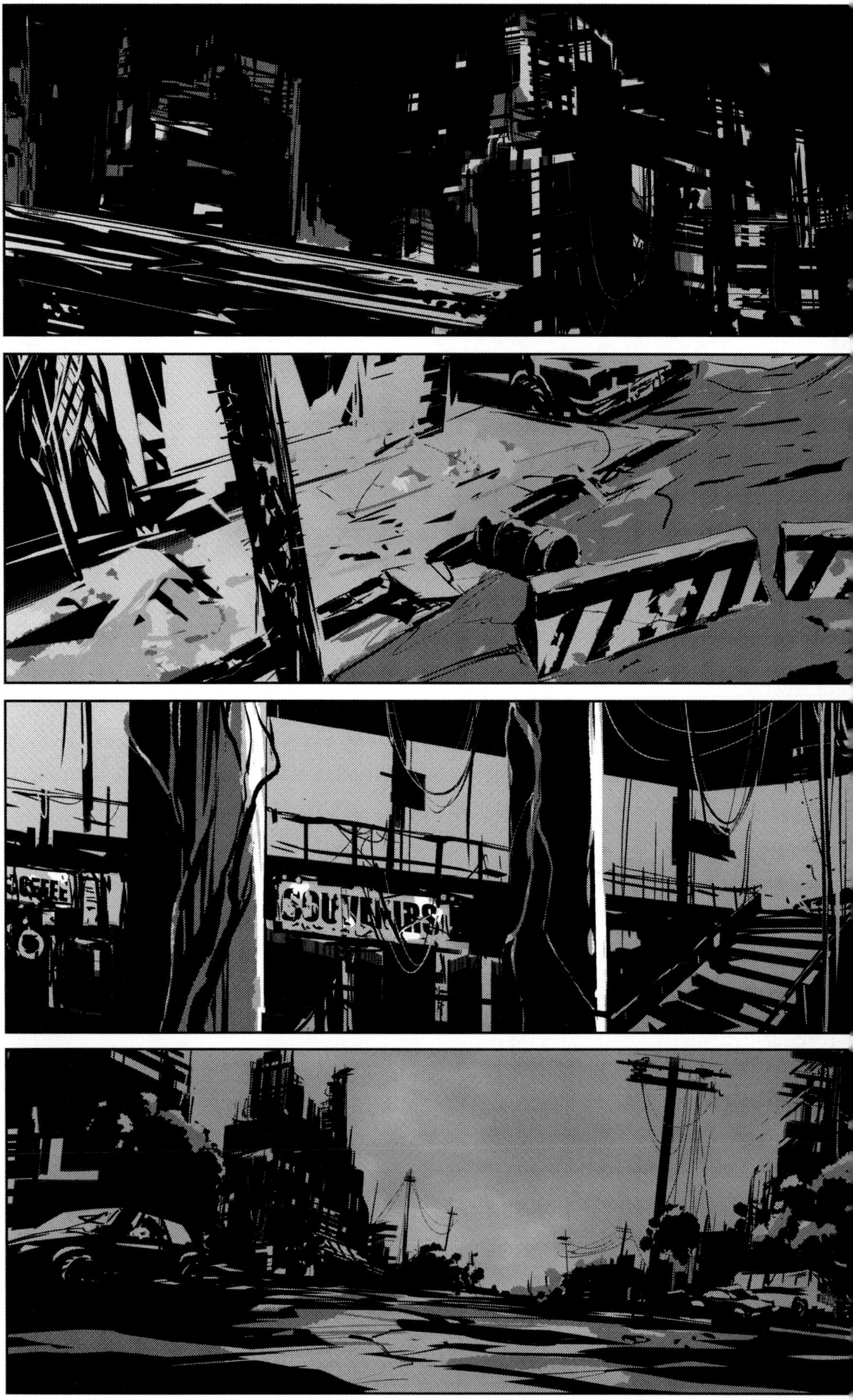
SOUVENIRS

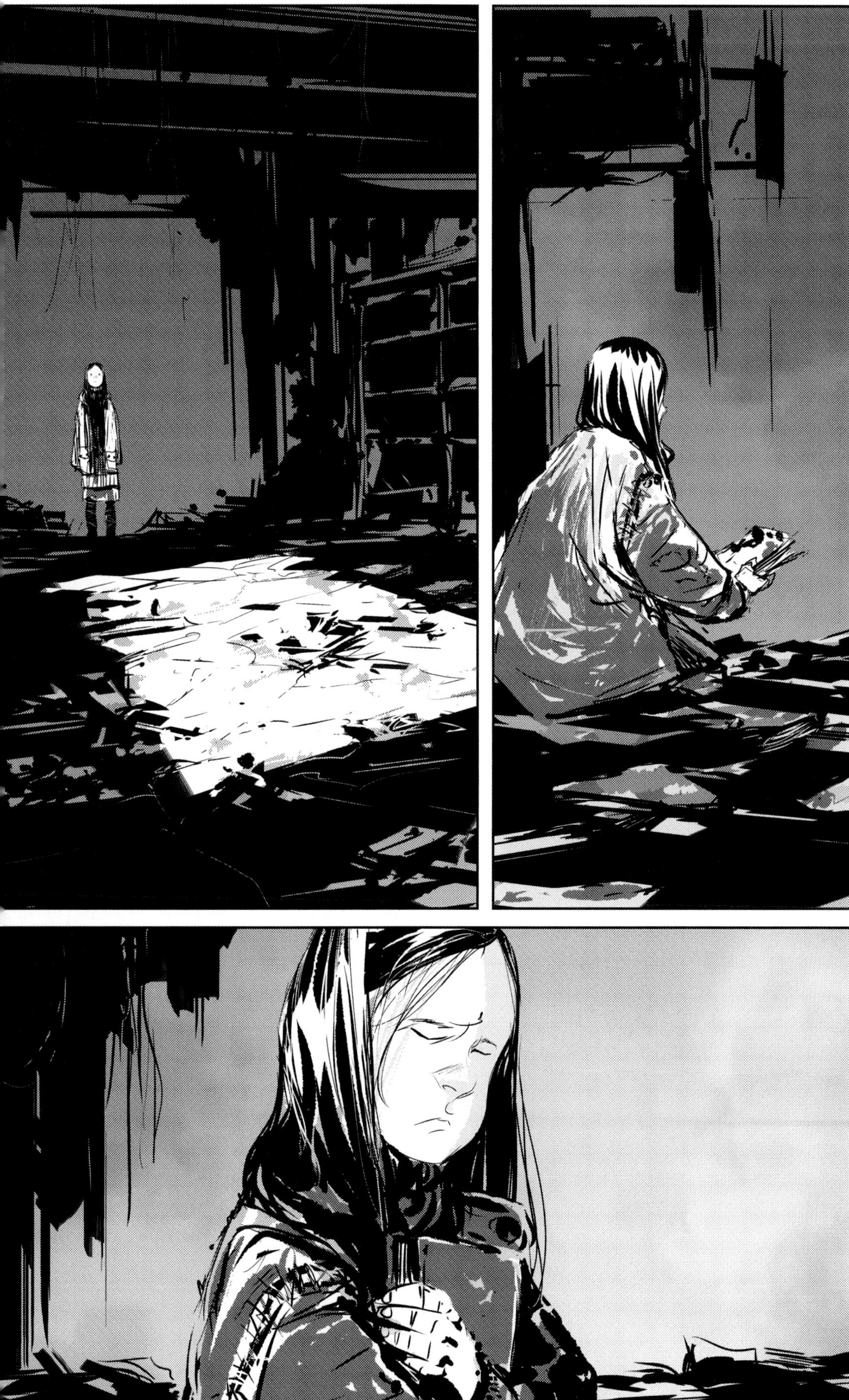

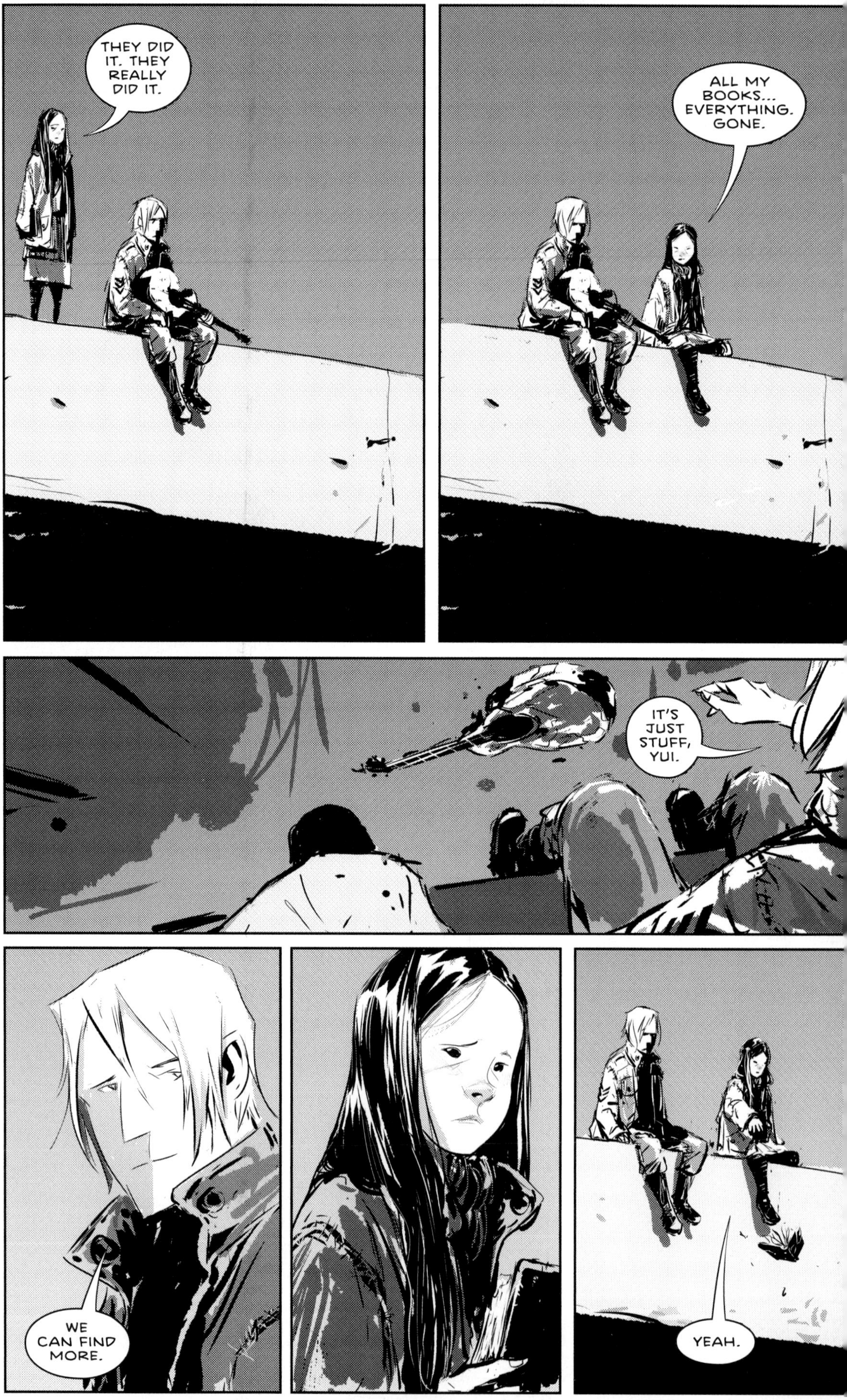
THEY DID IT. THEY REALLY DID IT.
ALL MY BOOKS... EVERYTHING. GONE.
IT'S JUST STUFF, YUI.
WE CAN FIND MORE.
YEAH.

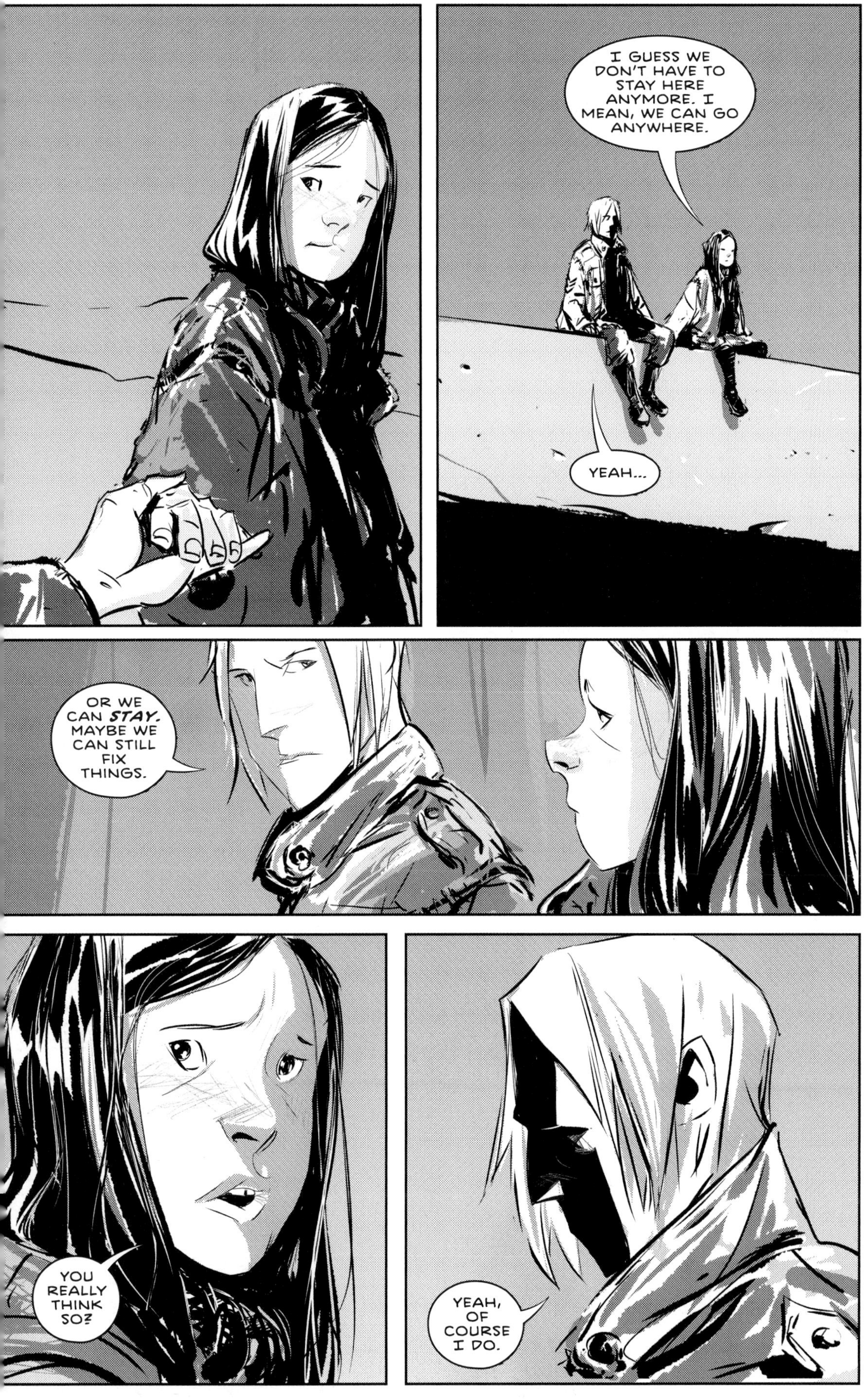
I GUESS WE DON'T HAVE TO STAY HERE ANYMORE. I MEAN, WE CAN GO ANYWHERE.
YEAH...
OR WE CAN STAY. MAYBE WE CAN STILL FIX THINGS.
YOU REALLY THINK SO?
YEAH, OF COURSE I DO.

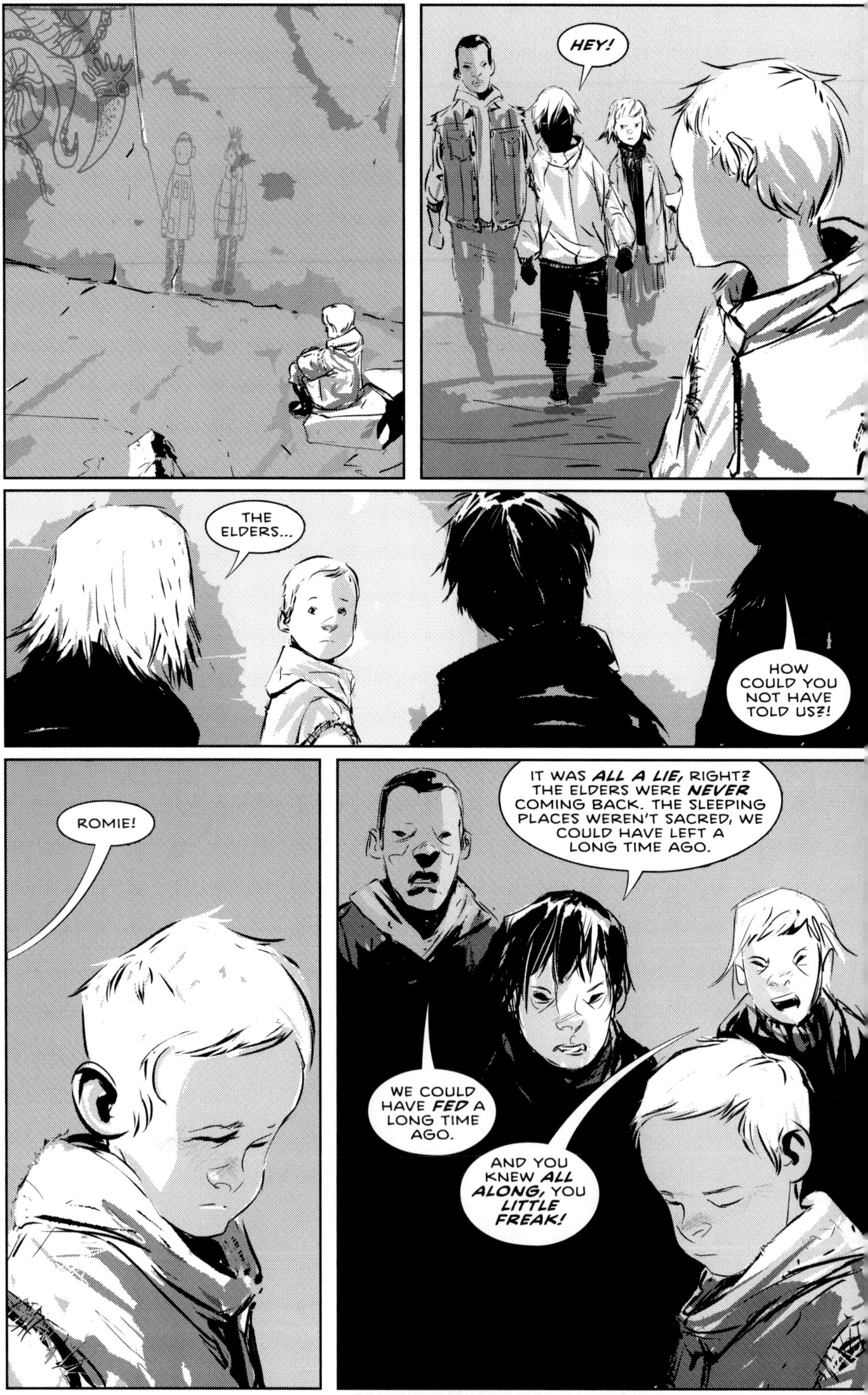
HEY!
THE ELDERS...
HOW COULD YOU NOT HAVE TOLD US?!
ROMIE!
IT WAS ALL A LIE, RIGHT? THE ELDERS WERE NEVER COMING BACK. THE SLEEPING PLACES WEREN'T SACRED, WE COULD HAVE LEFT A LONG TIME AGO.
WE COULD HAVE FED A LONG TIME AGO.
AND YOU KNEW ALL ALONG, YOU LITTLE FREAK!

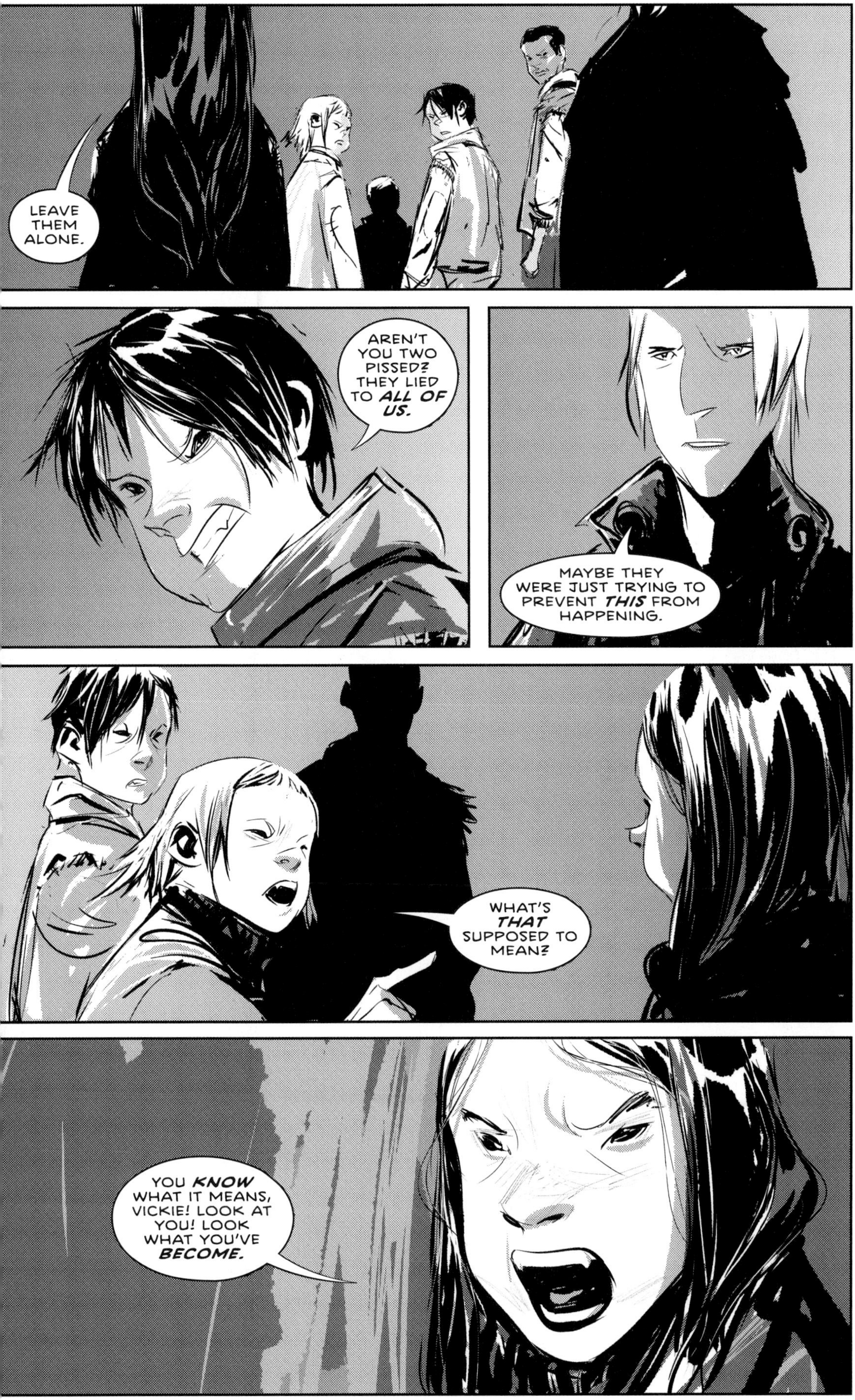
LEAVE THEM ALONE.
AREN'T YOU TWO PISSED? THEY LIED TO ALL OF US.
MAYBE THEY WERE JUST TRYING TO PREVENT THIS FROM HAPPENING.
WHAT'S THAT SUPPOSED TO MEAN?
YOU KNOW WHAT IT MEANS, VICKIE! LOOK AT YOU! LOOK WHAT YOU'VE BECOME.

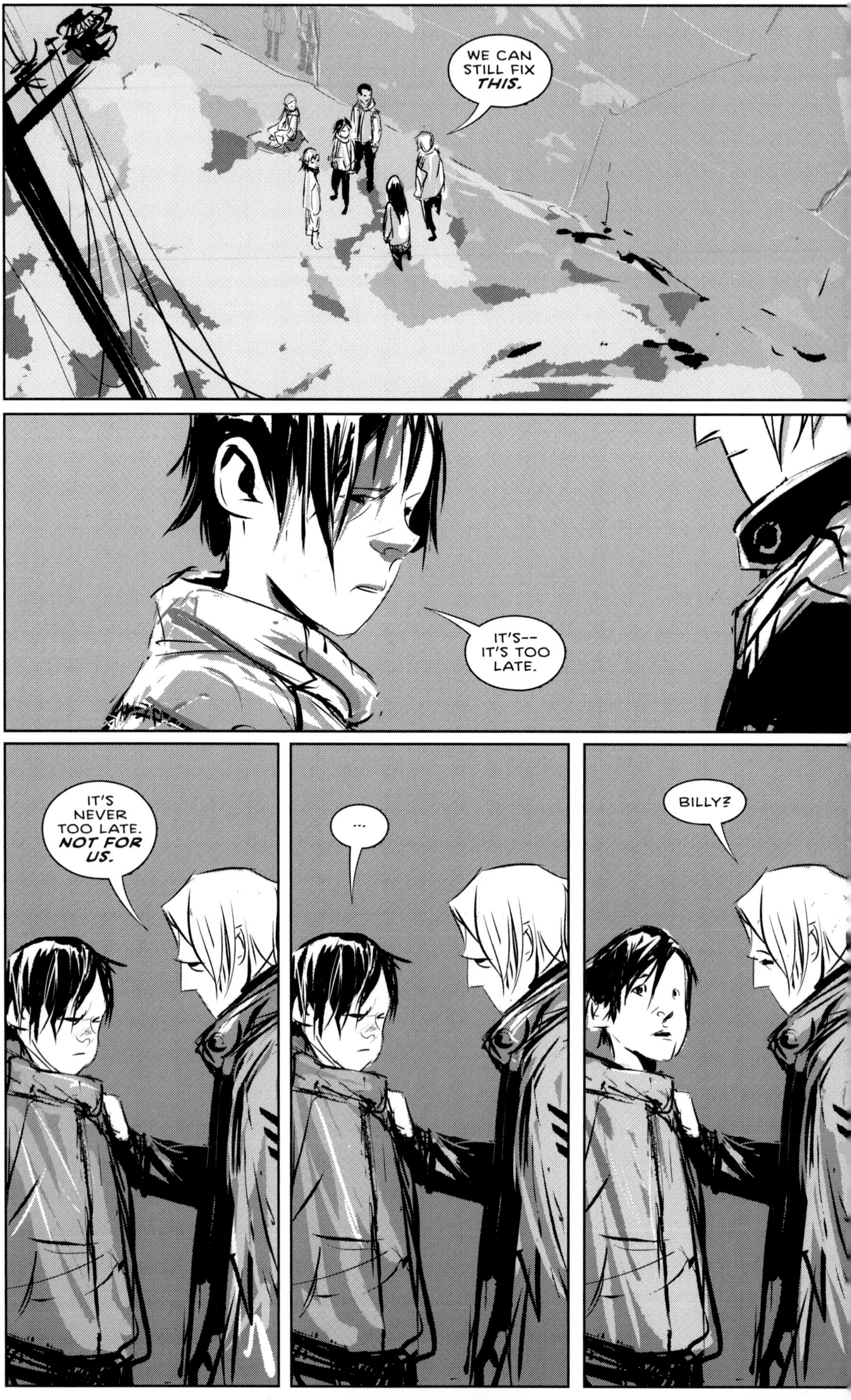

WE CAN STILL FIX *THIS.*
IT'S-- IT'S TOO LATE.
IT'S NEVER TOO LATE. *NOT FOR US.*
...
BILLY?

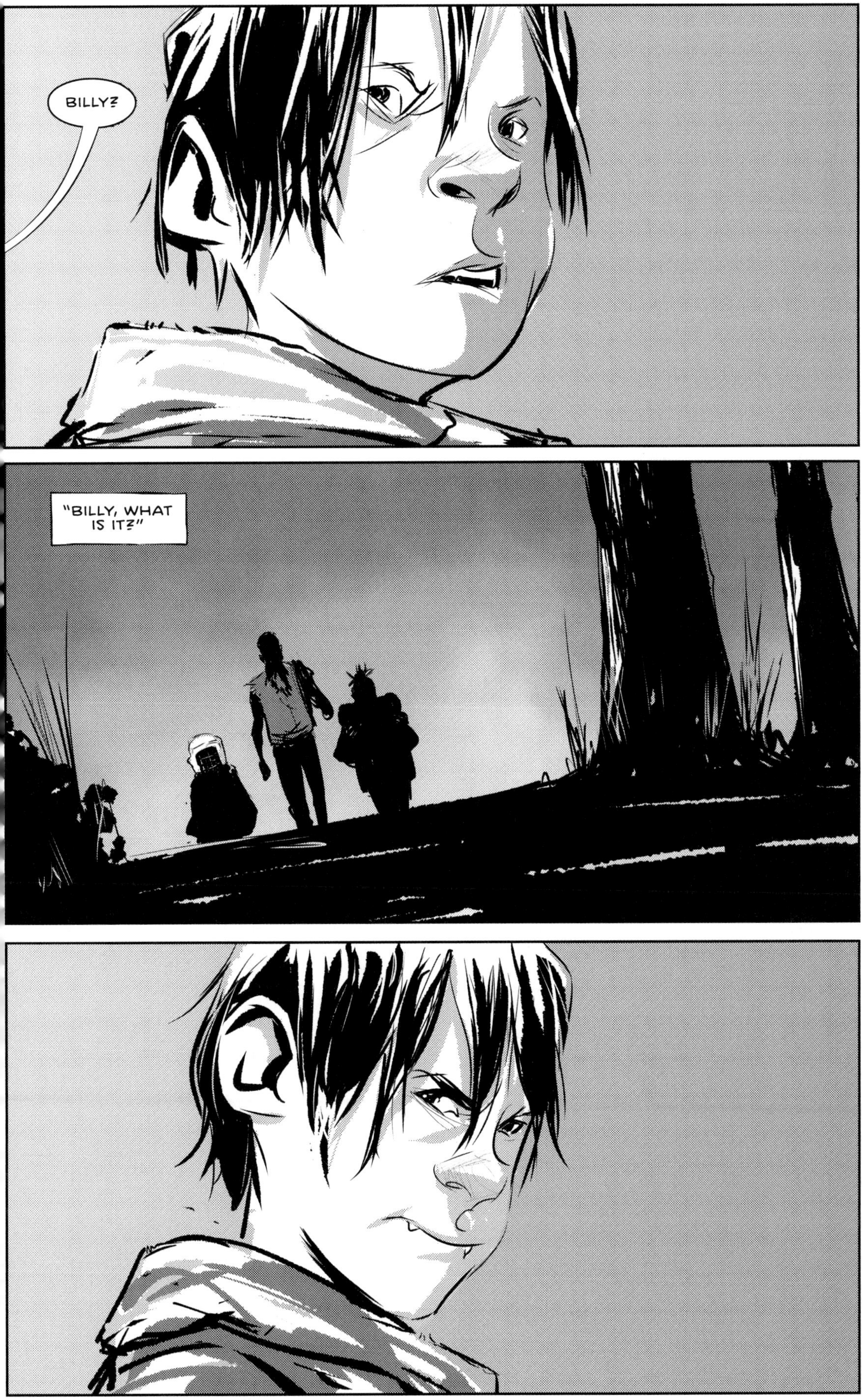
BILLY?
"BILLY, WHAT IS IT?"

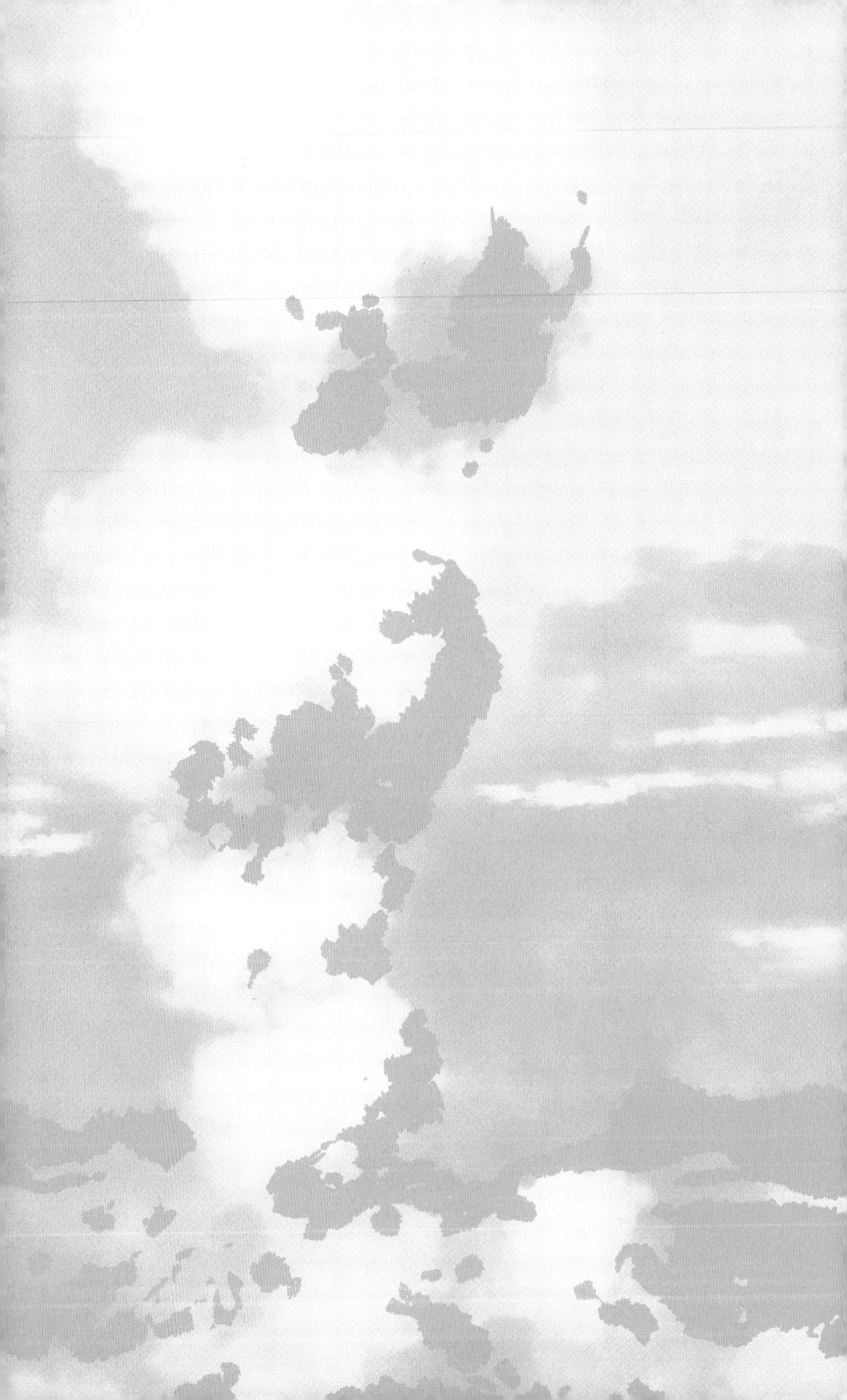

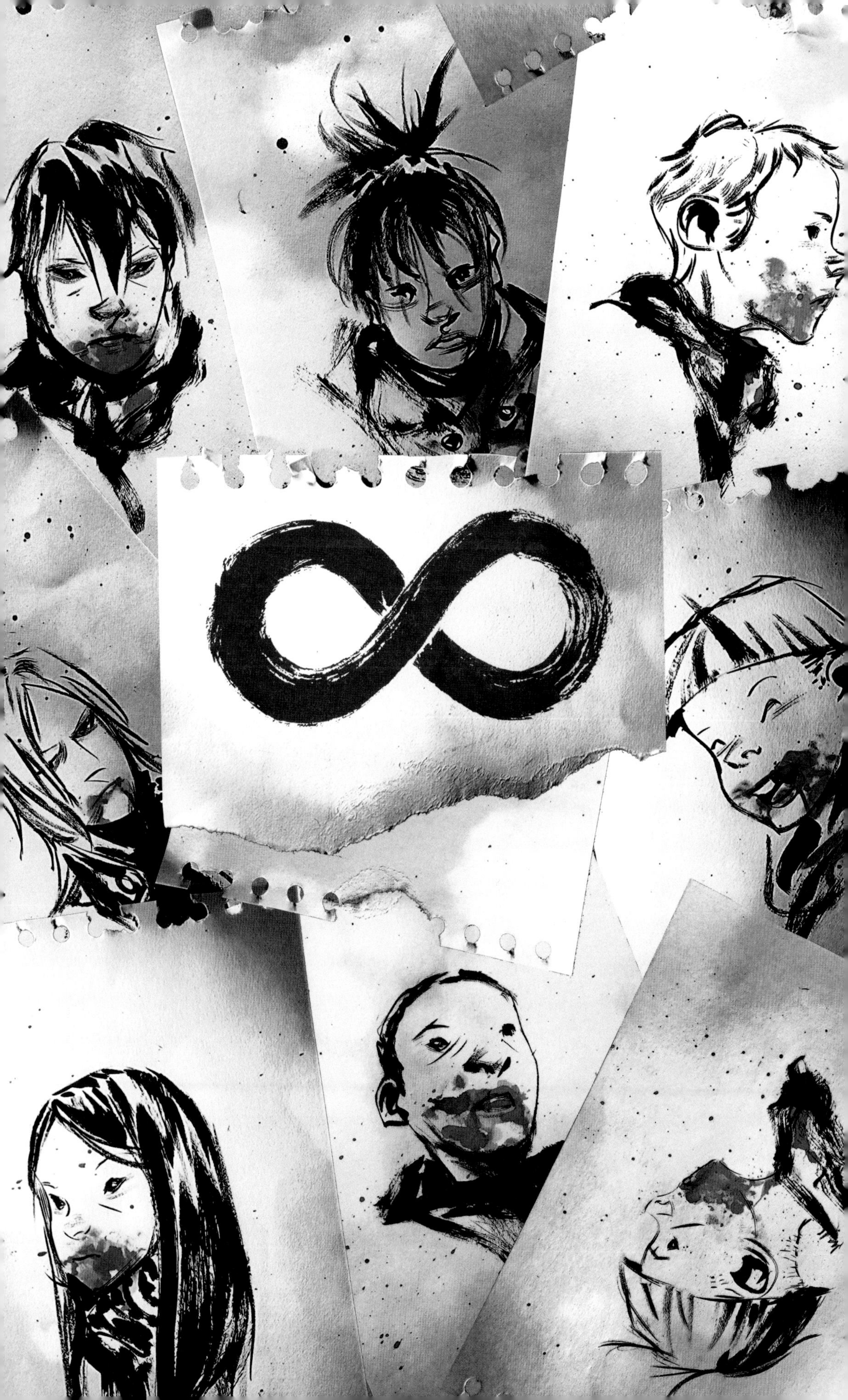

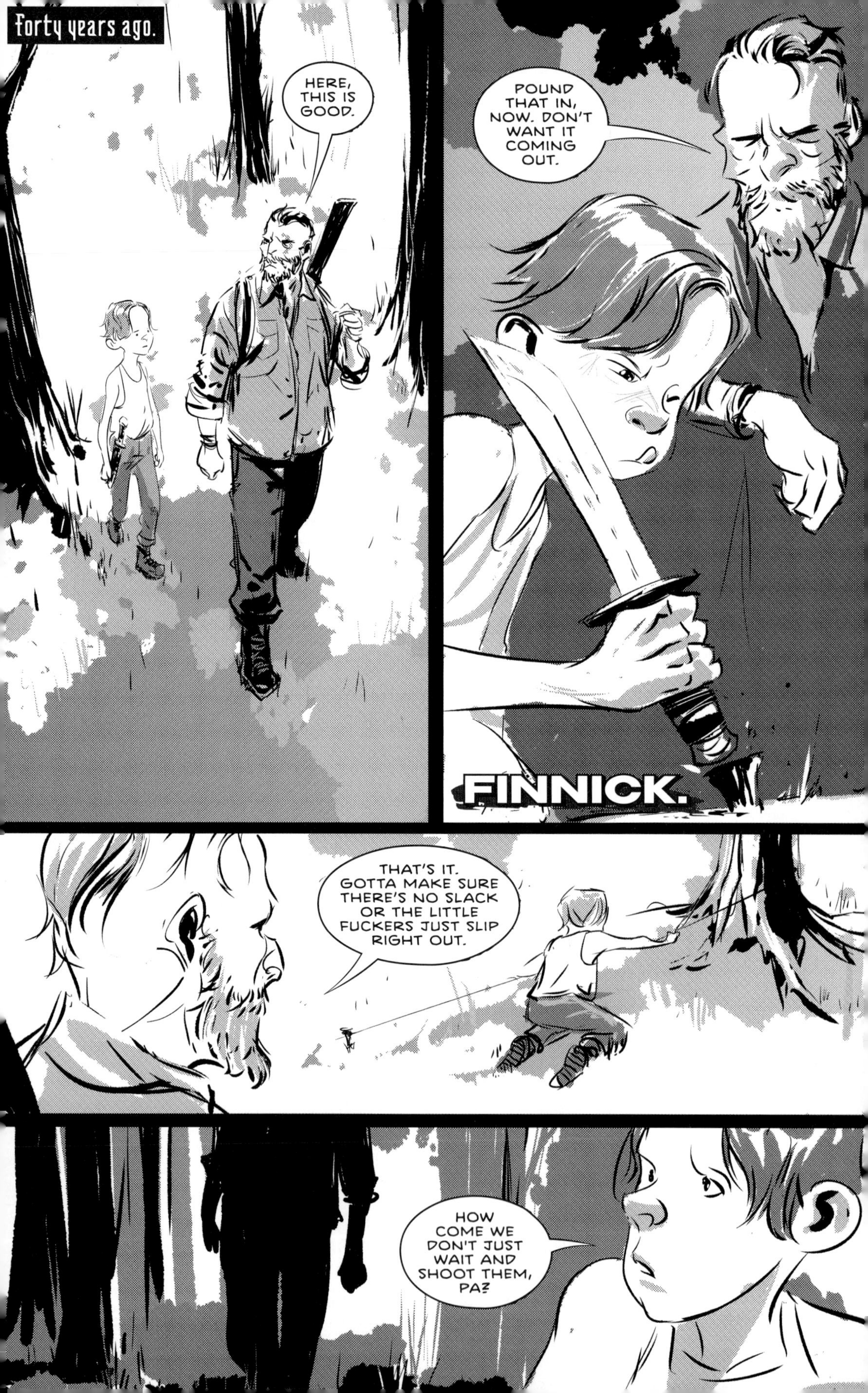
forty years ago.
HERE, THIS IS GOOD.
POUND THAT IN, NOW. DON'T WANT IT COMING OUT.
FINNICK.
THAT'S IT. GOTTA MAKE SURE THERE'S NO SLACK OR THE LITTLE FUCKERS JUST SLIP RIGHT OUT.
HOW COME WE DON'T JUST WAIT AND SHOOT THEM, PA?

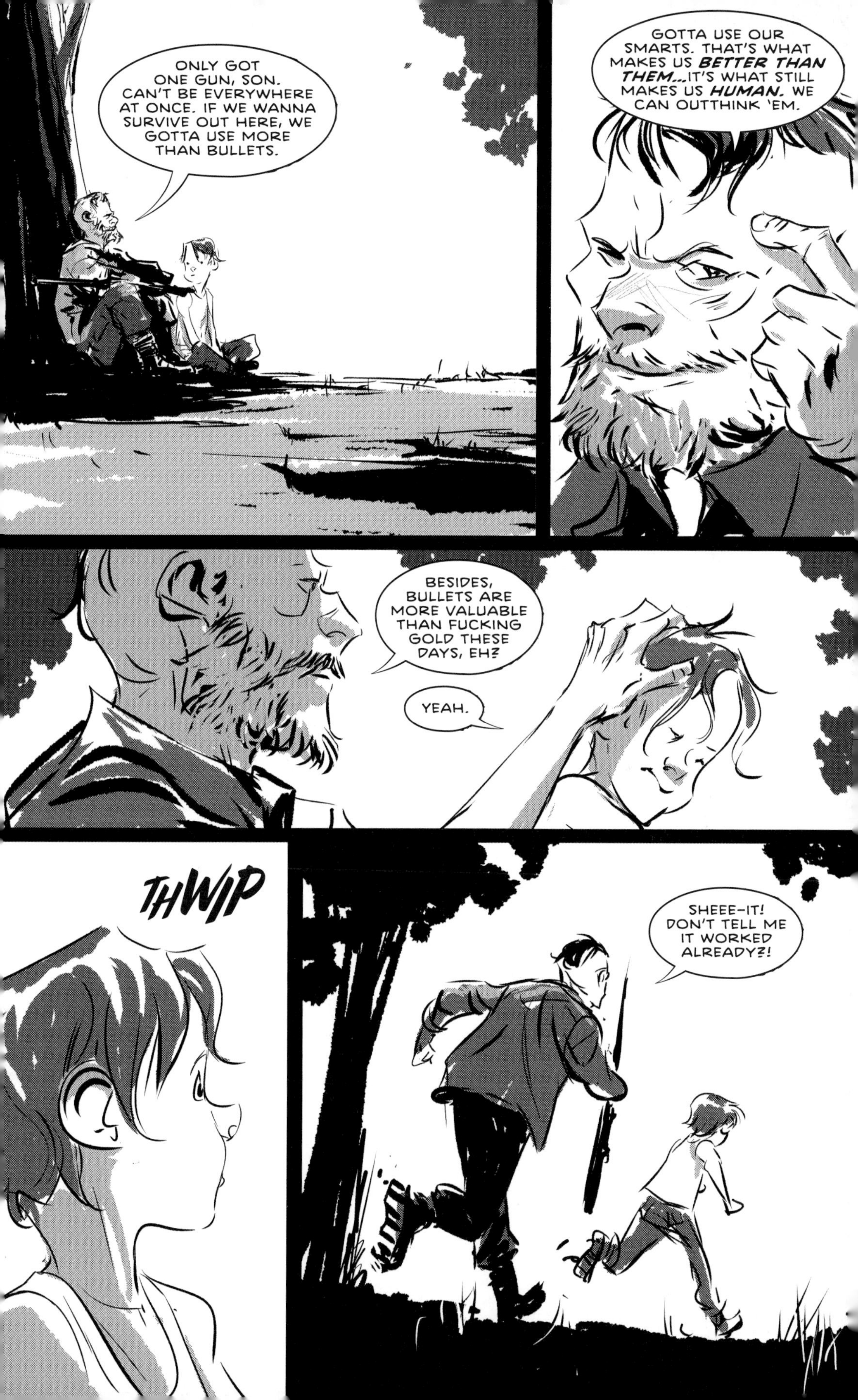
ONLY GOT ONE GUN, SON. CAN'T BE EVERYWHERE AT ONCE. IF WE WANNA SURVIVE OUT HERE, WE GOTTA USE MORE THAN BULLETS.
GOTTA USE OUR SMARTS. THAT'S WHAT MAKES US BETTER THAN THEM...IT'S WHAT STILL MAKES US HUMAN. WE CAN OUTTHINK 'EM.
BESIDES, BULLETS ARE MORE VALUABLE THAN FUCKING GOLD THESE DAYS, EH?
YEAH.
THWIP
SHEEE-IT! DON'T TELL ME IT WORKED ALREADY?!

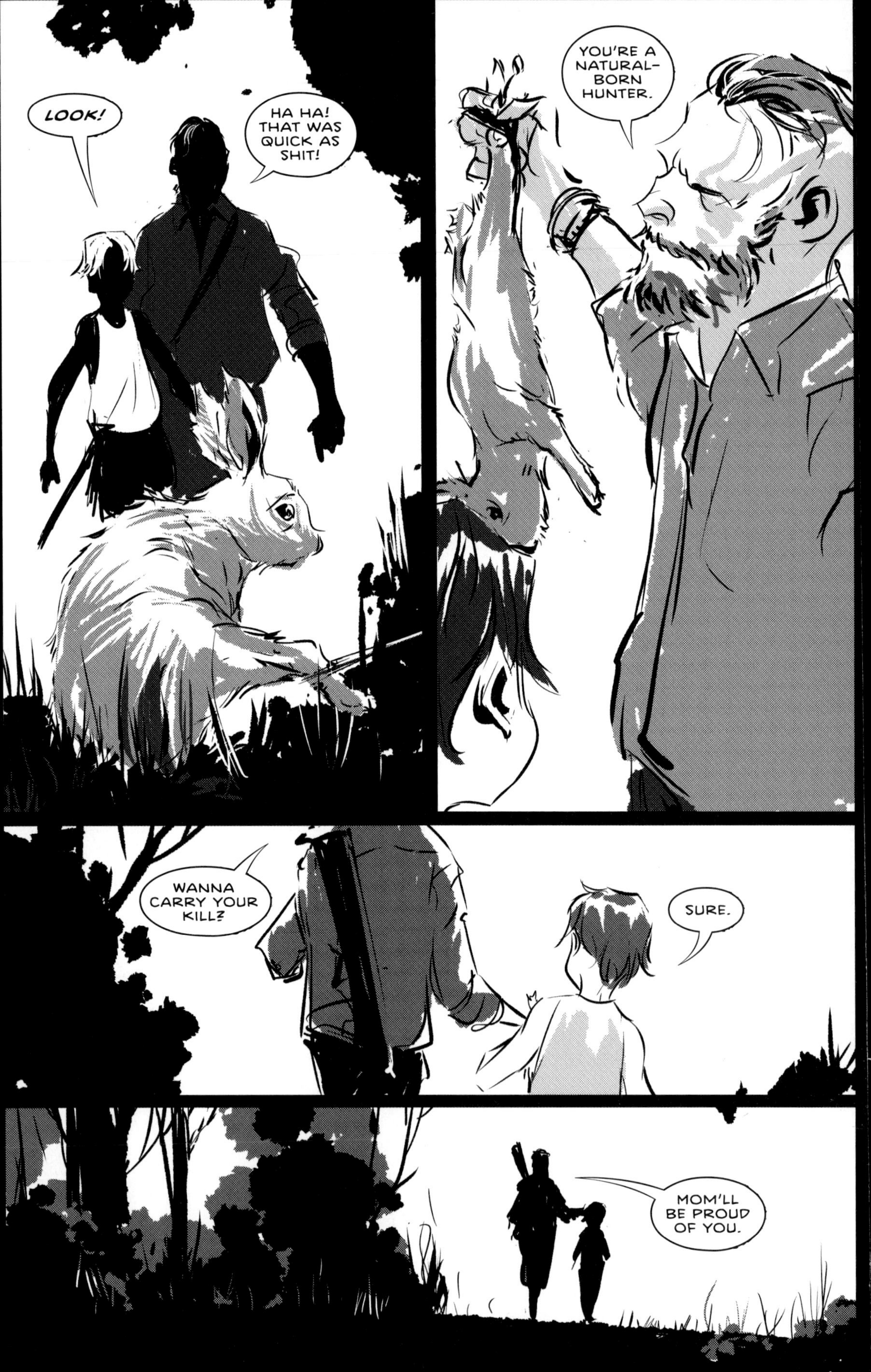
LOOK!
HA HA! THAT WAS QUICK AS SHIT!
YOU'RE A NATURAL-BORN HUNTER.
WANNA CARRY YOUR KILL?
SURE.
MOM'LL BE PROUD OF YOU.

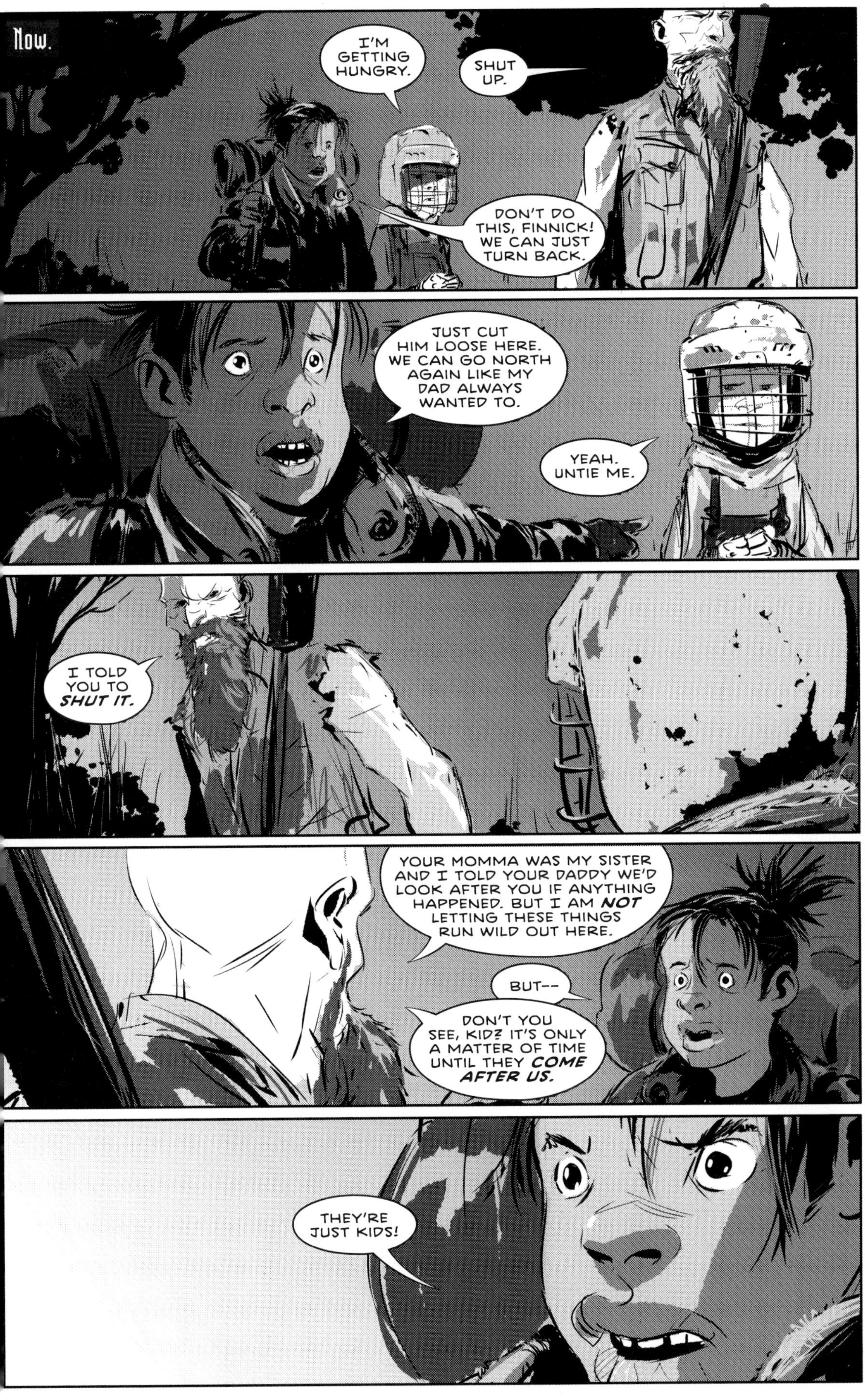
Now.
I'M GETTING HUNGRY.
SHUT UP.
DON'T DO THIS, FINNICK! WE CAN JUST TURN BACK.
JUST CUT HIM LOOSE HERE. WE CAN GO NORTH AGAIN LIKE MY DAD ALWAYS WANTED TO.
YEAH. UNTIE ME.
I TOLD YOU TO SHUT IT.
YOUR MOMMA WAS MY SISTER AND I TOLD YOUR DADDY WE'D LOOK AFTER YOU IF ANYTHING HAPPENED. BUT I AM NOT LETTING THESE THINGS RUN WILD OUT HERE.
BUT--
DON'T YOU SEE, KID? IT'S ONLY A MATTER OF TIME UNTIL THEY COME AFTER US.
THEY'RE JUST KIDS!

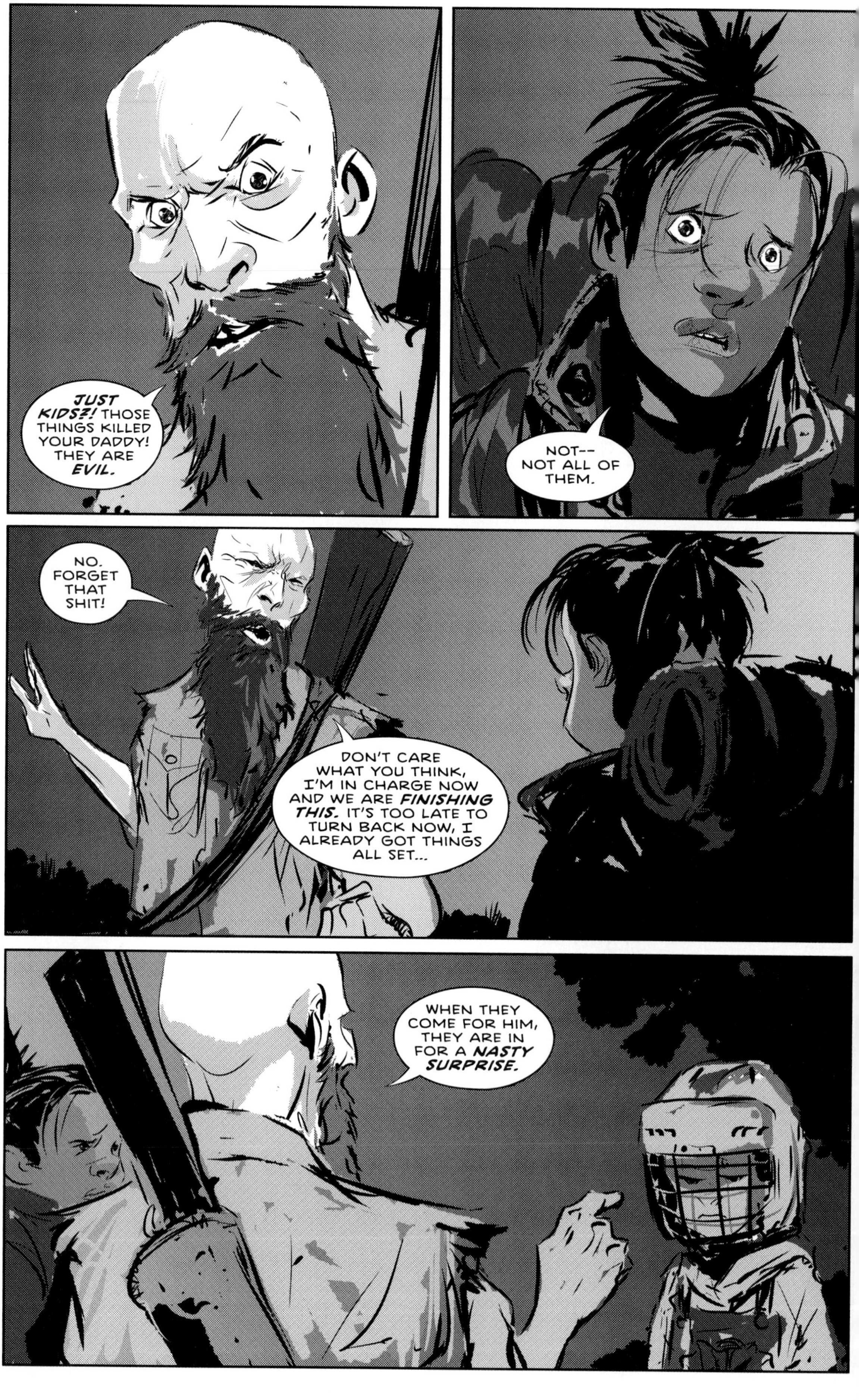
JUST KIDS?! THOSE THINGS KILLED YOUR DADDY! THEY ARE EVIL.
NOT-- NOT ALL OF THEM.
NO. FORGET THAT SHIT!
DON'T CARE WHAT YOU THINK, I'M IN CHARGE NOW AND WE ARE FINISHING THIS. IT'S TOO LATE TO TURN BACK NOW, I ALREADY GOT THINGS ALL SET...
WHEN THEY COME FOR HIM, THEY ARE IN FOR A NASTY SURPRISE.

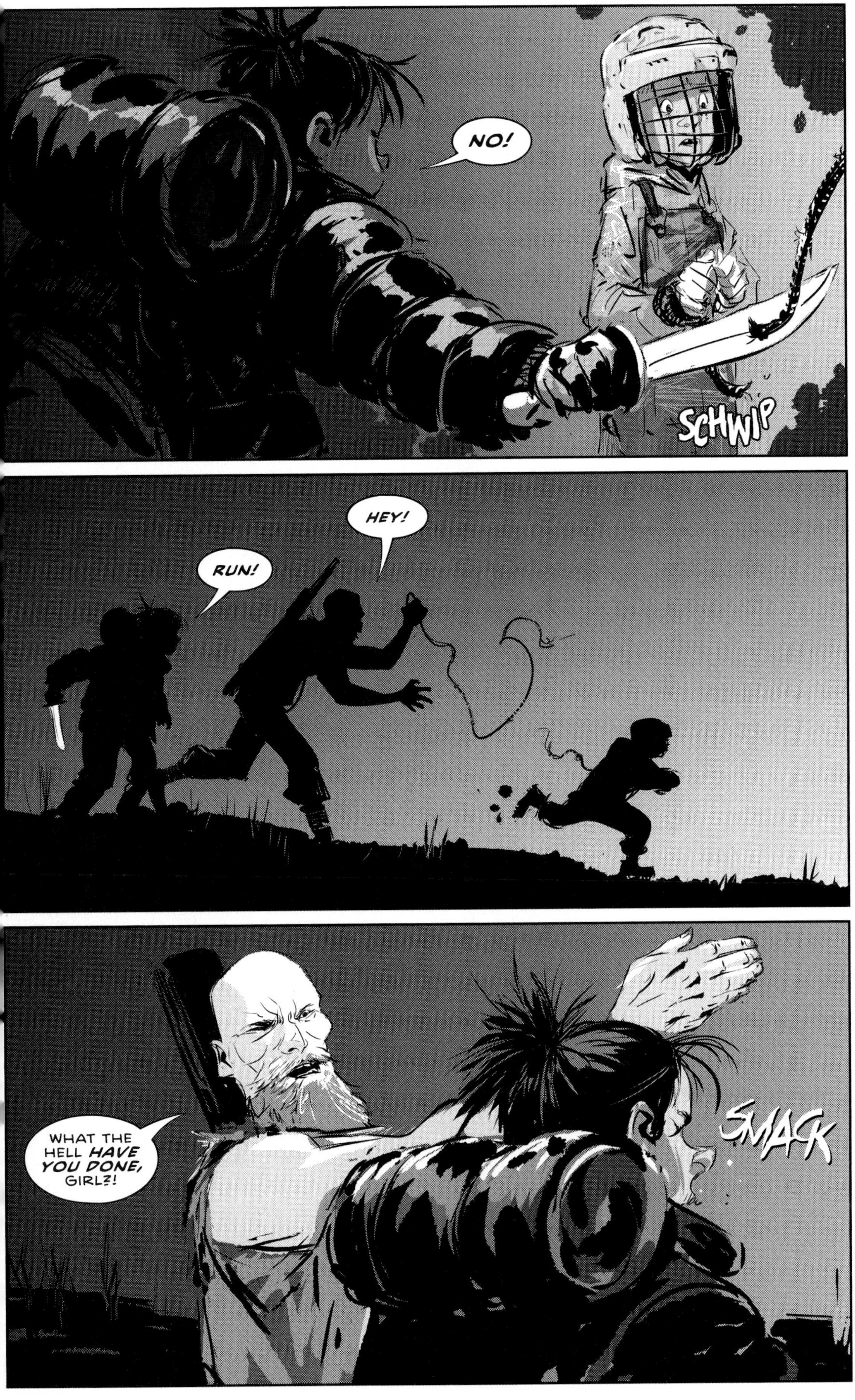
NO!
SCHWIP
RUN!
HEY!
WHAT THE HELL HAVE YOU DONE, GIRL?!
SMACK

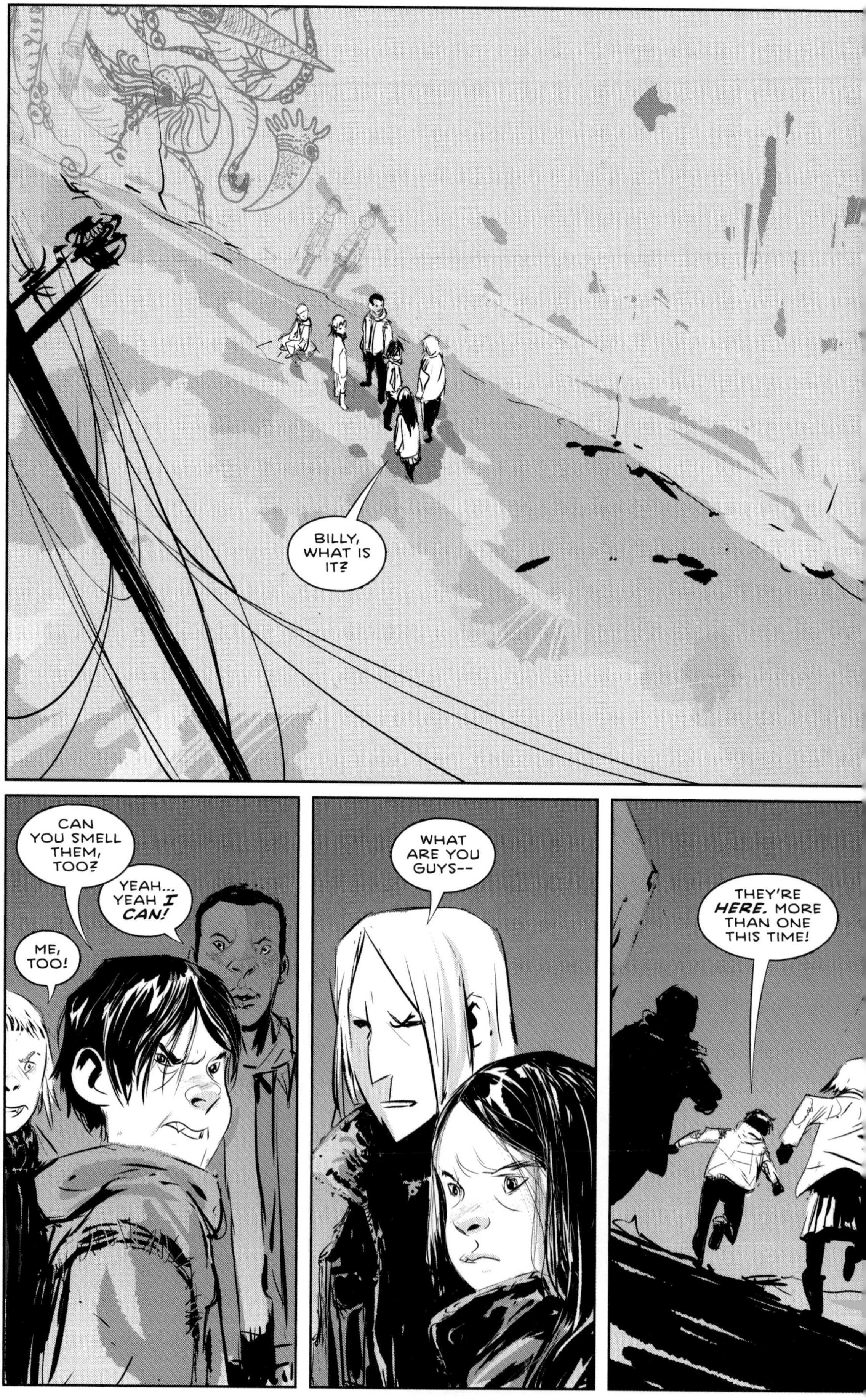
BILLY, WHAT IS IT?
CAN YOU SMELL THEM, TOO?
YEAH... YEAH *I CAN!*
ME, TOO!
WHAT ARE YOU GUYS--
THEY'RE *HERE.* MORE THAN ONE THIS TIME!

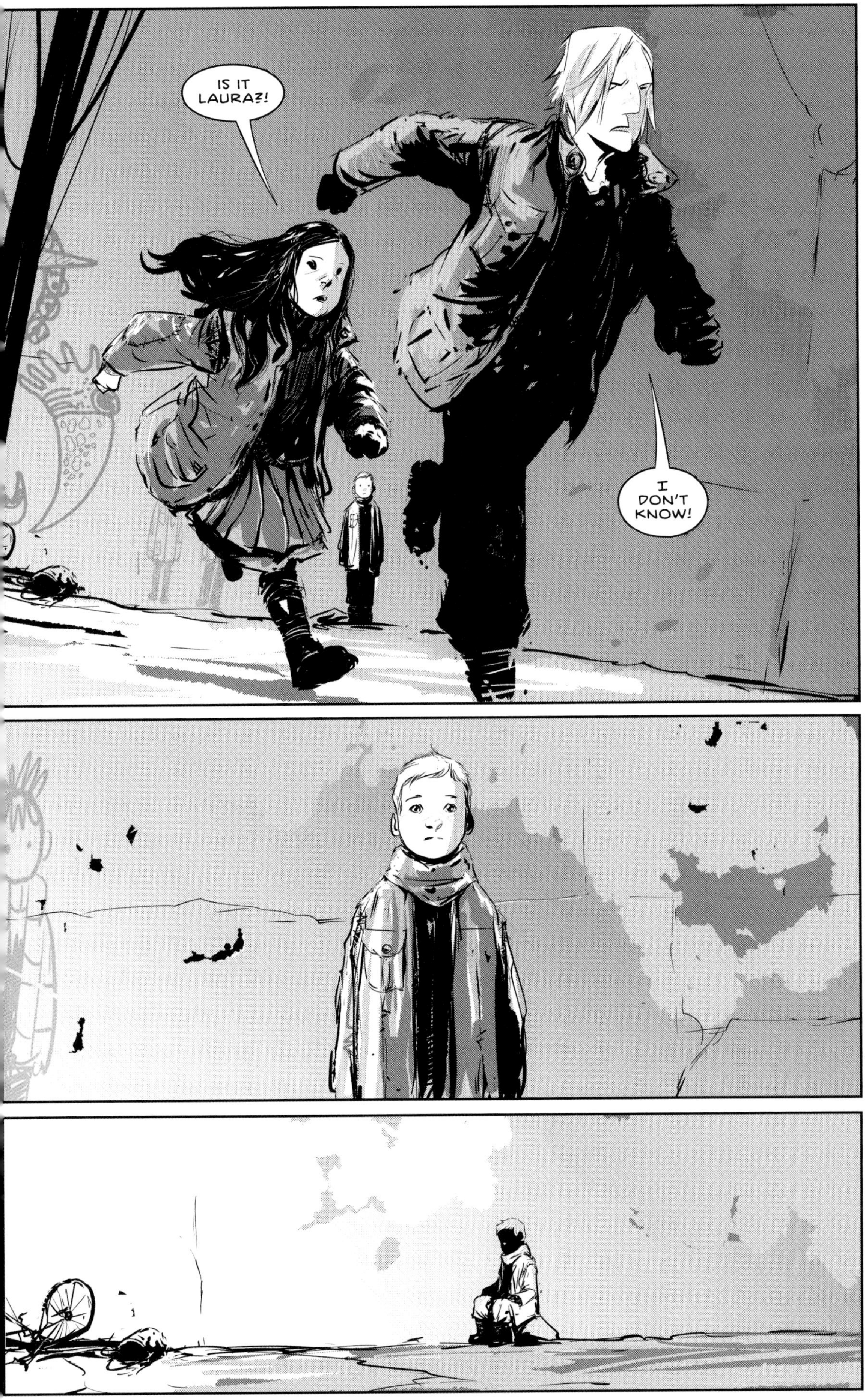
IS IT LAURA?!
I DON'T KNOW!

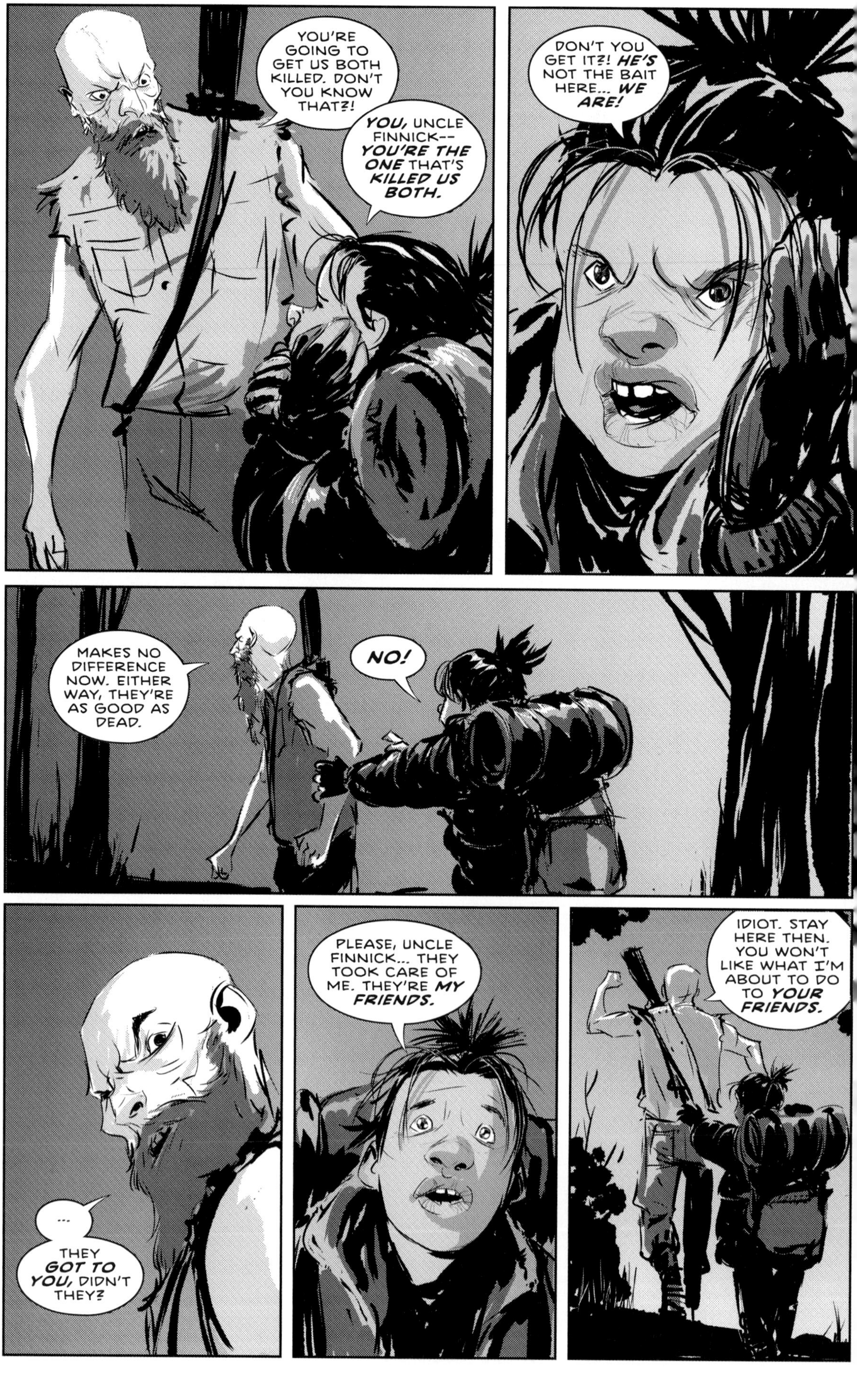
YOU'RE GOING TO GET US BOTH KILLED. DON'T YOU KNOW THAT?!
YOU, UNCLE FINNICK-- YOU'RE THE ONE THAT'S KILLED US BOTH.
DON'T YOU GET IT?! HE'S NOT THE BAIT HERE... WE ARE!
MAKES NO DIFFERENCE NOW. EITHER WAY, THEY'RE AS GOOD AS DEAD.
NO!
...
THEY GOT TO YOU, DIDN'T THEY?
PLEASE, UNCLE FINNICK... THEY TOOK CARE OF ME. THEY'RE MY FRIENDS.
IDIOT. STAY HERE THEN. YOU WON'T LIKE WHAT I'M ABOUT TO DO TO YOUR FRIENDS.

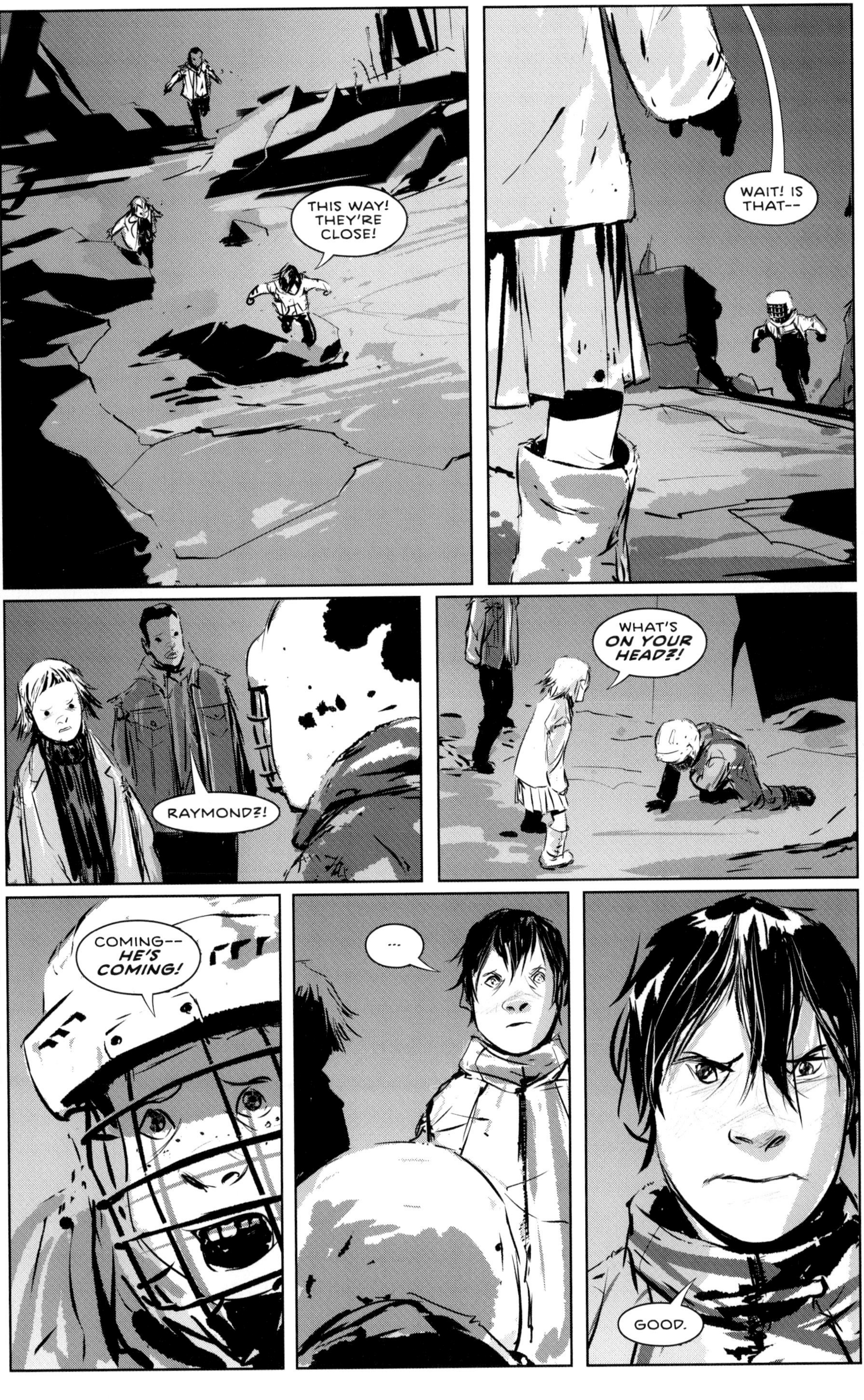
THIS WAY! THEY'RE CLOSE!
WAIT! IS THAT--
RAYMOND?!
WHAT'S ON YOUR HEAD?!
COMING-- HE'S COMING!
...
GOOD.

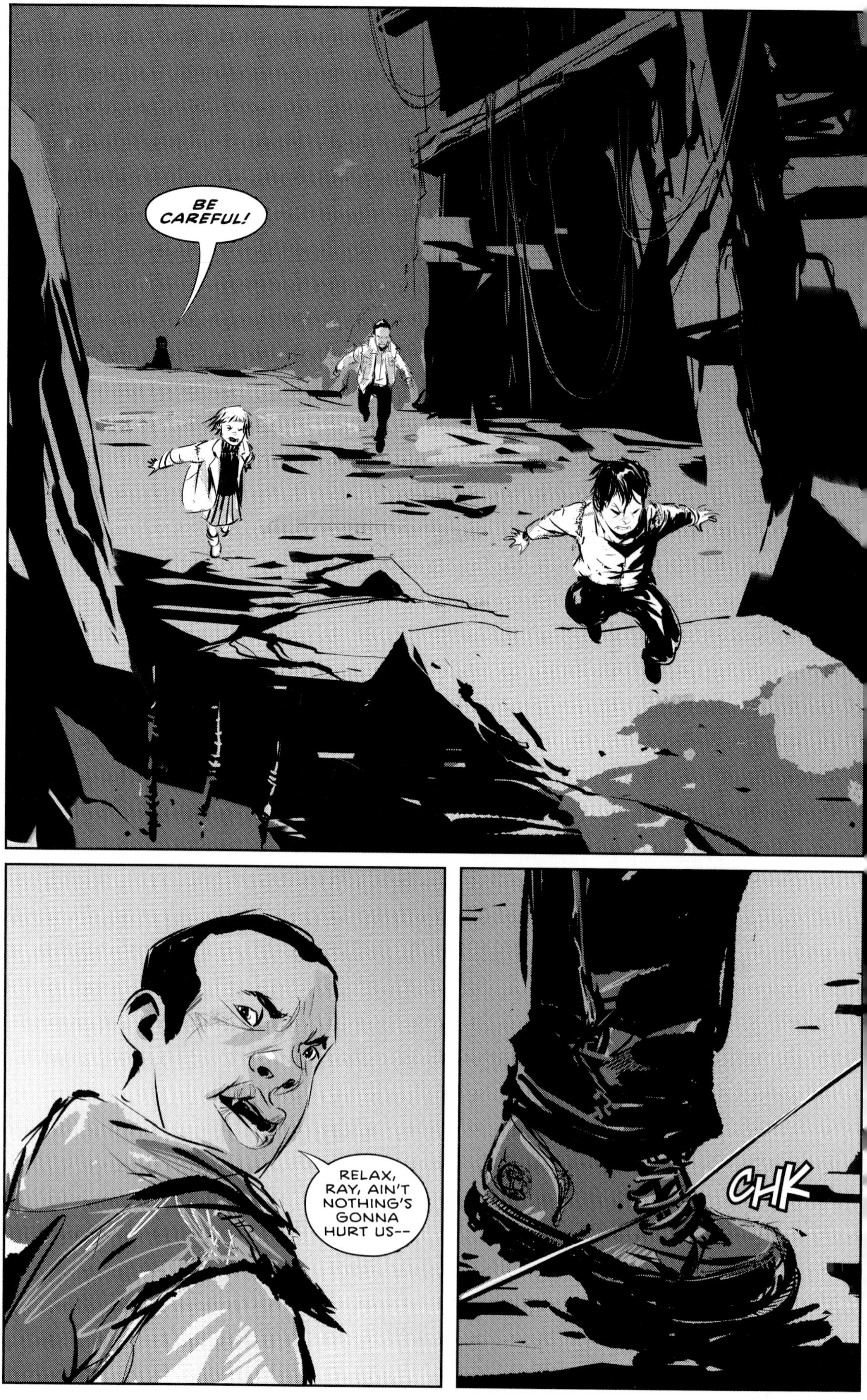
BE CAREFUL!
RELAX, RAY, AIN'T NOTHING'S GONNA HURT US--
CHK

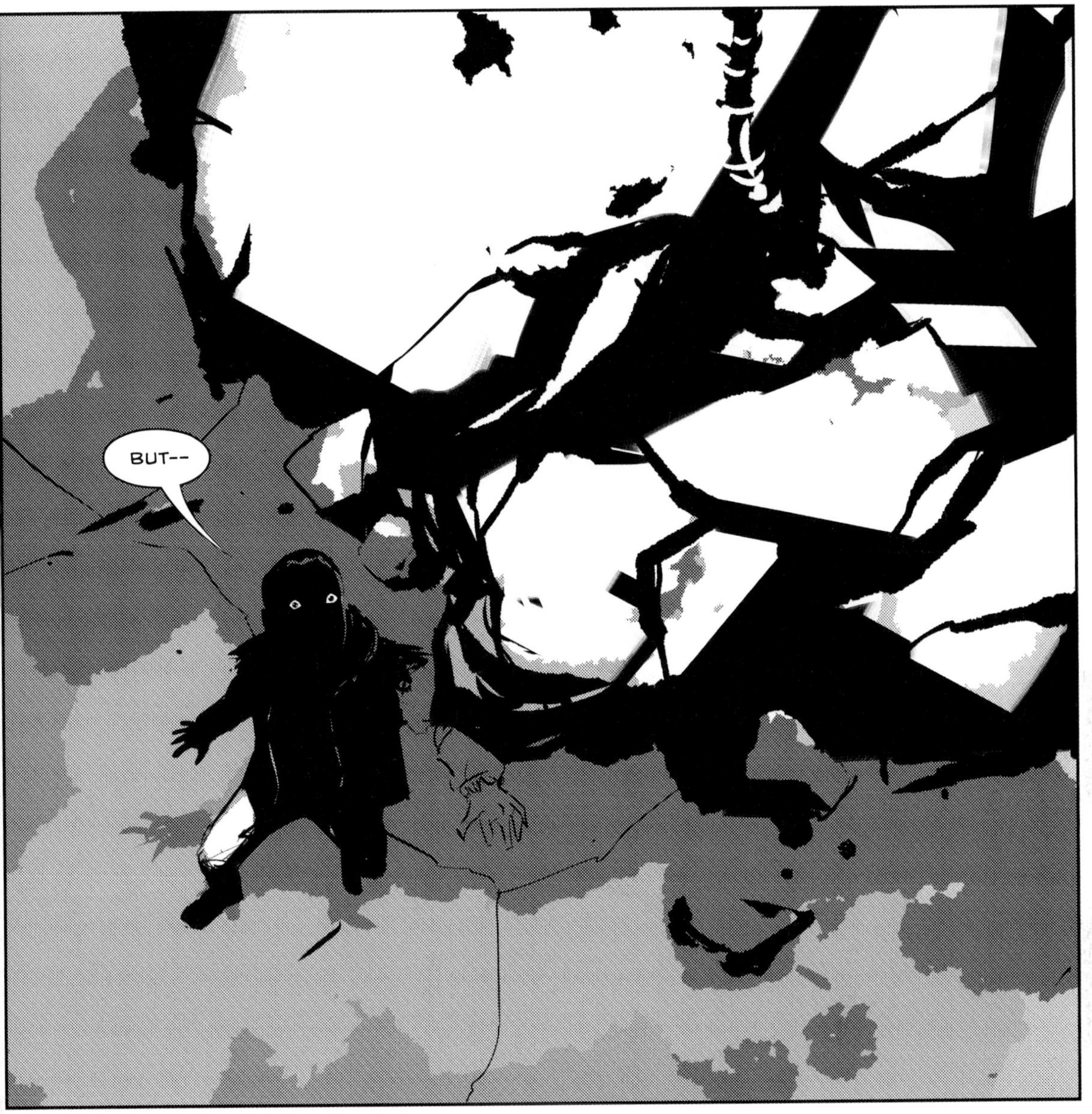
BUT--

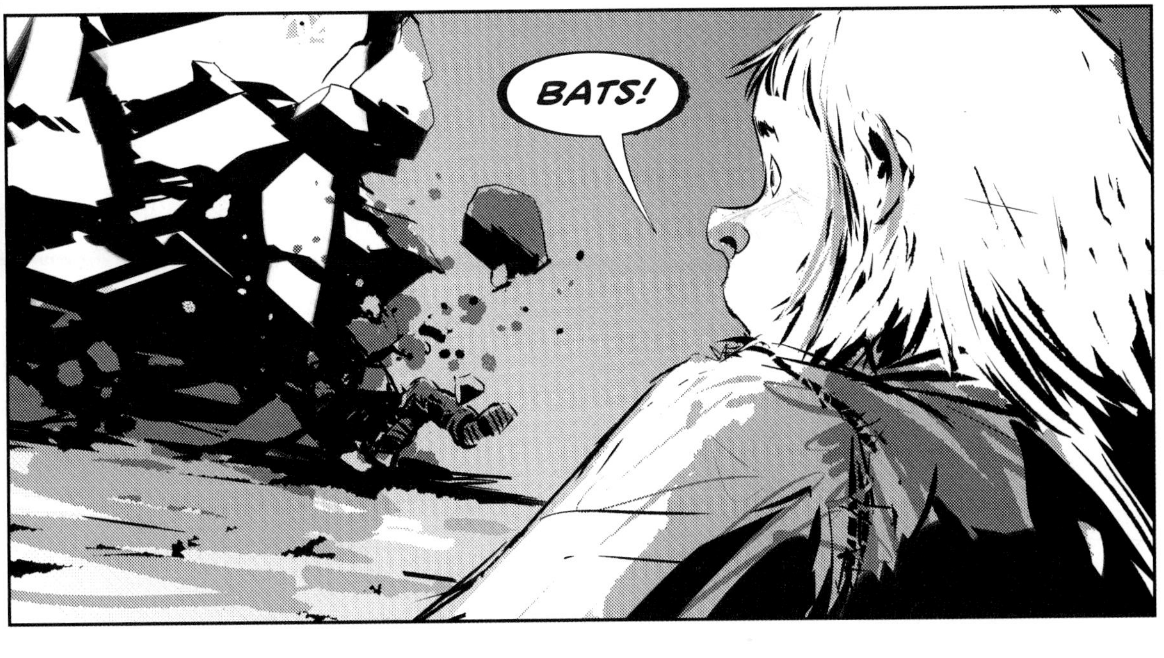
BATS!

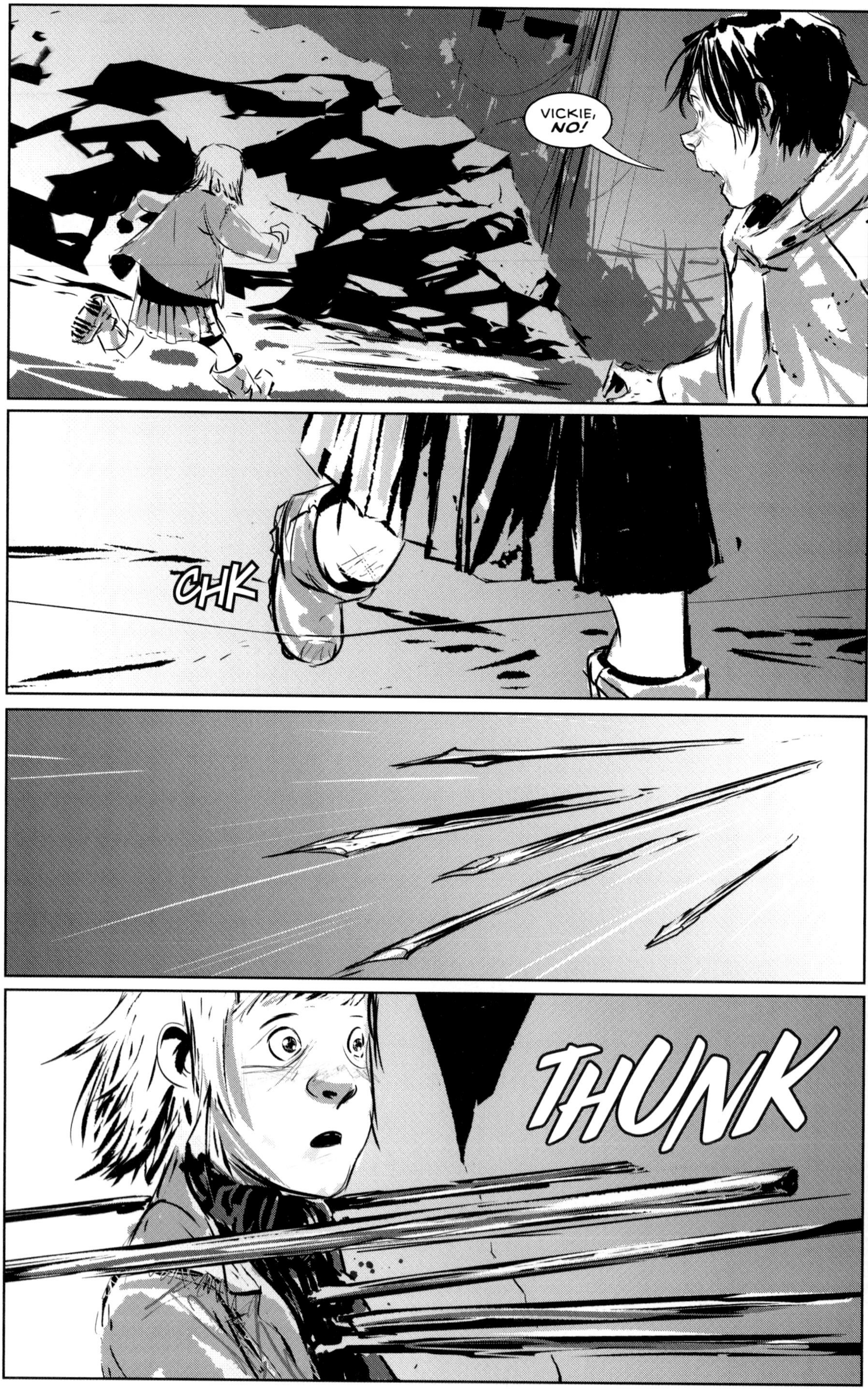
VICKIE, NO!
CHK
THUNK

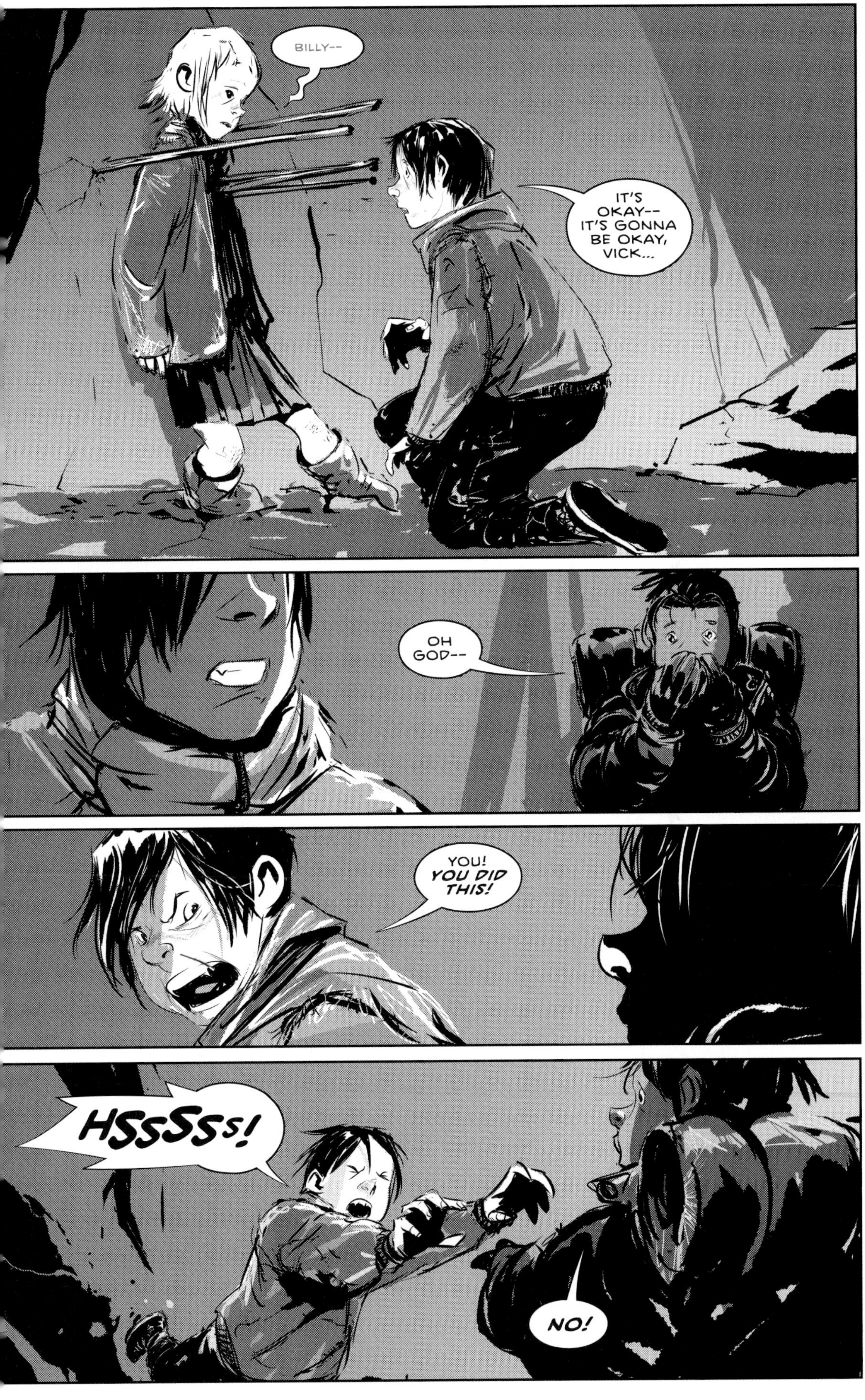
BILLY--
IT'S OKAY-- IT'S GONNA BE OKAY, VICK...
OH GOD--
YOU! *YOU DID THIS!*
HSsSSss!
NO!

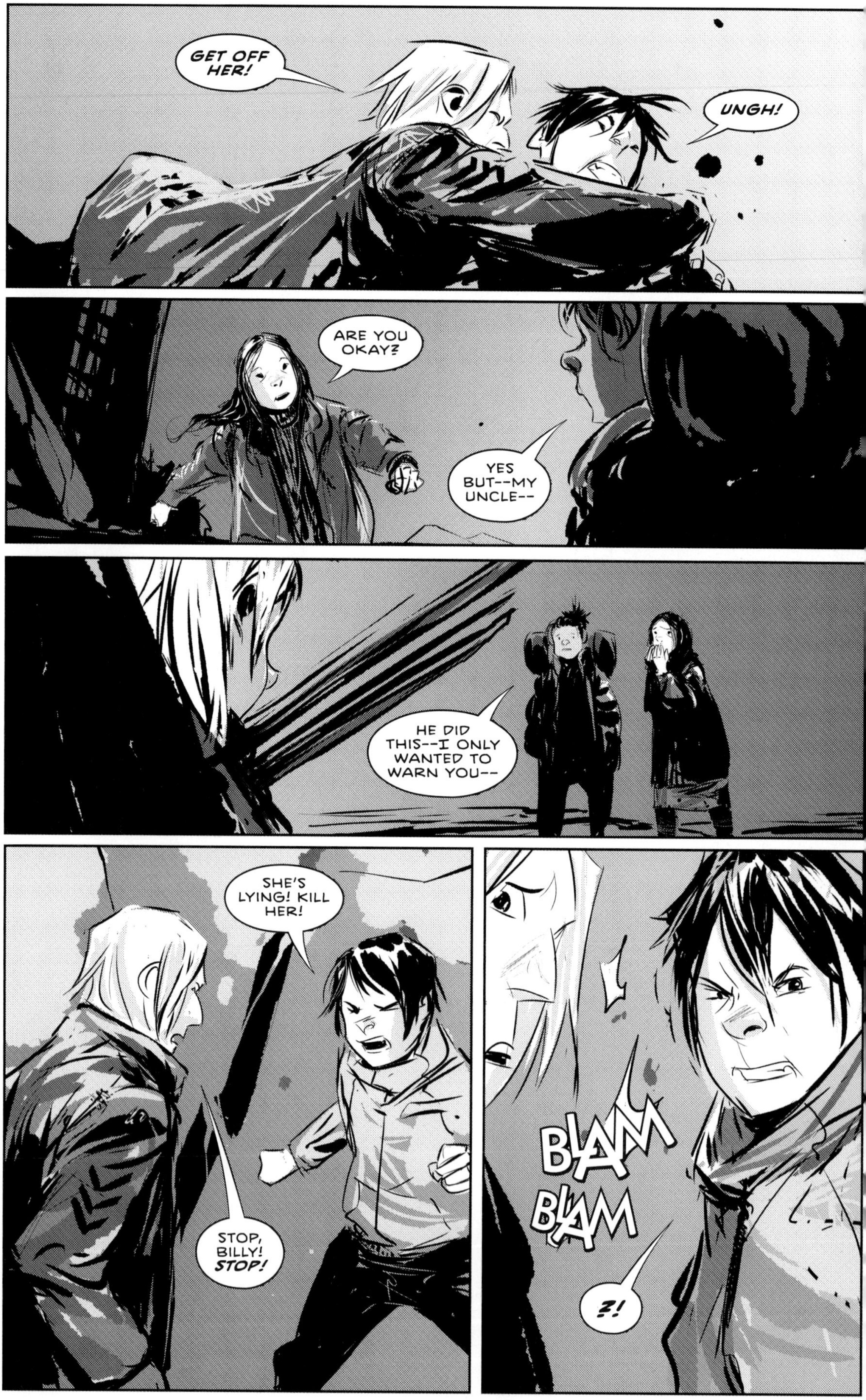
GET OFF HER!
UNGH!
ARE YOU OKAY?
YES BUT--MY UNCLE--
HE DID THIS--I ONLY WANTED TO WARN YOU--
SHE'S LYING! KILL HER!
STOP, BILLY! STOP!
BLAM
BLAM
?!

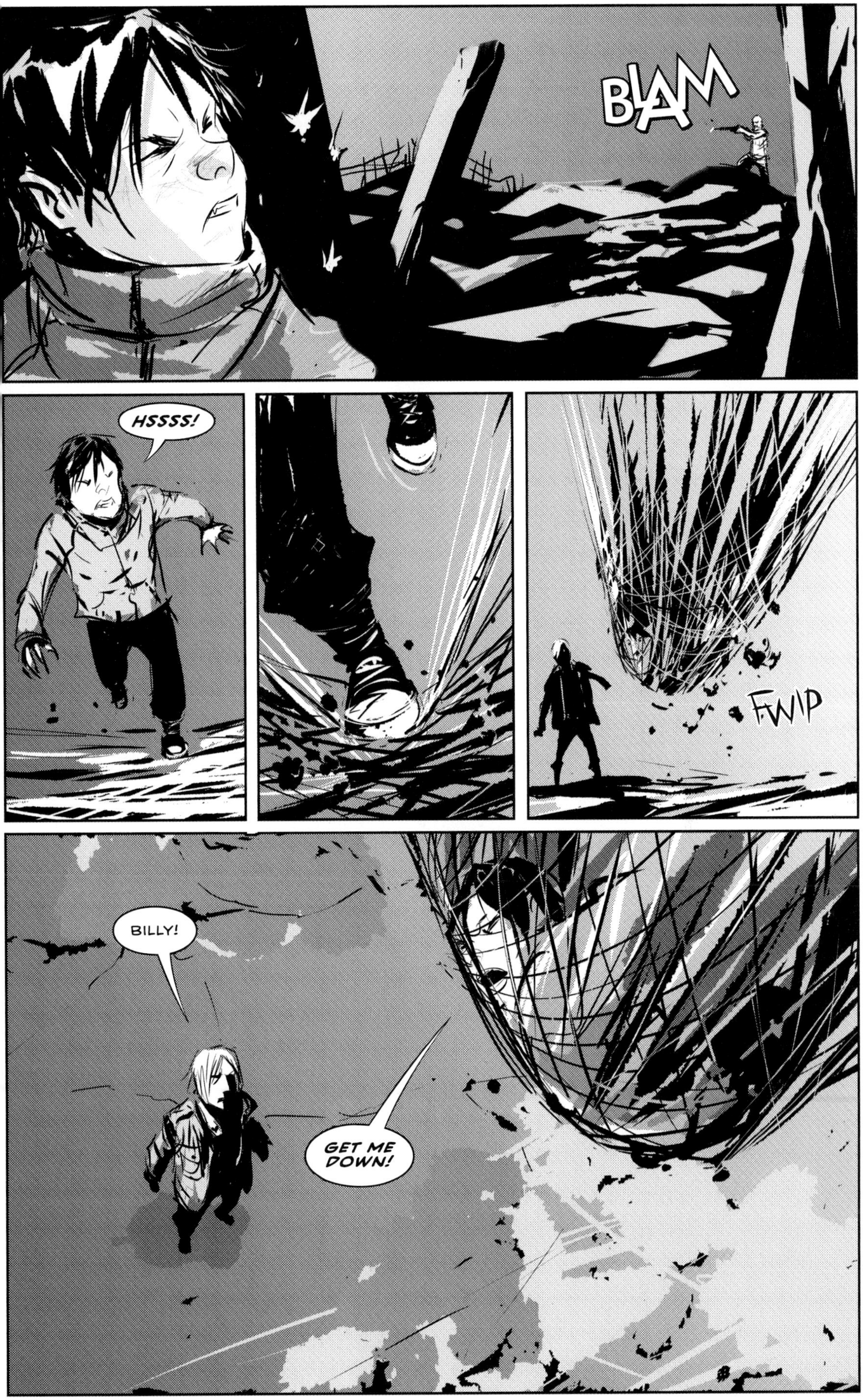
BLAM
HSSSS!
FWIP
BILLY!
GET ME DOWN!

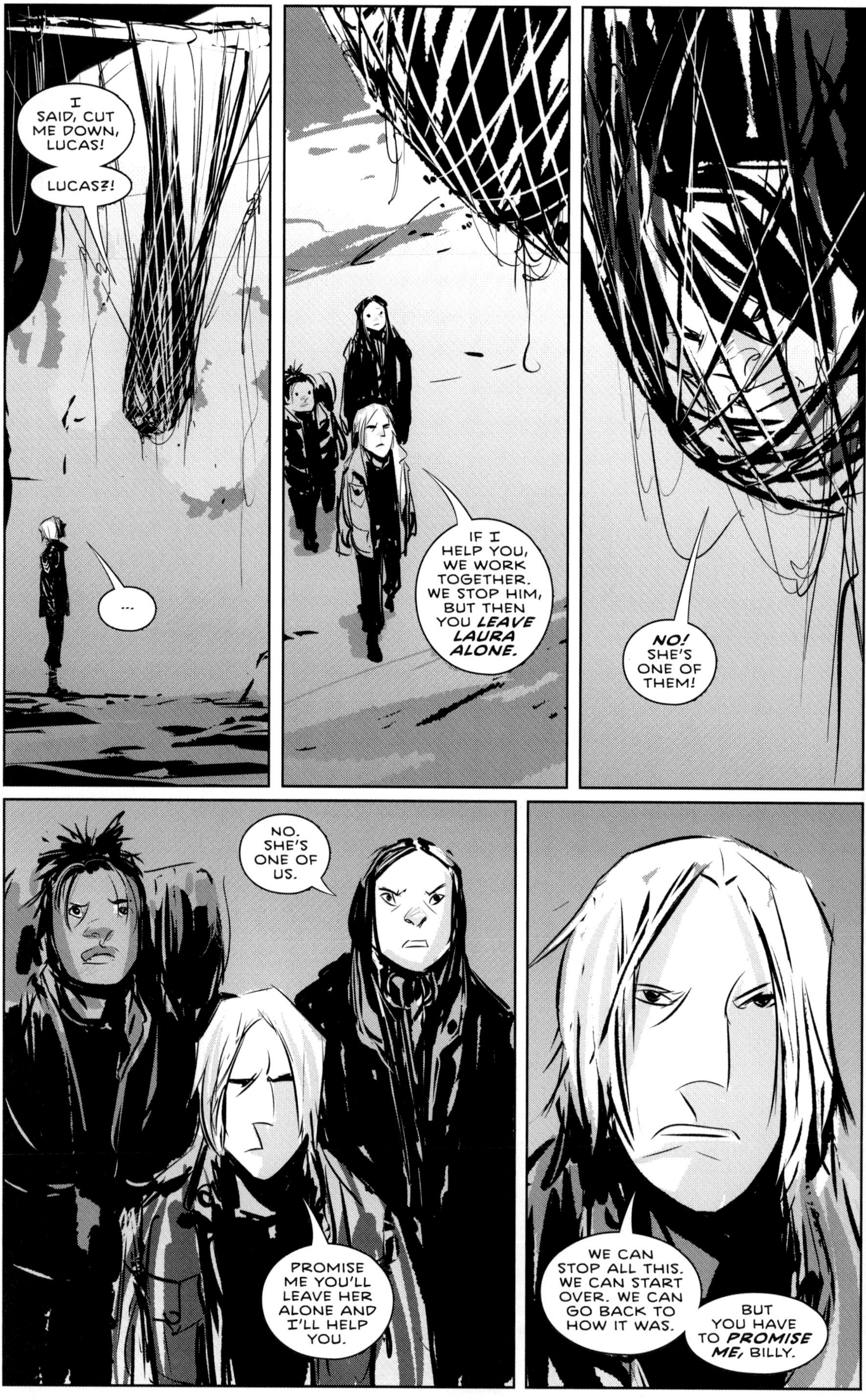
I SAID, CUT ME DOWN, LUCAS!
LUCAS?!
...
IF I HELP YOU, WE WORK TOGETHER. WE STOP HIM, BUT THEN YOU LEAVE LAURA ALONE.
NO! SHE'S ONE OF THEM!
NO. SHE'S ONE OF US.
PROMISE ME YOU'LL LEAVE HER ALONE AND I'LL HELP YOU.
WE CAN STOP ALL THIS. WE CAN START OVER. WE CAN GO BACK TO HOW IT WAS.
BUT YOU HAVE TO PROMISE ME, BILLY.

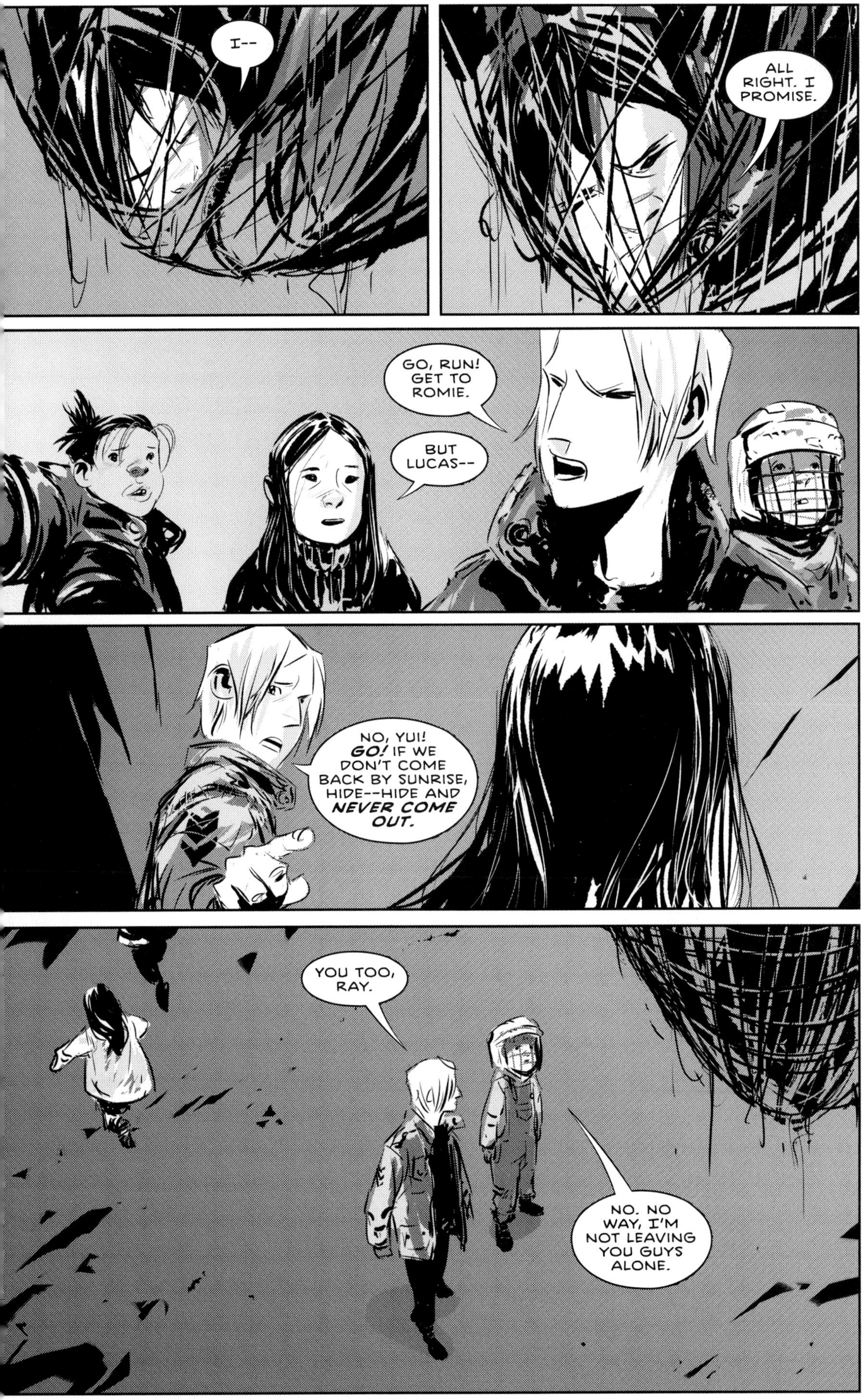
I--
ALL RIGHT. I PROMISE.
GO, RUN! GET TO ROMIE.
BUT LUCAS--
NO, YUI! GO! IF WE DON'T COME BACK BY SUNRISE, HIDE--HIDE AND NEVER COME OUT.
YOU TOO, RAY.
NO. NO WAY, I'M NOT LEAVING YOU GUYS ALONE.

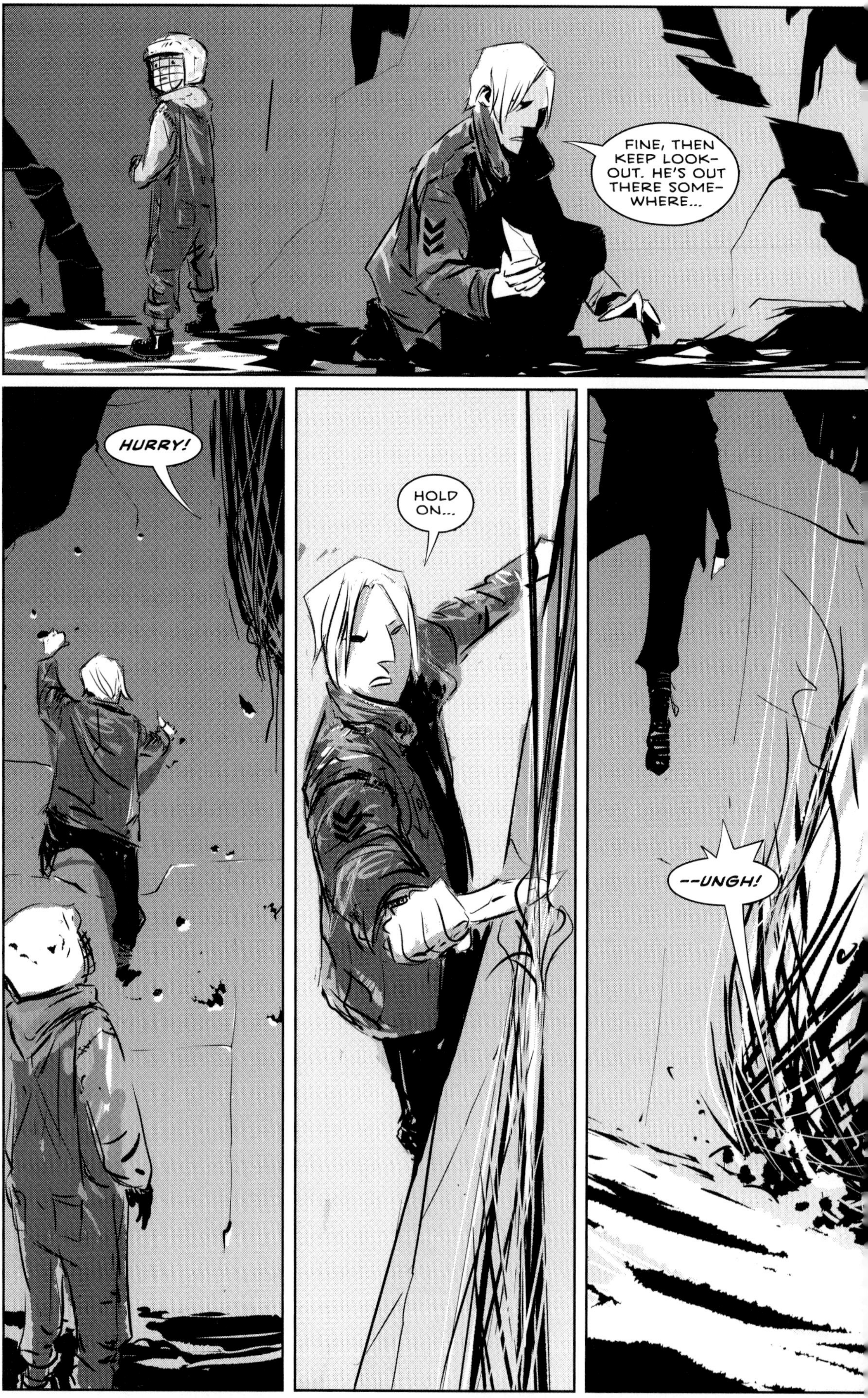
FINE, THEN KEEP LOOK-OUT. HE'S OUT THERE SOME-WHERE...
HURRY!
HOLD ON...
--UNGH!

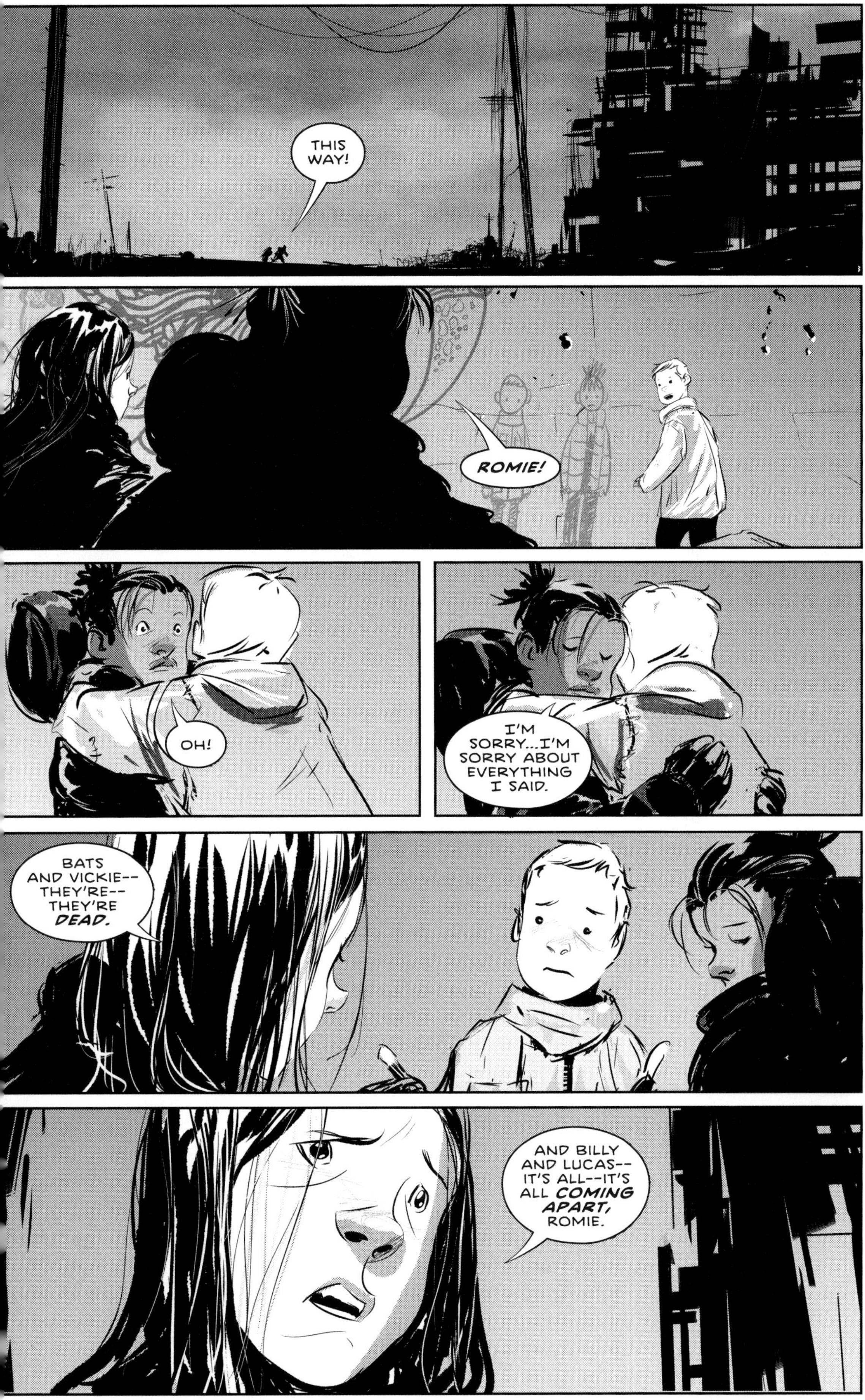
THIS WAY!
ROMIE!
OH!
I'M SORRY...I'M SORRY ABOUT EVERYTHING I SAID.
BATS AND VICKIE-- THEY'RE-- THEY'RE DEAD.
AND BILLY AND LUCAS-- IT'S ALL--IT'S ALL COMING APART, ROMIE.

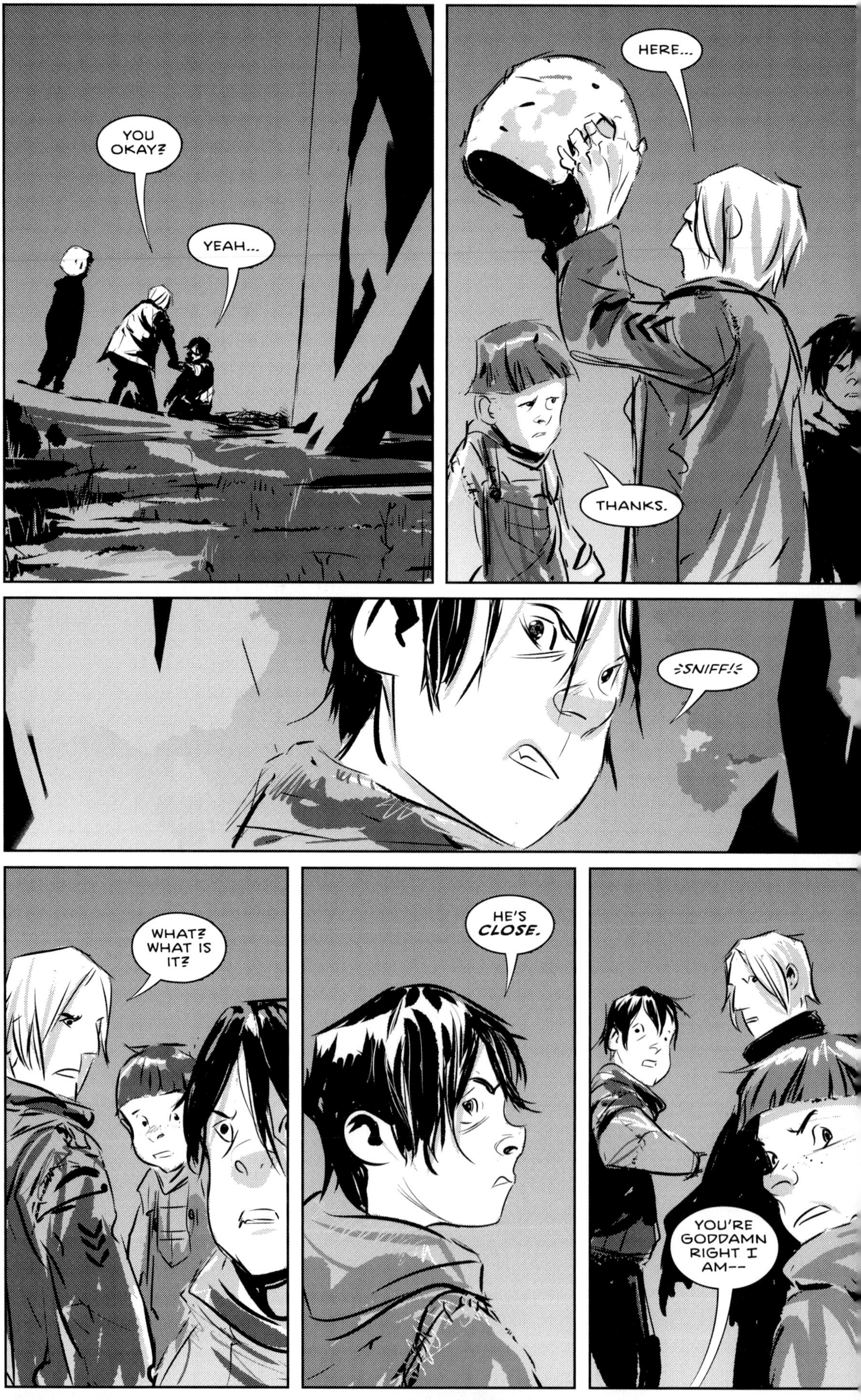
YOU OKAY?
YEAH...
HERE...
THANKS.
SNIFF!
WHAT? WHAT IS IT?
HE'S CLOSE.
YOU'RE GODDAMN RIGHT I AM--

WHOOOSH

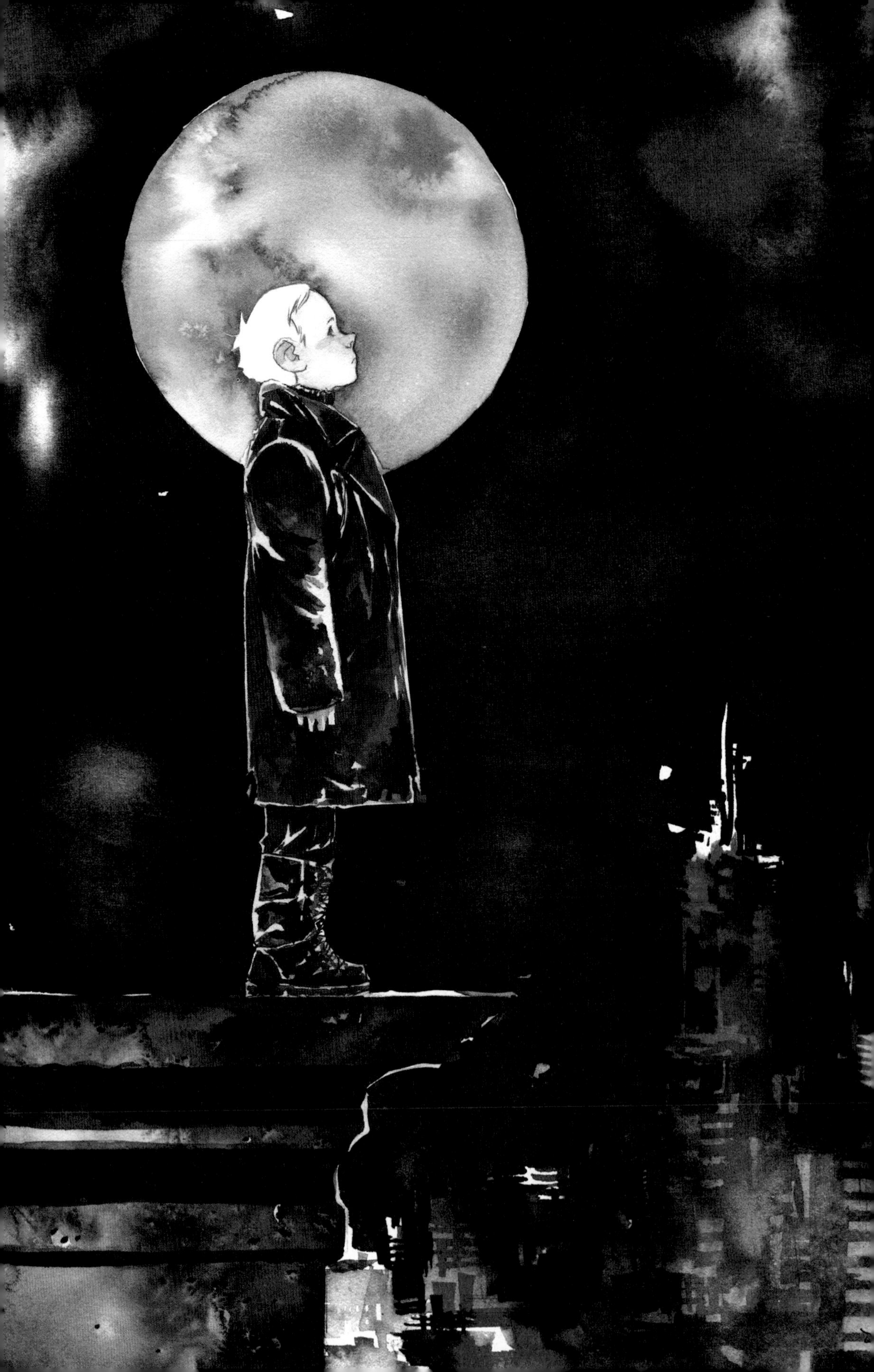

THIS IS THE
NIGHT...

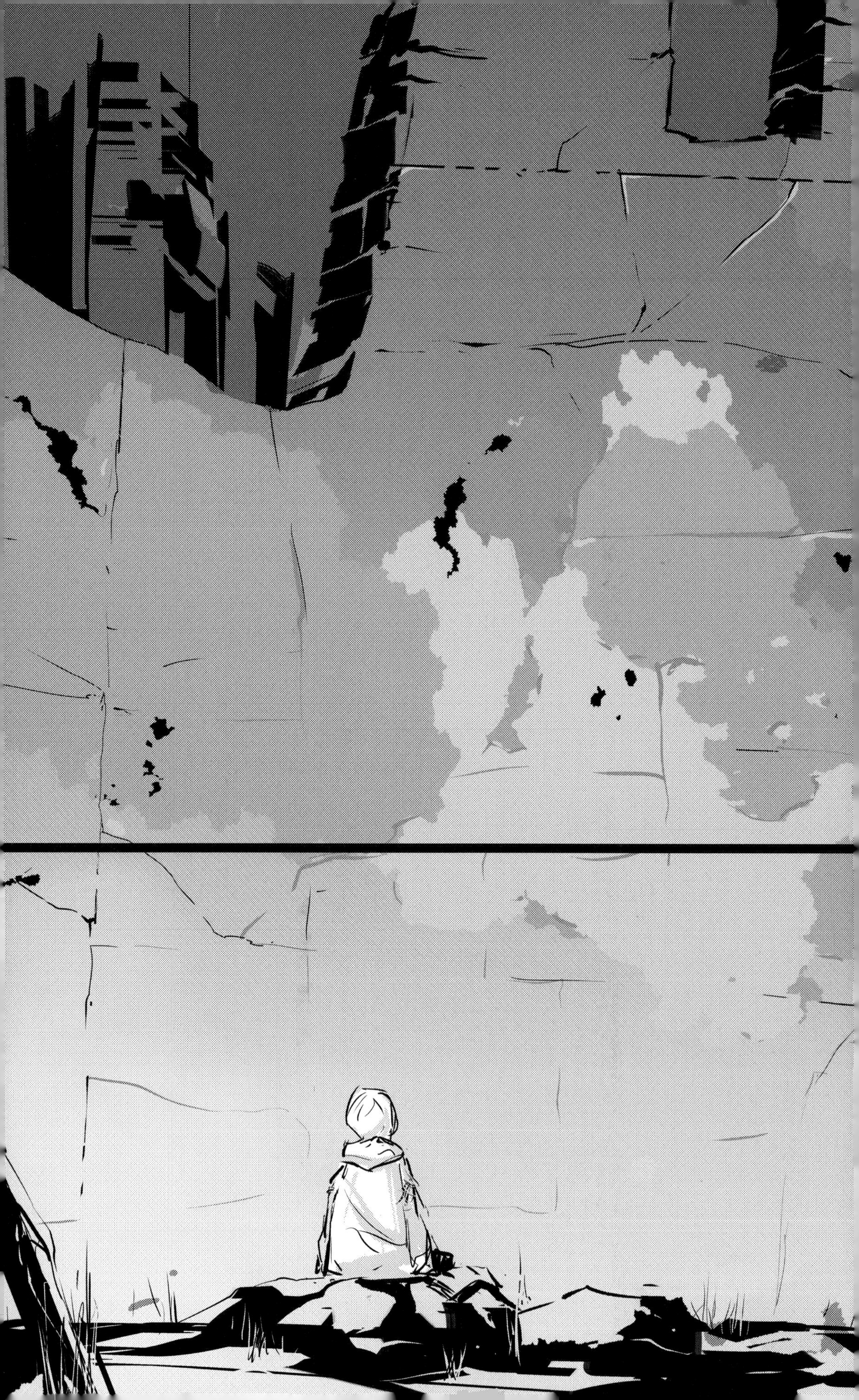

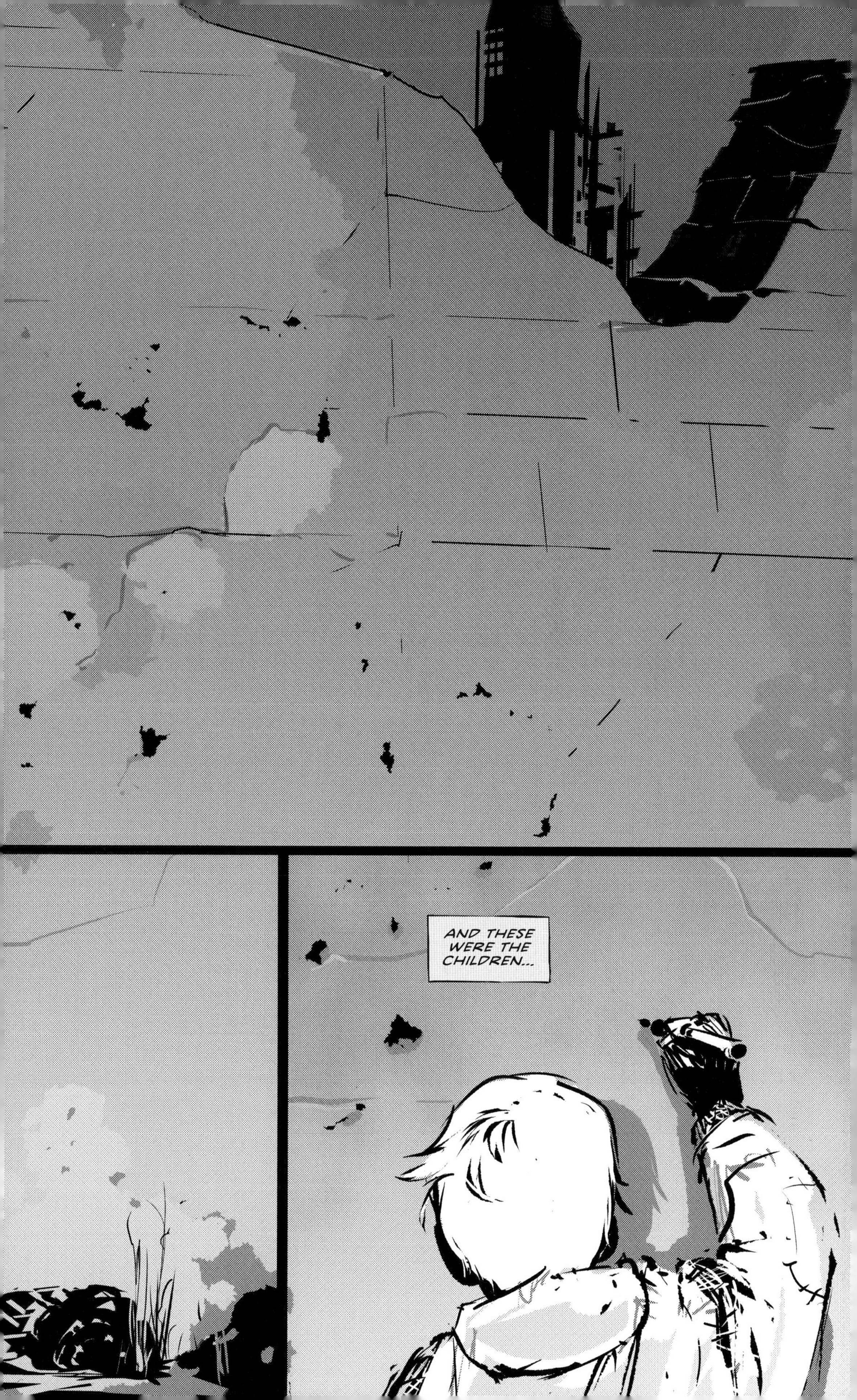
AND THESE WERE THE CHILDREN...

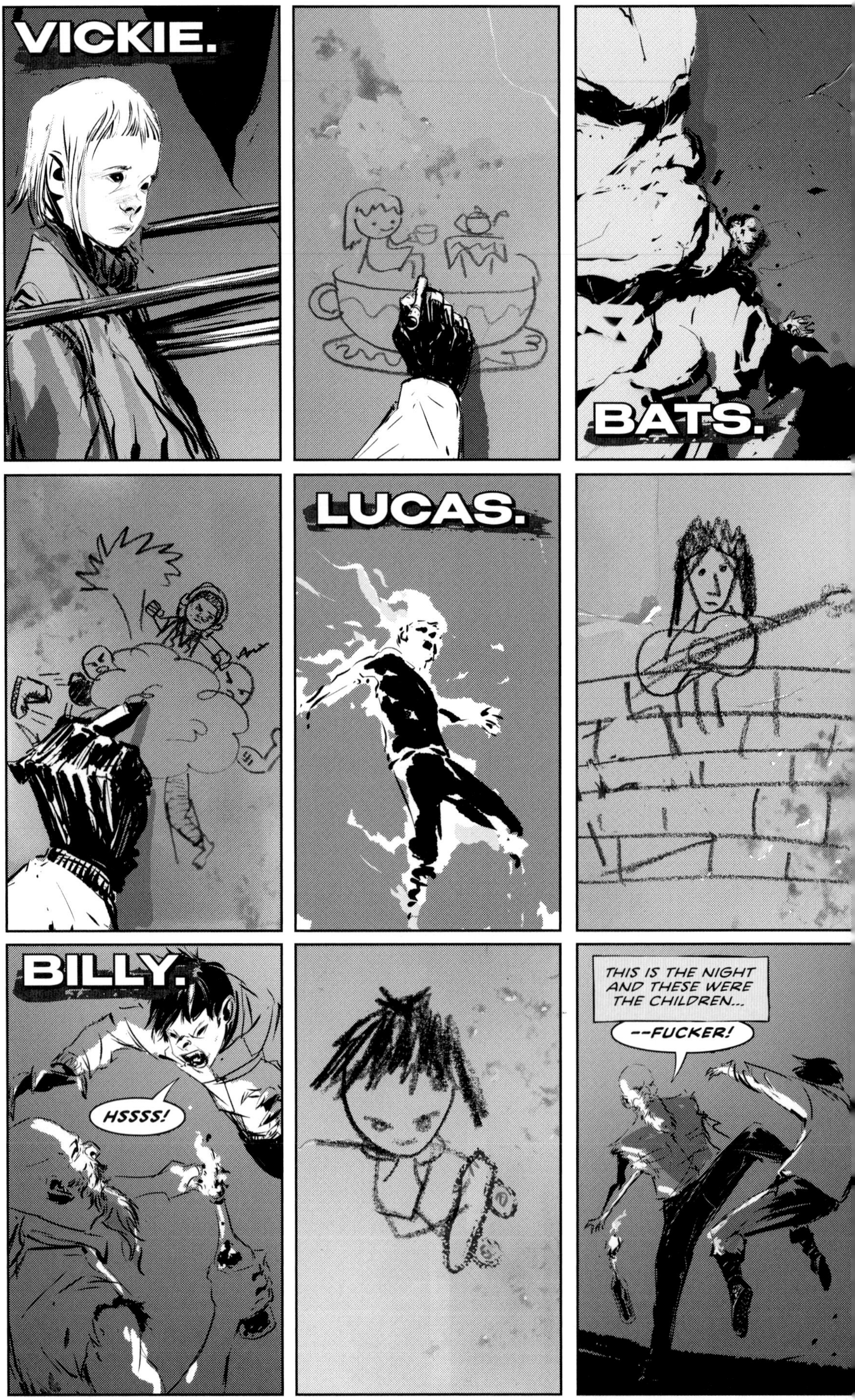
VICKIE.
BATS.
LUCAS.
BILLY.
HSSSS!
THIS IS THE NIGHT AND THESE WERE THE CHILDREN...
--FUCKER!

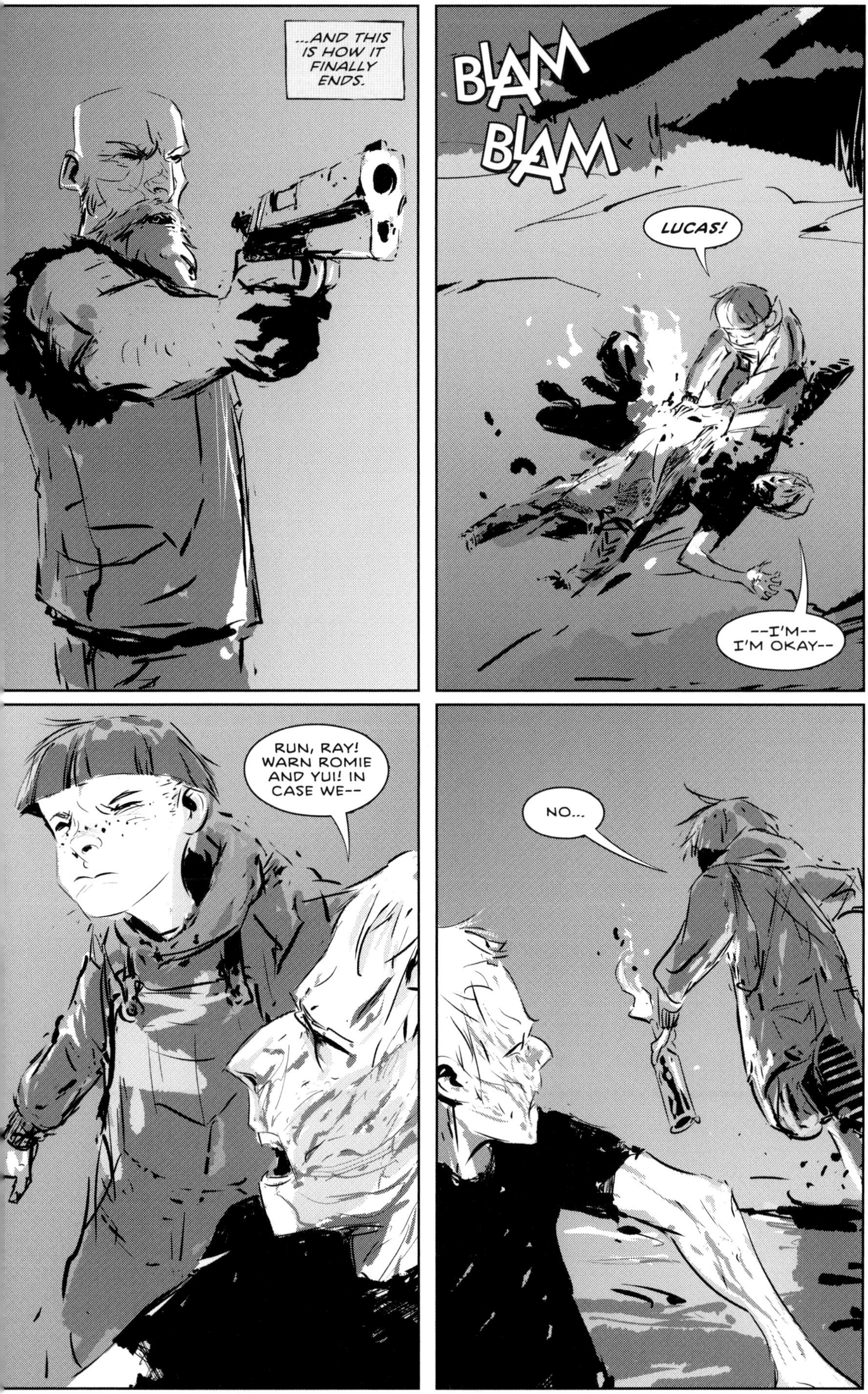
...AND THIS IS HOW IT FINALLY ENDS.
BLAM
BLAM
LUCAS!
--I'M-- I'M OKAY--
RUN, RAY! WARN ROMIE AND YUI! IN CASE WE--
NO...

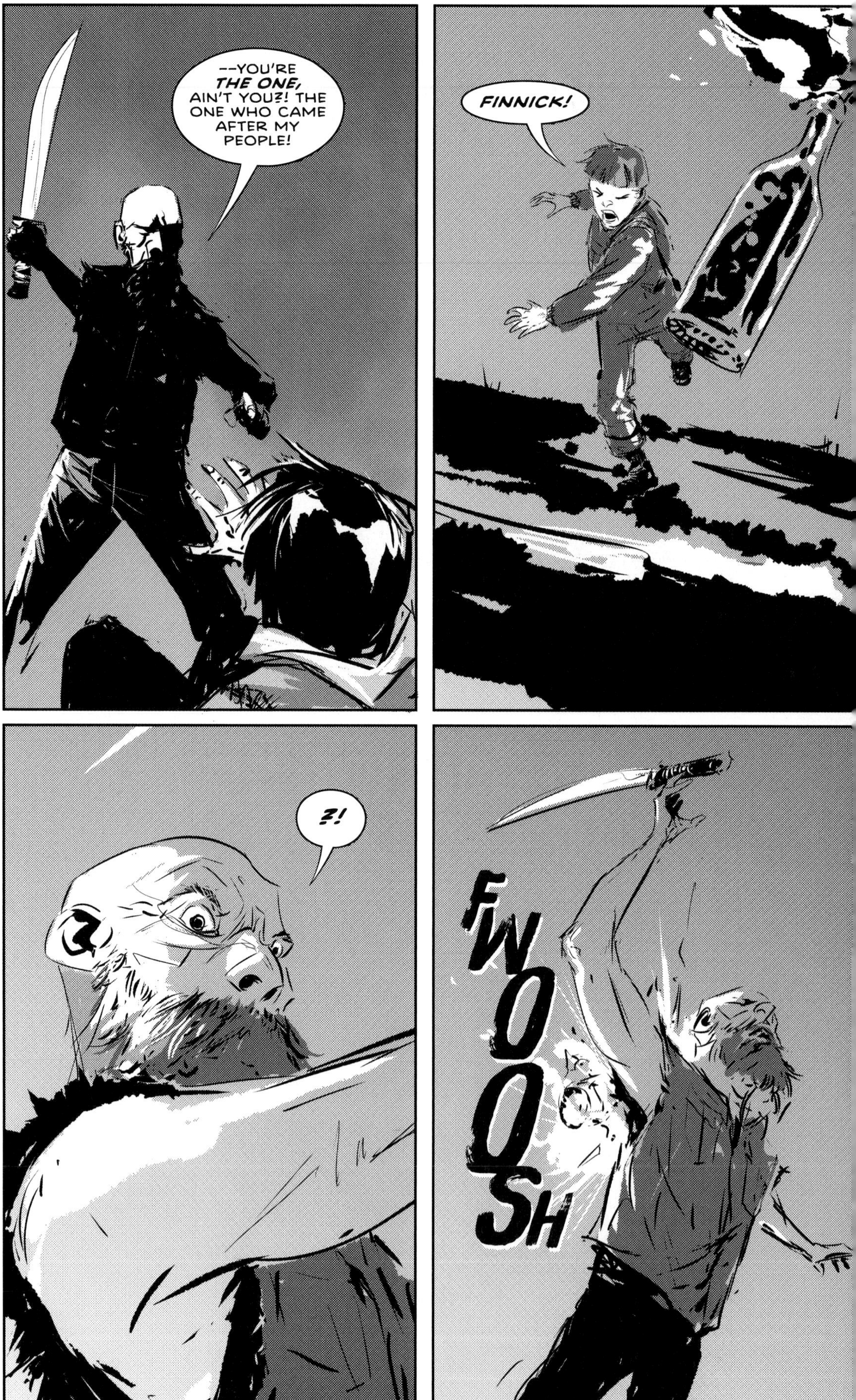

--YOU'RE THE ONE, AIN'T YOU?! THE ONE WHO CAME AFTER MY PEOPLE!
FINNICK!
?!
FWOOSH

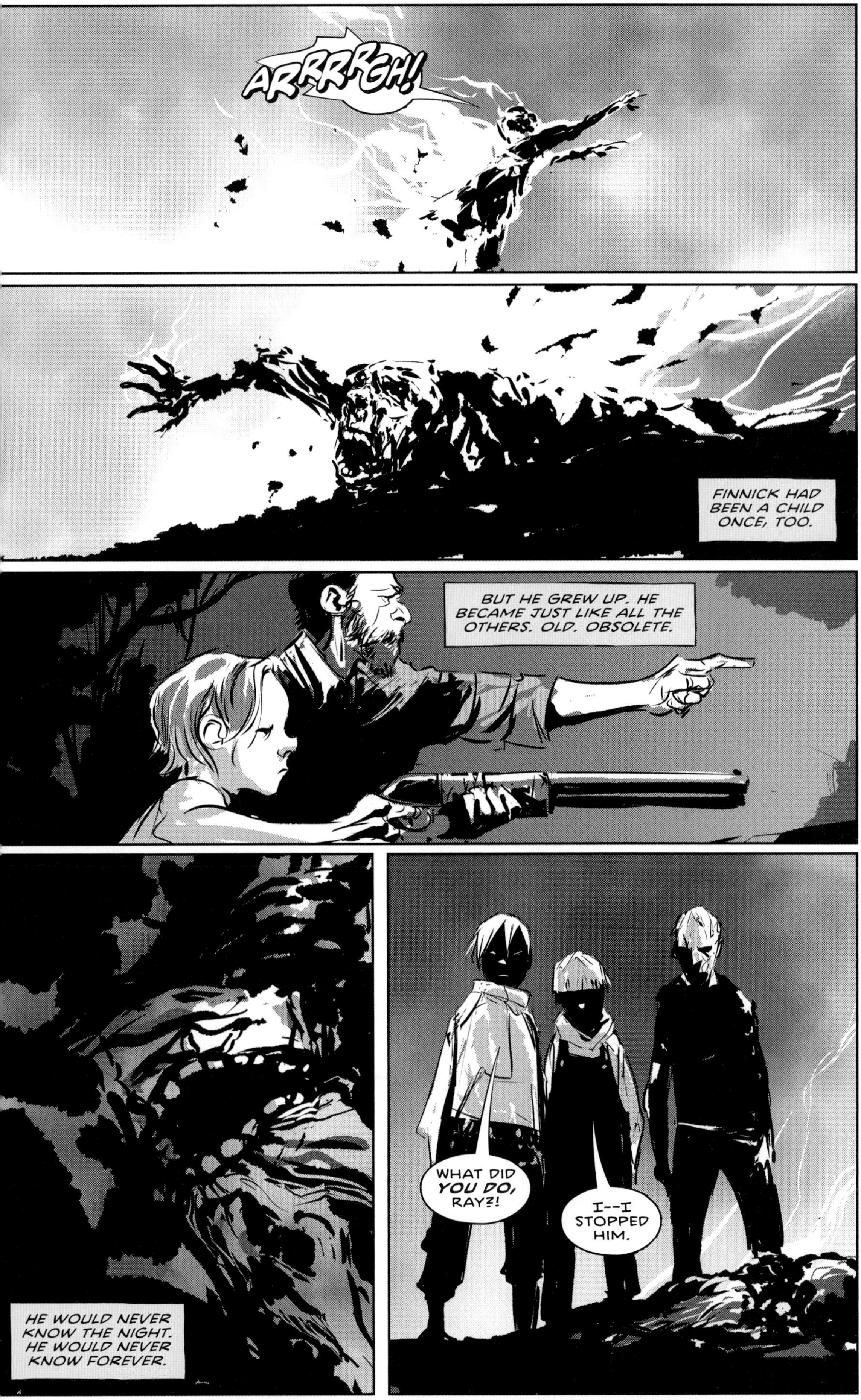
ARRRRGH!
FINNICK HAD BEEN A CHILD ONCE, TOO.
BUT HE GREW UP. HE BECAME JUST LIKE ALL THE OTHERS. OLD. OBSOLETE.
HE WOULD NEVER KNOW THE NIGHT. HE WOULD NEVER KNOW FOREVER.
WHAT DID YOU DO, RAY?!
I--I STOPPED HIM.

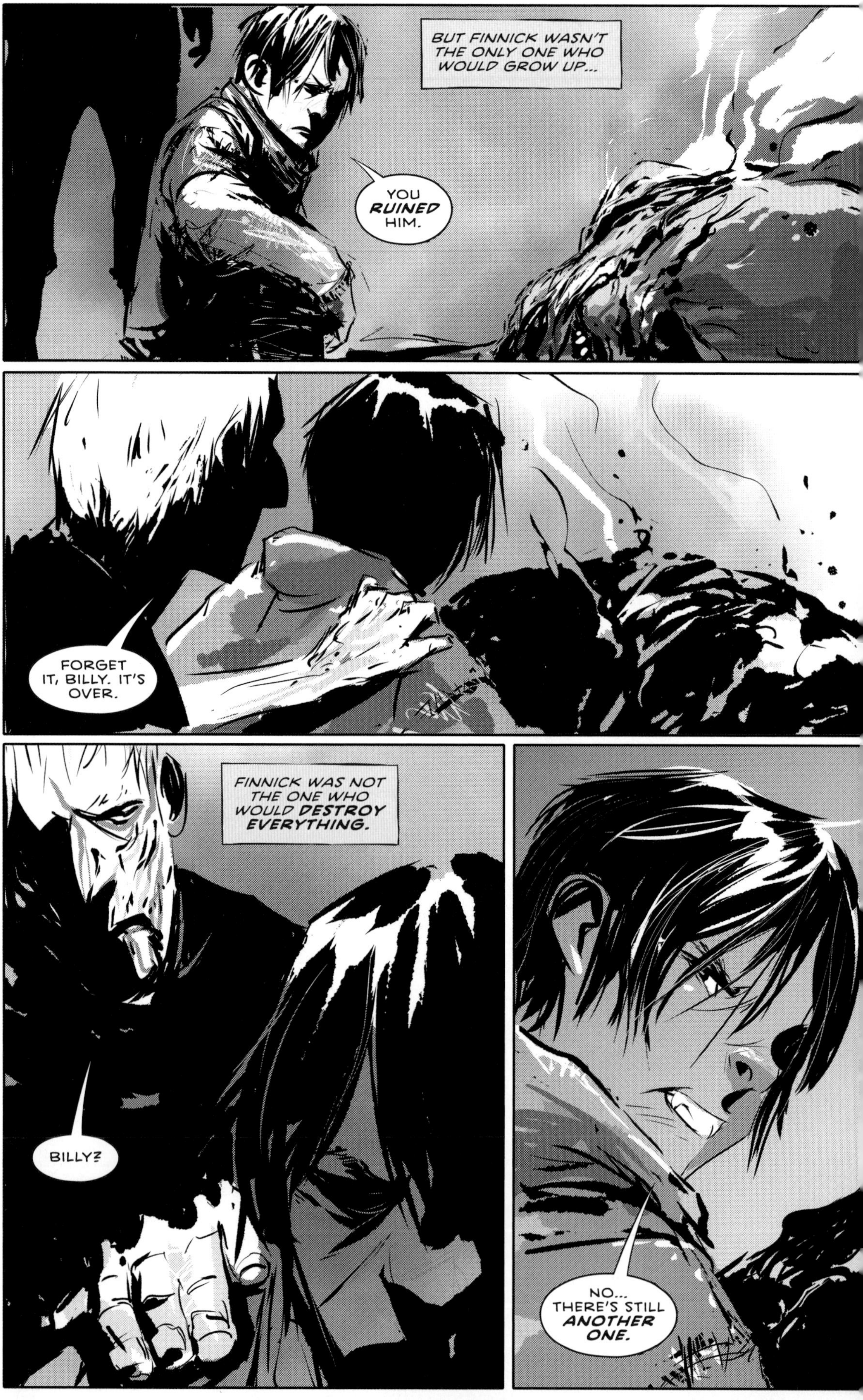
BUT FINNICK WASN'T THE ONLY ONE WHO WOULD GROW UP...
YOU RUINED HIM.
FORGET IT, BILLY. IT'S OVER.
FINNICK WAS NOT THE ONE WHO WOULD DESTROY EVERYTHING.
BILLY?
NO... THERE'S STILL ANOTHER ONE.

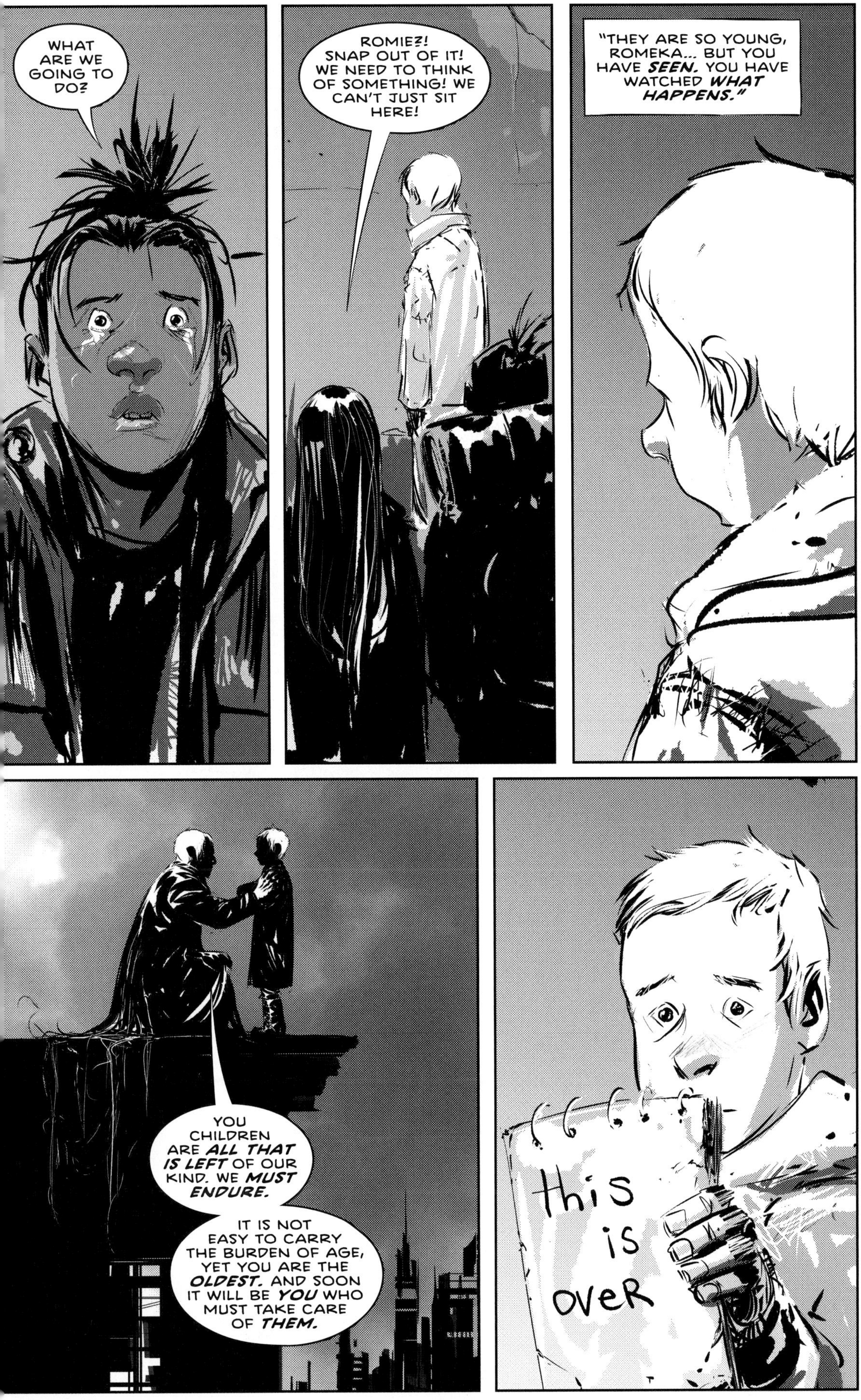
WHAT ARE WE GOING TO DO?
ROMIE?! SNAP OUT OF IT! WE NEED TO THINK OF SOMETHING! WE CAN'T JUST SIT HERE!
"THEY ARE SO YOUNG, ROMEKA... BUT YOU HAVE SEEN. YOU HAVE WATCHED WHAT HAPPENS."
YOU CHILDREN ARE ALL THAT IS LEFT OF OUR KIND. WE MUST ENDURE.
IT IS NOT EASY TO CARRY THE BURDEN OF AGE, YET YOU ARE THE OLDEST. AND SOON IT WILL BE YOU WHO MUST TAKE CARE OF THEM.
this is over

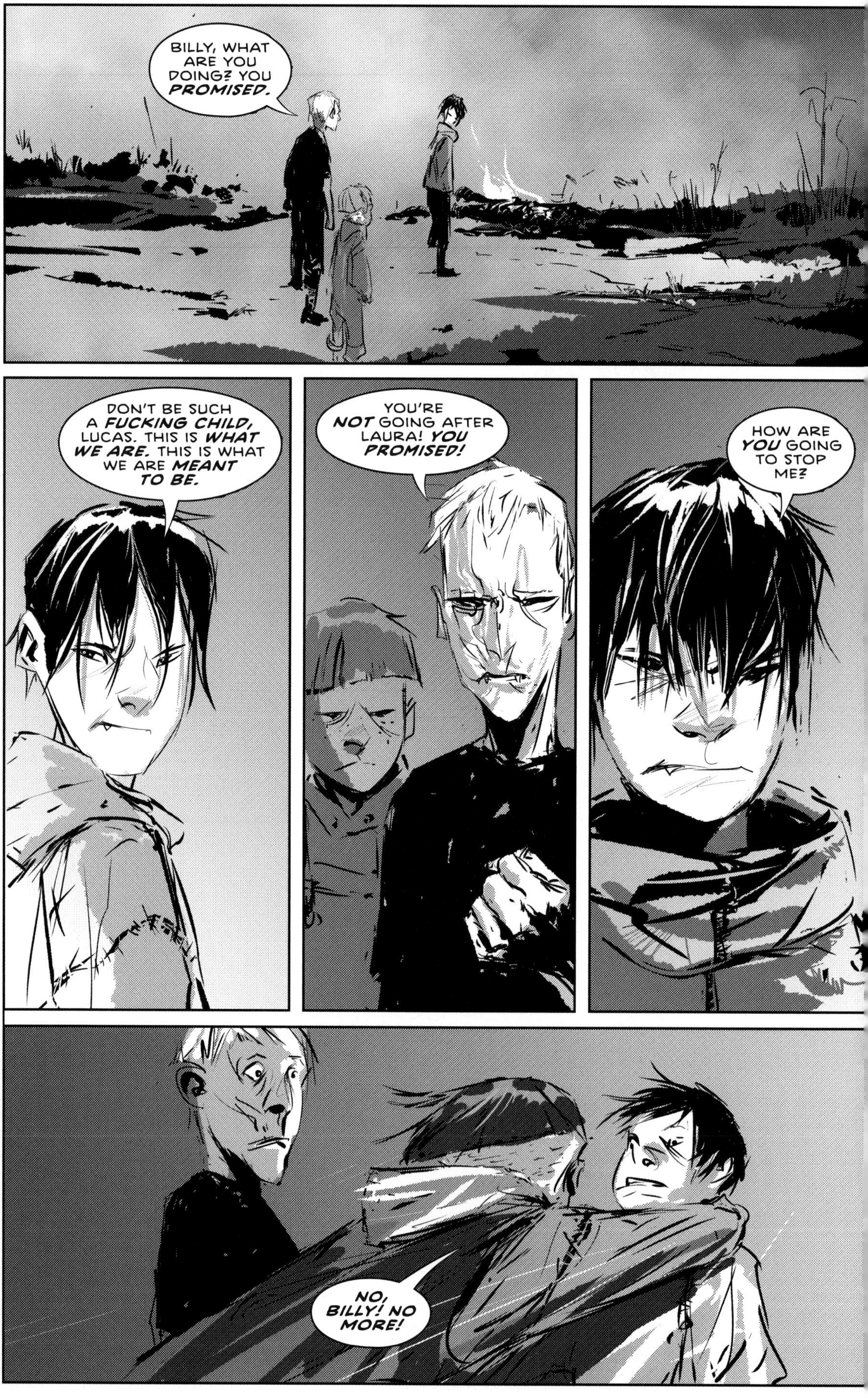
BILLY, WHAT ARE YOU DOING? YOU PROMISED.
DON'T BE SUCH A FUCKING CHILD, LUCAS. THIS IS WHAT WE ARE. THIS IS WHAT WE ARE MEANT TO BE.
YOU'RE NOT GOING AFTER LAURA! YOU PROMISED!
HOW ARE YOU GOING TO STOP ME?
NO, BILLY! NO MORE!

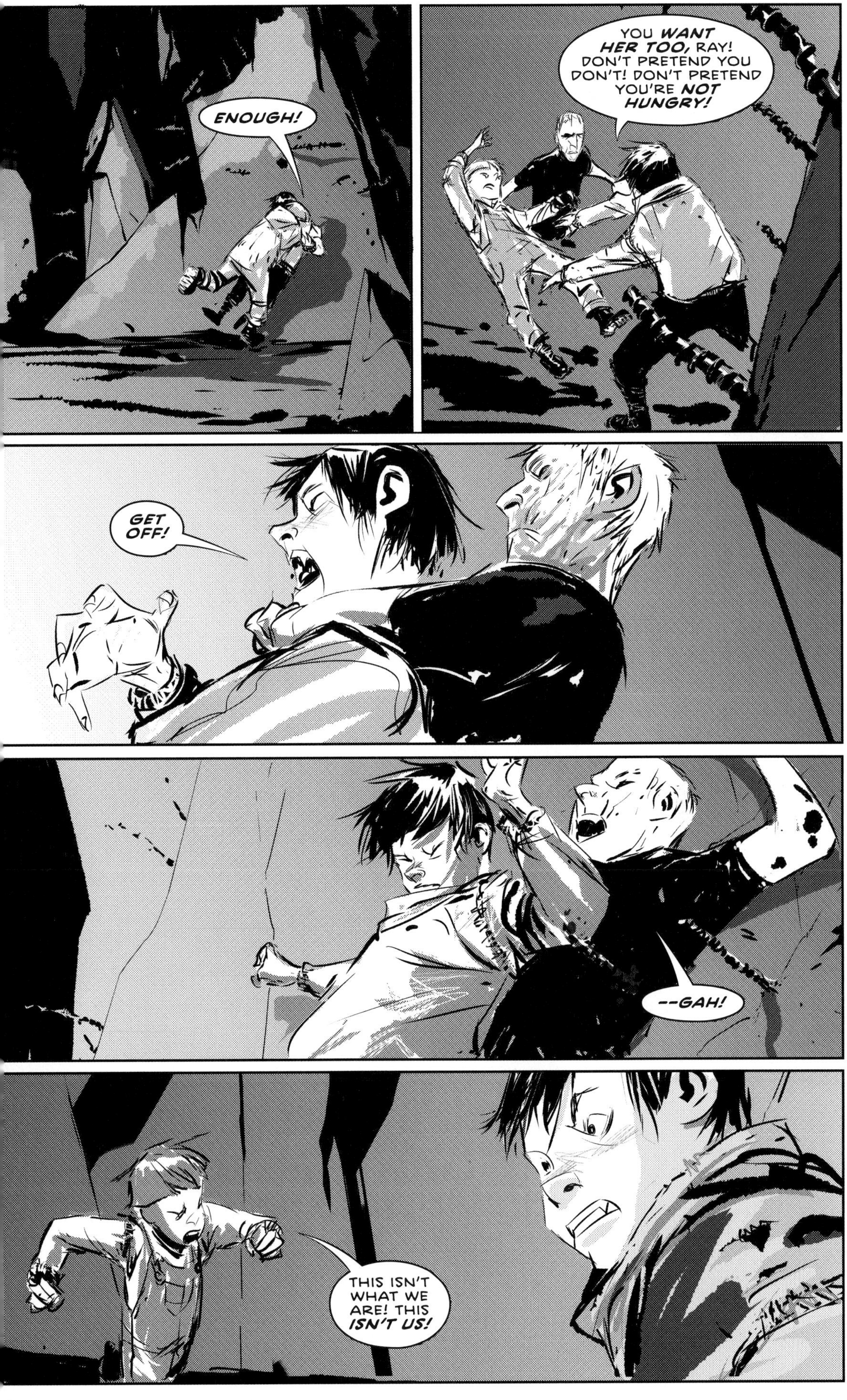
ENOUGH!
YOU WANT HER TOO, RAY! DON'T PRETEND YOU DON'T! DON'T PRETEND YOU'RE NOT HUNGRY!
GET OFF!
--GAH!
THIS ISN'T WHAT WE ARE! THIS ISN'T US!

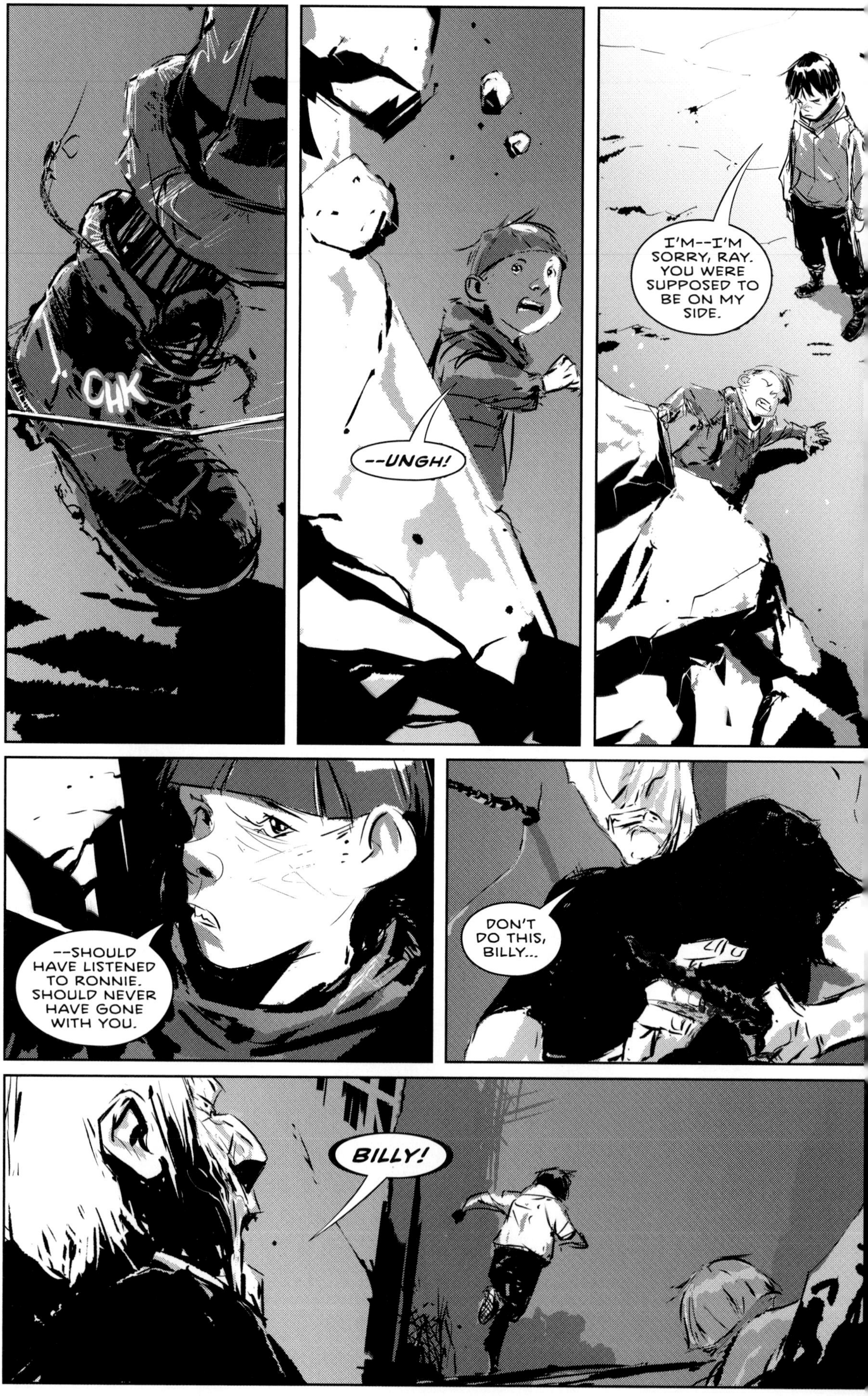
CHK
--UNGH!
I'M--I'M SORRY, RAY. YOU WERE SUPPOSED TO BE ON MY SIDE.
--SHOULD HAVE LISTENED TO RONNIE. SHOULD NEVER HAVE GONE WITH YOU.
DON'T DO THIS, BILLY...
BILLY!

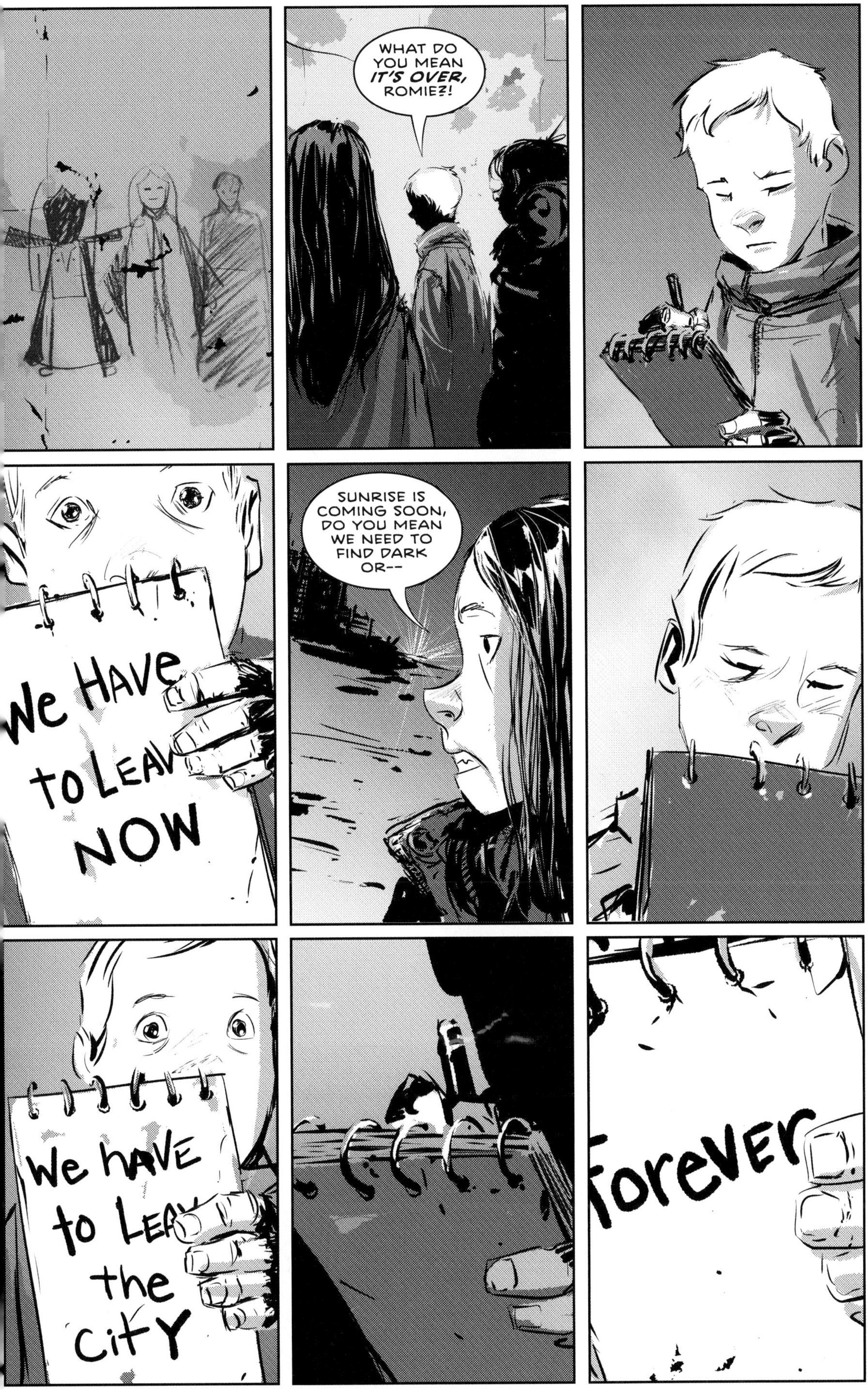
WHAT DO YOU MEAN *IT'S OVER,* ROMIE?!
We HAVE to LEAV
NOW
SUNRISE IS COMING SOON, DO YOU MEAN WE NEED TO FIND DARK OR--
We hAVE to LEA
the city
Forever

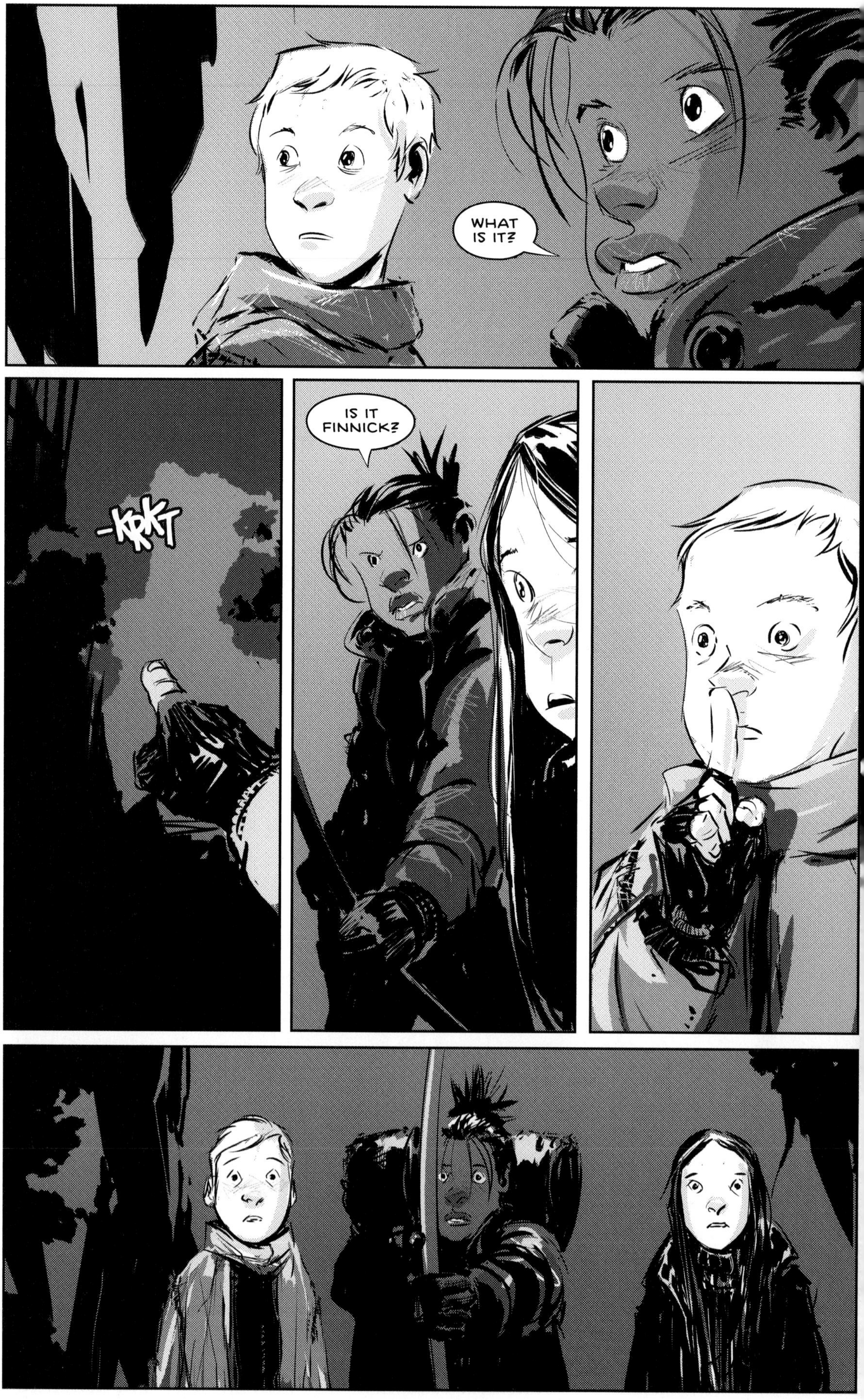
WHAT IS IT?
-KRKT
IS IT FINNICK?

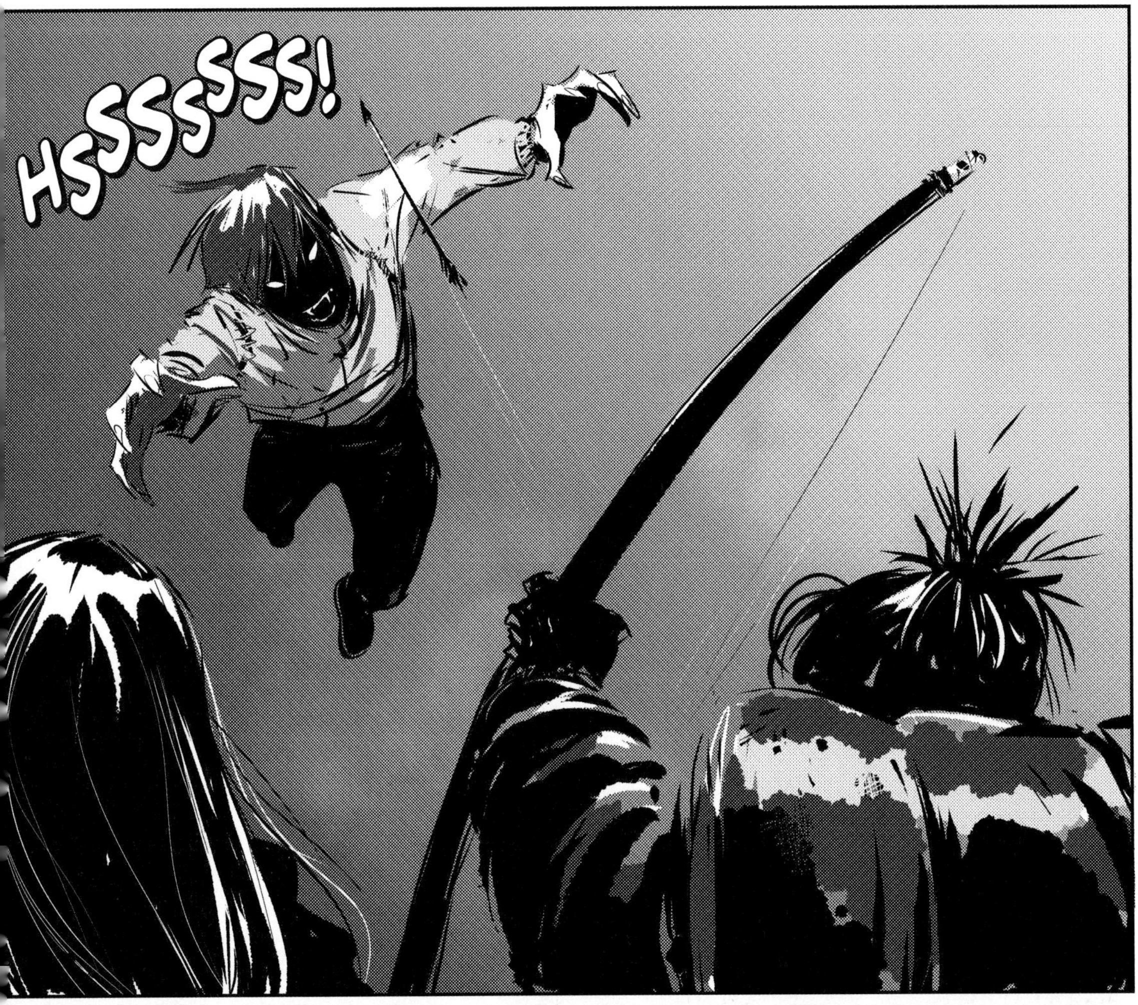
HSSSSSSS!

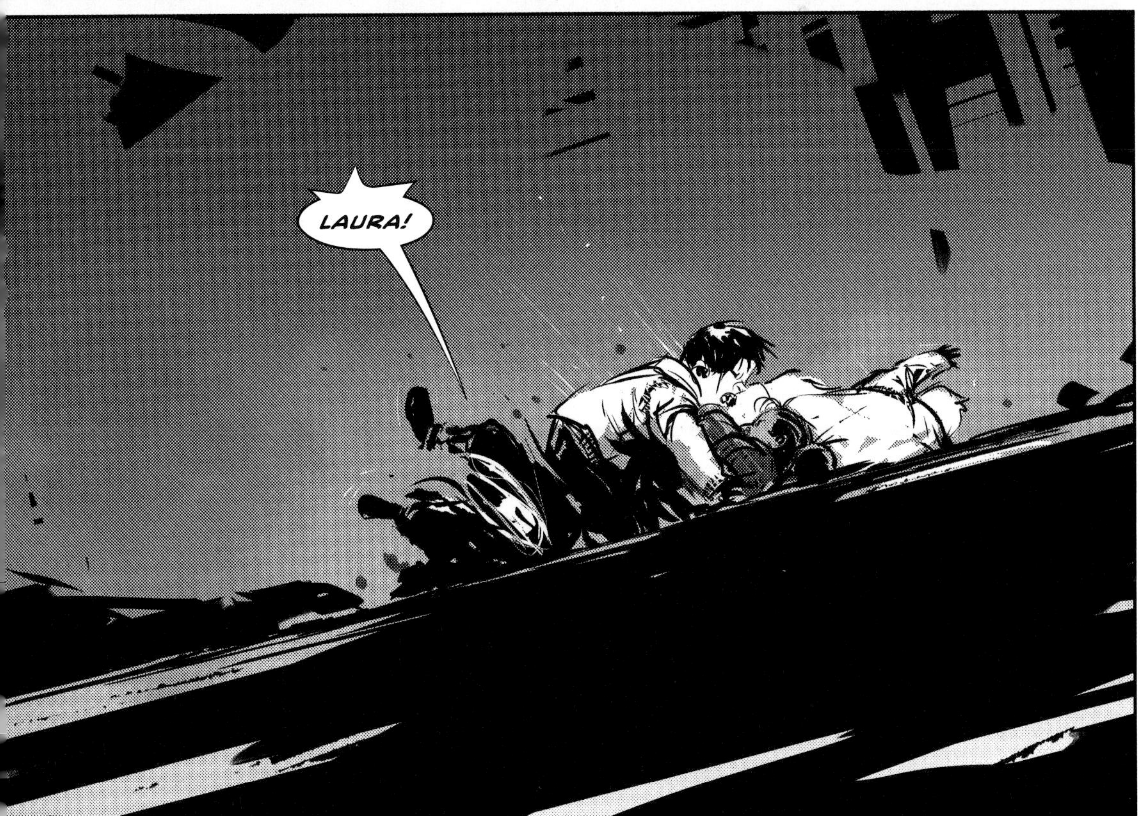
LAURA!

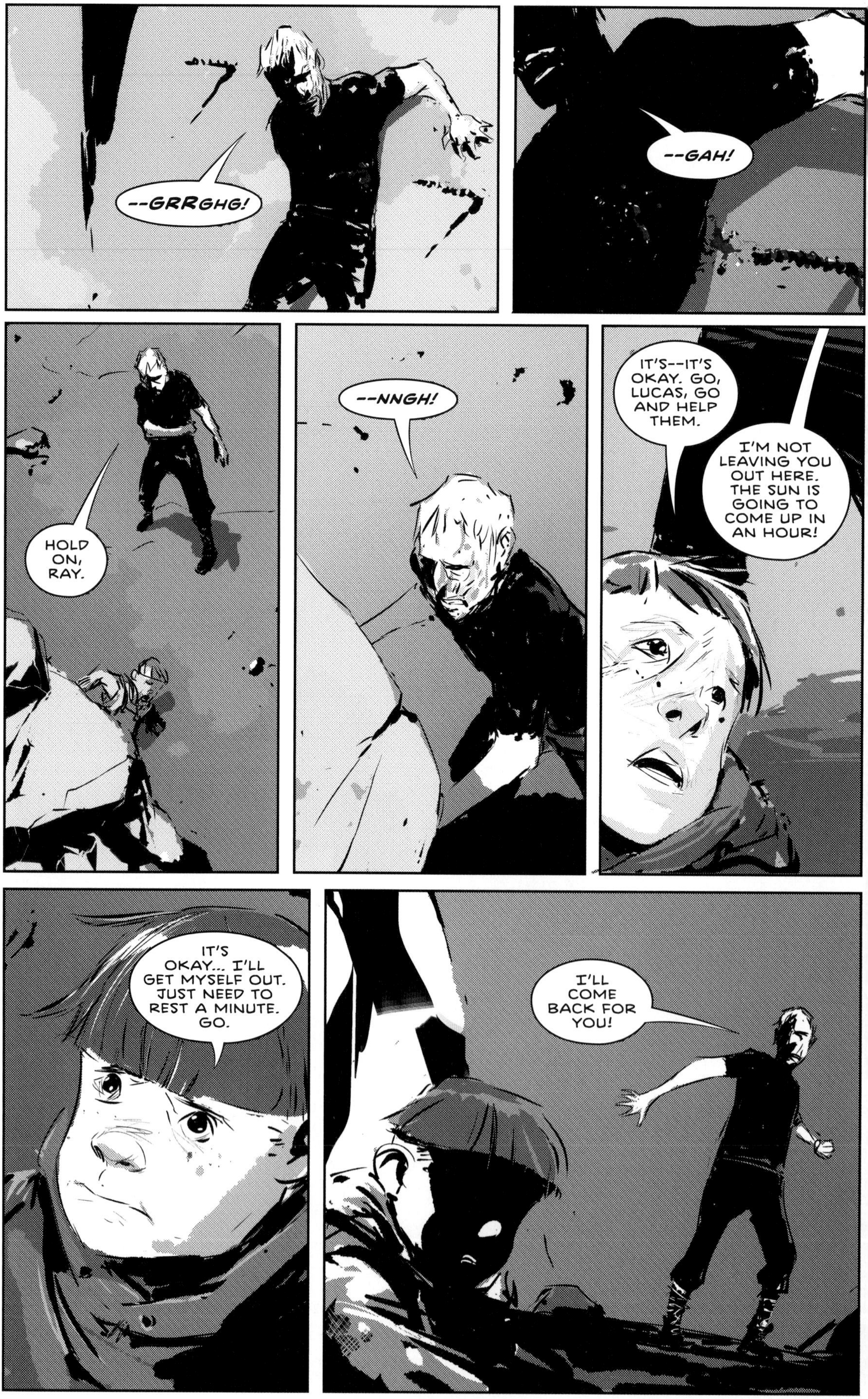
--GRRGHG!
--GAH!
HOLD ON, RAY.
--NNGH!
IT'S--IT'S OKAY. GO, LUCAS, GO AND HELP THEM.
I'M NOT LEAVING YOU OUT HERE. THE SUN IS GOING TO COME UP IN AN HOUR!
IT'S OKAY... I'LL GET MYSELF OUT. JUST NEED TO REST A MINUTE. GO.
I'LL COME BACK FOR YOU!

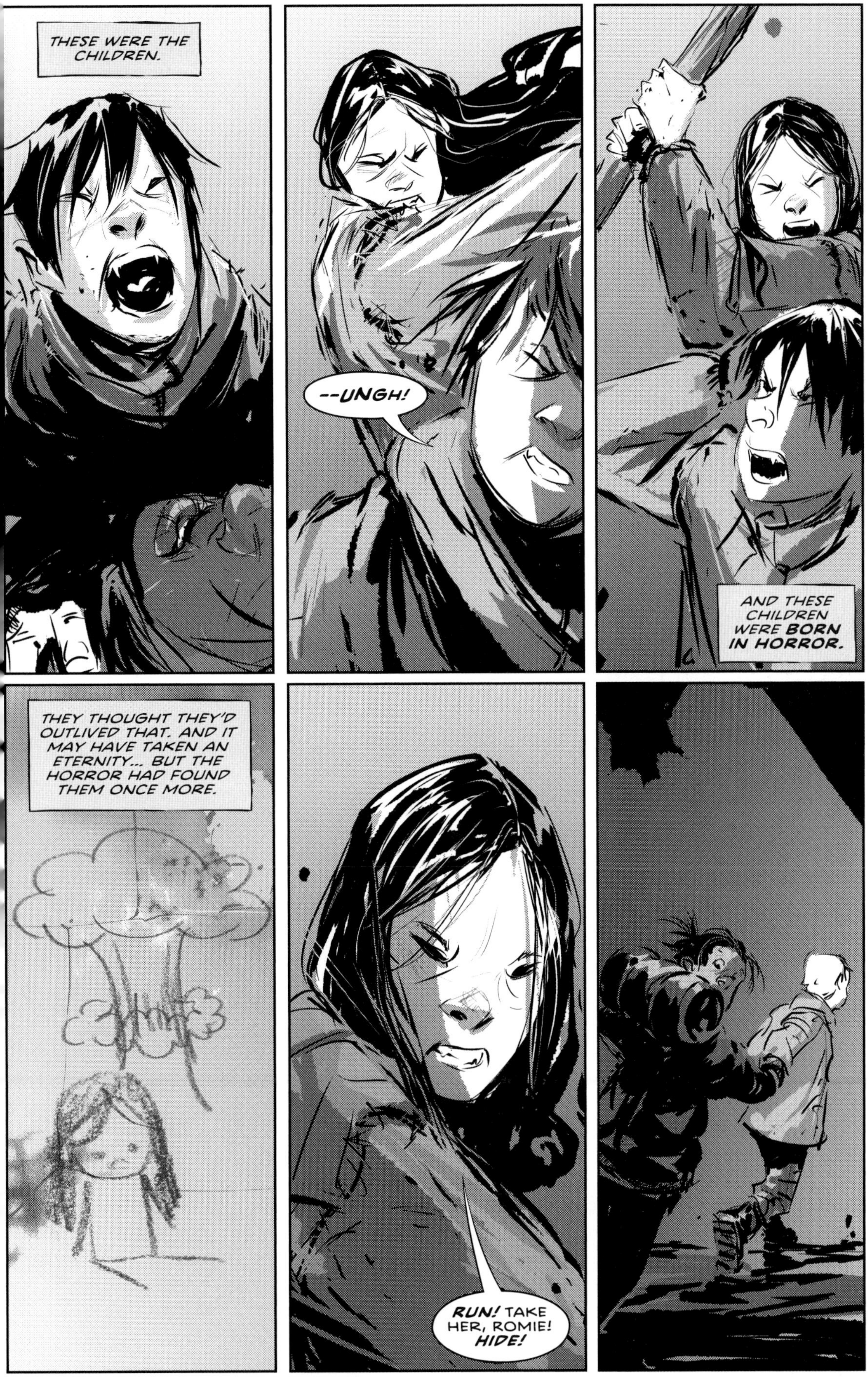
THESE WERE THE CHILDREN.
--UNGH!
AND THESE CHILDREN WERE BORN IN HORROR.
THEY THOUGHT THEY'D OUTLIVED THAT. AND IT MAY HAVE TAKEN AN ETERNITY... BUT THE HORROR HAD FOUND THEM ONCE MORE.
RUN! TAKE HER, ROMIE! HIDE!

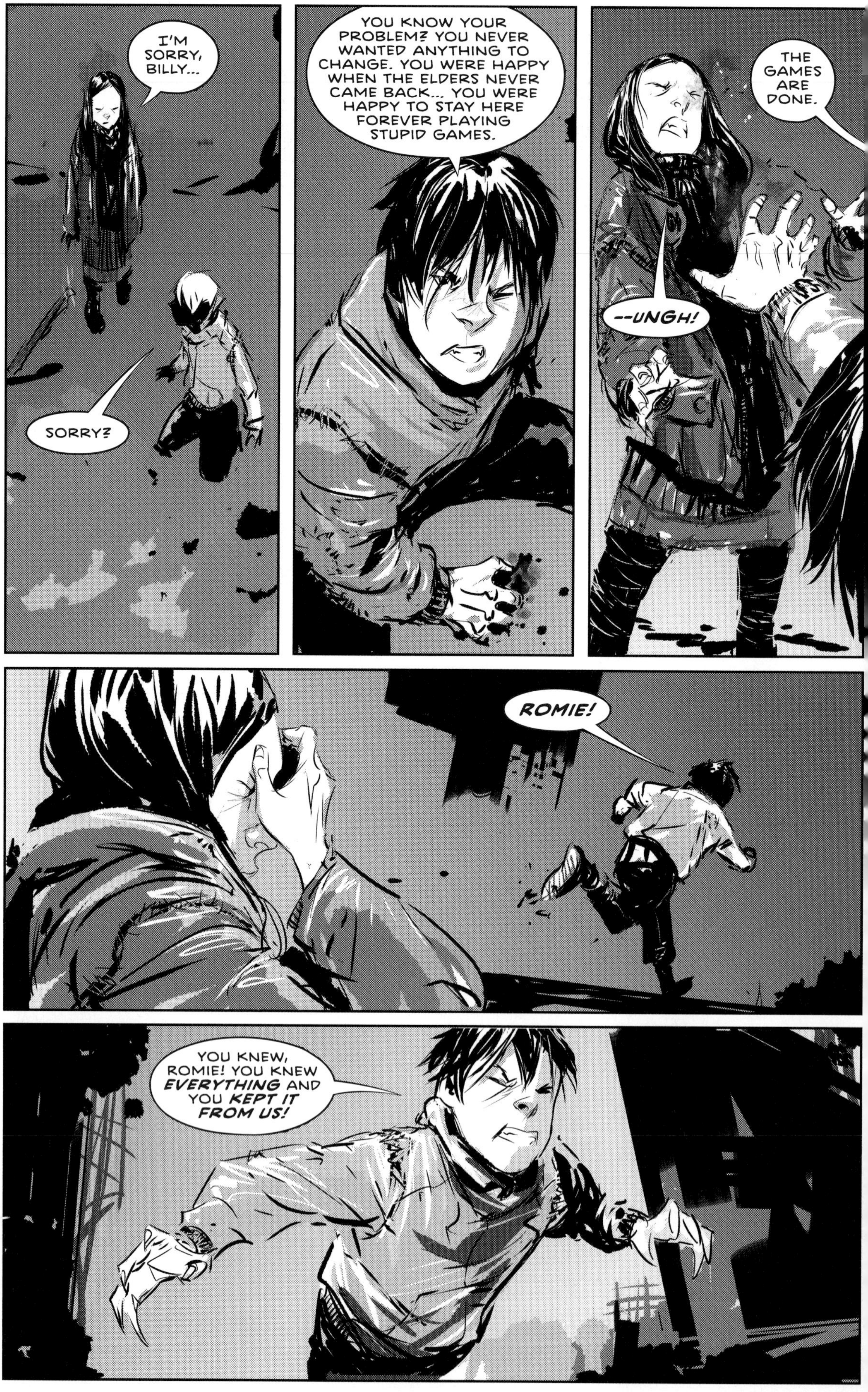
I'M SORRY, BILLY...
SORRY?
YOU KNOW YOUR PROBLEM? YOU NEVER WANTED ANYTHING TO CHANGE. YOU WERE HAPPY WHEN THE ELDERS NEVER CAME BACK... YOU WERE HAPPY TO STAY HERE FOREVER PLAYING STUPID GAMES.
THE GAMES ARE DONE.
--UNGH!
ROMIE!
YOU KNEW, ROMIE! YOU KNEW *EVERYTHING* AND YOU *KEPT IT FROM US!*

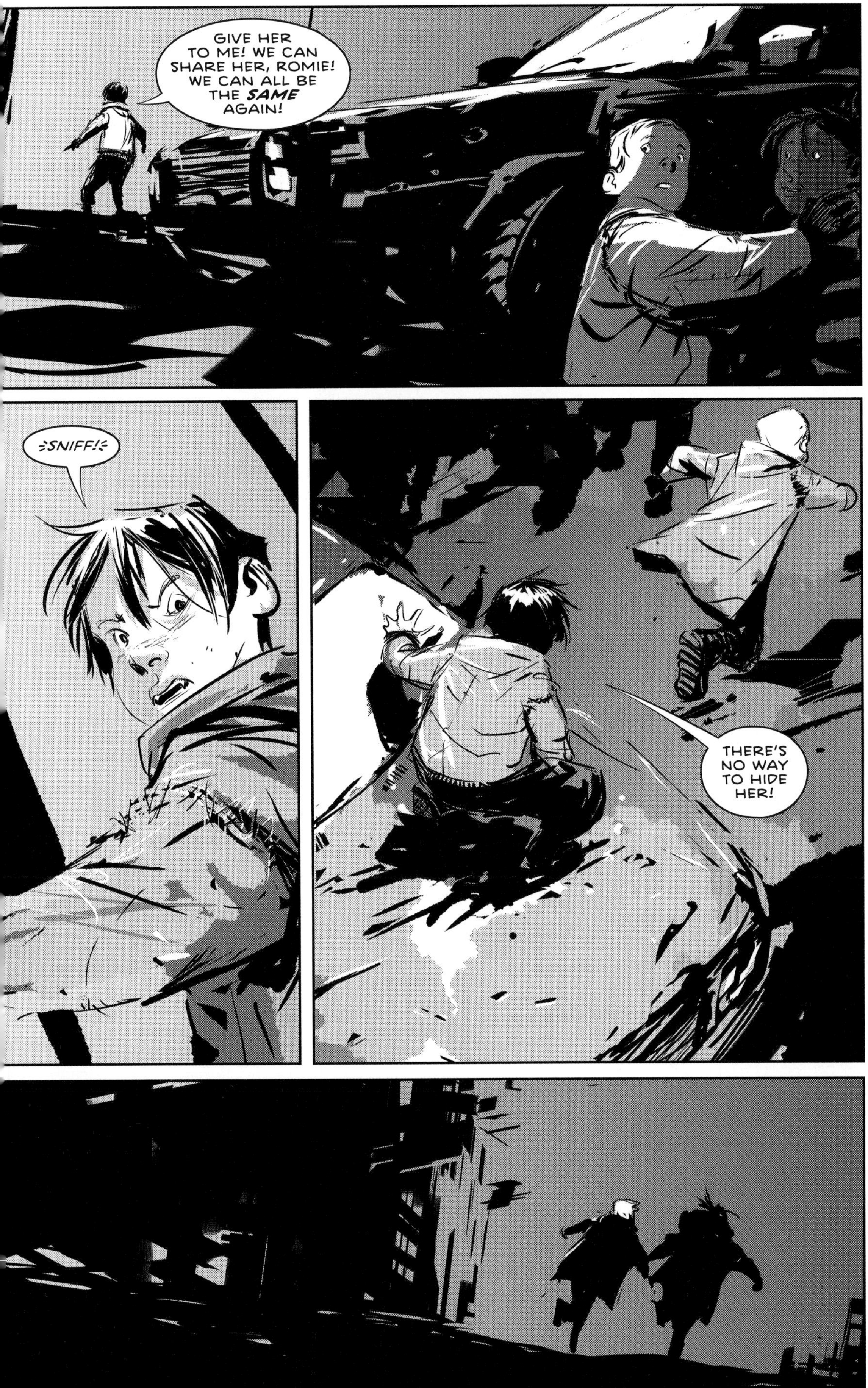
GIVE HER TO ME! WE CAN SHARE HER, ROMIE! WE CAN ALL BE THE SAME AGAIN!
SNIFF!
THERE'S NO WAY TO HIDE HER!

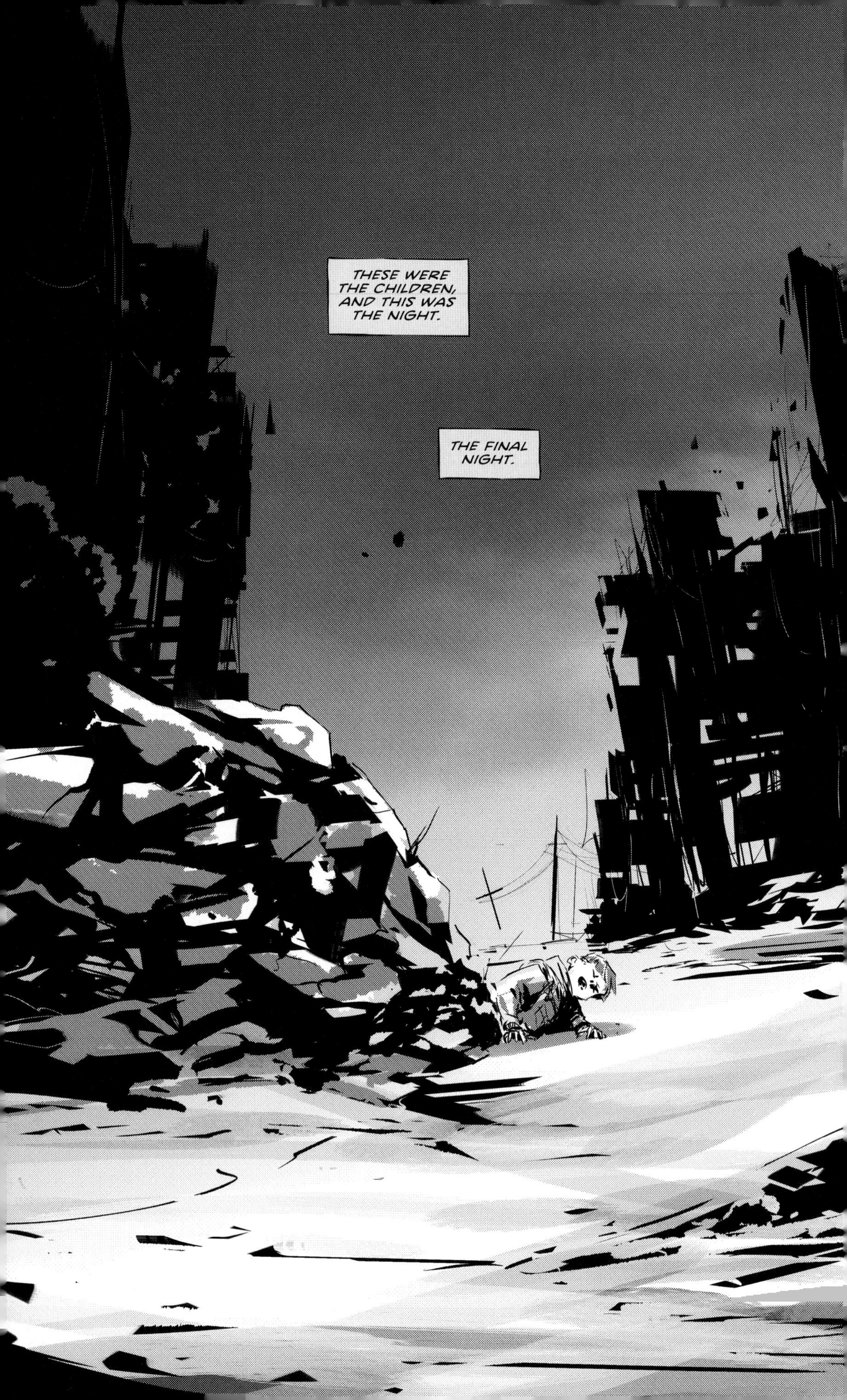
THESE WERE THE CHILDREN, AND THIS WAS THE NIGHT.
THE FINAL NIGHT.

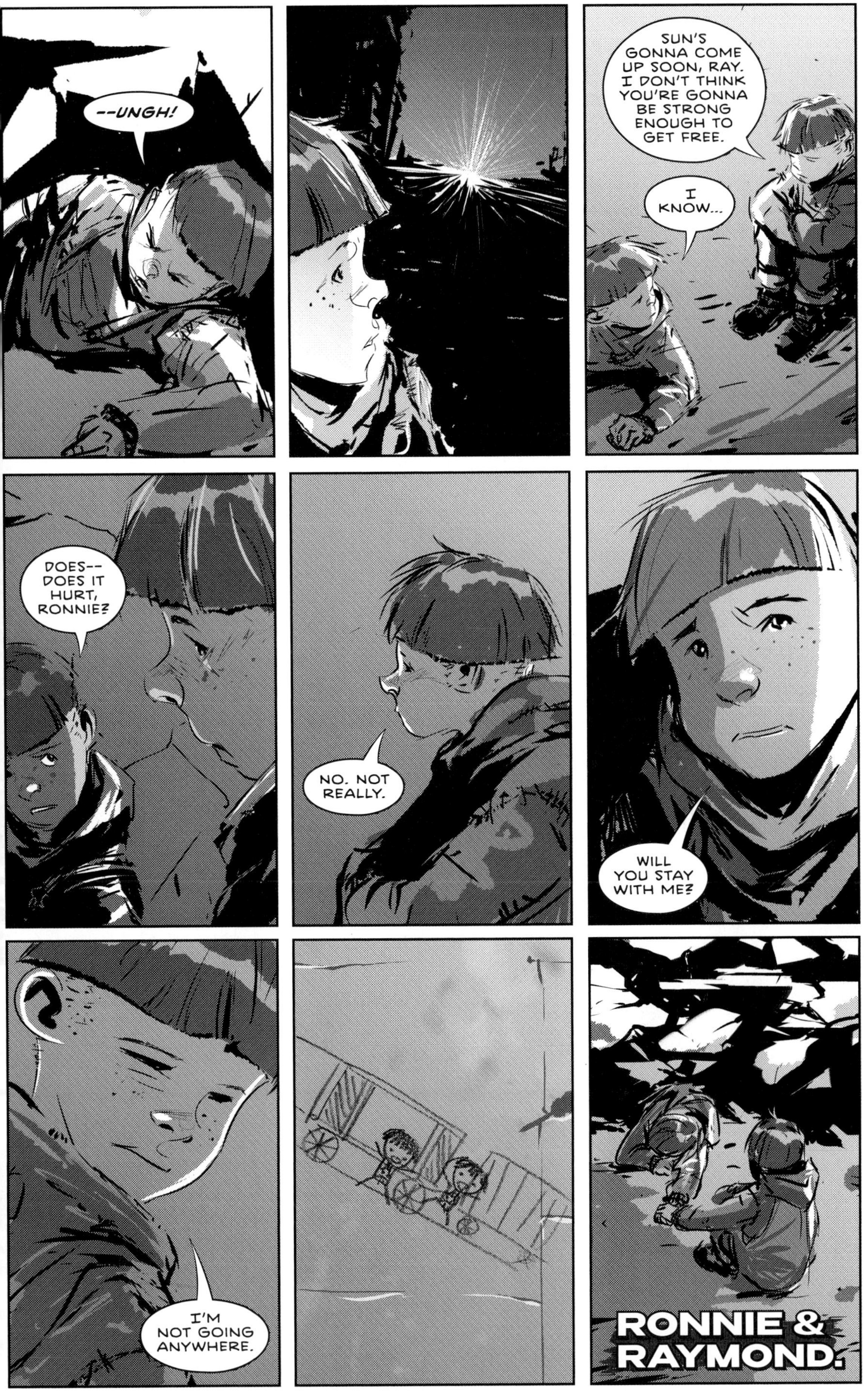
--UNGH!
SUN'S GONNA COME UP SOON, RAY. I DON'T THINK YOU'RE GONNA BE STRONG ENOUGH TO GET FREE.
I KNOW...
DOES-- DOES IT HURT, RONNIE?
NO. NOT REALLY.
WILL YOU STAY WITH ME?
I'M NOT GOING ANYWHERE.
RONNIE & RAYMOND.

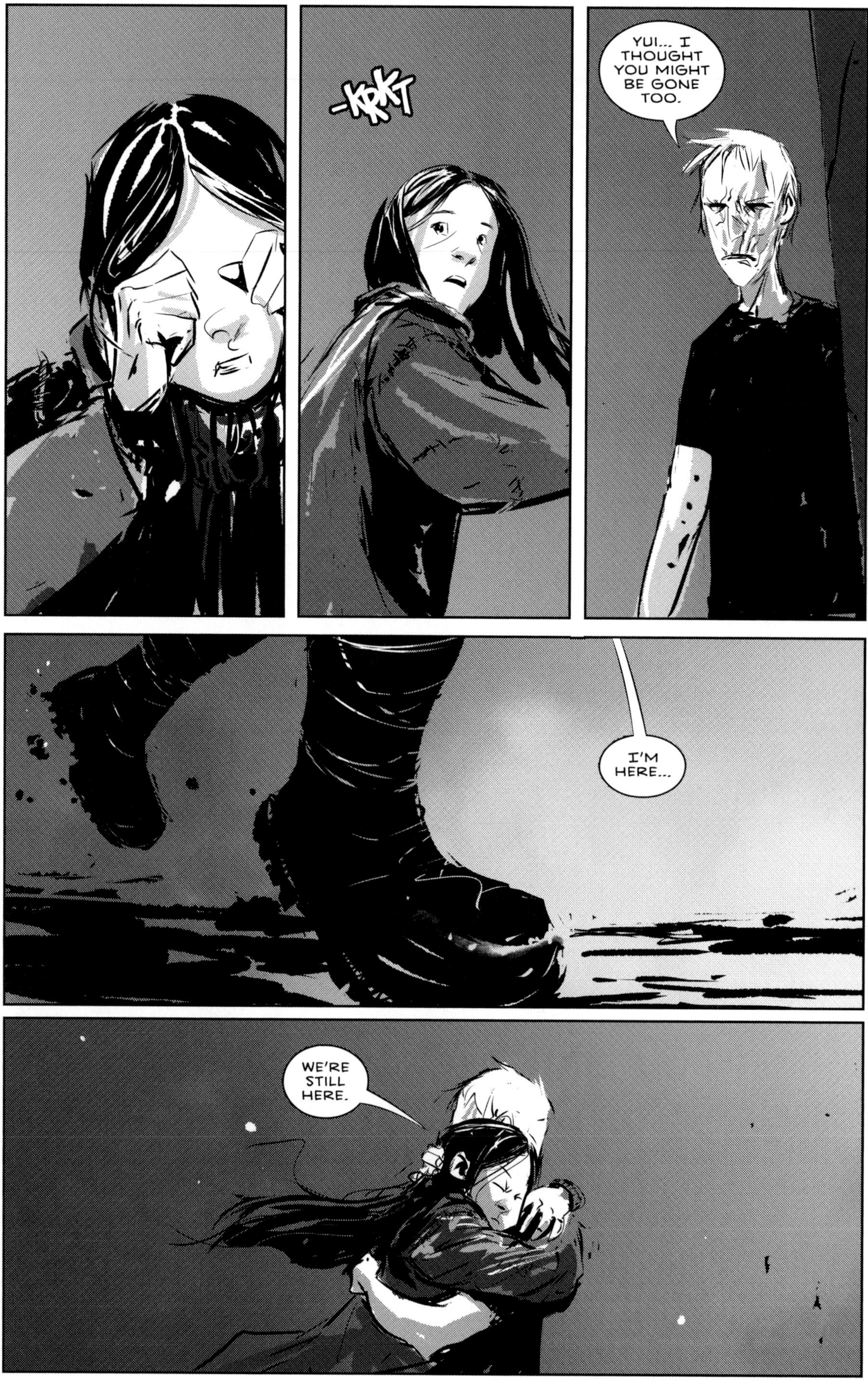
-KRKT
YUI... I THOUGHT YOU MIGHT BE GONE TOO.
I'M HERE...
WE'RE STILL HERE.

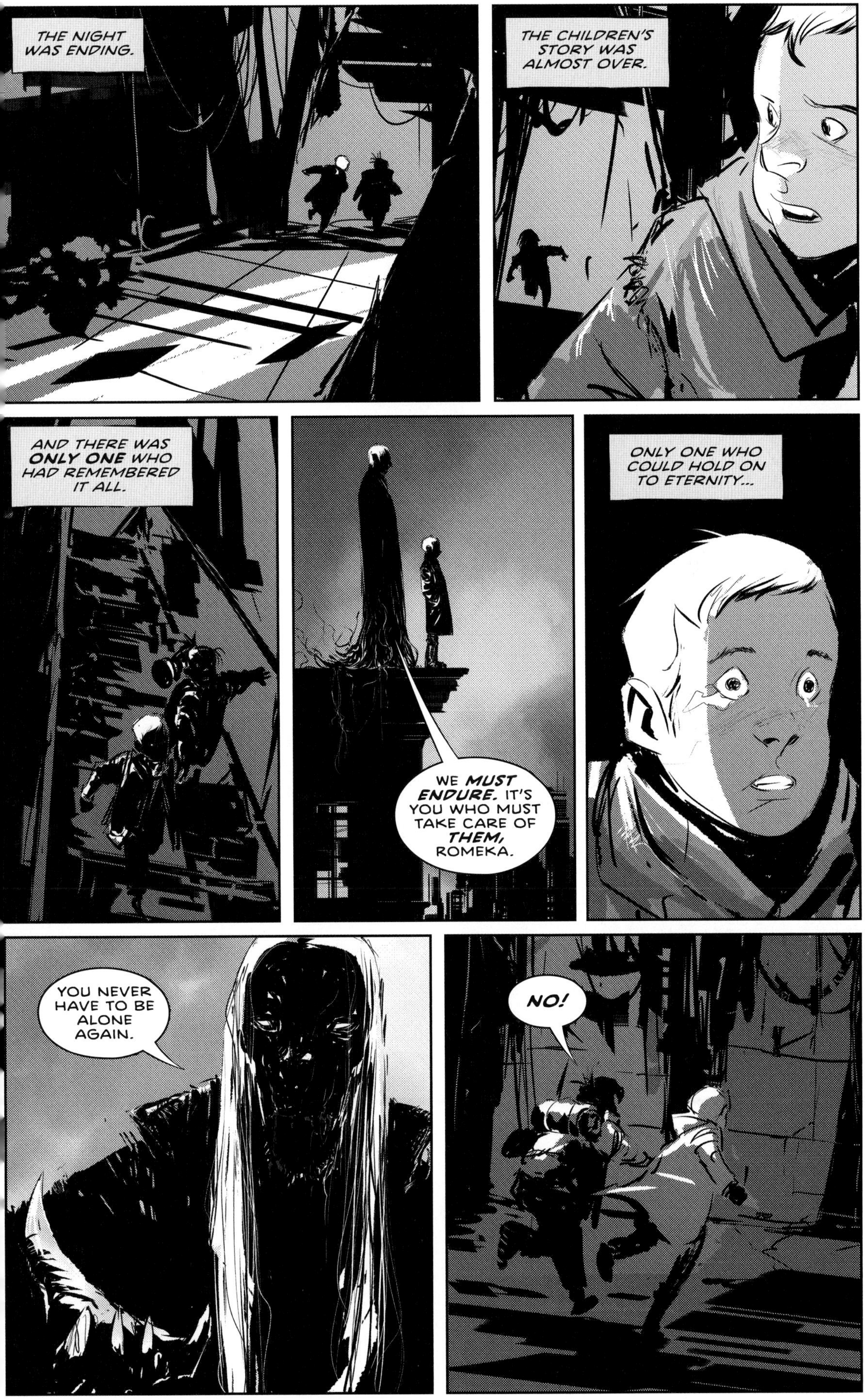
THE NIGHT WAS ENDING.
THE CHILDREN'S STORY WAS ALMOST OVER.
AND THERE WAS ONLY ONE WHO HAD REMEMBERED IT ALL.
WE MUST ENDURE. IT'S YOU WHO MUST TAKE CARE OF THEM, ROMEKA.
ONLY ONE WHO COULD HOLD ON TO ETERNITY...
YOU NEVER HAVE TO BE ALONE AGAIN.
NO!

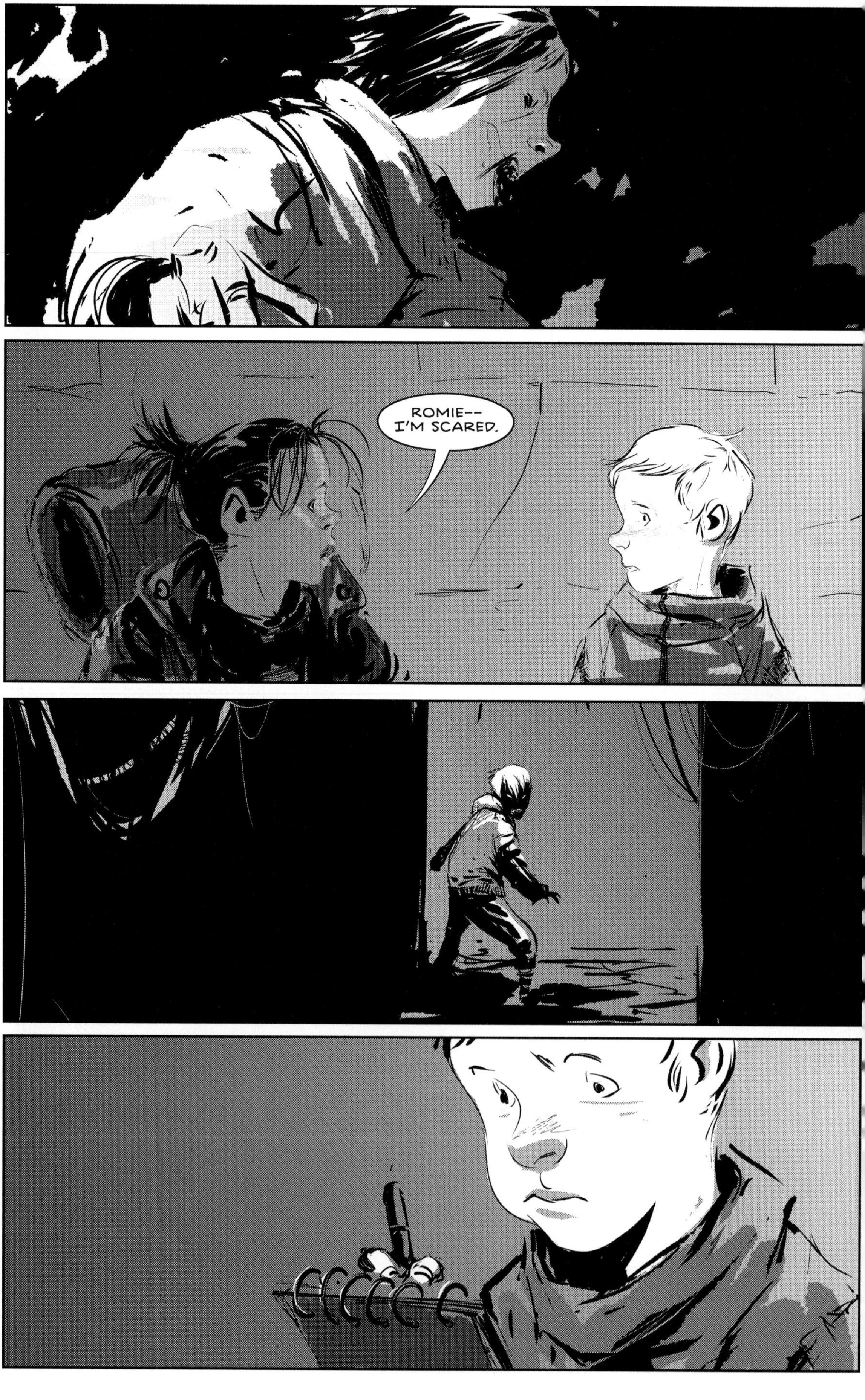
ROMIE--
I'M SCARED.

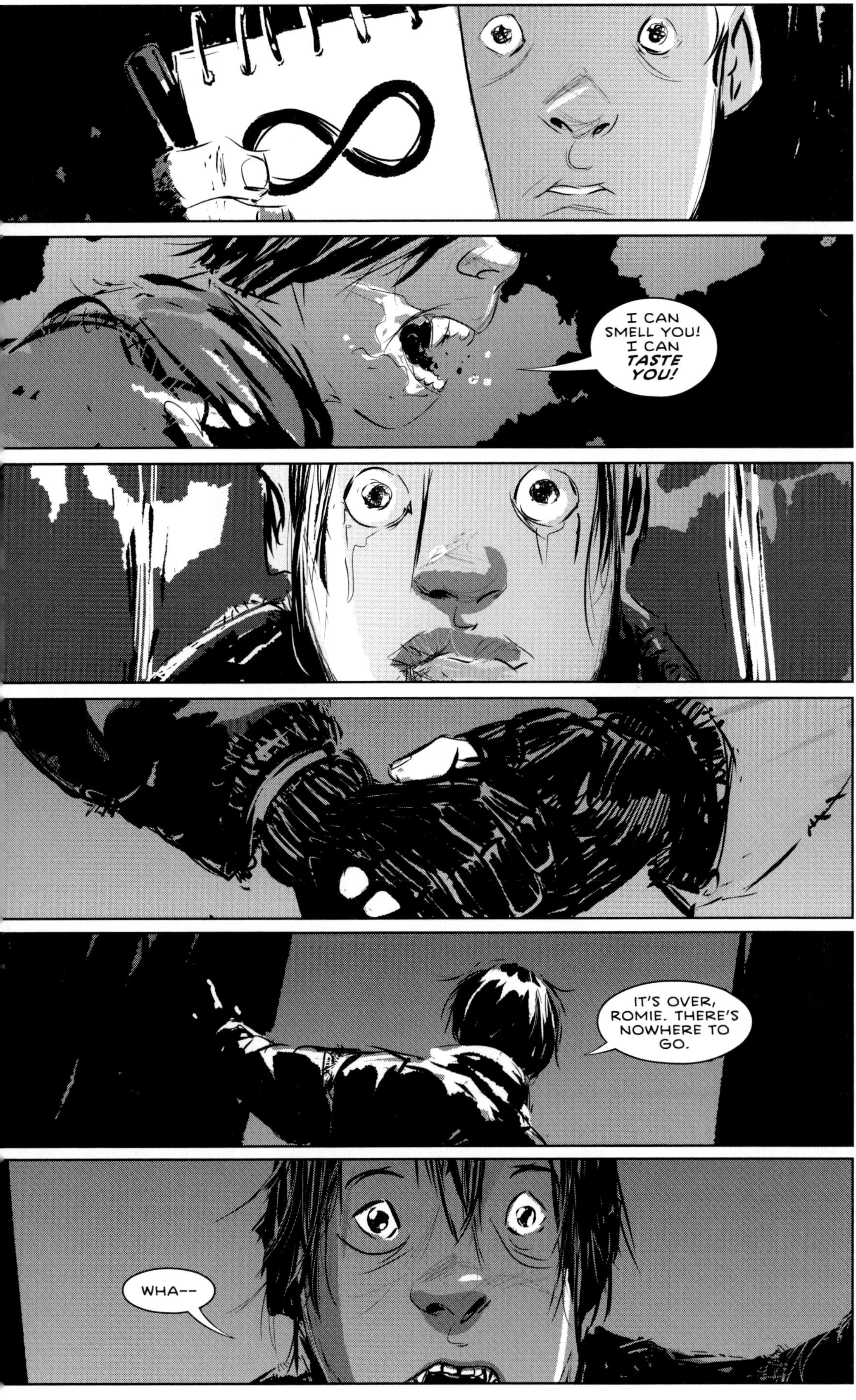
I CAN SMELL YOU! I CAN *TASTE YOU!*
IT'S OVER, ROMIE. THERE'S NOWHERE TO GO.
WHA--

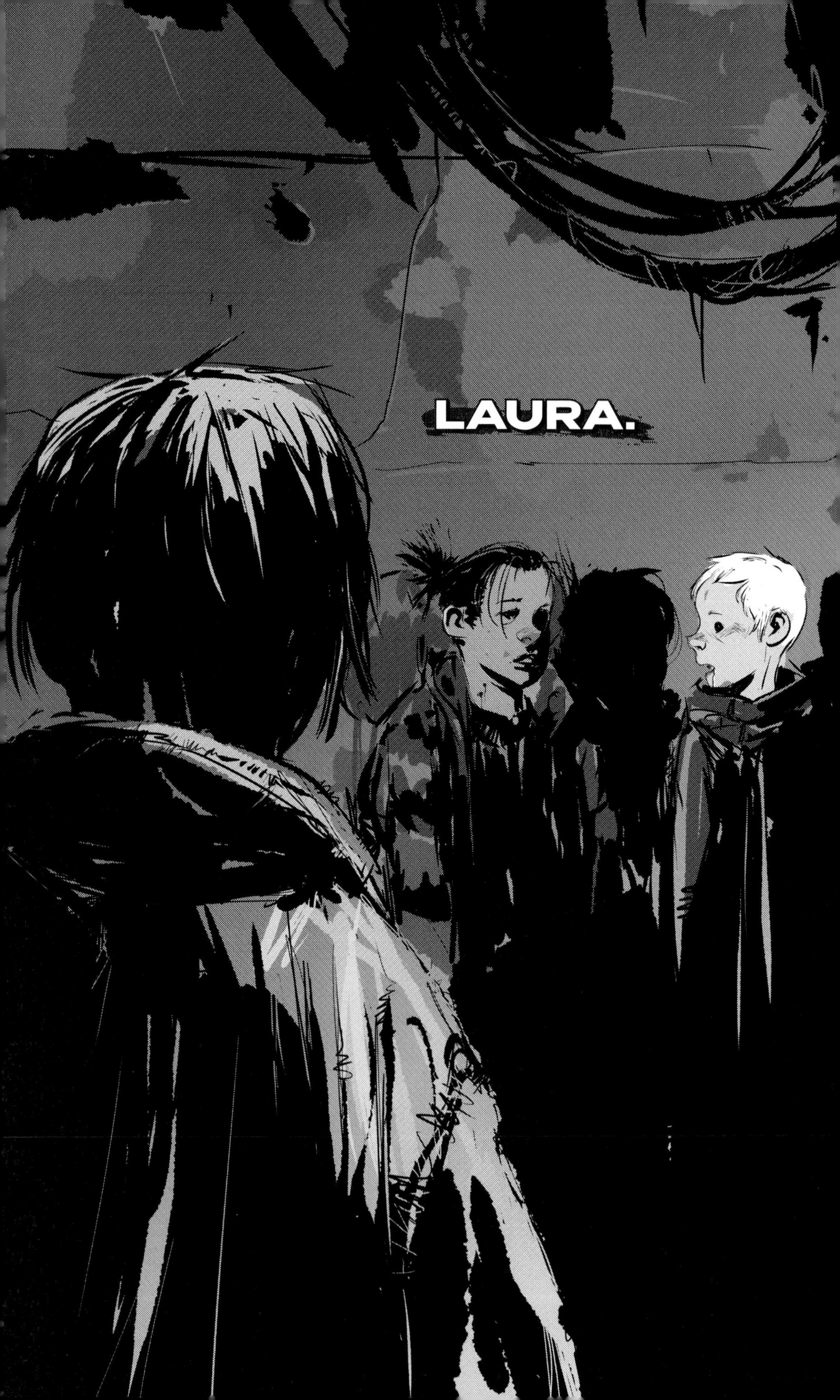
LAURA.

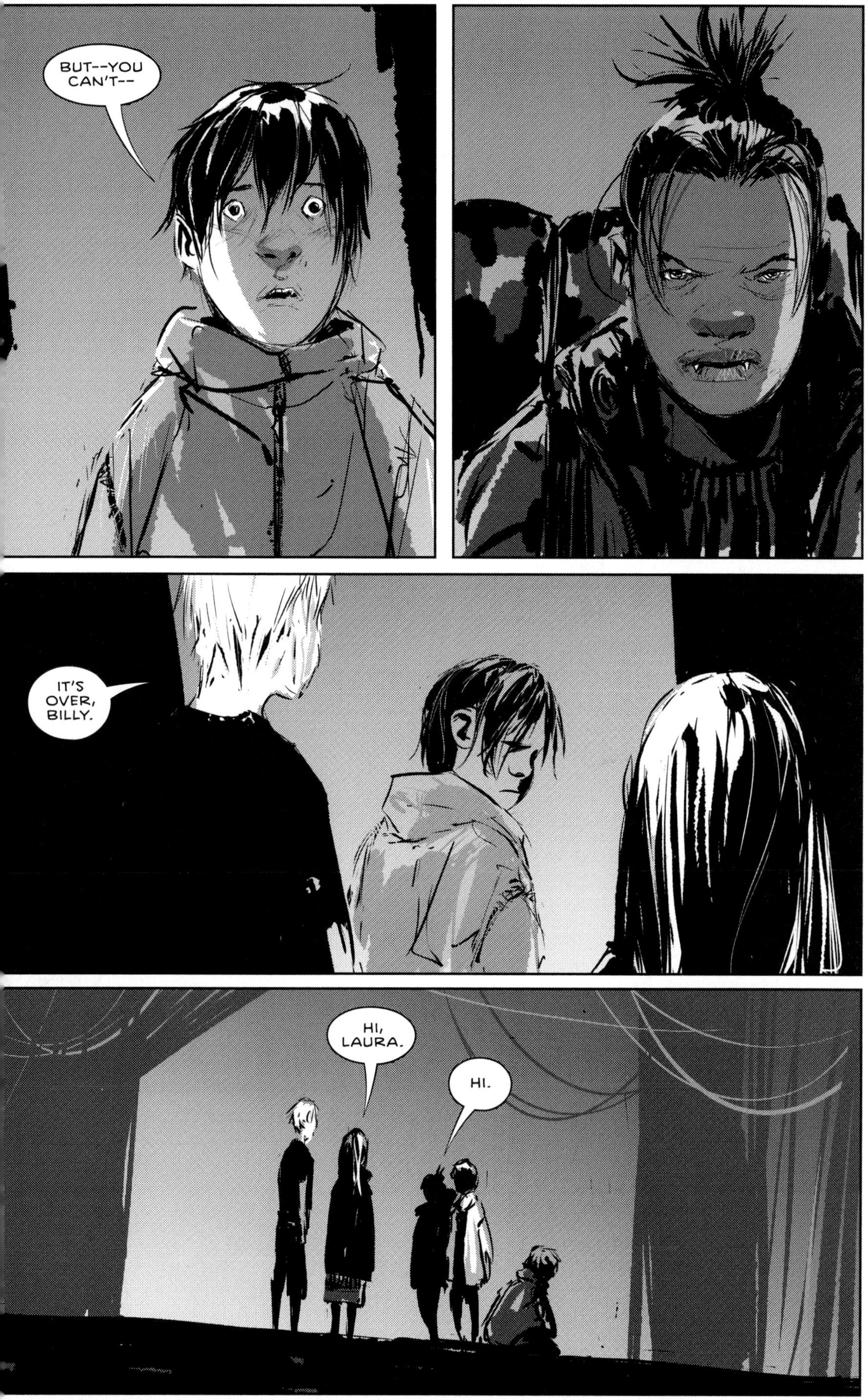
BUT--YOU CAN'T--
IT'S OVER, BILLY.
HI, LAURA.
HI.

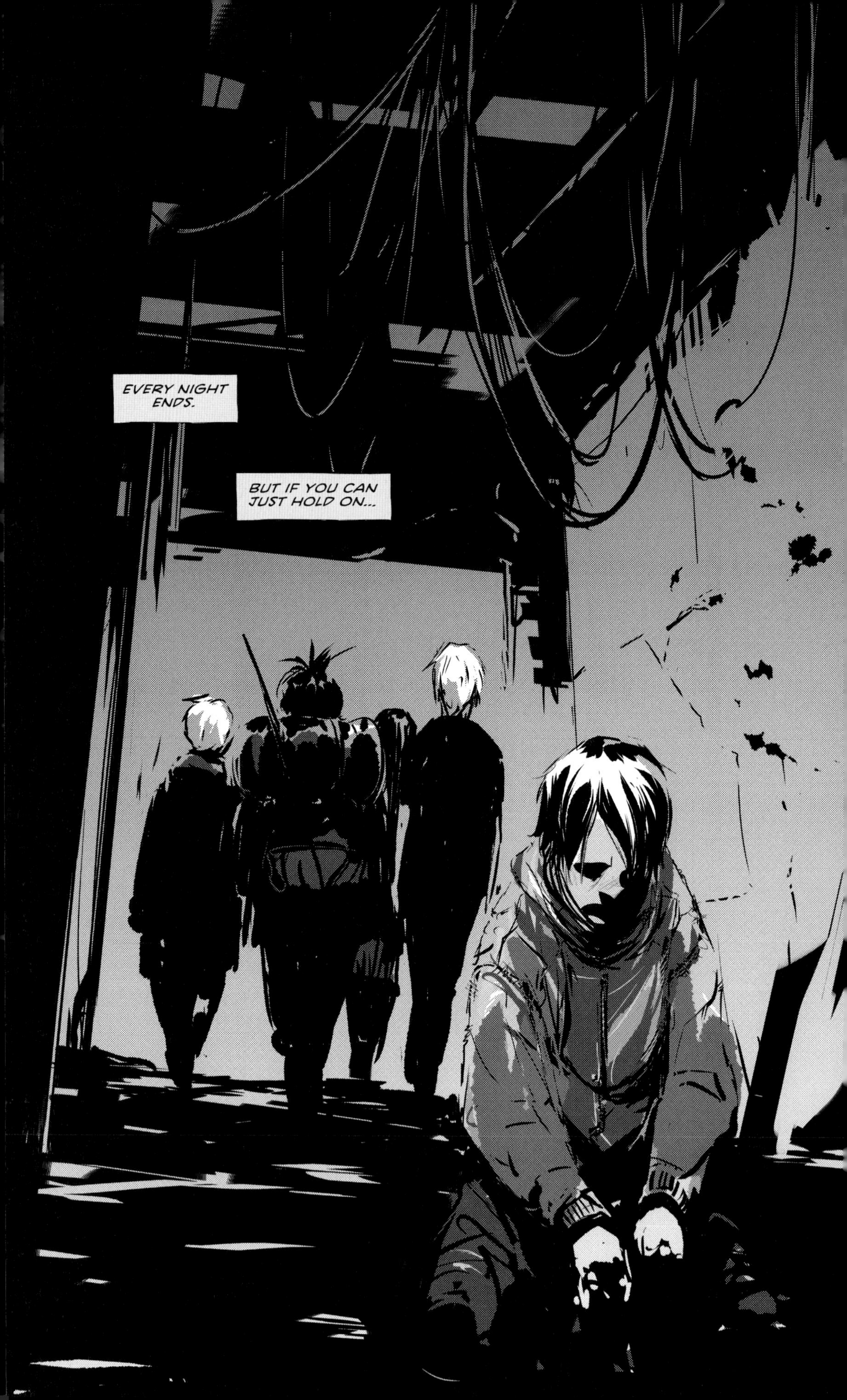
EVERY NIGHT ENDS.
BUT IF YOU CAN JUST HOLD ON...

ANOTHER ONE
ALWAYS COMES.

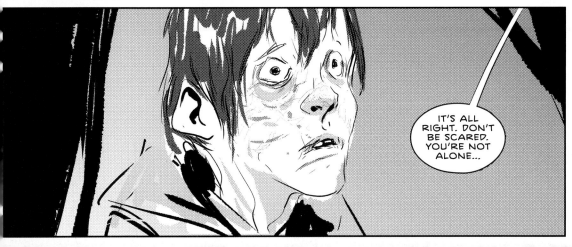

IT'S ALL
RIGHT. DON'T
BE SCARED.
YOU'RE NOT
ALONE...

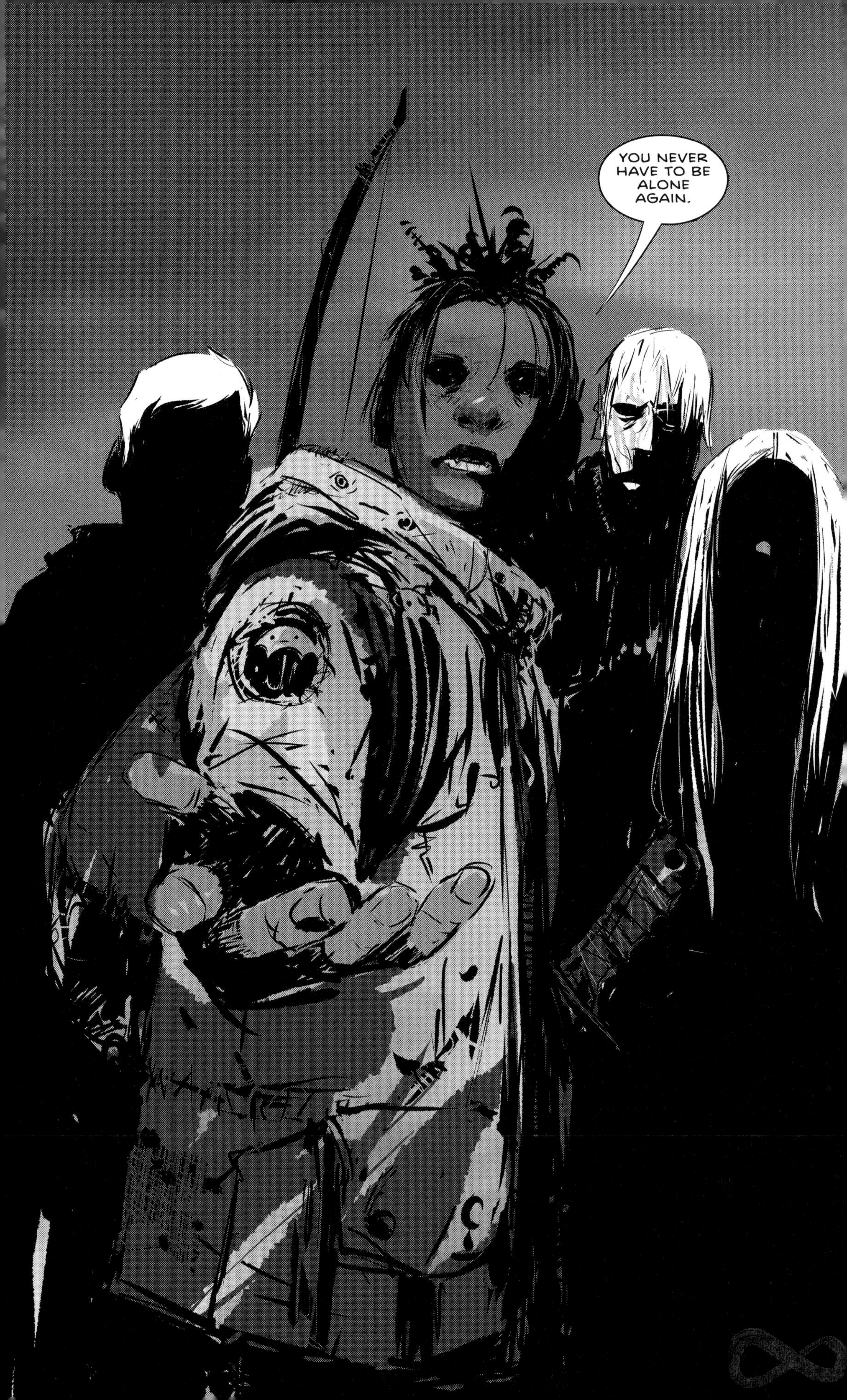
YOU NEVER HAVE TO BE ALONE AGAIN.

VARIANT
COVER
GALLERY

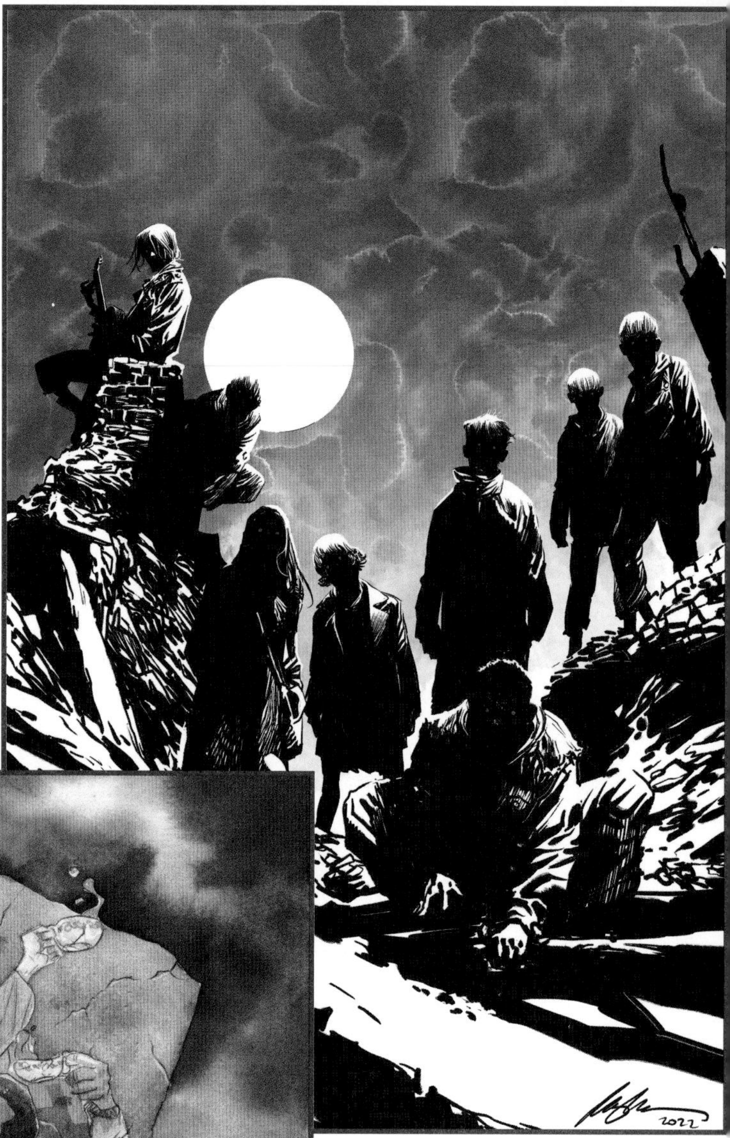

Rafael Albuquerque

Dustin Nguyen

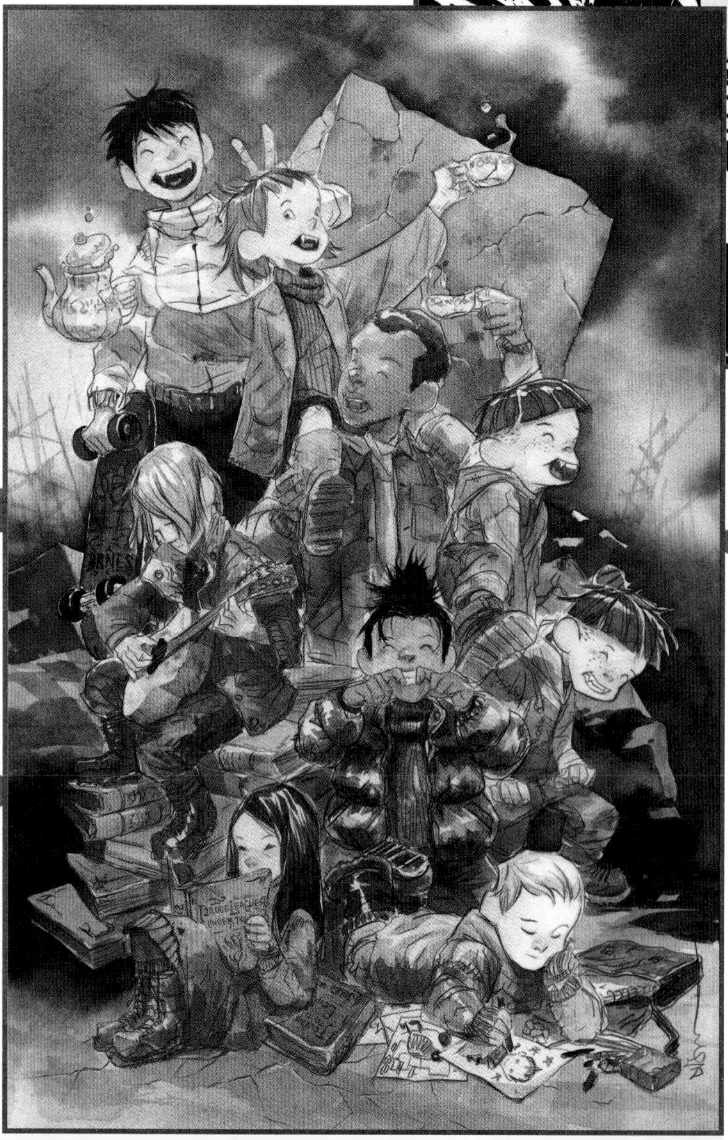

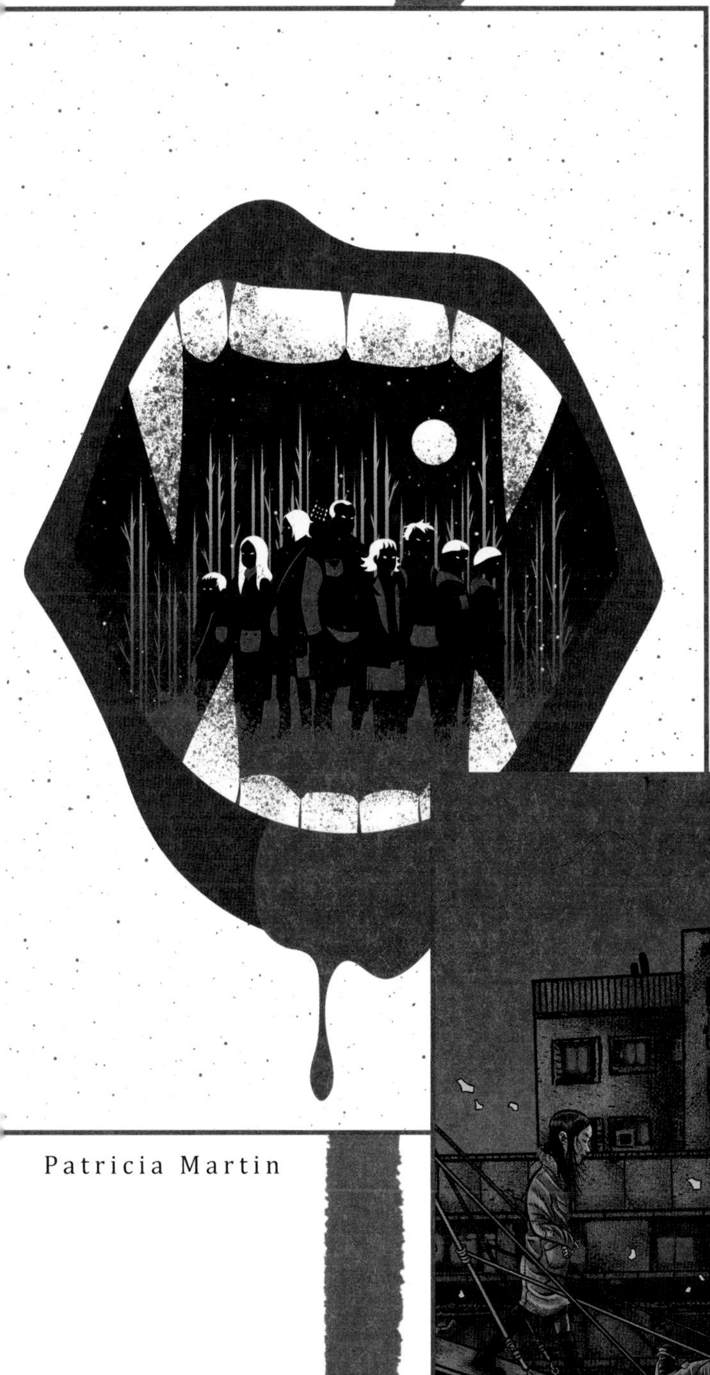

Patricia Martin

David Rubin

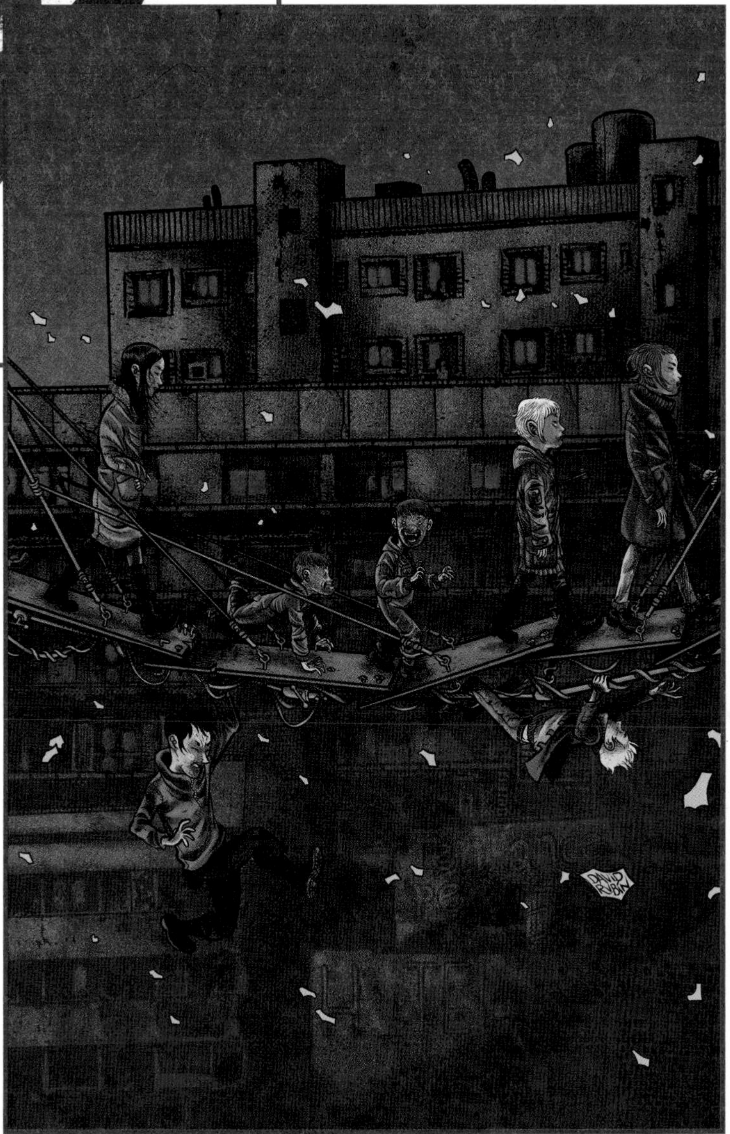
DAVID RUBIN

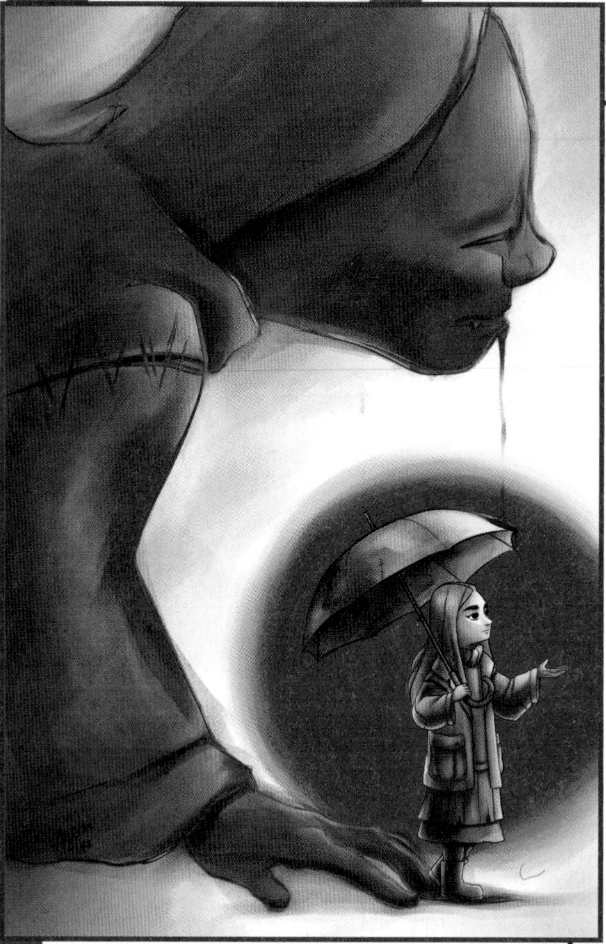

Agnes Garbowski

Jason Shawn Alexander

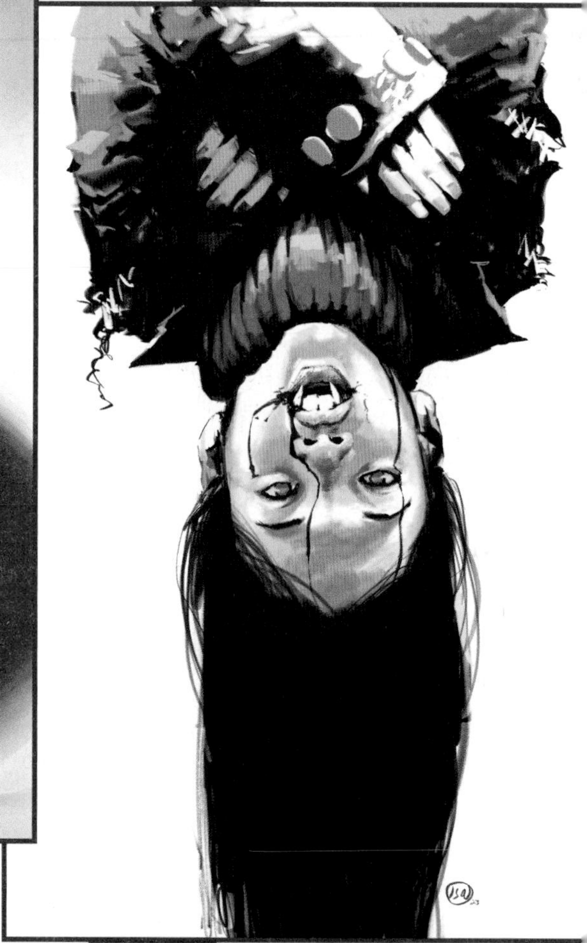

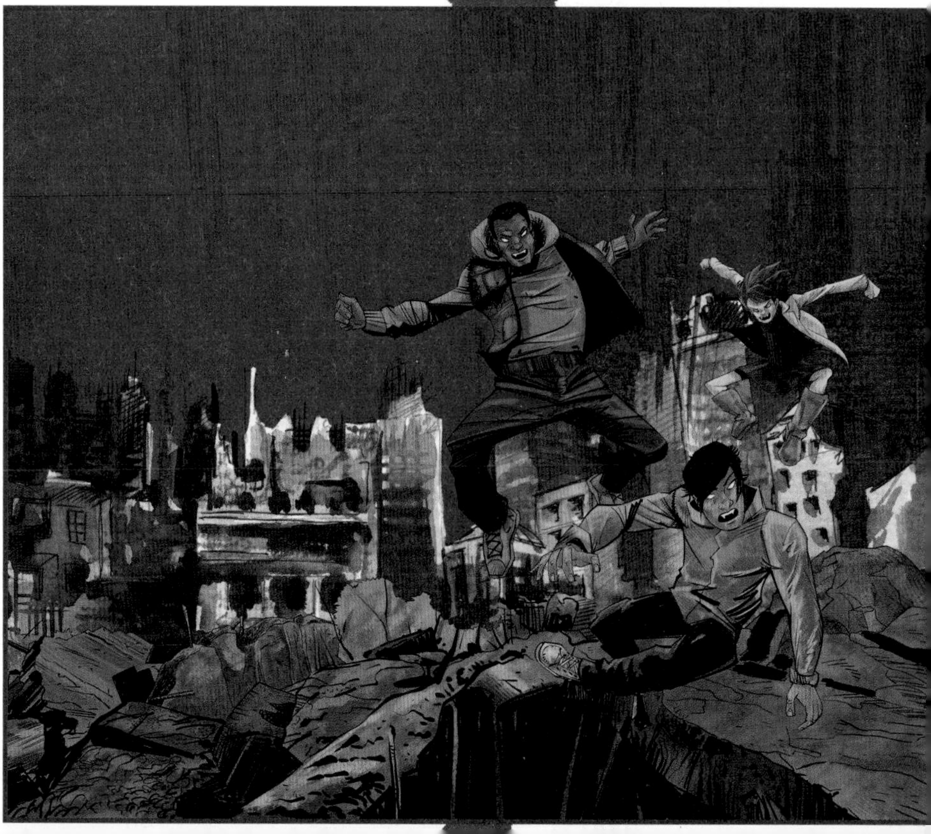

Steve Wands